1Q84: BOOK THREE

Haruki Murakami was born in Kyoto in 1949 and now lives near Tokyo. He is the author of many novels as well as short stories and non-fiction. His works include *Norwegian Wood, The Wind-Up Bird Chronicle, Kafka on the Shore, After Dark* and *What I Talk About When I Talk About Running*. His work has been translated into more than forty languages, and the most recent of his many international honours is the Jerusalem Prize, whose previous recipients include J.M. Coetzee, Milan Kundera, and V.S. Naipaul.

HARUKI MURAKAMI

1Q84

Book Three

TRANSLATED FROM THE JAPANESE BY
Philip Gabriel

VINTAGE BOOKS
London

Published by Vintage 2012

2 4 6 8 10 9 7 5 3 1

First published in three volumes with the title *1Q84* in 2009 and 2010
By Shinchosa Publishing Co Ltd, Tokyo

Adapted from the multi-volume Japanese edition with the
participation of the author

First published in Great Britain in 2011 by Harvill Secker

Vintage
Random House, 20 Vauxhall Bridge Road,
London SW1V 2SA

www.vintage-books.co.uk

Addresses for companies within The Random House Group Limited
can be found at: www.randomhouse.co.uk/offices.htm

The Random House Group Limited Reg. No. 954009

A CIP catalogue record for this book
is available from the British Library

ISBN 9780099549055

The Random House Group Limited supports The Forest Stewardship
Council (FSC®), the leading international forest certification organisation.
Our books carrying the FSC label are printed on FSC® certified paper. FSC
is the only forest certification scheme endorsed by the leading environmental
organisations, including Greenpeace. Our paper procurement policy can be
found at www.randomhouse.co.uk/environment

Design by Jim Smith Design

Typeset by Palimpsest Book Production Limited, Falkirk, Stirlingshire

Printed and bound by CPI Group (UK) Ltd, Croydon, CR0 4YY

It's a Barnum and Bailey world,
Just as phony as it can be,
But it wouldn't be make-believe
If you believed in me

"It's Only a Paper Moon"
BILLY ROSE & E.Y. "YIP" HARBURG

BOOK THREE

BOOK 3 OCTOBER–DECEMBER

1

USHIKAWA

Something Kicking at the
Far Edges of Consciousness

"I WONDER IF YOU WOULD MIND not smoking, Mr. Ushikawa," the
shorter man said.

Ushikawa gazed steadily at the man seated across the desk from
him, then down at the Seven Stars cigarette between his fingers. He
hadn't lit it yet.

"I'd really appreciate it," the man added politely.

Ushikawa looked puzzled, as if he were wondering how such an
object possibly found its way into his hand.

"Sorry about that," he said. "I won't light up. I just took it out
without thinking."

The man's chin moved up and down, perhaps a half inch, but his
gaze didn't waver. His eyes remained fixed on Ushikawa's. Ushikawa
stuck the cigarette back in its box, the box in a drawer.

The taller of the two men, the one with a ponytail, stood in the doorway, leaning so lightly against the door frame that it was hard to tell if he was actually touching it. He stared at Ushikawa as if he were a stain on the wall. *What a creepy pair,* Ushikawa thought. This was the third time he had met with these men, and they made him uneasy every time.

Ushikawa's cramped office had a single desk, and the shorter of the two men, the one with a buzz cut, sat across from him. He was the one who did the talking. Ponytail didn't say a word. Like one of those stone guardian dogs at the entrance to a Shinto shrine, he stood stock-still, not moving an inch, watching Ushikawa.

"It has been three weeks," Buzzcut noted.

Ushikawa picked up his desk calendar, checked what was written on it, and nodded. "Correct. It has been exactly three weeks since we last met."

"And in the meantime you haven't reported to us even once. As I've mentioned before, Mr. Ushikawa, every moment is precious. We have no time to waste."

"I completely understand," Ushikawa replied, fiddling with his gold lighter in place of the cigarette. "There's no time to waste. I am well aware of this."

Buzzcut waited for Ushikawa to go on.

"The thing is," Ushikawa said, "I don't like to talk in fits and starts. A little of this, a little of that. I would like to wait until I start to see the big picture and things begin to fall into place and I can see what's behind all this. Half-baked ideas can only lead to trouble. I know this sounds selfish, but that's the way I do things."

Buzzcut gazed coolly at Ushikawa. Ushikawa knew the man didn't think much of him, not that this really worried him much. As far as he could recall, no one had ever had a good impression of him. He was used to it. His parents and siblings had never liked him, and neither had his teachers or classmates. It was the same with his wife and children. If someone *did* like him, now *then* he would be concerned. But the other way around didn't faze him.

"Mr. Ushikawa, we would like to respect your way of doing things. And I believe we have done that. So far. But things are different this time. I'm sorry to say we don't have the luxury of waiting until we know all the facts."

"I understand," Ushikawa said, "but I doubt you've just been sitting back all this time waiting for me to get in touch. I suspect you've been running your own investigations?"

Buzzcut didn't respond. His lips remained pressed in a tight horizontal line, and his expression didn't give anything away. But Ushikawa could tell that he wasn't far from the truth. Over the past three weeks, their organization had geared up, and, although they had probably used different tactics from Ushikawa, they had been searching for the woman. But they must not have found anything, which is why they had turned up again in Ushikawa's office.

"It takes a thief to catch a thief," Ushikawa said, spreading his hands wide, as if disclosing some fascinating secret. "Try to hide something, and this thief can sniff it out. I know I'm not the most pleasant-looking person, but I do have a nose for things. I can follow the faintest scent to the very end. Because I'm a thief myself. I have to do things my way, at my own pace. I completely understand that time is pressing, but I would like you to wait a little longer. You have to be patient, otherwise the whole thing may collapse."

Ushikawa toyed with his lighter. Buzzcut's eyes patiently followed Ushikawa's movements, and then he looked up.

"I would appreciate it if you would tell me what you've found, even if it's incomplete. Granted, you have your own way of doing things, but if I don't take something concrete back to my superiors, we'll be in a tough spot. I think you're in a bit of a precarious situation yourself, Mr. Ushikawa."

These guys really are *up a creek,* Ushikawa realized. The two of them were martial arts experts, which is why they were selected to be Leader's bodyguards. Despite that, Leader had been murdered right under their noses. Not that there was actually any evidence that he had been

5

murdered – several doctors in the religion had examined the body and found no external injuries. But medical equipment within the religion was rudimentary at best. And time was of the essence. If a thorough, legal autopsy had been performed by a trained pathologist, they might very well have discovered evidence of foul play, but it was too late now. The body had been secretly disposed of within the Sakigake compound.

At any rate, these two bodyguards had failed in their assignment to protect Leader, and their position in the religion was shaky. Their role now was to locate this woman, after she had seemingly vanished into thin air. The order was out: leave no stone unturned until they found her. But so far they had come up empty-handed. They were trained bodyguards, but when it came to finding missing persons, they lacked the right skills.

"I understand where you're coming from," Ushikawa replied. "And I will tell you some things I've discovered. Not the whole story, but I can reveal parts of it."

Buzzcut sat there for a while, his eyes narrowed. And then he nodded. "That would be fine. We have uncovered a few details ourselves, things you may already be aware of, or perhaps not. We should share whatever information we have."

Ushikawa put the lighter down and tented his fingers on top of the desk.

"The young woman, Aomame," he began, "was asked to come to a suite at the Hotel Okura, and helped Leader to relax his muscles by working his body through a series of stretching exercises. This was at the beginning of September, on the evening of that tremendous thunderstorm. Aomame treated him for around an hour in a separate room, then left Leader while he slept. She told you to let him sleep undisturbed for two hours, and you followed her instructions. But Leader wasn't asleep. He was already dead. There were no external injuries, and it appeared to be a heart attack. Right after this, the woman vanished. She had cleared out of her apartment beforehand.

The place was empty. And the next day her resignation letter arrived at the sports club. Everything seemed to follow a preset plan. The inevitable conclusion is that this Miss Aomame was the one who murdered Leader."

Buzzcut nodded. It all sounded correct to him.

"Your goal is to get to the bottom of what actually occurred," Ushikawa added. "Whatever it takes, you need to catch this woman."

"If this Aomame really is the one who killed Leader, we need to know why, and who's behind it."

Ushikawa looked down at his ten fingers resting on the desk, as if they were some curious object he had never set eyes on before. He raised his head and looked at the man across from him.

"You've already run a background check on Aomame's family, correct? All of her family members are devout members of the Witnesses. Her parents are still quite active and they have continued to proselytize door to door. Her older brother, who is thirty-four, works at the religion headquarters in Odawara. He is married and has two children. His wife is also a devout Witness. Aomame is the only one in the family who left the religion – an apostate, they called her – and she was essentially disowned. I have found no evidence that the family has had any contact with her for nearly the last twenty years. I think it's impossible her family would hide her. At the age of eleven, she cut all ties with her family, and has been on her own pretty much ever since. She lived with her uncle for a while, but since she entered high school she has effectively been independent. Quite an impressive feat. And quite a strong-willed woman."

Buzzcut didn't say a word. He might have already had all this information.

"There is no way that the Witnesses are involved," Ushikawa went on. "They are well known to be pacifists, following the principle of nonresistance. It's not possible that their organization itself was aiming to take Leader's life. On that we can be agreed, I think."

Buzzcut nodded. "The Witnesses aren't involved in this. That much

I know. Just to be sure, though, we had a talk with her brother. We took *every possible precaution*. But he didn't know anything."

"By *every possible precaution* you don't mean ripping off his finger-nails, do you?"

Buzzcut ignored the question.

"Don't look so upset," Ushikawa said. "I'm joking. I'm sure her brother knew nothing about her actions or her whereabouts. I'm a born pacifist myself and would never do something so harsh, but that much I can figure out. Aomame has nothing to do with either her family or the Witnesses. Still, she couldn't have pulled off something this complicated on her own. Things were carefully arranged, and she just followed the plan. And that was also a pretty nimble vanishing act she pulled. She had to have a lot of help and a generous amount of funding. There's got to be someone – or some organization – who is backing her, someone who wanted Leader dead. They're the ones that plotted all this. Agreed?"

Buzzcut nodded. "Generally speaking, yes."

"But there's no clue what sort of organization we're talking about," Ushikawa said. "I assume you checked out her friends and acquaint-ances?"

Buzzcut silently nodded.

"And – let me guess – you found no friends to speak of," Ushikawa said. "No friends, no boyfriend. She has a few acquaintances at work, but outside of work she doesn't hang out with anybody. At least I wasn't able to find any evidence of her having any close relationship with anyone. Why would that be? She is a young, healthy, decent-looking woman."

Ushikawa glanced at Ponytail, standing by the door, seemingly frozen in time. He was devoid of all expression to begin with, so what was there to change? Does this guy even have a name? Ushikawa wondered. He wouldn't be surprised if he didn't.

"You two are the only ones who have actually seen Miss Aomame," Ushikawa said. "How about it? Did you notice anything unusual about her?"

Buzzcut shook his head slightly. "As you said, she is a fairly attractive young woman. Not beautiful enough to turn heads, though. A very quiet, calm person. She seemed quite confident in her abilities as a physical therapist. But nothing else really leapt out at us. It's strange, in fact, how little of an impression her outward appearance made. I can't even remember much about her face."

Ushikawa again glanced over at Ponytail by the door. Perhaps he had something to add? But he didn't look like he was about to open his mouth.

Ushikawa looked back at Buzzcut. "I'm sure you checked out Miss Aomame's phone record for the past few months?"

Buzzcut shook his head. "We haven't done that yet."

"You should," Ushikawa smiled. "It's definitely worth checking out. People call all sorts of places and get all sorts of calls. Investigate a person's phone records and you get a good idea of the kind of life they lead. Miss Aomame is no exception. It's no easy thing to get ahold of private phone records, but it can be done. It takes a thief to catch one, right?"

Buzzcut was silent, waiting for him to continue.

"In looking over Miss Aomame's phone records, several facts came to light. Quite unusually for a woman, she doesn't like talking on the phone. There weren't so many calls, and those that she made didn't last long. Occasionally there were some long calls, but these are the exception. Most of the calls were to her workplace, but since she works freelance half the time, she also made calls related to private business – in other words, appointments she made directly with clients rather than going through the sports club desk. There were quite a few calls like that. But as far as I could tell, none of them were suspicious."

Ushikawa paused, and as he examined the nicotine stains on his fingers from a number of angles, he thought about cigarettes. He lit an imaginary cigarette, inhaled the imaginary smoke, and exhaled.

"There were two exceptions, however. Two calls were to the police.

Not 911 calls, but to the Traffic Bureau in the Shinjuku police station. And there were several calls from the station to her. She doesn't drive, and policemen can't afford private lessons at an expensive gym. So it must mean she has a friend working in that division. Who it is, though, I have no idea. One other thing that bothered me is that she had several long conversations with an unknown number. The other party always called her. She never once called them. I tried everything but couldn't trace the number. Obviously there are numbers that can be manipulated so that the party's name remains undisclosed. But even these, with some effort, should be traceable. I tried my best, but I couldn't find out anything. It's locked up tight. Quite extraordinary, really."

"This other person, then, can do things that aren't ordinary."

"Exactly. Professionals are definitely involved."

"Another thief," Buzzcut said.

Ushikawa rubbed his bald, misshapen head with his palm, and grinned. "That's right. Another thief – and a pretty formidable one at that."

"So at least we understand that professionals are backing her," Buzzcut commented.

"Correct. Miss Aomame is connected to some sort of organization. And this isn't some organization run by amateurs in their spare time."

Buzzcut lowered his eyelids halfway and studied Ushikawa. Then he turned around, toward the door. His eyes met Ponytail's, and Ponytail gave a slight single nod to indicate he understood their conversation. Buzzcut turned his gaze back to Ushikawa.

"So?" Buzzcut asked.

"So –" Ushikawa said, "it's my turn to ask you the questions. Do you have any idea which group or organization might want to rub out Leader?"

Buzzcut's long eyebrows became one as he frowned. Three wrinkles appeared above his nose.

"Listen, Mr. Ushikawa. Think about it. We are a religious organization.

We seek a peaceful heart and a spiritual life. We live in harmony with nature, spending our days farming and in religious training. Who could possibly view us as an enemy? What is there to gain?"

A vague smile played around the corners of Ushikawa's mouth. "There are fanatics in every area of life. Who knows what kind of ideas fanatics will come up with?"

"We have no idea who could be behind this," Buzzcut replied, his face blank, ignoring Ushikawa's sarcasm.

"What about Akebono? There are still members of that group at large, aren't there?"

Buzzcut shook his head once more, this time decisively, meaning this was impossible. Anyone connected with Akebono must have been so thoroughly crushed that there were no fears about them. So there was no trace of Akebono left.

"Fine. So you have no idea who it could be either. The reality is, though, that some organization somewhere targeted your Leader and took his life. Very cleverly, very efficiently. And then they vanished, leaving nothing behind. Like smoke."

"And we have to find out who is behind this."

"Without getting the police involved."

Buzzcut nodded. "This is our problem, not a legal problem."

"Fine," Ushikawa said. "Understood. You've made that clear. But there's one more thing I would like to ask you."

"Go ahead," Buzzcut said.

"How many people within your religion know that Leader has died?"

"There would be the two of us," Buzzcut said. "And the two other people who helped transport the body. Subordinates of mine. Only five of the council know about this. That would make nine people. We haven't told his three shrine maidens yet, but they will find out soon enough. They serve him personally, so we can't hide it from them for very long. And then there's you, Mr. Ushikawa. Of course you know about it too."

"So all together, thirteen people."

Buzzcut didn't reply.

Ushikawa sighed deeply. "May I speak frankly?"

"Please do," Buzzcut said.

"I know it doesn't do much good to say this now," Ushikawa said, "but when you found out Leader was dead you should have contacted the police immediately. You should have made his death public. This kind of major event can't be hidden forever. Any secret known by more than ten people isn't a secret anymore. You could soon find yourself in a lot of trouble."

Buzzcut's expression didn't change. "It is not my job to decide. I just follow orders."

"So who makes the decisions?"

No reply.

"The person who has taken over for Leader?"

Buzzcut maintained his silence.

"Fine," Ushikawa said. "Someone above you instructed you to take care of Leader's corpse behind closed doors. In your organization, orders from above can't be questioned. But from a legal standpoint this clearly involves willful destruction and disposal of a dead body, which is quite a serious crime. You're aware of this, I'm sure."

Buzzcut nodded.

Ushikawa sighed deeply again. "I mentioned this before, but if by some chance the police get involved, please make it clear that I was never informed of Leader's death. Criminal charges are the last thing I need."

"You were never told about Leader's death," Buzzcut said. "We hired you as an outside investigator to locate a woman named Aomame, that's all. You have done nothing illegal."

"That works," Ushikawa said.

"You know, we had no desire to have an outsider like yourself find out about Leader's death. But you're the one who conducted the initial background check on Aomame, the one who cleared her. So you're already involved. We need your help to locate her. And we need you to keep the whole thing confidential."

"Keeping secrets is what my profession is all about. There is nothing to worry about. I assure you that no one else will ever hear about this from me."

"If it does get out, and we find out that you were the source, this could lead to something unpleasant."

Ushikawa looked down at his desk again, at the ten plump fingers resting on it. He looked surprised to discover that these fingers were his.

"Something unpleasant," he repeated, and looked up.

Buzzcut's eyes narrowed slightly. "Above all we have to keep Leader's death a secret. And we're not concerned about the means we use to accomplish this."

"I will keep your secret. Rest assured," Ushikawa said. "So far, we've worked together perfectly well. I've done a number of things behind the scenes that would have been hard for you to do openly. The work hasn't always been easy, but the compensation is more than adequate. So okay – double zippers on my mouth. I have no religious beliefs, but Leader helped me personally, so I am doing all I possibly can to locate Miss Aomame. I will do my utmost to uncover what is behind this. And I'm starting to see some progress. So please, be patient for just a while longer. Before too long, I should have some good news."

Buzzcut shifted ever so slightly in his chair. Standing by the door, Ponytail shifted in tandem, moving his weight to his other leg.

"Is this all the information you're able to share?" Buzzcut asked.

Ushikawa mulled this over. "As I said, Miss Aomame called the Traffic Bureau of the Shinjuku Metropolitan Police Precinct twice, and the other party called her a number of times. I don't know the other party's name yet. It's the police. I can't just ask them. But an idea did flash through this inept brain of mine. There was something I remembered about the Traffic Bureau in the Shinjuku Precinct. I thought about it a lot, wondering what it was that was clinging to the edges of my pathetic memory. It took quite some time before it came to me. It's no fun growing old, no fun at all. The drawers where you store memories get harder to open. I used to be able to just yank them open with no problem, but this time it took me a good week before it finally dawned on me."

Ushikawa stopped talking, and a theatrical smile rose to his lips. He gazed at Buzzcut, who waited patiently for him to go on.

"In August of this year, a young female police officer with the Traffic Bureau in the Shinjuku Precinct was found strangled to death in a love hotel in Maruyama Ward, in Shibuya. Stark naked, handcuffed with her own police-issue handcuffs. Naturally this caused a scandal. The phone conversations between Miss Aomame and the Shinjuku Precinct were in the several months before this incident. There were no calls at all after the murder. What do you think? Too much to see this as mere coincidence?"

Buzzcut was silent for a while, then finally spoke. "So you're saying that the person Aomame contacted was this female police officer who was murdered?"

"The officer's name was Ayumi Nakano. Age twenty-six. A very charming-looking young woman. She came from a police family. Her father and older brother were both in the force. She was a fairly top-ranked officer. Needless to say, the police have tried very hard to locate the murderer, but with no luck so far. I apologize for being so forward with this question, but is there any chance that you might know something about this incident?"

Buzzcut's eyes, staring at Ushikawa, were cold, as if only minutes ago he had been extracted from a glacier. "I'm not sure what you mean," he said. "Are you thinking that we may in some way be involved in this incident? That one of us took this female police officer to a disreputable hotel, handcuffed her, and strangled her to death?"

Ushikawa pursed his lips and shook his head. "Don't be absurd! The thought never crossed my mind. All I'm asking is whether you have any ideas about this case. Anything at all. I would welcome even the smallest clue. No matter how hard I try to squeeze out whatever I can from this brain of mine, I can't find a connection between these two murders."

Buzzcut gazed at Ushikawa for a time, as if measuring something. Then he slowly let out his breath. "I understand. I will let my superiors know," he said. He took out a pocket notebook and made some notes. "Ayumi Nakano. Twenty-six. Traffic Bureau, Shinjuku Precinct. Possibly connected with Aomame."

"Exactly."

"Anything else?"

"There's one more thing. Someone within your religion must have brought up Miss Aomame's name. Someone who knew of a fitness trainer in Tokyo who was very good at stretching exercises. As you pointed out, I was hired to investigate the woman's background. I'm not trying to excuse myself, but I did my absolute best. Yet I didn't find anything out of the ordinary, nothing at all suspicious. She's as clean as they come. And you all asked her to come to the suite at the Hotel Okura. So who was it who recommended her in the first place?"

"I don't know."

"You don't know?" Ushikawa exclaimed. He looked like a child who has just heard a word he doesn't understand. "You mean that while someone within your religion must have first raised Miss Aomame's name, no one can recall who it was? Is that what you're saying?"

"Correct," Buzzcut replied, his expression unchanged.

"That's pretty weird," Ushikawa said, in a tone that reflected just how odd he found it.

Buzzcut didn't say a word.

"So we don't know when her name came up, or from whom, and things went forward seemingly on their own. Is that what you're saying?"

"To tell you the truth, the one who most enthusiastically supported the idea was Leader himself," Buzzcut said, choosing his words carefully. "Within the leadership, some thought it might be dangerous to allow a complete stranger to take care of Leader like that. As bodyguards we felt the same way. But Leader wasn't worried. In fact, he is the one who insisted that we go forward with it."

Ushikawa picked up his lighter again, flipped open the top, and flicked it on, as if testing it. Then he quickly snapped the top shut.

"I always heard Leader was a very cautious person," he said.

"He was. Very careful, very cautious," Buzzcut said. Silence continued for a time.

"There is one more thing I would like to ask," Ushikawa said. "About Tengo Kawana. He was seeing an older, married woman named Kyoko Yasuda. She came to his apartment once a week, and they would spend some intimate time together. He's young, so that's only to be expected. But suddenly one day her husband calls him, telling him she won't be paying him any more visits. And he hasn't heard a peep from her since."

Buzzcut frowned. "I don't understand why you're telling me this. Are you saying that Tengo Kawana was involved in all this?"

"I wouldn't go that far. It's just that something has been bothering me. Whatever the circumstances might be, you would expect the woman to at least give him a call. But she hasn't gotten in touch. She just vanished, without a trace. Loose ends bother me, so that's why I posed the question, to be on the safe side. Do you know anything about this?"

"Personally, I have no knowledge about this woman," Buzzcut said in a flat tone. "Kyoko Yasuda. She had a relationship with Tengo Kawana."

"She was married, and ten years older than him."

Buzzcut noted down the name in his notebook. "I will let my superiors know."

"That's fine," Ushikawa said. "By the way, have you located the whereabouts of Eriko Fukada?"

Buzzcut raised his head and stared at Ushikawa as if he were examining a crooked picture frame. "And why should we know where Eriko Fukada is?"

"You're not interested in locating her?"

Buzzcut shook his head. "It is not our concern. She is free to go wherever she wants."

"And you're not interested in Tengo Kawana either?"

"He has nothing to do with us."

"At one time it seemed like you were quite interested in both of them," Ushikawa said.

Buzzcut narrowed his eyes for a moment, then opened his mouth. "At this point we are focused solely on Aomame."

"Your focus shifts from day to day?"

Buzzcut's lips parted a fraction, but he didn't reply.

"Mr. Buzzcut, have you read the novel Eriko Fukada wrote, *Air Chrysalis*?"

"No, I have not. In the religion we are strictly forbidden to read anything other than books on Sakigake doctrine. We can't even touch them."

"Have you ever heard the term *Little People*?"

"No," Buzzcut said, without missing a beat.

"That's fine," Ushikawa replied.

Their conversation came to an end. Buzzcut slowly rose from his chair and straightened the collar of his jacket. Ponytail took one step forward from the wall.

"Mr. Ushikawa, as I mentioned before, time is of the essence." Buzzcut stood and looked down at Ushikawa, who had remained seated. "We have to locate Aomame as soon as possible. We are doing our very best, and we need you to do the same, from a different angle. If Aomame isn't found, it could be bad for both of us. You are, after all, one of the few who know an important secret."

"With great knowledge comes great responsibility."

"Exactly," Buzzcut replied without a trace of emotion. He turned and swiftly exited the room. Ponytail followed Buzzcut out, noiselessly shutting the door.

*   *   *

After they had left, Ushikawa pulled open a desk drawer and switched off the tape recorder inside. He opened the lid of the recorder, extracted the cassette tape, and wrote the date and time on it with a ballpoint pen. For a man with his sort of odd looks, his handwriting was neat and graceful. He grabbed the pack of Seven Stars cigarettes beside him, extracted one, and lit it with his lighter. He took a long puff, exhaled deeply toward the ceiling, then closed his eyes for a moment. He opened his eyes and looked over at the wall clock. The clock showed 2:30. *What a creepy pair indeed,* Ushikawa told himself once more.

If Aomame isn't found, it could be bad for both of us, Buzzcut had said.

Ushikawa had twice visited the headquarters of Sakigake, deep in the mountains of Yamanashi Prefecture, and had seen the huge incinerator in the woods behind the compound. It was built to burn garbage and waste, but since it operated at an extremely high temperature, if you threw a human corpse inside there wouldn't be a single bone left. He knew that in fact several people's bodies had been disposed of in this way. Leader's body was probably one of them. Naturally enough, Ushikawa didn't want to suffer the same fate. Someday he would die, but if possible he would prefer something a bit more peaceful.

But there were some facts that Ushikawa hadn't revealed. Ushikawa preferred not to show all his cards at once. It was okay to show them a few of the lower-value cards, but the face cards he kept hidden. One needed some insurance – like the secret conversation he had recorded. When it came to this kind of game, Ushikawa was an expert. These young bodyguards had nowhere near the experience he had.

Ushikawa had gotten ahold of Aomame's private client list. As long as you don't mind the time and effort, and you know what you're doing, you can get ahold of almost any kind of information. Ushikawa had made a decent enough investigation of the backgrounds of the twelve private clients. Eight women and four men, all of them of high social standing and fairly well off. Not a single one the type who would lend a hand to an assassin. But one of them, a wealthy woman in her seventies, provided a safe house for women escaping domestic violence. She allowed battered women to live in a two-story apartment building on the extensive grounds of her estate, next door to her house.

This was, in itself, a wonderful thing to do. There was nothing suspicious about it. Yet something bothered Ushikawa, kicking around the edges of his consciousness. And as this vague notion rattled around in his mind, Ushikawa tried to pinpoint what it was. He was equipped with an almost animal-like sense of smell, and he trusted his intuition more than anything. His sense of smell had saved him a few times. *Violence* was perhaps the keyword here. This elderly woman had a special awareness of the violent, and thus went out of her way to protect those who were its victims.

Ushikawa had actually gone over to see this safe house. The wooden apartment building was on a rise in Azabu, prime real estate. It was a fairly old building, but had character. Through the grille of the front gate, he saw a beautiful flower bed in front of the entrance, and an extensive garden. A large oak cast a shadow onto the ground. A small die-cut plate glass was set into the front door. It was the kind of building that was fast disappearing from Tokyo.

For all its tranquillity, the building was heavily secured. The walls around it were high, and topped with barbed wire. The solid metal gate was securely locked, and a German shepherd patrolled the grounds and barked loudly if anyone approached. There were several cameras set up to scan the vicinity. Hardly any pedestrians walked on the road in front of the apartment building, so one couldn't loiter there long. It was a quiet residential area, with several embassies nearby. If a strange-looking man like Ushikawa were seen loitering, someone would be sure to question his presence.

The security was a little too tight. For a place meant to shelter battered women, they went a bit overboard. Ushikawa felt he would have to find out all there was to know about this safe house. No matter how tightly it was guarded, he would somehow have to pry it open. No – the more tightly it was guarded, the more he had to pry it open. And to do so, he would have to wrack his brain to come up with a plan.

Ushikawa recalled the part of his conversation with Buzzcut concerning the Little People.

"Have you ever heard the term Little People?"

"No."

The reply had come a little too fast. If you had never heard that name before, you would normally pause a beat before answering. Little People? You would let the sound roll around in your mind for a second to see if anything clicked. And then you would reply. That's what most people would do.

Buzzcut had heard the term *Little People* before. Ushikawa didn't know if he knew what it meant or what it was, but it was definitely not the first time he'd heard it.

Ushikawa extinguished his now stubby cigarette. He was lost in thought for a while, and then he pulled out a new cigarette and lit it. He had decided years ago not to worry about getting lung cancer. If he wanted to concentrate, he had to get some nicotine into his system. Who knew what his fate was, even two or three days down the road? So what was the point in worrying about how his health would be fifteen years from now?

As he smoked his third Seven Stars, an idea came to him. *Ah!* he thought. *This might actually work.*

2

AOMAME

Alone, but Not Lonely

WHEN IT GOT DARK SHE SAT on a chair on the balcony and gazed out at the playground across the street. This was the most important part of her daily schedule, the focal point of her life. On sunny days, cloudy days, even when it rained, she kept a close watch, without missing a day. As October came around, the air grew cooler. On cold nights she wore many layers, kept a blanket for her legs, and sipped hot cocoa. She watched the slide until ten thirty, then took a leisurely bath to warm herself up, and went to bed.

Of course, there was a possibility that Tengo might appear even in the daytime. But most likely he wouldn't. If he was going to show up at the park, it would be after the mercury-vapor lamp went on and the moon was in the sky. Aomame had a quick supper, dressed so she could run outside, straightened her hair, then sat down on a garden chair and fixed her gaze on the slide. She always had an automatic pistol and a pair of small Nikon binoculars with her. Fearing that Tengo might appear if she went inside to the bathroom, she restricted her drinks to the hot cocoa.

Aomame kept up her watch without missing a day. She didn't read, didn't listen to music, just stared at the park, her ears poised to catch any sound outside. She rarely even changed her position in the chair. She would raise her head from time to time and – if it was a cloudless night – look at the sky to make sure there were still two moons. And then she would quickly shift her gaze back to the park. As Aomame kept a close watch on the park, the moons kept a close watch over her.

But Tengo didn't come.

Not many people visited the playground at night. Occasionally young lovers would appear. They would sit on a bench, hold hands, and, like a pair of tiny birds, exchange a few short, nervous kisses. But the park was too small, and too well lit. Soon they would grow restless and move on. Someone might show up to use the public toilet, find the door locked, and go away disappointed (or perhaps angry). The occasional office worker on his way home from work would sometimes sit alone on the bench, head bowed, undoubtedly hoping to sober up. Or maybe he just didn't want to go straight home. And there was an old man who took his dog for a walk late at night. Both the dog and the man were taciturn, and looked like they had given up all hope.

Most of the time, though, the playground was empty at night. Not even a cat ran across it. Just the mercury-vapor lamp's anonymous light illuminating the swings, the slide, the sandbox, the locked public toilet. When Aomame looked at this scene for a long time, she began to feel as if she had been abandoned on a deserted planet. Like that movie that showed the world after a nuclear war. What was the title?

On the Beach.

Still, Aomame sat there, her mind focused as she kept watch over the playground. As if she were a sailor who had climbed a tall mast and was scanning the vast ocean in search of schools of fish, or the ominous shadow of a periscope. Her watchful pair of eyes were on the lookout for one thing only – Tengo Kawana.

Perhaps Tengo lived in some other town, and had just happened to be passing by that night. In that case, the chances of his revisiting this park were close to zero. But Aomame didn't think so. When he sat on the slide that night, something about his manner, and his clothes, made her feel that he was taking a late-night stroll in the neighborhood, that he had stopped by the park and climbed up the slide. Probably to get a better look at the moons. Which meant he must live within walking distance.

In the Koenji District it wasn't easy to find a place to see the moon. The area was mostly flat, with hardly any tall buildings from which you could look at the sky. This made the slide in the playground a decent place to do so. It was quiet, and no one would bother you. If he decided he wanted to look at the moon again, he would show up – Aomame was certain of it. But then the next moment a thought struck her: *Things might not work out that easily. Maybe he's already found a better place to view the moon.*

Aomame gave a short, decisive shake of her head. She shouldn't overthink things. *The only choice I have is to believe that Tengo will return to this playground, and to wait here patiently until he does. I can't leave – this is the only point of contact between him and me.*

Aomame hadn't pulled the trigger.

It was the beginning of September. She was standing in a turnout on the Metropolitan Expressway No. 3, in the midst of a traffic jam, bathed in bright morning sunlight as she stuck the black muzzle of a Heckler & Koch in her mouth. Dressed in a Junko Shimada suit and Charles Jourdan high heels.

People were watching her from their cars, as if something was about to occur but they had no idea what. There was a middle-aged woman in a silver Mercedes coupe. There were suntanned men looking down at her from the high cab of a freight truck. Aomame planned to blow her brains out right before their very eyes with a 9mm bullet. Taking her life was the only way she could vanish from this 1Q84 world. That way she would be able to save Tengo's life. At least Leader had promised that. He had promised that much, and sought his own death.

Aomame didn't find it particularly disappointing that she had to die. Everything, she felt, had already been decided, ever since she was first pulled into this 1Q84 world. *I'm just following the plan that has already been laid out. Continuing to live, alone, in this unreasonable world – where there are two moons in the sky, one large, one small, where something called Little People control the destiny of others – what meaning could it have anyway?*

In the end, though, she didn't pull the trigger. At the last moment she relaxed her right index finger and removed the muzzle from her mouth. Like a person surfacing from deep under water she took a long breath, and exhaled, as if replacing every molecule of air within her.

She stopped moving toward death because she had heard a distant voice. At that point, she was in a soundless space. From the moment she put pressure on the trigger, all noise around her vanished. She was wrapped in silence, as if at the bottom of a pool. Down there, death was neither dark nor fearful. Like amniotic fluid to a fetus, it was natural, self-evident. *This isn't so bad,* Aomame thought, and almost smiled. That was when she heard a voice.

The voice sounded far away, as if coming from a distant time. She didn't recognize it. It reached her only after many twists and turns, and in the process it lost its original tone and timbre. What was left was a hollow echo, stripped of meaning. Still, within that sound, Aomame could detect a warmth she hadn't felt for years. The voice seemed to be calling her name.

She relaxed her finger on the trigger, narrowed her eyes, and listened carefully, trying to hear the words the voice was saying. But all she could make out, or thought that she made out, was her name. The rest was wind whistling through a hollow space. In the end the voice grew distant, lost any meaning at all, and was absorbed into the silence.

The void enveloping her disappeared, and, as if a cork had been pulled, the noise and clamor around her rushed in. And she no longer wanted to die.

Maybe I can see Tengo one more time at that little playground, she thought. *I can die after that. I'll take a chance on that happening. Living – not dying – means the possibility of seeing Tengo again. I want to live,* she decided. It was a strange feeling. *Had she ever experienced that feeling before in her life?*

She released the hammer of the automatic pistol, set the safety, and put it inside her shoulder bag. She straightened up, put on her sunglasses, and walked in the opposite direction of traffic back to her taxi. People silently watched her, in her high heels, striding down the expressway. She didn't have to walk for long. Even in the traffic jam, her taxi had managed to inch forward and had come up to where she was now standing.

Aomame knocked on the window and the driver lowered it.

"Can I get in again?"

The driver hesitated. "That thing you put in your mouth over there looked like a pistol."

"It was."

"A real one?"

"No way," Aomame replied, curling her lips.

The driver opened the door, and she climbed in. She took the bag off her shoulder and laid it on the seat and wiped her mouth with her handkerchief. She could still taste the metal and the residue of gun oil.

"So, did you find an emergency stairway?" the driver asked.

Aomame shook her head.

"I'm not surprised. I never heard of an emergency stairway anywhere around here," the driver said. "Would you still like to get off at the Ikejiri exit?"

"Yes, that would be fine," Aomame replied.

The driver rolled down his window, stuck his hand out, and pulled over into the right lane in front of a large bus. The meter in the cab was unchanged from when she had gotten out.

Aomame leaned back against the seat, and, breathing slowly, she gazed at the familiar Esso billboard. The huge tiger was looking in her direction, smiling, with a gas hose in his paw. *Put a Tiger in Your Tank*, the ad read.

"Put a tiger in your tank," she whispered.

"Excuse me?" the driver said, glancing at her in the rearview mirror.

"Nothing. Just talking to myself."

I think I'll stay alive here a bit longer, and see with my own eyes what's going to happen. I can still die after that – it won't be too late. Probably.

The day after she gave up on killing herself, Tamaru called her. So Aomame told him that the plan had changed – that she was going to stay put, and not change her name or get plastic surgery.

On the other end of the line Tamaru was silent. Several theories noiselessly aligned themselves in his mind.

"In other words, you're saying you don't want to move to another location?"

"Correct," Aomame replied. "I would like to stay here for the time being."

"That place is not set up to hide someone for an extended period."

"If I stay inside and don't go out, they shouldn't find me."

"Don't underestimate them," Tamaru said. "They will do everything they can to pinpoint who you are and hunt you down. And you won't be the only one in danger. It could involve those around you. If that happens, I could be put in a difficult position."

"I'm very sorry about that. But I need a bit more time."

"*A bit more time?* That's a little vague," Tamaru said.

"That's the only way I can put it."

Tamaru was silent, in thought. He seemed to have sensed how firm her decision was.

"I have to keep my priorities straight," he said. "Do you understand that?"

"I think so."

Tamaru was silent again, and then continued.

"All right. I just wanted to make sure I wasn't misunderstanding. Since you insist on staying, you must have your reasons."

"I do," Aomame said.

Tamaru briefly cleared his throat. "As I have told you before, we have committed to take you someplace safe, and far away – to erase any trail, change your face and name. Maybe it won't be a total transformation, but as close to total as we can manage. I thought we were agreed on this."

"Of course I understand. I'm not saying I don't like the plan itself. It's just that something unexpected occurred, and I need to stay put for a while longer."

"I am not authorized to say yes or no to this," Tamaru said, making a faint sound in the back of his throat. "It might take a while to get an answer."

"I'll be here," Aomame said.

"Glad to hear it," Tamaru said, and hung up.

The phone rang the next morning, just before nine. Three rings, then it stopped, and rang again. It had to be Tamaru.

Tamaru launched right in without saying hello. "Madame also is concerned about you staying there for very long. It is just a safe house, and it is not totally secure. Both of us agree that it's best to move you somewhere far away, somewhere more secure. Do you follow me?"

"I do."

"But you are a calm, cautious person. You don't make stupid mistakes, and I know you are committed. We trust you implicitly."

"I appreciate that."

"If you insist that you want to stay in that place for a *bit* longer then you must have your reasons. We don't know what your rationale is, but I'm sure it's not just a whim. So she is thinking that she would like to follow your wishes as much as she can."

Aomame said nothing.

Tamaru continued. "You can stay there until the end of the year. But that's the limit."

"After the first of the year, then, I need to move to another place."

"Please understand we are doing our very best to respect your wishes."

"I understand," Aomame said. "I'll be here until the end of the year, then I will move."

But this wasn't her real intention. She didn't plan to take one step out of this apartment until she saw Tengo again. If she mentioned this now, though, complications would set in. She could delay things for over three months, until the end of the year. After that she would consider what to do next.

"Fine," Tamaru said. "We'll deliver food and other necessities once a week. At one p.m. each Tuesday the supply masters will stop by. They have a key, so they can get in on their own. They will only go to the kitchen, nowhere else. While they are at the apartment, I want you to go into the back bedroom and lock the door. Don't show your face, or speak. When they're leaving, they will ring the doorbell once. Then you can come out of the bedroom. If there's anything special you need, let me know right now and I'll have it included in the next delivery."

"It would be nice to have equipment so I could do some strength training," Aomame said. "There's only so much you can do exercising and stretching without equipment."

"Full-scale gym equipment is out of the question, but we could supply some home equipment, the kind that doesn't take up much space."

"Something very basic would be fine," Aomame said.

"A stationary bike and some auxiliary equipment for strength training. Would that do it?"

"That would be great. If possible, I'd also like to get a metal softball bat."

Tamaru was silent for a few seconds.

"A bat has many uses," Aomame explained. "Just having it next to me makes me calm. It's like I grew up with a bat in my hand."

"Okay. I'll get one for you," Tamaru said. "If you think of anything else you need, write it on a piece of paper and leave it on the kitchen counter. I'll make sure you get it the next time we bring supplies."

"Thank you. But I think I have everything I need."

"How about books and videos and the like?"

"I can't think of anything I particularly want."

"How about Proust's *In Search of Lost Time*?" Tamaru asked. "If you've never read it this would be a good opportunity to read the whole thing."

"Have you read it?"

"No, I've never been in jail, or had to hide out for a long time. Someone once said unless you have those kinds of opportunities, you can't read the whole of Proust."

"Do you know anybody who has read the whole thing?"

"I've known some people who have spent a long period in jail, but none were the type to be interested in Proust."

"I'd like to give it a try," Aomame said. "If you can get ahold of those books, bring them the next time you bring supplies."

"Actually, I already got them for you," Tamaru said.

The so-called supply masters came on Tuesday afternoon at one p.m. on the dot. As instructed, Aomame went into the back bedroom, locked it from the inside, and tried not to make a sound. She heard the front door being unlocked and people opening the door and coming in. Aomame had no idea what kind of people these "supply masters" were. From the sounds they made she got the feeling there were two of them, but she didn't hear any voices. They carried in several boxes and silently went about putting things away. She heard them at the sink, rinsing off the food they had bought and then stacking it in the fridge. They must have decided beforehand who would be in charge of what. They unwrapped some boxes, and she could hear them folding up the wrapping paper and containers. It sounded like they were wrapping up the kitchen garbage as well. Aomame couldn't take the bag of garbage downstairs to the collection spot, so she had to have somebody take it for her.

The people seemed to do their work efficiently, with no wasted effort. They tried not to make any unnecessary noise, and their footsteps, too, were quiet. They were finished in about twenty minutes. Then they opened the front door and left. She heard them lock the front door from the outside, and then the doorbell rang once as a signal. To be on the safe side, Aomame waited fifteen minutes. Then she exited the bedroom, made sure no one else was there, and locked the dead bolt on the front door.

The large fridge was crammed full of a week's worth of food. This time it wasn't the kind of food you popped in the microwave, but mostly fresh groceries: a variety of fruits and vegetables; fish and meat; tofu, wakame, and natto. Milk, cheese, and orange juice. A dozen eggs. So there wouldn't be any extra garbage, they had taken everything out of their original containers and then neatly rewrapped them in plastic wrap. They had done a good job understanding the type of food she normally ate. *How would they know this?* she wondered. A stationary bicycle was set down next to the window, a small but high-end model. The digital display on it showed speed, distance, and calories burned. You could also monitor rpms and heart rate. There was a bench press to work on abs, deltoids, and triceps, the kind of equipment that was easy to assemble and disassemble. Aomame was quite familiar with it. It was the newest type, a very simple design yet very effective. With these two pieces of equipment she would have no trouble keeping in shape.

A metal bat in a soft case was there as well. Aomame took it out of the case and took a few swings. The shiny, new silver bat swished sharply through the air. The old familiar heft of it calmed her. The feel of the bat in her hands brought back memories of her teenage years, and the time she had spent with Tamaki Otsuka.

All seven volumes of *In Search of Lost Time* were piled up on the dining table. They were not new copies, but they appeared to be unread. Aomame flipped through one. There were several magazines, too – weekly and monthly magazines – and five brand-new videos, still in their plastic wrap. She had no idea who had chosen them, but they were all new movies she had never seen. She was not in the habit of going to movie theaters, so there were always a lot of new films that she missed.

There were three brand-new sweaters in a large department-store shopping bag, in different thicknesses. There were two thick flannel shirts, and four long-sleeved T-shirts. All of them were in plain fabric and simple designs. They were all the perfect size. There were also some thick socks and tights. If she was going to be here until December, she would need them. Her handlers knew what they were doing.

She took the clothes into the bedroom and folded them to store in drawers or hung them on hangers in the closet. She had gone back to the kitchen and was drinking coffee when the phone rang. It rang three times, stopped, then rang again.

"Did you get everything?" Tamaru asked.

"Yes, thank you. I think I have everything I need now. The exercise equipment is more than enough. Now I just have to crack open Proust."

"If there is anything that we've overlooked, don't hesitate to tell me."

"I won't," Aomame said. "Though I don't think it would be easy to find anything you have overlooked."

Tamaru cleared his throat. "This might not be my business, but do you mind if I give you a warning?"

"Go right ahead."

"Unless you have experienced it, being shut up in a small place by yourself, unable to see or talk to anyone else, is not the easiest thing in the world. No matter how tough a person might be, eventually he is going to make a sound. Especially when someone is after you."

"I haven't been living in very spacious places up till now."

"That could be an advantage," Tamaru said. "Still, I want you to be very careful. If a person remains tense for a long time he might not notice it himself, but it's like his nerves are a piece of rubber that has been stretched out. It's hard to go back to the original shape."

"I'll be careful," Aomame said.

"As I said before, you are a very cautious person. You're practical and patient, not overconfident. But no matter how careful a person might be, once your concentration slips, you will definitely make one or two mistakes. Loneliness becomes an acid that eats away at you."

"I don't think I'm lonely," Aomame declared. She said this half to Tamaru, and half to herself. "I'm all alone, but I'm not lonely."

There was silence on the other end of the phone, as if Tamaru were giving serious thought to the difference between being alone and being lonely.

"At any rate I'll be more cautious than I have been," Aomame said. "Thank you for the advice."

"There is one thing I'd like you to understand," Tamaru said. "We will do whatever we can to protect you. But if some emergency situation arises – what that might be, I don't know – you may have to deal with it yourself. I can run over there as fast as possible and still might not make it in time. Depending on the situation, I may not be able to get there at all. For instance, if it is no longer desirable for us to have a connection with you."

"I understand completely. I plan to protect myself. With the bat, and with the *thing you gave me.*"

"It's a tough world."

"Wherever there's hope there's a trial," Aomame said.

Tamaru was silent again for a moment, and then spoke. "Have you heard about the final tests given to candidates to become interrogators for Stalin's secret police?"

"No, I haven't."

"A candidate would be put in a square room. The only thing in the room is an ordinary small wooden chair. And the interrogator's boss gives him an order. He says, 'Get this chair to confess and write up a report on it. Until you do this, you can't leave this room.'"

"Sounds pretty surreal."

"No, it isn't. It's not surreal at all. It's a real story. Stalin actually did create that kind of paranoia, and some ten million people died on his watch – most of them his fellow countrymen. And we *actually* live in that kind of world. Don't ever forget that."

"You're full of heartwarming stories, aren't you."

"Not really. I just have a few set aside, just in case. I never received a formal education. I just learned whatever looked useful, as I experienced it. *Wherever there's hope there's a trial.* You're exactly right. Absolutely. Hope, however, is limited, and generally abstract, while there are countless trials, and they tend to be concrete. That is also something I had to learn on my own."

"So what kind of confession did the interrogator candidates extract from the chairs?"

"That is a question definitely worth considering," Tamaru said. "Sort of like a Zen koan."

"Stalinist Zen," Aomame said.

After a short pause, Tamaru hung up.

That afternoon she worked out on the stationary bike and the bench press. Aomame enjoyed the moderate workout, her first in a while. Afterward she showered, then made dinner while listening to an FM station. In the evening she checked the TV news (though not a single item caught her interest). After the sun had set she went out to the balcony to watch the playground, with her usual blanket, binoculars, and pistol. And her shiny brand-new bat.

If Tengo doesn't show up by then, she thought, *I guess I will see out this enigmatic year of 1Q84 in this corner of Koenji, one monotonous day after another. I'll cook, exercise, check the news, and work my way through Proust – and wait for Tengo to show up at the playground. Waiting for him is the central task of my life. Right now that slender thread is what is barely keeping me alive. It's like that spider I saw when I was climbing down the emergency stairway on the Metropolitan Expressway No. 3. A tiny black spider that had spun a pathetic little web in a corner of the grimy steel frame and was silently lying in wait. The wind from under the bridge had blown the spider web, which hung there precariously, tattered and full of dust. When I first saw it, I thought it was pitiful. But right now I'm in the same situation.*

I have to get ahold of a recording of Janáček's Sinfonietta. I need it when I'm working out. It makes me feel connected. It's as if that music is leading me to something. To what, though, I can't say. She made a mental note to add that to the next list of supplies.

It was October now. There were less than three months left of her reprieve. The clock kept ticking away, ceaselessly. Aomame sank down into her garden chair and continued to watch the slide in the playground through the plastic blinds. The little children's playground looked pale under the mercury-vapor lamp. The scene made Aomame think of deserted hallways in an aquarium at night. Invisible, imaginary fish were swimming noiselessly through the trees, never halting their silent movements. And two moons hung in the sky, waiting for Aomame's acknowledgment.

"Tengo," she whispered. "Where are you?"

3

TENGO
The Animals All Wore Clothes

IN THE AFTERNOONS TENGO WOULD VISIT his father in the hospital, sit next to his bed, open the book he brought, and read aloud. After reading five pages he would take a short break, then read five more pages. He read whatever book he happened to be reading on his own at the time. Sometimes it was a novel, or a biography, or a book on the natural sciences. What was most important was the act of reading the sentences aloud, not the contents.

Tengo didn't know if his father actually heard his voice. His face never showed any reaction. This thin, shabby-looking old man had his eyes closed, and he was asleep. He didn't move at all, and his breathing wasn't audible. He was breathing, but unless you brought your ear very close, or held a mirror up to his nose to see if it clouded, you couldn't really tell. The liquid in the IV drip went into his body, and a tiny amount of urine oozed out the catheter. The only thing that revealed that he was alive was this silent, slow movement in and out. Occasionally a nurse would shave his beard with an electric razor and use a tiny pair of scissors with rounded-off tips to clip the white hairs growing out of his ears and nose. She would trim his eyebrows as well. Even though he was unconscious, these continued to grow. As he watched his father, Tengo started to have doubts about the difference between a person being alive and being dead. *Maybe there really wasn't much of a difference to begin with,* he thought. *Maybe we just decided, for convenience's sake, to insist on a difference.*

At three the doctor came and gave Tengo an update on his father's condition. The explanation was always concise, and it was nearly the same from one day to the next. There was no change. The old man was simply asleep, his life gradually fading away. In other words, death was approaching, slowly but certainly, and there was nothing medically speaking that could be done. Just let him lie here, quietly sleeping. That's about all the doctor could say.

In the evenings two male nurses would come and take his father to an examination room. The male nurses differed depending on the day, but both of them were taciturn. Perhaps the masks they wore had something to do with it, but they never said a word. One of them looked foreign. He was short and dark skinned, and was always smiling at Tengo through his mask. Tengo could tell he was smiling by his eyes. Tengo smiled back and nodded.

Anywhere from a half hour to an hour later, his father would be brought back to his room. Tengo had no idea what kind of examinations they were conducting. While his father was gone he would go to the cafeteria, have some hot green tea, and stay about fifteen minutes before going back to the hospital room. All the while he held on to the hope that when he returned an air chrysalis would once again materialize, with Aomame as a young girl lying inside. But all that greeted him in the gloomy hospital room was the smell of a sick person and the depressions left behind in the empty bed.

Tengo stood by the window and looked at the scene outside. Beyond the garden and lawn was the dark line of the pine windbreak, through which came the sound of waves. The rough waves of the Pacific. It was a thick, darkish sound, as if many souls were gathered, each whispering his story. They seemed to be seeking more souls to join them, seeking even more stories to be told.

Before this, in October, Tengo had twice taken day trips, on his days off, to the sanatorium in Chikura. He would take the early-morning express train. Once there, he would sit beside his father's bed, and talk to him sometimes. There was nothing even close to a response. His father just lay there, faceup, sound asleep. Tengo spent most of his time gazing out the window. As evening approached he waited for something to happen, but nothing ever did. The sun would silently sink, and the room would be wrapped in the gathering gloom. He would ultimately give up, leave, and take the last express train back to Tokyo.

Maybe I should be more patient, stay with him longer, Tengo thought once. *Maybe visiting him for the day and then leaving isn't enough. What's needed, perhaps, is a deeper commitment.* He had no concrete evidence that this was true. He just felt that way.

After the middle of November he took the vacation leave he had accumulated, telling the cram school that his father was in critical condition and he needed to look after him. This in itself wasn't a lie. He asked a classmate from college to take over his classes. He was one of the relatively few people with whom Tengo had kept in touch, albeit just once or twice a year. Even in the math department, which had more than its share of oddballs, this guy was particularly odd, as well as smart beyond compare. After graduating, though, he didn't get a job or go on to grad school. Instead, when he felt like it, he taught math at a private cram school for junior high students. Other than that, he read, went fly fishing, and did whatever he wanted. Tengo happened to know, however, that he was a very capable teacher. The thing was, he was tired of being so capable. Plus, he was from a wealthy family and there was no need for him to force himself to work. He had substituted for Tengo once before and the students had liked him. Tengo called him and explained the situation, and he immediately agreed to step in.

There was also the question of what to do about Fuka-Eri. Tengo couldn't decide if leaving this naive girl behind in his apartment for a long time was the right thing to do. And besides, she was trying to hide out, to stay out of sight. So he asked her directly. "Are you okay on your own here for a while? Or would you like to go someplace else, temporarily?"

"Where are you going," Fuka-Eri asked, a serious look in her eyes.

"To the cat town," Tengo explained. "My father won't regain consciousness. He's been in a deep sleep for a while. They say he might not last long."

He didn't say a word about the air chrysalis appearing in the hospital room bed one evening. Or how Aomame appeared inside as a young girl, asleep. Or how the air chrysalis was exactly as Fuka-Eri had described it in her novel, down to the last detail. Or how he was secretly hoping that it would again appear before him.

Fuka-Eri narrowed her eyes, pursed her lips, and stared straight at Tengo, as if trying to make out a message written in tiny letters. Almost unconsciously he touched his face, but it didn't feel as though something was written on it.

"That's fine," Fuka-Eri said after a while, and she nodded several times. "Do not worry about me. I will stay at home." After thinking for a moment she added, "Right now there is no danger."

"Right now there is no danger," Tengo repeated.

"Do not worry about me," she said again.

"I'll call you every day."

"Do not get abandoned in the cat town."

"I'll be careful," Tengo said.

Tengo went to the supermarket and bought enough food so Fuka-Eri wouldn't have to go shopping, all things that would be simple to prepare. Tengo was well aware that she had neither the ability nor the desire to do much cooking. He wanted to avoid coming back in two weeks to a fridge full of mushy, spoiled food.

He stuffed a vinyl bag full of clothes and toiletries, a few books, pens, and paper. As usual he took the express train from Tokyo Station, changed to a local train at Tateyama, and got off at Chikura. He went to the tourist information booth in front of the station to look for a fairly inexpensive hotel. It was the off-season, so he had no trouble finding a room in a simple Japanese-style inn that catered mainly to people coming to fish. The cramped but clean room smelled of fresh tatami. The fishing harbor was visible from the second-floor window. The charge for the room, which included breakfast, was cheaper than he had expected.

"I don't know yet how long I'll be staying," Tengo said, "but I'll go ahead and pay for three days." The proprietress of the inn had no objection. The doors shut at eleven, and bringing a woman to his room would be problematic, she explained in a roundabout way. All this sounded fine to him. Once he settled into his room, he phoned the sanatorium. He told the nurse (the same middle-aged nurse he had met before) that he would like to visit his father at three p.m. and asked if that would be convenient. That would be fine, she replied. "Mr. Kawana just sleeps all the time," she said.

Thus began Tengo's days at the cat town beside the sea. He would get up early, take a walk along the shore, watch the fishing boats go in and out of the harbor, then return to the inn for breakfast. Breakfast was exactly the same every day – dried horse mackerel and fried eggs, a quartered tomato, seasoned dried seaweed, miso soup with shijimi clams, and rice – but for some reason it tasted wonderful every morning. After breakfast he would sit at a small desk and write. He hadn't written in some time and found the act of writing with his fountain pen enjoyable. Working in an unfamiliar place, away from your daily routine, was invigorating. The engines of the fishing boats chugged monotonously as they pulled into the harbor. Tengo liked the sound.

The story he was writing began with a world where there were two moons in the sky. A world of Little People and air chrysalises. He had borrowed this world from Fuka-Eri's *Air Chrysalis,* but by now it was entirely his own. As he wrote, his mind was living in that world. Even when he lay down his pen and stood up from the desk, his mind remained there. There was a special sensation of his body and his mind beginning to separate, and he could no longer distinguish the real world from the fictional. The protagonist of the story who entered the cat town probably experienced the same sensation. Before he knew it, the world's center of gravity had shifted. And the protagonist would (most likely) be unable to ever board the train to get out of town.

At eleven Tengo had to leave his room so they could clean it. When the time came he stopped writing, went out, walked to the front of the station, and drank coffee in a nearby coffee shop. Occasionally he would have a light sandwich, but usually he ate nothing. He would then pick up the morning paper and check it closely to see if there was any article that might have something to do with him. He found no such article. *Air Chrysalis* had long since disappeared from the bestseller lists. Number one on the list now was a diet book entitled *Eat as Much as You Want of the Food You Love and Still Lose Weight.* What a great title. The whole book could be blank inside and it would still sell.

After he finished his coffee and was done with the paper, Tengo took the bus to the sanatorium. He usually arrived between one thirty and two. He chatted a bit with the nurse who was always at the front desk. When Tengo began staying in the town and visiting his father every day, the nurses grew kinder to him, and treated him in a friendly way – as warmly as the prodigal son's family must have welcomed him back home.

One of the younger nurses always gave an embarrassed smile whenever she saw Tengo. She seemed to have a crush on him. She was petite, wore her hair in a ponytail, and had big eyes and red cheeks. She was probably in her early twenties. But ever since the air chrysalis had appeared with the sleeping girl inside, all Tengo could think about was Aomame. All other women were faint shadows in comparison. An image of Aomame was constantly playing at the edges of his mind. Aomame was alive somewhere in this world – he could *feel* it. He knew she must be searching for him, which is why on that evening she chose to find him. She had not forgotten him either.

If what I saw wasn't an illusion.

Sometimes he remembered his older girlfriend, and wondered how she was. *She's irretrievably lost now,* her husband had said on the phone. She can no longer visit your home. *Irretrievably lost.* Even now those words gave Tengo an uncomfortable, uneasy feeling. They had an undeniably ominous ring.

Still, she became less and less of a presence in his mind as time went on. He could recall the afternoons they had spent together only as events in the past, undertaken to fulfill certain goals. Tengo felt guilty about this. But before he had known it, gravity had changed. It had shifted, and it wouldn't be going back to its original location.

When he arrived at his father's room, Tengo would sit in the chair next to his bed and briefly greet him. Then he would explain, in chronological order, what he had done since the previous night. He hadn't done much. He had gone back to town on the bus, had a simple dinner at a restaurant, drunk a beer, returned to the inn, and read. He'd gone to bed at ten. In the morning he would take a walk, eat breakfast, and work on his novel for about two hours. He repeated the same things every day, but even so, Tengo gave the unconscious man a detailed report on all his activities. There was no response from his listener. It was like talking to a wall. A formality he had to go through. Still, sometimes simple repetition has meaning.

Then Tengo would read from the book he had brought along. He didn't stick to just one book. He would read aloud the book that he himself was reading at the time. If a manual for an electric lawn mower had been his current reading material, that's what he would have read. Tengo read in a deliberately clear voice, slowly, so that it was easy to understand. That was the one thing he made sure to do.

The lightning outside grew steadily stronger and for a while the greenish light illuminated the road, but there was no rumble of thunder. Maybe there was thunder, but he felt unfocused. It was as if he couldn't hear it. Rainwater flowed in small rivers along the road. After wading through the water, customers came into the shop, one after another.

His friend turned and stared. He went strangely quiet. There was a sudden commotion as customers pushed toward them, making it hard to breathe.

Someone cleared his throat, perhaps because a piece of food had gotten stuck; it was a strange voice, more of a snuffling cough, as if it were a dog.

Suddenly there was a huge flash of lightning that shone all the way inside the place, illuminating the people on the dirt floor. And just then a clap of thunder sounded, ready to crack the roof. Surprised, he stood up, and the crowd of people at the entrance turned as one to face him. Then he saw that theirs were the faces of animals – dogs or foxes, he wasn't sure – and the animals all wore clothes, and some of them had long tongues hanging out, licking around the corners of their mouths.

Tengo read to there and looked at his father's face. "The end," he said. The story stopped there.

No reaction.

"What do you think?"

As expected, there was no response from his father.

Sometimes he would read what he himself had written that

morning. After he had read it, he would rewrite in ballpoint pen the parts he wasn't satisfied with, and reread the parts he had edited. If he still wasn't satisfied at the way it sounded, he would rewrite it again, and then read the new version.

"The rewritten version is better," he said to his father, as if hoping he would agree. His father, predictably, didn't express an opinion. He didn't say that it was better, or that the earlier version was better, or that there really wasn't much of a difference between the two. The lids on his sunken eyes were shut tight, like a sad house with its heavy shutters lowered.

Sometimes Tengo would stand up from his chair and stretch and go to the window and look at the scenery outside. After several overcast days, it was raining. The continual afternoon rain made the pine windbreak dark and heavy. He couldn't hear the waves at all. There was no wind, just the rain falling straight down from the sky. A flock of black birds flew by in the rain. The hearts of those birds were dark, and wet, too. The inside of the room was also wet. Everything there, pillows, books, desk, was damp. But oblivious to it all – to the weather, the damp, the wind, the sound of the waves – his father continued in an uninterrupted coma. Like a merciful cloak, paralysis enveloped his body. After a short break Tengo went back to reading aloud. In the damp, narrow room, that was all he was able to do.

When he tired of reading aloud, Tengo sat there, gazing at the form of his sleeping father and trying to surmise what kinds of things were going through his brain. Inside – in the inner parts of that stubborn skull, like an old anvil – what sort of consciousness lay hidden there? Or was there nothing left at all? Was it like an abandoned house from which all the possessions and appliances had been moved, leaving no trace of those who had once dwelled there? Even if it was, there should be the occasional memory or scenery etched into the walls and ceilings. Things cultivated over such a long time don't just vanish into nothingness. As his father lay on this plain bed in the sanatorium by the shore, at the same time he might very well be surrounded by scenes and memories invisible to others, in the still darkness of a back room in his own vacant house.

The young nurse with the red cheeks would come in, smile at Tengo, then take his father's temperature, check how much remained in the IV drip, and measure the amount of urine he had produced. She would note all the numbers down on a clipboard. Her actions were automatic and brisk, as if prescribed in a training manual. Tengo watched this series of movements and wondered how she must feel to live her life in this sanatorium by the sea, taking care of senile old people whose prognosis was grim. She looked young and healthy. Beneath her starched uniform, her waist and her breasts were compact but ample. Golden down glistened on her smooth neck. The plastic name tag on her chest read *Adachi*.

What could possibly have brought her to this remote place, where oblivion and listless death lay hovering over everything? Tengo could tell she was a skilled and hardworking nurse. She was still young and worked quite efficiently. She could have easily worked in some other field of health care, something more lively and engaging, so why did she choose this sad sort of place to work? Tengo wondered. He wanted to find out the reason and the background. If he did ask her, he knew she would be honest. He could sense that about her. But it would be better not to get involved, Tengo decided – this was, after all, the cat town. Some day he would have to get on the train and go back to the world from which he came.

The nurse finished her tasks, put the clipboard back, and gave Tengo an awkward smile.

"His condition is unchanged. The same as always."

"So he's stable," Tengo said in as cheerful a voice as he could manage. "To put a positive spin on it."

A half-apologetic smile rose to her lips and she inclined her head just a touch. She glanced at the book on his lap. "Are you reading that to him?"

Tengo nodded. "I doubt he can hear it, though."

"Still, it's a good thing to do," the nurse said.

"Maybe it is, or maybe it isn't, but I can't think of anything else I can do."

"But not everybody else would do that."

"Most people have busier lives than I do," Tengo said.

The nurse looked like she was about to say something, but she hesitated. In the end she didn't say a thing. She looked at his sleeping father, and then at Tengo.

"Take care," she said.

"Thanks," Tengo answered.

After Nurse Adachi left, Tengo waited a while, then began reading aloud once more.

In the evening, when his father was wheeled on a gurney to the examination room, Tengo went to the cafeteria, drank some tea, then phoned Fuka-Eri from a pay phone.

"Is everything okay?" Tengo asked her.

"Yes, everything is okay," she said. "Just like always."

"Everything's fine with me, too. Doing the same thing every day."

"But time is moving forward."

"That's right," Tengo said. "Every day time moves forward one day's worth."

And what has gone forward can't go back to where it came from.

"The crow came back again just a little while ago," Fuka-Eri said. "A big crow."

"In the evening that crow always comes up to the window."

"Doing the same thing every day."

"That's right," Tengo said. "Just like us."

"But it doesn't think about time."

"Crows can't think about time. Probably only humans have the concept of time."

"Why," she asked.

"Humans see time as a straight line. It's like putting notches on a long straight stick. The notch here is the future, the one on this side is the past, and the present is this point right here. Do you understand?"

"I think so."

"But actually time isn't a straight line. It doesn't have a shape. In all senses of the term, it doesn't have any form. But since we can't picture something without form in our minds, for the sake of convenience we understand it as a straight line. At this point, humans are the only ones who can make that sort of conceptual substitution."

"But maybe we are the ones who are wrong."

Tengo mulled this over. "You mean we may be wrong to see time as a straight line?"

No response.

"That's a possibility. Maybe we're wrong and the crow is right. Maybe time is nothing at all like a straight line. Perhaps it's shaped like a twisted doughnut. But for tens of thousands of years, people have probably been seeing time as a straight line that continues on forever. And that's the concept they based their actions on. And until now they haven't found anything inconvenient or contradictory about it. So as an experiential model, it's probably correct."

"Experiential model," Fuka-Eri repeated.

"After taking a lot of samples, you come to view one conjecture as actually correct."

Fuka-Eri was silent for a time. Tengo had no idea if she had understood him or not.

"Hello?" Tengo said, checking if she was still there.

"How long will you be there," Fuka-Eri asked, omitting the question mark.

"You mean how long will I be in Chikura?"

"Yes."

"I don't know," Tengo answered honestly. "All I can say right now is that I'll stay here until certain things make sense. There are some things I don't understand. I want to stay for a while and see how they develop."

Fuka-Eri was silent on the other end again. When she was silent it was like she wasn't there at all.

"Hello?" Tengo said again.

"Don't miss the train," Fuka-Eri said.

"I'll be careful," Tengo replied, "not to be late for the train. Is everything okay with you?"

"One person came here a while ago."

"What kind of person?"

"An N – H – K person."

"A fee collector from NHK?"

"Fee collector," she asked, again without the question mark.

"Did you talk to him?" Tengo asked.

"I did not understand what he was saying."

She apparently had no idea what NHK was. The girl lacked some essential cultural knowledge.

"It will take too long to explain over the phone," Tengo said, "but basically it's a large organization. A lot of people work there. They go around to all the houses in Japan and collect money every month. You and I don't need to pay, because we don't receive anything from them. I hope you didn't unlock the door."

"No, I did not unlock it. Like you told me."

"I'm glad."

"But he said, 'You are a thief.'"

"You don't need to worry about that," Tengo said.

"We have not stolen anything."

"Of course we haven't. You and I haven't done anything wrong."

Fuka-Eri was again silent on the other end of the line.

"Hello?" Tengo said.

Fuka-Eri didn't reply. She might have already hung up. Though he didn't hear any sound that indicated this.

"Hello?" Tengo repeated, this time more loudly.

Fuka-Eri coughed lightly. "That person knew a lot about you."

"The fee collector?"

"Yes. The N – H – K person."

"And he called you a thief."

"No. He didn't mean me."

"He meant me?"

Fuka-Eri didn't reply.

"Anyway," Tengo said, "I don't have a TV. So I'm not stealing anything from NHK."

"But that person was very angry that I didn't unlock the door."

"It doesn't matter. Let him be angry. But no matter what happens, no matter what anyone tells you, never, ever unlock the door."

"I won't unlock it."

After saying this, Fuka-Eri suddenly hung up. Or perhaps it wasn't so sudden. Perhaps for her, hanging up the phone at that point was an entirely natural, even logical act. To Tengo's ear, though, it sounded abrupt. But Tengo knew that even if he were to try his hardest to guess what Fuka-Eri was thinking and feeling, it wouldn't do any good. As an experiential model.

Tengo hung up the phone and went back to his father's room.

His father had not been brought back to his room yet. The bed still had a depression in it from his body. No air chrysalis was there. In the room, darkened by the dim, chill dusk, the only thing present was the slight trace of the person who had occupied it until moments ago.

Tengo sighed and sat down on the chair. He rested his hands on his lap and gazed for a long while at the depression in the sheets. Then he stood, went to the window, and looked outside. The rain had stopped, and the autumn clouds lingered over the pine windbreak. It would be a beautiful sunset, the first in some time.

Tengo had no idea why the fee collector *knew a lot* about him. The last time an NHK fee collector had come around had been about a year ago. At that time he had stood at the door and politely explained to the man that there was no TV in his apartment. He never watched TV, he continued. The fee collector hadn't been convinced, but he had left without saying any more, muttering some snide remark under his breath.

Was it the same fee collector who had come today? He had the impression that that man had also said something about his being a *thief*. It was a bit odd that the same collector would show up a year later and say he *knew a lot* about Tengo. They had only stood at the door and chatted for five minutes or so, that's all.

Whatever. What was important was that Fuka-Eri had kept the door locked. The fee collector wouldn't be paying another visit anytime soon. He had a quota to meet and had to be tired of standing around quarreling with people who refused to pay their subscription fees. In order not to waste time, he would skip the troublesome customers' places and collect the fees from people who didn't have a problem paying.

Tengo looked again at the hollow his father had left in the bed, and he remembered all the pairs of shoes his father had worn out. As his father had pounded the Tokyo pavement collecting fees, he had consigned countless pairs of shoes to oblivion. All of the shoes looked the same – cheap, no-nonsense leather shoes, black, with thick soles. He had worn them hard, until they were worn out and falling apart, the heels warped out of shape. As a boy, every time Tengo saw these terribly misshapen shoes it pained him. He didn't feel sorry for his father, but for the shoes. They reminded him of a pitiful work animal, driven as hard as possible and hovering on the verge of death.

But come to think of it, wasn't his father now like a work animal about to die? No different from a worn-out pair of leather shoes?

Tengo gazed out the window again as the colors of the sunset deepened in the western sky. He remembered the air chrysalis emitting a faint, pale light, and Aomame, as a young girl, sleeping inside.

Would that air chrysalis ever appear here again?

Was time really a straight line?

"It seems I've reached a deadlock," Tengo mumbled to the wall. "There are too many variables. Even for a former child prodigy, it's impossible to find an answer."

The walls didn't have a response. Nor did they express an opinion. They simply, and silently, reflected the color of the setting sun.

4

USHIKAWA

Occam's Razor

USHIKAWA FOUND IT HARD TO GET his head around the idea that the elderly dowager who lived in a mansion in Azabu could somehow be involved with the assassination of Sakigake's Leader. He had dug up background information on her. She was a well-known figure in society, so the investigation had not taken much effort. Her husband had been a prominent businessman in the postwar era, influential in the political sphere. His business focused mainly on investments and real estate, though he had also branched out into large-scale retail stores and transport-related businesses. After her husband's death in the mid-1950s, the woman had taken over his company. She had a talent for managing business, as well as an ability to sense impending danger. In the late 1960s she felt that the company had overextended itself, so she deliberately sold – at a high price – its stock in various fields, and systematically downsized the business. She put all her physical and mental strength into the remaining areas. Thanks to this, she was able to weather the era of the oil shock that occurred soon after with minimal damage and set aside a healthy amount of liquid assets. She knew how to turn other people's crises into golden opportunities for herself.

She was retired now and in her mid-seventies. She had an abundance of money, which allowed her to live in comfort in her spacious mansion, indebted to no one. But why would a woman like that deliberately plot to murder someone?

Even so, Ushikawa decided to dig a little deeper. One reason was that he couldn't find anything else that even resembled a clue. The second reason was that there was something about this safe house that bothered him. There was nothing especially unnatural about providing a free shelter for battered women. It was a sound and useful service to society. The dowager had the financial resources, and the women must be very grateful to her for her kindness. The problem was that the security at that apartment building – the heavy locked gate, the German shepherd, the surveillance cameras – was too tight for a facility of its type. There was something excessive about it.

The first thing Ushikawa did was check the deed for the land and the house that the dowager lived in. This was public information, easily ascertained by a trip to city hall. The deed to both the land and the house were in her name alone. There was no mortgage. Everything was quite clear-cut. As private assets, the property tax would come to quite a sum, but she probably didn't mind paying such an amount. The future inheritance tax would also be huge, but this didn't seem to bother her, which was unusual for such a wealthy person. In Ushikawa's experience, nobody hated paying taxes more than the rich.

After her husband's death, she continued to live alone in that enormous mansion. No doubt she had a few servants, so she wasn't totally alone. She had two children, and her son had taken over the company. The son had three children. Her daughter had married and died fifteen years ago of an illness. She left no children behind.

This much was easy to find out. But once he tried to dig deeper into the woman's background, a solid wall loomed up out of nowhere, blocking his way. Beyond this, all paths were closed. The wall was high, and the door had multiple locks. What Ushikawa did know was that this woman wanted to keep anything private about her completely out of public view. And she had poured considerable effort and money into carrying out that policy. She never responded to any sort of inquiry, never made any public statements. And no matter how many materials he raked through, not once did he come up with a photograph of her.

The woman's number was listed in the Minato Ward phone book. Ushikawa's style was to tackle things head on, so he went ahead and dialed it. Before the phone had rung twice, a man picked up.

Ushikawa gave a phony name and the name of some investment firm and said, "There's something I would like to ask the lady of the house about, regarding her investment funds."

The man replied, "She isn't able to come to the phone. But you can tell me whatever she needs to know." His businesslike tone sounded mechanical, manufactured.

"It's company policy not to reveal these things to anyone other than the client," Ushikawa explained, "so if I can't speak with her directly now, I can mail the documents to her. She will have them in a few days."

"That would be fine," the man said, and hung up.

Ushikawa wasn't particularly disappointed that he couldn't speak to the dowager. He wasn't expecting to. What he really wanted to find out was how concerned she was about protecting her privacy. Extremely so, it would appear. She seemed to have several people with her in the mansion who kept a close guard over her. The tone of this man who answered the phone – her secretary, most likely – made this clear. Her name was printed in the telephone directory, but only a select group could actually speak to her. All others were flicked away, like ants who had crawled into the sugar bowl.

Pretending to be looking for a place to rent, he made the rounds of local real estate agencies, indirectly asking about the apartment building used as the safe house. Most of the agents had no idea there was an apartment building at that address. This neighborhood was one of the more upscale residential areas in Tokyo. These agents only dealt with high-end properties and couldn't be bothered with a two-story, wooden apartment building. One look at Ushikawa's face and clothes, too, and they essentially gave him the cold shoulder. If a three-legged, water-logged dog with a torn-off tail and mange had limped in the door, they would have treated it more kindly than they treated him.

Just when he was about to give up, a small local agency that seemed to have been there for years caught his eye. The yellowed old man at the front desk said, "Ah, that place," and volunteered information. The man's face was shriveled up, like a second-rate mummy, but he knew every nook and cranny of the neighborhood and always jumped at the chance to bend someone's ear.

"That building is owned by Mr. Ogata's wife, and yes, in the past it was rented out as apartments. Why she happened to have that building, I don't really know. Her circumstances did not exactly demand that she manage an apartment building. I imagine she mostly used it to house their employees. I don't know much about it now, but it seems to be used for battered women, kind of like those *kakekomidera,* temples in the old days that sheltered wives running away from abusive husbands. Anyway, it isn't going to fatten a real estate agent's wallet."

The old man laughed, with his mouth shut. He sounded like a woodpecker.

"A *kakekomidera,* eh?" Ushikawa said. He offered him a Seven Stars cigarette. The old man took it, let Ushikawa light it for him with his lighter, and took a deep, appreciative drag on it. This is exactly what the Seven Stars must long for, Ushikawa mused – to be enjoyed so thoroughly.

"Women whose husbands smack them around and run away, their faces all puffed up, they – they take shelter there. They don't have to pay rent."

"Like a kind of public service," Ushikawa said.

"Yes, that sort of thing. They had this extra apartment building so they used it to help people in trouble. She's tremendously wealthy, so she could do whatever she wanted, without worrying about making money. Not like the rest of us."

"But why did Mrs. Ogata start doing that? Was there something that led up to it?"

"I don't know. She's so rich that maybe it's like a hobby?"

"Well, even if it is a hobby," Ushikawa said, beaming, "that's a wonderful thing, to help people in trouble like that. Not everyone with money to burn takes the initiative to help others."

"Of course it's a nice thing to do," the old man agreed. "Years ago I used to hit my old lady all the time, so I'm not one to talk." He opened his mouth, showing off his missing teeth, and guffawed, as if hitting your wife every once in a while were one of life's notable pleasures.

"So I take it that several people live there now?" Ushikawa asked.

"I go past there when I take a walk every morning, but you can't see anything from outside. But it does seem like a few people are living there. I guess there will always be men in the world who beat their wives."

"There are always far more people in the world who make things worse, rather than help out."

The old man guffawed again loudly, his mouth wide open. "You got that right. There are a lot more people who do bad things than do good."

The old man seemed to have taken a liking to Ushikawa. This made Ushikawa uncomfortable.

"By the way, what sort of person is Mrs. Ogata?" Ushikawa asked, trying to sound casual.

"I really don't know that much about her," the old man replied, knitting his brow like the spirit of an old, withered tree. "She lives a very quiet, reserved life. I've done business here for many years, but at most I've just caught glimpses of her from afar. When she goes out she always has a chauffeur, and her maids do all the shopping. She has a man who is like her personal secretary and he takes care of most everything. I mean, she's a well-bred, wealthy woman, and you can't expect her to talk with the hoi polloi." The old man frowned, and from the midst of those wrinkles came a wink, directed at Ushikawa.

By hoi polloi, the old man with the yellowed face seemed to be talking about a group composed primarily of two people: himself and Ushikawa.

Ushikawa asked another question. "How long has Mrs. Ogata been active in providing a safe house for victims of domestic violence?"

"I'm not really sure. I've only heard from others that the place is a kind of *kakekomidera*. But about four years ago, people started to go in and out of that apartment building. Four or five years, something like that." The old man lifted the teacup to his lips and drank his cold tea. "It was about then that they built a new gate and the security got tighter. It's a safe house, after all, and if anyone can just wander in, the folks who live there won't be able to relax."

The old man seemed to come back to the present. He looked at Ushikawa a bit suspiciously. "So – you said you're looking for a reasonably priced place to rent?"

"That's correct."

"Then you better try somewhere else. This neighborhood is full of expensive mansions and even if there are places for rent that come on the market, they're all high-end rentals aimed at foreigners who work in the embassies. A long time ago there were a lot of regular people who lived around here, ones who weren't so wealthy. As a matter of fact, finding places for them is how our business got started. But there aren't any affordable houses left, so I'm thinking of closing the business. Land prices in Tokyo have skyrocketed and small fry like me can't handle it anymore. Unless you have bags of cash to spare, I suggest you try elsewhere."

"I'll do that," Ushikawa said. "The truth is, I am a bit strapped. I'll try some other location."

The old man breathed out cigarette smoke and a sigh. "But once Mrs. Ogata passes, you can bet that mansion will disappear. That son of hers is a real go-getter, and there's no way he's going to let a prime piece of real estate like that in a premium area just sit around. He'll knock it down in a flash and put up an ultra-high-end condo. He may very well be drawing up the blueprints as we speak."

"If that happens this whole neighborhood won't be quite as serene as it is now."

"Yup, you won't recognize it."

"You mentioned her son. What business is he in?"

"Basically he's in real estate. The same as me. But the difference between us is like chalk and cheese. Like a Rolls-Royce and an old bicycle. He takes a huge amount of capital and then makes investments on his own, one after another. He licks up all the honey himself, without leaving a drop behind. Nothing spills over in my direction, I can tell you that. The world sucks, that's for sure."

"I was just walking around a while ago and wandered all around the outskirts of that mansion. I was impressed. It's quite a place."

"Well, it's definitely the best residence in this neighborhood. When I picture those beautiful willow trees being chopped down, it hurts." The old man shook his head as if he really were in pain. "I can only hope that Mrs. Ogata lives a little longer."

"I hear you," Ushikawa agreed.

Ushikawa found a listing for the Center for Victims of Domestic Violence in the phone book and decided to contact them. It was a nonprofit organization, run by volunteers and headed by several lawyers. Ushikawa made an appointment in the name of his phony office, the New Japan Foundation for the Advancement of Scholarship and the Arts. He led them to believe he might be a potential donor, and they set the time for the appointment.

Ushikawa proffered his business card (which was the same as the one he had given to Tengo) and explained how one of the purposes of his foundation was to pinpoint an outstanding nonprofit organization that was making a real contribution to society, and provide them with a grant. Though he couldn't reveal who the sponsor was, the grant could be used in any way the recipient wished. The only requirement was to submit a simple report by the end of the year.

Ushikawa's appearance didn't inspire any goodwill or trust, and the young lawyer he spoke with eyed him warily at first. However, they were chronically short on funds, and had to accept any support, no matter the source.

"I'll need to know more about your activities," Ushikawa said. The lawyer explained how they had started the organization. Ushikawa found this history boring, but he listened carefully, his expression one of devoted interest. He made all the appropriate noises, nodded in all the right places, and kept his expression docile and open. As he did, the lawyer warmed up to him. Ushikawa was a highly trained listener, adopting such a sincere and receptive manner that he almost always succeeded in putting the other person at ease.

He found the opportunity to casually nudge the conversation in the direction of the safe house. For the unfortunate women who are running away from domestic violence, he asked, if they can't find an appropriate place to go, where do they end up living? He put on an expression that showed his deep sympathy for these women whose fate was like that of leaves tossed about in some outrageously strong wind.

"In instances like that we have several safe houses where they can go," the young lawyer replied.

"Safe houses?"

"Temporary refuges. There aren't many, but there are places that charitable people have offered us. One person has even provided an entire apartment building for us to use."

"An entire apartment building," Ushikawa said, sounding impressed. "I guess some people can be quite generous."

"That's right. Whenever our activities are covered in newspapers or magazines, inevitably we'll get a call from people wanting to help out. Without offers from people like that, we would never be able to keep this organization going, since we depend almost entirely on contributions."

"What you're doing is very meaningful," Ushikawa said.

The lawyer flashed him a vulnerable smile. *Nobody's easier to fool,* Ushikawa thought, *than the person who is convinced that he is right.*

"How many women would you say are living in that apartment building now?"

"It depends, but – let's see – I would say usually four or five," the lawyer said.

"About that charitable person who provided that apartment building," Ushikawa said, "how did this person get involved? I'm thinking there must have been some event that led up to this interest."

The lawyer tilted his head. "I really don't know. Though in the past this person was, it seems, involved in similar activities, on an individual level. As far as we're concerned, we're just grateful for this individual's kindness. We don't ask the reasons behind it."

"Of course," Ushikawa nodded. "I assume you keep the locations of your safe houses secret?"

"Correct. We have to make sure that the women are protected, plus many of our donors prefer to remain anonymous. I mean, we're dealing with acts of violence, after all."

They talked for a while longer, but Ushikawa was unable to extract any more useful information. What Ushikawa knew were the following facts: the Center for Victims of Domestic Violence had begun operations in earnest four years ago. Not long afterward, a certain "donor" had contacted them and offered them use of a vacant apartment building as a safe house. The donor had read about their activities in the newspaper. The donor had set one condition, namely, that the donor's name never be revealed. Still, from what was said, Ushikawa could deduce that, beyond any doubt, the "donor" was the elderly dowager living in Azabu, the one who owned the old apartment building.

"Thank you so much for taking the time to speak with me," Ushikawa said warmly to the idealistic young lawyer. "Your organization is certainly making a valuable contribution. I'll present what I have learned here to our board of directors. We should be getting in touch with you fairly soon. In the meantime, my very best wishes for your continued success."

Next, Ushikawa began to investigate the death of the dowager's daughter. The daughter had married an elite bureaucrat in the Ministry of Transport and was only thirty-six when she died. He didn't know the cause yet. Not long after she died, her husband left the Ministry of Transport. These were the only facts Ushikawa had unearthed so far. He didn't know why the husband had left the ministry, or what sort of life he had led afterward. The Ministry of Transport was not the sort of government office that willingly revealed information regarding its inner workings to ordinary citizens. But Ushikawa had a sharp sense of smell, and something smelled fishy. He couldn't believe that losing his wife would have made the man so overcome with grief that he would quit his job and go into hiding.

Ushikawa knew there weren't many thirty-six-year-old women who died of illness. Not that there weren't some. No matter how old you are, or how blessed your circumstances, you can suddenly fall ill and die – from cancer, a brain tumor, peritonitis, acute pneumonia. The human body is a fragile thing. But for an affluent woman of thirty-six to join the ranks of the dead – in all likelihood it was not a natural death, but either an accident or suicide.

Let me speculate here, Ushikawa said to himself. *Following the famous rule of Occam's razor, I'll try to find the simplest possible explanation. Eliminate all unnecessary factors, boil it all down to one logical line, and then look at the situation.*

Let's say the dowager's daughter didn't die of illness but by suicide. Ushikawa rubbed his hands together as he pondered this. *It wouldn't be too hard to pretend that a suicide was actually death by illness, especially for someone with money and influence. Take this a step further and say that this daughter was the victim of domestic violence, grew despondent, and took her own life. Certainly not an impossibility. It was a well-known fact that certain members of the so-called elite had disgusting personalities and dark, twisted tendencies, as if they had taken more than the share of darkness allotted to them.*

If that were the case, what would the rich old dowager do? Would she call it fate, say that nothing else could be done, and give up? Not very likely. She would take suitable revenge against whatever force had driven her daughter to her untimely end. Ushikawa felt he had a better understanding of the dowager. She was a daring, bright woman, with a clear vision and a strong will. And she would spare neither fortune nor influence to avenge the death of the one she loved.

Ushikawa had no way of knowing what kind of retaliation she had actually taken toward her daughter's husband, since all trace of him had vanished into thin air. He didn't think that the dowager had gone so far as to take the man's life. But he had no doubt that she had taken some sort of decisive action. And it was hard to believe that she had left any trail behind.

Ushikawa's conjectures thus far seemed to make sense, though he had no proof. His theory, however, did clear up a lot of questions. Licking his lips, Ushikawa vigorously rubbed his hands together. Beyond this point, though, things started to get a little hazy.

The dowager had set up the safe house to sublimate her desire for revenge, turning it into something more useful and positive. Then, at the sports club she frequented, she got to know the young instructor Aomame, and somehow – he had no idea how – they came to a secret understanding. After meticulous preparation, Aomame got access to the suite at the Hotel Okura and murdered Leader. The method she used was unclear. Aomame might be quite proficient in murdering people using a special technique. As a result, despite being closely guarded by two very dedicated and able bodyguards, Leader wound up dead.

Up to this point, the threads tying his conjectures held together – barely – but when it came to linking Sakigake's Leader to the center for battered women, Ushikawa was at a total loss. At this point his thought process hit a roadblock and a very sharp razor neatly severed all the threads.

What Sakigake wanted from Ushikawa at this point were answers to two questions: Who planned the murder of Leader? and Where was Aomame?

Ushikawa was the one who had run the original background check on Aomame, and he had found nothing suspicious about her at all. But after she had left, Leader expired. And right after that, Aomame disappeared. *Poof* – like a gust of smoke in the wind. Sakigake had to have been very upset with Ushikawa, convinced that his investigation hadn't been thorough enough.

But in fact, as always, his investigation left nothing to be desired. As he had told Buzzcut, Ushikawa was a stickler for making sure all the bases were covered. He could be faulted for not having checked her phone records beforehand, but unless there was something extraordinarily suspicious about a situation, that wasn't something he normally did. And as far as he could tell from his investigations, there wasn't a single suspect thing about Aomame.

Ushikawa didn't want them to be upset with him forever. They paid him well, but they were a dangerous bunch. Ushikawa was one of the few who knew how they had secretly disposed of Leader's body, which made him a potential liability. He knew he had to come up with something concrete to show them so they would know he was a valuable resource, someone worth keeping alive.

He had no proof that the old dowager from Azabu was mixed up in Leader's murder. At this point it was pure speculation. He did know that some deep secret lay hidden inside that mansion with its magnificent willows. Ushikawa's sense of smell told him this, and his job was to bring that truth to light. It wouldn't be easy. The place was under heavy guard, with professionals involved.

Yakuza?

Perhaps. Businessmen, those involved in real estate in particular, are often involved in secret negotiations with yakuza. When the going gets rough, the yakuza get called in. It was possible the old dowager might be making use of their influence. But Ushikawa wasn't very certain of this – the old dowager was too well bred to deal with people like them. Also, it was hard to imagine that she would use yakuza to protect women who were victims of domestic violence. Probably she had her own security apparatus in place, one that she paid for herself. Her own personal system she had refined. It would cost her, but then, she wasn't hurting for funds. And this system of hers might employ violence when there was a perceived need.

If Ushikawa's hypothesis was correct, then Aomame must have gone into hiding somewhere far away, with the aid of the old dowager. They would have carefully erased any trail, given her a new identity and a new name, possibly even a new face. If that was the case, then it would be impossible for Ushikawa's painstaking little private investigation to track her down.

At this point the only thing to do was to try to learn more about the dowager. His hope was that he would run across a seam that would lead him to discover something about Aomame's whereabouts. Things might work out, and then again they might not. But Ushikawa had some strong points: his sharp sense of smell and his tenaciousness. He would never let go of something once he latched onto it. *Besides these,* he asked himself, *what other talents do I have worth mentioning? Do I have other abilities I can be proud of?*

Not one, Ushikawa answered himself, convinced he was right.

5

AOMAME

No Matter How Long You Keep Quiet

AOMAME DIDN'T FIND IT PAINFUL TO be shut away, living a monotonous, solitary existence. She got up every day at six thirty and had a simple breakfast. Then she would spend an hour or so doing laundry, ironing, or mopping the floor. For an hour and a half in the morning she used the equipment Tamaru had obtained for her to do a strenuous workout. As a fitness instructor she was well versed in how much stimulation all the various muscles needed every day – how much exercise was just right, and how much was excessive.

Lunch was usually a green salad and fruit. The afternoon was spent sitting on the sofa and reading, or taking a short nap. In the evening she would spend an hour preparing dinner, which she would finish before six. Once the sun set, she would be out on the balcony, seated on her garden chair, keeping watch over the playground. Then to bed at ten thirty. One day was the same as the next, but she never felt bored.

She was not very social to begin with, and never had a problem going long stretches without seeing or talking with other people. Even when she was in elementary school, she seldom talked with her class-mates. More accurately, unless it was absolutely necessary, no one else ever spoke to her.

Compared with the harsh days of her childhood, being holed up in a neat little apartment, not talking to anybody, was nothing. Compared with staying silent while those around her chatted away, it was much easier – and more natural – to be silent in a place where she was all alone. And besides, she had a book she should read. She had started reading the Proust volumes that Tamaru had left for her. She read no more than twenty pages a day. She read each and every word carefully, working her way through each day's reading. Once she finished that section, she read something else. And just before bed she made sure to read a few pages of *Air Chrysalis*. This was Tengo's writing, and it had become a sort of manual she followed to live in 1Q84.

She also listened to music. The elderly dowager had sent over a box of classical music cassettes: Mahler symphonies, Haydn chamber music, Bach keyboard pieces – all varieties and types of classical music. There was a tape of Janáček's *Sinfonietta* as well, which she had specifically requested. She would listen to the *Sinfonietta* once a day as she noise-lessly went through her exercise routine.

Autumn quietly deepened. She had the feeling that her body was slowly becoming transparent. Aomame tried her best to keep her mind clear of any thoughts, but it was impossible not to think of anything. Nature abhors a vacuum. At the very least, though, she felt that now there was nothing for her to hate. There was no need to hate her classmates and teacher anymore. Aomame was no longer a helpless child, and no one was forcing her to practice a religion now. There was no need to hate the men who beat up women. The anger she had felt before, like a high tide rising up within her – the overwrought emotions that sometimes made her want to smack her fists against the closest wall – had vanished before she'd realized it. She wasn't sure why, but those feelings were entirely gone. She was grateful for this.

As much as possible, she wanted never to hurt anyone, ever again. Just as she didn't want to hurt herself.

On nights when she found it hard to sleep, she thought of Tamaki Otsuka and Ayumi Nakano. When she closed her eyes, the memory of holding their bodies close came rushing back to her. Both of them had had soft, lustrous skin and warm bodies. Gentle, profound bodies, with fresh blood coursing through them, hearts beating regular, blessed beats. She could hear them sigh softly and giggle. Slender fingers, hardened nipples, smooth thighs. . . . But these two women were no longer in the world.

Like dark, soft water, sadness took over Aomame's heart, soundlessly, and with no warning. The best antidote at a time like this was to just shut off that stream of memories and think only of Tengo. Focus, and recall the touch of the ten-year-old boy's hand as she had held it for a fleeting moment. And then she called forth from memory the thirty-year-old Tengo sitting on top of the slide, she imagined what it would feel like to be held in those large, strong arms.

He was almost within reach.

Maybe if I hold out my hand the next time, I really will be able to reach him. In the darkness she closed her eyes and immersed herself in that possibility. She gave herself up to her longing.

But if I never do see him again, she thought, her heart trembling, *then what?* Things had been a whole lot simpler when there was no actual point of contact between them. Meeting the adult Tengo had been a mere dream, an abstract hypothesis. But now that she had seen the *real* him before her very eyes, his presence was more concrete, more powerful, than it had ever been before. She *had* to see him, to have him hold her, caress every part of her. Just the very thought that this might not come to pass made her feel as if her heart and body were being ripped in two.

Maybe back there in front of the Esso tiger on the billboard, I should

AOMAME | NO MATTER HOW LONG YOU KEEP QUIET

have shot that 9mm bullet into my skull. Then I wouldn't have to live like this, feeling such sadness and pain. But she just couldn't pull the trigger. She had heard a voice. From far off, someone calling her name. *I might be able to see Tengo again,* she had thought – and once this thought had struck her, she had to go on living. Even if what Leader had said was true, that doing so would make things dangerous for Tengo, she had no other choice. She had felt an unbearably strong surge of the life force, beyond the bounds of logic. The upshot was that she was burning with a fierce desire for him. It was a thirst that wouldn't quit, and a premonition of despair.

A realization struck her. *This is what it means to live on. When granted hope, a person uses it as fuel, as a guidepost to life. It is impossible to live without hope.* Aomame's heart clenched at the thought, as if every bone in her body were suddenly creaking and screaming out.

She sat at the dining table and picked up the automatic pistol. She pulled back the slide, sending a bullet into the chamber, thumbed back the hammer, and stuck the muzzle in her mouth. Just a touch more pressure with her trigger finger and all this sadness would disappear. *Just a touch more. One more centimeter. No, if I pull my finger just five millimeters toward me, I will shift over to a silent world where there are no more worries. The pain will only last an instant. And then there will be a merciful nothingness.* She closed her eyes. The Esso tiger from the billboard, gas hose in hand, grinned at her. *Put a Tiger in Your Tank.*

She pulled the hard muzzle out of her mouth and slowly shook her head.

I can't die. In front of the balcony is the playground. The slide is there, and as long as I have the hope that Tengo will show up again, I won't be able to pull this trigger. This possibility drew her back from the brink. One door closed inside her heart and another door opened, quietly, without a sound. Aomame pulled the slide again, ejecting the bullet, set the safety, and placed the pistol back on the table. When she closed her eyes she sensed something in the darkness, a faint light, fading away by the moment. What it could be, she had no idea.

She sat down on the sofa and focused on the pages of *Swann's Way*. She imagined the scenes depicted in the story, trying hard not to let other thoughts intrude. Outside a cold rain had started to fall. The weather report on the radio said a gentle rain would continue until the next morning. A weather front was stalled out in the Pacific – like a lonely person, lost in thought, oblivious of time.

Tengo won't be coming, she thought. The sky was covered from one end to the other with thick clouds, blocking out the moon. Still she would probably go out onto the balcony, a hot cup of cocoa in hand, and watch the playground. She would keep binoculars and the pistol nearby, wear something decent enough so that she could quickly run outside, and gaze at the slide in the rain. This was the only meaningful act she could undertake.

At three p.m., someone at the entrance of the building rang her bell. Aomame ignored it. It wasn't possible that anyone would be visiting her. She had the kettle on for tea, but to be on the safe side she switched off the gas and listened. The bell rang three or four times and then was silent.

About five minutes later a bell rang again. This time it was the doorbell to her apartment. Now someone was inside the building, right outside her door. The person may have followed a resident inside, or else had rung somebody else's bell and talked their way in. Aomame kept perfectly still. *If somebody comes, don't answer,* Tamaru had instructed her. *Set the dead bolt and don't make a sound.*

The doorbell must have rung ten times. A little too persistent for a salesman – they usually give up at three rings. As she held her breath, the person began to knock on the door with his fist. It wasn't that loud a sound, but she could sense the irritation behind it. "Miss Takai," a low, middle-aged man's voice said. A slightly hoarse voice. "Miss Takai. Can you please answer the door?"

Takai was the fake name on the mailbox.

"Miss Takai, I know this isn't a good time, but I would like to see you. Please."

The man paused for a moment, waiting for a response. When there was none, he knocked on the door again, this time a little louder.

"I know you're inside, Miss Takai, so let's cut to the chase and open the door. I know you're in there and can hear me."

Aomame picked up the automatic pistol from the table and clicked off the safety. She wrapped the pistol in a towel and held it by the grip.

She had no idea who this could be, nor what he could possibly want. His anger seemed directed at her – why, she had no clue – and he was determined to get her to open the door. Needless to say, in her present position this was the last thing she wanted.

The knocking finally stopped and the man's voice echoed again in the hallway.

"Miss Takai, I am here to collect your NHK fee. That's right, good old NHK. I know you're at home. No matter how much you try to stay quiet, I can tell. Working this job for so many years, I know when someone is really out, and when they're just pretending. Even when a person tries to stay very quiet, there are still signs he's there. People breathe, their hearts beat, their stomachs continue to digest food. Miss Takai, I know you're in there, and that you're waiting for me to give up and leave. You're not planning to open the door or answer me. Because you don't want to pay the subscription fee."

The man's voice was louder than it needed to be, and it reverberated down the hallway of the building. That was his intention – calling out the person's name so loudly that it would make them feel ridiculed and embarrassed. And so it would be a warning to all the neighbors. Aomame kept perfectly silent. She wasn't about to respond. She put the pistol back on the table. Just to be sure, though, she kept the safety off. The man could just be pretending to be an NHK fee collector. Seated at the dining table, she stared at the front door.

She wanted to stealthily pad over to the door, look through the peephole, and check out what kind of person he was. But she was glued to the chair. Better not do anything unnecessary – after a while he would give up and leave.

The man, however, seemed ready to deliver an entire lecture.

"Miss Takai, let's not play hide and seek anymore, okay? I'm not doing this because I like to. Even I have a busy schedule. Miss Takai, I know you watch TV. And everyone who watches TV, without exception, has to pay the NHK subscription fee. You may not like it, but that's the law. Not paying the fee is the same as stealing, Miss Takai, you don't want to be treated as a thief because of something as petty as this, do you? This is a fancy building you live in, and I don't think you will have any trouble paying the fee. Right? Hearing me proclaim this to the world can't be much fun for you."

Normally Aomame wouldn't care if an NHK fee collector was making a racket like this. But right now she was in hiding, trying to keep out of sight. She didn't want anything to attract the attention of other residents. But there was nothing she could do about it. She had to keep still and wait until he went away.

"I know I'm repeating myself, Miss Takai, but I am sure you're in there, listening to me. And you're thinking this: Why, of all places, did you have to choose *my* apartment to stand outside of? I wonder, too, Miss Takai. It's probably because I don't like people pretending not to be at home. Pretending not to be at home is just a temporary solution, isn't it? I want you to open the door and tell me to my face that you don't have any intention of paying the NHK fee. You would feel much better, and so would I. That would leave some room for discussion. Pretending to be out is not the way to go. It's like a pitiful little rat hiding in the dark. It only sneaks out when people aren't around. What a miserable way to live your life."

This man's lying, Aomame thought. *That's just ridiculous, that he can sense when somebody is at home. I haven't made a sound. His real goal is to just stand in front of a random apartment, make a racket, and intimidate all the other residents, to make people decide they would prefer to pay the fee than to have him plant himself outside their door like that. This man must have tried the same tactics elsewhere and had good results.*

"Miss Takai, I know you find me unpleasant. I can understand perfectly what you're thinking. And you're right – I *am* an unpleasant person. I'm aware of that. But you have to understand, Miss Takai, that pleasant people don't make good fee collectors. There are tons of people in the world who have decided they aren't going to pay the NHK subscription fee, and if you're going to collect from people like that you can't always act so nice. I would rather leave with no problem, just say, *Is that right? You don't want to pay the fee? I understand. Sorry to bother you.* But I can't. Collecting the fee is my job, and besides, personally I don't like it when people pretend not to be at home."

The man stopped and paused. And then he knocked on the door ten times in a row.

"Miss Takai, you must be finding this annoying. Aren't you starting to feel like a real thief by now? Think about it. We're not talking about a lot of money here. Enough to buy a modest dinner at your neighborhood chain restaurant. Just pay it, and you won't be treated like a thief. You won't have anyone yelling at you outside or banging on your door anymore. Miss Takai, I know you're hiding in there. You think you can hide and get away from me forever. Well – go ahead and try. You can keep as quiet as you like, but one of these days somebody is going to find you. You can't act so sneaky forever. Consider this: there are people a whole lot poorer than you all over Japan who faithfully pay their fee every month. Is that fair?"

Fifteen knocks on the door followed. Aomame counted them.

"I get it, Miss Takai. You're pretty stubborn too. Fine. I'll be going now. I can't stand outside here forever. But rest assured, I'll be back. Once I decide on something, I don't give up easily. And I don't like people pretending to be out. I'll be back, and I'll knock on your door. I'll keep banging on your door until the whole world has heard it. I promise you this, a promise just between you and me. All right? Well, I'll be seeing you soon."

She didn't hear any footsteps. Perhaps he had on rubber soles. Aomame stayed still there for five minutes, staring at the door. The hallway outside was quiet again, and she couldn't hear a thing. She crept to the front door, summoned her courage, and peered out the peephole. No one was there.

She reset the safety on the pistol and took some deep breaths to get her heart rate back down. She switched on the gas, heated up water, made green tea, and drank it. *It was only an NHK collector,* she told herself. But there was something malicious, sick even, about his voice. Whether this was directed at her personally or at the fictitious Miss Takai, she couldn't tell. Still, that husky voice and persistent knock disturbed her, like something clammy sticking to your bare skin.

Aomame undressed and took a shower. She carefully scrubbed herself in the hot water. After she finished and had put on clean clothes, she felt a bit better. The clammy sensation was gone. She sat down on the sofa and drank the rest of the tea. She tried to read her book but couldn't concentrate on the words. Fragments of the man's voice came back to her.

"You think you can hide and get away from me forever. Well – go ahead and try. You can keep as quiet as you like, but one of these days somebody is going to find you."

She shook her head. The man just said whatever nonsense popped into his head, yelling things just to make people feel bad. *He doesn't know a thing about me – what I've done, why I'm here.* Still, her heart wouldn't stop pounding.

You can keep as quiet as you like, but one of these days somebody is going to find you.

The fee collector's words sounded like they had deeper implications. *Maybe it was just a coincidence,* she thought, *but that man knew exactly what to say to upset me.* Aomame gave up reading and closed her eyes as she lay on the sofa.

Tengo, where are you? she wondered. She said it out loud. "Tengo, where are you?" *Find me now. Before someone else does.*

6

TENGO

By the Pricking of My Thumbs

TENGO LED A VERY ORDERLY LIFE in the small town by the sea. Once his days fell into a pattern, he tried his best to keep them that way. He wasn't sure why he did so, but it seemed important. In the morning he would take a walk, work on his novel, then go to see his father in the sanatorium and read whatever he had at hand. Then he would go back to his room and sleep. One day followed the next like the monotonous rhythm of the work songs farmers sing as they plant their rice paddies.

There were several warm nights, followed by surprisingly cold ones. Autumn advanced a step, then retreated, but was steadily deepening. The change in seasons didn't bring any change to Tengo's life, however – he simply modeled each day on the one preceding it. He tried his best to become an invisible observer, staying quiet, keeping the effect of his presence to a minimum, silently waiting for *that time* to come. As the days passed, the difference between one day and the next grew fainter. A week passed, then ten days. But the air chrysalis never materialized. In the afternoon when his father was at the examination room, the only thing on his bed was the small, pitiful, person-shaped depression.

Was that just a one-time event? Tengo thought, biting his lip as he sat in the small room in the gathering twilight. *A special revelation never to appear again? Or did I just see an illusion?* No one answered him. The only sound that reached him was the roar of the far-off sea, and the wind blowing through the pine windbreak.

Tengo wasn't certain that he was doing the right thing. Maybe the time he was spending here, in this room in a sanatorium in a town far from Tokyo, was meaningless. Even if it was, though, he didn't think he could leave. Here in this room, he had seen the air chrysalis, and inside, in a faint light, the small sleeping figure of Aomame. He had *touched* it. Even if this was a one-time event, even if it was nothing more than a fleeting illusion, he wanted to stay as long as he possibly could, tracing with his mind's eye the scene as he had witnessed it.

Once they discovered that he was not going back to Tokyo, the nurses began to act more friendly. They would take a short break between tasks and stop to chat. If they had a free moment they came to his father's room to talk with him. They brought him tea and cakes. Two nurses alternated in caring for Tengo's father – Nurse Omura, who was in her mid-thirties (she was the one who wore her hair up with a ballpoint pen stuck through her bun), and Nurse Adachi, who had rosy cheeks and wore her hair in a ponytail. Nurse Tamura, a middle-aged nurse with metal-framed glasses, usually staffed the reception desk, but if they happened to be shorthanded she would pitch in and care for his father too. All three of them seemed to take a personal interest in Tengo.

Except for his special hour at twilight, Tengo had plenty of time on his hands and talked with them about all kinds of things. It was more like a question-and-answer session, though, with the nurses asking questions about his life and Tengo responding as honestly as he could.

The nurses talked about their own lives as well. All three had been born in this area, had entered nursing school after high school, and had become nurses. They all found work at the sanatorium monotonous and boring, the working hours long and irregular, but they were happy to be able to work in their hometown. The work was much less stressful than being at a general hospital, where they would face life-and-death situations on a daily basis. The old people in the sanatorium gradually lost their memory and died, not really understanding their situation. There was little blood, and the staff minimized any pain. No one was brought there by ambulance in the middle of the night, and there were no distraught, sobbing families to deal with. The cost of living was low in the area, so even with a salary that wasn't the most generous they were able to comfortably get by. Nurse Tamura, the one with glasses, had lost her husband five years earlier in an accident, and lived in a nearby town with her mother. Nurse Omura, who wore the ballpoint pen in her hair, had two little boys and a husband who drove a cab. Young Miss Adachi lived in an apartment on the outskirts of town with her sister, who was three years older and worked as a hair stylist.

"You are such a kind person, Tengo," Nurse Omura said as she changed an IV bag. "There's no one else I know who comes here to read aloud to an unconscious patient."

The praise made Tengo uncomfortable. "I just happen to have some vacation days," he said. "But I won't be here all that long."

"No matter how much free time someone might have, they don't come to a place like this because they want to," she said. "Maybe I shouldn't say this, but these are patients who will never recover. As time passes it makes people get more and more depressed."

"My father asked me to read to him. He said he didn't mind what I read. This was a long time ago, when he was still conscious. Besides, I don't have anything else to do, so I might as well come here."

"What do you read to him?"

"All kinds of things. I just pick whatever book I'm in the midst of reading, and read aloud from wherever I've left off."

"What are you reading right now?"

"Isak Dinesen's *Out of Africa*."

The nurse shook her head. "Never heard of it."

"It was written in 1937. Dinesen was from Denmark. She married a Swedish nobleman, moved to Africa just before the First World War, and they ran a plantation there. After she divorced him, she continued to run the plantation on her own. The book is about her experiences at the time."

The nurse took his father's temperature, noted it on his chart, then returned the ballpoint pen to her hair and brushed back her bangs. "I wonder if I could hear you read for a bit," she said.

"I don't know if you'll like it," Tengo said.

She sat down on a stool and crossed her legs. They were sturdy looking, fleshy, but nicely shaped. "Just go ahead and read, if you would."

Tengo slowly began to read from where he had left off. It was the kind of passage that was best read slowly, like time flowing over the African landscape.

When in Africa in March the long rains begin after four months of hot, dry weather, the richness of growth and the freshness and fragrance everywhere are overwhelming.

But the farmer holds back his heart and dares not trust to the generosity of nature, he listens, dreading to hear a decrease in the roar of the falling rain. The water that the earth is now drinking in must bring the farm, with all the vegetable, animal and human life on it, through four rainless months to come.

It is a lovely sight when the roads of the farm have all been turned into streams of running water, and the farmer wades through the mud with a singing heart, out to the flowering and dripping coffee-fields. But it happens in the middle of the rainy season that in the evening the stars show themselves through the thinning clouds; then he stands outside his house and stares up, as if hanging himself on to the sky to milk down more rain. He cries to the sky: "Give me enough and more than enough. My heart is bared to thee now, and I will not let thee go except thou bless me. Drown me if you like, but kill me not with caprices. No *coitus interruptus,* heaven, heaven!"

"*Coitus interruptus?*" the nurse asked, frowning.
"She's the kind of person who doesn't mince words."
"Still, it seems awfully graphic to use when you're addressing God."
"I'm with you on that," Tengo said.

Sometimes a cool, colourless day in the months after the rainy season calls back the time of the *marka mbaya,* the bad year, the time of the drought. In those days the Kikuyu used to graze their cows round my house, and a boy amongst them who had a flute, from time to time played a short tune on it. When I have heard this tune again, it has recalled in one single moment all our anguish and despair of the past. It has got the salt taste of tears in it. But at the same time I found in the tune, unexpectedly surprisingly, a vigour, a curious sweetness, a song. Had those hard times really had all these in them? There was youth in us then, a wild hope. It was during those long days that we were all of us merged into a unity, so that on another planet we shall recognize one another, and the things cry to each other, the cuckoo clock and my books to the lean-fleshed cows on the lawn and the sorrowful old Kikuyus: "You also were there. You also were part of the Ngong farm." That bad time blessed us and went away.

"That's a wonderful passage," the nurse said. "I can really picture the scene. Isak Dinesen's *Out of Africa,* you said?"

"That's right."

"You have a nice voice, too. It's deep, and full of emotion. Very nice for reading aloud."

"Thanks."

The nurse sat on the stool, closed her eyes for a while, and breathed quietly, as if she were still experiencing the afterglow of the passage. Tengo could see the swell of her chest under her uniform rise and fall as she breathed. As he watched this, Tengo remembered his older girlfriend. Friday afternoons, undressing her, touching her hard nipples. Her deep sighs, her wet vagina. Outside, beyond the closed curtains, a tranquil rain was falling. She was feeling the heft of his balls in her hand. But these memories didn't arouse him. The scenery and emotions were distant and vague, as though seen through a thin film.

Some time later the nurse opened her eyes and looked at Tengo. Her eyes seemed to read his thoughts. But she was not accusing him. A faint smile rose to her lips as she stood up and looked down at him.

"I have to be going." She patted her hair to check that the ballpoint pen was there, spun around, and left the room.

Every evening he called Fuka-Eri. Nothing really happened today, she would tell him. The phone had rung a few times, but she followed instructions and didn't answer. "I'm glad," Tengo told her. "Just let it ring."

When Tengo called her he would let it ring three times, hang up, then immediately dial again, but she didn't always follow this arrangement. Most of the time she picked up on the first set of rings.

"We have to follow our plan," Tengo cautioned her each time this happened.

"I know who it is. There is no need to worry," Fuka-Eri said.

"You know it's me calling?"

"I don't answer the other phone calls."

I guess that's possible, Tengo thought. He himself could sense when a call was coming in from Komatsu. The way it rang was sort of nervous and fidgety, like someone tapping their fingers persistently on a desktop. But this was, after all, just a feeling. It wasn't as if he knew who was on the phone.

Fuka-Eri's days were just as monotonous as Tengo's. She never set foot outside the apartment. There was no TV, and she didn't read any books. She hardly ate anything, so at this point there was no need to go out shopping.

"Since I'm not moving much there's not much need to eat," Fuka-Eri said.

"What are you doing by yourself every day?"

"Thinking."

"About what?"

She didn't answer the question. "There's a crow that comes, too."

"The crow comes once every day."

"It comes many times, not just once," she said.

"Is it the same crow?"

"Yes."

"Nobody else comes?"

"The N-H-K person came again."

"Is it the same NHK person as before?"

"He says, *Mr. Kawana, you're a thief,* in a loud voice."

"You mean he yells that right outside my door?"

"So everyone else can hear him."

Tengo pondered this for a moment. "Don't worry about that. It has nothing to do with you, and it's not going to cause any harm."

"He said he knows you are hiding in here."

"Don't let it bother you," Tengo said. "He can't tell that. He's just saying it to intimidate me. NHK people do that sometimes."

Tengo had witnessed his father do exactly the same thing any number of times. A Sunday afternoon, his father's voice, filled with malice, ringing out down the hallway of a public housing project.

Threatening and ridiculing the resident. Tengo lightly pressed the tips of his fingers against his temple. The memory brought with it a heavy load of other baggage.

As if sensing something from his silence, Fuka-Eri asked, "Are you okay."

"I'm fine. Just ignore the NHK person, okay?"

"The crow said the same thing."

"Glad to hear it," Tengo said.

Ever since he saw two moons in the sky, and an air chrysalis materializing on his father's bed in the sanatorium, nothing surprised Tengo very much. Fuka-Eri and the crow exchanging opinions by the window-sill wasn't hurting anybody.

"I think I'll be here a little longer. I can't go back to Tokyo yet. Is that all right?"

"You should be there as long as you want to be."

And then she hung up. Their conversation vanished in an instant, as if someone had taken a nicely sharpened hatchet to the phone line and chopped it in two.

Afterward Tengo called the publishing company where Komatsu worked. He wasn't in. He had put in a brief appearance around one p.m. but then had left, and the person on the phone had no idea where he was or if he was coming back. This wasn't that unusual for Komatsu. Tengo left the number for the sanatorium, saying that was where he could be found during the day, and asked that Komatsu call back. If he had left the inn's number and Komatsu ended up calling in the middle of the night, that would be a problem.

The last time he had heard from Komatsu had been near the end of September, just a short talk on the phone. Since then Komatsu hadn't been in touch, and neither had Tengo. For a three-week period starting at the end of August, Komatsu had disappeared. He had called the publisher with some vague excuse, claiming he was ill and needed time off to rest, but hadn't called afterward, as if he were a missing person. Tengo was concerned, but not overly worried. Komatsu had always done his own thing. Tengo was sure that he would show up before long and saunter back into the office.

Such self-centered behavior was usually forbidden in a corporate environment. But in Komatsu's case, one of his colleagues always smoothed things over so he didn't get in trouble. Komatsu wasn't the most popular man, but somehow there always seemed to be a willing person on hand, ready to clean up whatever mess he left behind. The publishing house, for its part, was willing, to a certain extent, to look the other way. Komatsu was self-centered, uncooperative, and insolent, but when it came to his job, he was capable. He had handled, on his own, the bestseller *Air Chrysalis.* So they weren't about to fire him.

As Tengo had predicted, one day Komatsu simply returned, without explaining why he was away or apologizing for his absence, and came back to work. Tengo heard the news from another editor he worked with who happened to mention it.

"So how is Mr. Komatsu feeling?" Tengo asked the editor.

"He seems fine," the man replied. "Though he seems less talkative than before."

"Less talkative?" Tengo asked, a bit surprised.

"How should I put it – he's *less sociable* than before."

"Was he really quite sick?"

"How should I know?" the editor said, apathetically. "He says he's fine, so I have to go with that. Now that he's back we've been able to take care of the work that has been piling up. While he was away there were all sorts of things to do with *Air Chrysalis* that were a real pain, things I had to take care of in his absence."

"Speaking of *Air Chrysalis,* are there any developments in the case of the missing author, Fuka-Eri?"

"No, no updates. No progress at all, and not any idea where the author is. Everybody is at their wits' end."

"I've been reading the newspapers but haven't seen a single mention of it recently."

"The media has mostly backed off the story, or maybe they're deliberately distancing themselves from it. And the police don't appear to be actively pursuing the case. Mr. Komatsu will know the details, so he would be the one to ask. But as I said, he has gotten a bit less talkative. Actually he's not himself at all. He used to be brimming with confidence, but he has toned that down, and has gotten more intro-spective, I guess you would say, just sitting there half the time. He's more difficult to get along with, too. Sometimes it seems like he has totally forgotten that there are other people around, like he is all by himself inside a hole."

"Introspective," Tengo said.

"You'll know what I mean when you talk with him."

Tengo had thanked him and hung up.

A few days later, in the evening, Tengo called Komatsu. He was in the office. Just like the editor had told him, the way Komatsu spoke had changed. Usually the words slipped out smoothly without a pause, but now there was awkwardness about him, as if he were preoccupied. *Something must be bothering him,* Tengo thought. At any rate, this was no longer the cool Komatsu he knew.

"Are you completely well now?" Tengo asked.

"What do you mean?"

"Well, you took a long break from work because you weren't feeling well, right?"

"That's right," Komatsu said, as if he had just recalled the fact. A short silence followed. "I'm fine now. I'll tell you all about it sometime, before long. I can't really explain it at this point."

Sometime, before long. Tengo mulled over the words. There was something odd about the sound of Komatsu's voice. The sense of distance that you would normally expect was missing, and his words were flat, without any depth.

Tengo found an appropriate point in the conversation to say good-bye, and hung up. He decided not to bring up *Air Chrysalis* or Fuka-Eri. Something in Komatsu's tone indicated he was trying to avoid these topics. Had Komatsu ever had trouble discussing anything before?

This phone call, at the end of September, was the last time he had spoken to Komatsu. More than two months had passed since then. Komatsu usually loved to have long talks on the phone. Tengo was, as it were, the wall against which Komatsu hit a tennis ball. Maybe he was going through a period when he just didn't want to talk to anyone, Tengo surmised. Everybody has times like that, even somebody like Komatsu. And Tengo, for his part, didn't have anything pressing he had to discuss with him. *Air Chrysalis* had stopped selling and had practically vanished from the public eye, and Tengo knew exactly where the missing Fuka-Eri happened to be. If Komatsu had something he needed to discuss, then he would surely call. No calls simply meant he didn't have anything to talk about.

But Tengo was thinking that it was getting about time to call him. *I'll tell you all about it sometime, before long.* Komatsu's words had stuck with him, oddly enough, and he couldn't shake them.

Tengo called his friend who was subbing for him at the cram school, to see how things were going.

"Everything's fine," his friend replied. "How is your father doing?"

"He has been in a coma the whole time," Tengo explained. "He's breathing, and his temperature and blood pressure are low but stable. But he's unconscious. I don't think he's in any pain. It's like he has gone over completely to the dream world."

"Not such a bad way to go," his friend said, without much emotion. What he was trying to say was *This might sound a little insensitive, but depending on how you look at it, that's not such a bad way to die.* But he had left out such prefatory remarks. If you study for a few years in a mathematics department, you get used to that kind of abbreviated conversation.

"Have you looked at the moon recently?" Tengo suddenly asked. This friend was probably the only person he knew who wouldn't find it suspicious to be asked, out of the blue, about the moon.

His friend gave it some thought. "Now that you mention it, I don't recall looking at the moon recently. What's going on with the moon?"

"When you have a chance, would you look at it for me? And tell me what you think."

"What I think? From what standpoint?"

"Any standpoint at all. I would just like to hear what you think when you see the moon."

A short pause. "It might be hard to find the right way to express what I think about it."

"No, don't worry about expression. What's important are the most obvious characteristics."

"You want me to look at the moon and tell you what I think are the most obvious characteristics?"

"That's right," Tengo replied. "If nothing strikes you, then that's fine."

"It's overcast today, so I don't think you can see the moon, but when it clears up I'll take a look. If I remember."

Tengo thanked him and hung up. *If he remembers.* This was one of the problems with math department graduates. When it came to areas they weren't interested in, their memory was surprisingly short-lived.

When visiting hours were over and Tengo was leaving the sanatorium he said good-bye to Nurse Tamura, the nurse at the reception desk. "Thank you. Good night," he said.

"How many more days will you be here?" she asked, pressing the bridge of her glasses on her nose. She seemed to have finished her shift, because she had changed from her uniform into a pleated dark purple skirt, a white blouse, and a gray cardigan.

Tengo came to a halt and thought for a minute. "I'm not sure. It depends on how things go."

"Can you still take time off from your job?"

"I asked somebody to teach my classes for me, so I should be okay for a while."

"Where do you usually eat?" the nurse asked.

"At a restaurant in town," he replied. "They only provide breakfast at the inn so I go someplace nearby and eat their set meal, or a rice bowl, that sort of thing."

"Is it good?"

"I wouldn't say that. Though I don't really notice what it tastes like."

"That won't do," the nurse said, looking displeased. "You have to eat more nutritious food. I mean, look – these days your face reminds me of a horse sleeping standing up."

"A horse sleeping standing up?" Tengo asked, surprised.

"Horses sleep standing up. You've never seen that?"

Tengo shook his head. "No, I never have."

"Their faces look like yours," the middle-aged nurse said. "Go check out your face in the mirror. At first glance you can't tell they're asleep, but if you look closely you will see that their eyes are open, but they aren't seeing anything."

"Horses sleep with their eyes open?"

The nurse nodded deeply. "Just like you."

For a moment Tengo did think about going to the bathroom and looking at himself in the mirror, but he decided against it. "I understand. I'll try to eat better from now on."

"Would you care to go out to get some *yakiniku*?"

"*Yakiniku?*" Tengo didn't eat much meat. He didn't usually crave it. But now that she had brought it up, he thought it might be good to have some meat for a change. His body might indeed be crying out for more nourishment.

"All of us were talking about going out now to eat some *yakiniku*. You should join us."

"All of us?"

"The others finish work at six thirty and we'll meet afterward. There will be three of us. Interested?"

The other two were Nurse Omura and Nurse Adachi. The three of them seemed to enjoy spending time together, even after work. Tengo considered the idea of going out to eat *yakiniku* with them. He didn't want to disrupt his simple lifestyle, but he couldn't think of a plausible excuse in order to refuse. It was obvious to them that in a town like this Tengo would have plenty of free time on his hands.

"If you don't think I'll be a bother."

"Of course you won't," the nurse said. "I don't invite people out if I think they'll be a bother. So don't hesitate to come with us. It will be nice to have a healthy young man along for a change."

"Well, healthy I definitely am," Tengo said in an uncertain voice.

"That is the most important thing," the nurse declared, giving it her professional opinion.

It wasn't easy for all three nurses to be off duty at the same time, but once a month they managed it. The three of them would go into town, eat something nutritious, have a few drinks, sing karaoke, let loose, and blow off some steam. They definitely needed a change of scenery. Life in this rural town was monotonous, and with the exception of the doctors and other nurses at work, the only people they saw were the elderly, those devoid of memory and signs of life.

The three nurses ate and drank a lot, and Tengo couldn't keep up. As they got livelier, he sat beside them, quietly eating a moderate amount of grilled meat and sipping his draft beer so he didn't get drunk. After they left the *yakiniku* place, they went to a bar, bought a bottle of whiskey, and belted out karaoke. The three nurses took turns singing their favorite songs, then teamed up to do a Candies number, complete with choreographed steps. Tengo was sure they had practiced, they were that good. Tengo wasn't into karaoke, but he did manage one Yosui Inoue song he vaguely remembered.

Nurse Adachi was normally reserved, but after a few drinks, she turned animated and bold. Once she got a bit tipsy, her red cheeks turned a healthy tanned color. She giggled at silly jokes and leaned back, in an entirely natural way, on Tengo's shoulder. Nurse Omura had changed into a light blue dress and had let down her hair. She looked three or four years younger and her voice dropped an octave. Her usually brisk, businesslike manner was subdued, and she moved languidly, as if she had taken on a different personality. Only Nurse Tamura, with her metal-framed glasses, looked and acted the same as always.

"My kids are staying with a neighbor tonight," Nurse Omura explained. "And my husband has to work the night shift. You have to take advantage of times like this to just go out and have fun. It's important to get away from it all sometimes. Don't you agree, Tengo?"

The three nurses had started calling him by his first name. Most people around him seemed to do that naturally. Even his students called him "Tengo" behind his back.

"Yes, that's for sure," Tengo agreed.

"We just have to get out sometimes," Nurse Tamura said, sipping a glass of Suntory Old whiskey and water. "We're just flesh and blood, after all."

"Take off our uniforms, and we're just ordinary women," Miss Adachi said, and giggled at her comment.

"Tell me, Tengo," Nurse Omura said. "Is it okay to ask this?"

"Ask what?"

"Are you seeing anybody?"

"Yes, tell us," Nurse Adachi said, crunching down on some corn nuts with her large, white teeth.

"It's not an easy thing to talk about," Tengo said.

"We don't mind if it's not easy to talk about," the experienced Nurse Tamura said. "We have lots of time, and we would love to hear about it. I'm dying to hear this hard-to-talk-about story."

"Tell us, tell us!" Nurse Adachi said, clapping her hands lightly and giggling.

"It's not all that interesting," Tengo said. "It's kind of trite and pointless."

"Well, then just cut to the chase," Nurse Omura said. "Do you have a girlfriend, or not?"

Tengo gave in. "At this point, I'm not seeing anyone."

"Hmm," Nurse Tamura said. She stirred the ice in her glass with a finger and licked it. "That won't do. That won't do at all. A young, vigorous man like yourself without a girlfriend, it's such a waste."

"It's not good for your body, either," the large Nurse Omura said. "If you keep it stored inside you for a long time, you'll go soft in the head."

Young Nurse Adachi was still giggling. "You'll go soft in the head," she said, and poked her forehead.

"I did have someone until recently," Tengo said, somewhat apologetically.

"But she left?" Nurse Tamura said, pushing up the bridge of her glasses.

Tengo nodded.

"You mean she dumped you?"

"I don't know," Tengo said, inclining his head. "Maybe she did. I think I probably was dumped."

"By any chance is that person – a lot older than you?" Nurse Tamura asked, her eyes narrowed.

"Yes, she is," Tengo said. How did she know that?

"Didn't I tell you?" Nurse Tamura said, looking proudly at the other two nurses. They nodded.

"I told the others that," Nurse Tamura said, "that you were going out with an older woman. Women can sniff out these things."

"Sniff, sniff," went Nurse Adachi.

"On top of that, maybe she was already married," Nurse Omura said in a lazy tone. "Am I right?"

Tengo hesitated for a moment and then nodded. Lying was pointless.

"You bad boy," Nurse Adachi said, and poked him in the thigh.

"Ten years older," Tengo said.

"Goodness!" Nurse Omura exclaimed.

"Ah, so you had an experienced, older married woman loving you," Nurse Tamura, herself a mother, said. "I'm envious. Maybe I should do that myself. And comfort lonely, gentle young Tengo here. I might not look it, but I still have a pretty decent body."

She grabbed Tengo's hand and was about to press it against her breasts. The other two women managed to stop her. Even if you were letting your hair down, there was a line that shouldn't be crossed between nurses and a patient's relative. That's what they seemed to think – or else they were afraid that someone might spot them. It was a small town, and rumors spread quickly. Maybe Nurse Tamura's husband was the jealous type. Tengo had enough problems and didn't want to get caught up in any more.

"You're really something," Nurse Tamura said, wanting to change the subject. "You come all this way here, sit by your father's bedside for hours a day reading aloud to him . . . Not many people would do that."

Young Nurse Adachi tilted her head a bit. "I agree, he really is something. I really respect you for that."

"You know, we're always praising you," Nurse Tamura said.

Tengo's face reddened. He wasn't in this town to nurse his father. He was staying here hoping to again see the air chrysalis, and the faint light it gave off, and inside it, the sleeping figure of Aomame. That was the only reason he remained here. Taking care of his unconscious father was only a pretext. But he couldn't reveal the truth. If he did, he would have to start by explaining an air chrysalis.

"It's because I never did anything for him up till now." Awkwardly, he scrunched up his large frame in the narrow wooden chair, sounding uncomfortable. But the nurses found his attitude appealingly humble.

Tengo wanted to tell them he was sleepy so he could get up and go back to his inn, but he couldn't find the right opportunity. He wasn't the type, after all, to assert himself.

"Yes, but –" Nurse Omura said, and cleared her throat. "To get back to what we were talking about, I wonder why you and that married woman ten years older than you broke up. I imagine you were getting along all right? Did her husband find out or something?"

"I don't know the reason," Tengo said. "At one point she just stopped calling, and I haven't heard from her since."

"Hmm," Nurse Adachi said. "I wonder if she was tired of you."

Nurse Omura shook her head. She held one index finger pointing straight up and turned to her younger colleague. "You still don't know anything about the world. You don't get it at all. A forty-year-old married woman who snags a young, vigorous, delicious young man like this one and enjoys him to the fullest doesn't then just up and say *Thanks. It was fun. Bye!* It's impossible. Of course, the other way around happens sometimes."

"Is that right?" Nurse Adachi said, inclining her head just a fraction. "I guess I'm a bit naive."

"Yes, that's the way it is," Nurse Omura declared. She looked at Tengo for a while, as if stepping back from a stone monument to examine the words chiseled into it. Then she nodded. "When you get a little older you'll understand."

"Oh, my – it's been simply ages," Nurse Tamura said, sinking deeper into her chair.

For a time the three nurses were lost in a conversation about the sexual escapades of someone he didn't know (another nurse, he surmised). With his glass of whiskey and water in hand, Tengo surveyed these three nurses, picturing the three witches in *Macbeth*. The ones who chant "Fair is foul, and foul is fair," as they fill Macbeth's head with evil ambitions. But Tengo wasn't seeing the three nurses as evil beings. They were kind and straightforward women. They worked hard and took good care of his father. Overworked, living in this small, less-than-stimulating fishing town, they were just letting off steam, as they did once every month. But when he witnessed how the energy in these three women, all of different generations, was converging, he couldn't help but envision the moors of Scotland – a gloomy, overcast sky, a cold wind and rain howling through the heath.

In college he had read *Macbeth* in English class, and somehow a few lines remained with him.

> *By the pricking of my thumbs,*
> *Something wicked this way comes,*
> *Open, locks,*
> *Whoever knocks!*

Why should he remember only these lines? He couldn't even recall who spoke them in the play. But they made Tengo think of that persistent NHK collector, knocking at the door of his apartment in Koenji. Tengo looked at his own thumbs. They didn't feel pricked. Still, Shakespeare's skillful rhyme had an ominous ring to it.

> *Something wicked this way comes . . .*

Tengo prayed that Fuka-Eri wouldn't unlock the door.

7

USHIKAWA

I'm Heading Your Way

FOR A WHILE USHIKAWA HAD TO give up collecting more information on the elderly dowager in Azabu. The security around her was just too tight, and he knew he would come smack up against a high wall whatever direction he went in. He wanted to find out more about the safe house, but it was too risky hanging out in the neighborhood any longer. There were security cameras, and given his looks, Ushikawa was too conspicuous. Once the other party was on its guard, things could get a bit sticky, so he decided to stay away from the Willow House and try a different approach.

The only different approach he could come up with, though, was to reinvestigate Aomame. He had already asked a PI firm he had worked with to collect more information on her, and he did some of the legwork himself, questioning people involved with her. Nothing suspicious or opaque surfaced. Ushikawa frowned, sighing deeply. *I must have overlooked something,* he thought. *Something critical.*

* * *

Ushikawa took out an address book from a drawer of his desk and dialed a number. Whenever he needed information that could only be obtained illegally, this was the number he called. The man on the other end lived in a much darker world than Ushikawa. As long as you paid, he could dig up almost any information you needed. The more tightly guarded the information, the higher the fee.

Ushikawa was after two pieces of information. One was personal background on Aomame's parents, who were still devout members of the Witnesses. Ushikawa was positive that the Witnesses had a central database with information on all their members. They had numerous followers throughout Japan, with much coming and going between the headquarters and the regional branches. Without a centralized database, the system wouldn't run smoothly. Their headquarters was located in the suburbs of Odawara. They owned a magnificent building on a generous plot of land, and had their own factory to print pamphlets, and an auditorium and guest facilities for followers from all over the country. All their information was sourced from this location, and you could be sure it was under strict control.

The second piece of information was Aomame's employment record at the sports club. Ushikawa wanted to know the details of her job there, and the names of her personal clients. This kind of information wouldn't be as closely guarded. Not that you could waltz in, say, "I wonder if you would mind showing me Miss Aomame's file, please?," and have them gladly hand it over.

Ushikawa left his name and phone number on the machine. Thirty minutes later he got a call back.

"Mr. Ushikawa," a hoarse voice said.

Ushikawa related the particulars of what he was looking for. He had never actually met the man. They always did business by phone, with materials sent over by special delivery. The man's voice was a bit husky, and he occasionally cleared his throat. He might have had something wrong with it. There was always a perfect silence on the other end of the line, as if he were phoning from a soundproof room.

93

All Ushikawa could hear was the man's voice, and the grating sound of his breathing. Beyond that, nothing. The sounds he heard were all a bit exaggerated. *What a creepy guy,* Ushikawa thought each time. *The world is sure full of creepy guys,* he mused, knowing full well that, objectively speaking, this category would include himself. He had secretly nicknamed the man Bat.

"In both cases, then, you're after information concerning the name Aomame, right?" Bat said huskily, and cleared his throat.

"Correct. It's an unusual name."

"You want every bit of information I can get?"

"As long as it involves the name Aomame, I want it all. If possible, I would also like a photo of her, with a clear shot of her face."

"The gym should be easy. They aren't expecting anyone to steal their information. The Witnesses, though, are a different story. They're a huge organization, with a lot of money, and tight security. Religious organizations are some of the hardest groups to crack. They keep things tight to protect their members' personal security, and there are always tax issues involved."

"Do you think you can do it?"

"There are ways to pry open the door. What is more difficult is making sure you close it afterward. If you don't do that, you'll have a homing missile chasing you."

"You make it sound like a war."

"That's exactly what it is. Some pretty scary things might pop out," the man rasped. Ushikawa could tell from his tone of voice that this battle was something he enjoyed.

"So, you'll take it on for me?"

The man lightly cleared his throat. "All right. But it'll cost you."

"How much are we talking about, roughly?"

The man gave him an estimate. Ushikawa had to swallow before he accepted. He had put aside enough of his own funds to cover it, and if the man came through, he could get reimbursed later on.

"How long will it take?"

"I assume this is a rush job?"

"Correct."

"It's hard to give an exact estimate, but I'm thinking a week to ten days."

"Fine," Ushikawa said. He would have to let Bat determine the pace.

"When I've gathered the material, I'll call you. I'll definitely get in touch before ten days are up."

"Unless a missile catches up with you," Ushikawa said.

"Exactly," Bat said, totally blasé.

After he hung up, Ushikawa hunched over his desk, turning things over in his mind. He had no idea how Bat would gather the information via some *back door*. Even if he asked, he knew he wouldn't get an answer. The only thing for sure was that his methods weren't legal. He would start by trying to bribe somebody inside. If necessary he might try trespassing. If computers were involved, things could get complicated.

There were only a few government offices and companies that managed information by computer. It cost too much and took too much effort. But a religious organization of national scale would have the resources to computerize. Ushikawa himself knew next to nothing about computers. He did understand, however, that computers were becoming an indispensable tool for gathering information. Earlier ways of finding information – going to the National Diet Library, sitting at a desk with piles of bound, small-sized editions of old newspapers, or almanacs – might soon become a thing of the past. The world might be reduced to a battlefield, the smell of blood everywhere, where computer managers and hackers fought it out. No, "the smell of blood" isn't accurate, Ushikawa decided. It was a war, so there was bound to be some bloodshed. But there wouldn't be any smell. What a weird world. Ushikawa preferred a world where smells and pain still existed, even if the smells and pain were unendurable. Still, people like Ushikawa might become out-of-date relics.

But Ushikawa wasn't pessimistic. He had an innate sense of intuition, and his unique olfactory organ let him sniff out and distinguish all sorts of odors. He could physically feel, in his skin, how things were trending. Computers couldn't do this. This was the kind of ability that couldn't be quantified or systematized. Skillfully accessing a heavily guarded computer and extracting information was the job of a hacker. But deciding which information to extract, and sifting through massive amounts of information to find what is useful, was something only a flesh-and-blood person could do.

Maybe I am just an ugly, middle-aged, outdated man, Ushikawa thought. *Nope, no maybes about it. I am, without a doubt, one ugly, middle-aged, outdated man. But I do have a couple of talents nobody else has. And as long as I have these talents, no matter what sort of weird world I find myself in, I'll survive.*

I'm going to get you, Miss Aomame. You are quite clever, to be sure. Skilled, and cautious. But I'm going to chase after you until I catch you. So wait for me. I'm heading your way. Can you hear my footsteps? I don't believe you can. I'm like a tortoise, hardly making a sound. But step by step, I am getting closer.

But Ushikawa felt something else pressing on him from behind. Time. Pursuing Aomame meant simultaneously shaking off time, which was in pursuit of him. He had to track her down quickly, clarify who was backing her, and present it all, nice and neat, on a plate to the people from Sakigake. He had been given a limited amount of time. It would be too late to find out everything, say, three months from now. Up until recently he had been a very valuable person to them. Capable and accommodating, well versed in legal matters, a man they could count on to keep his mouth shut. Someone who could work off the grid. But in the end, he was simply a hired jack-of-all-trades. He wasn't one of them, a member of their family. He was a man without a speck of religious devotion. If he became a danger to the religion, they might eliminate him with no qualms whatever.

While he waited for Bat to return his call, Ushikawa went to the library to look into the history and activities of the Witnesses. He took notes and made copies of relevant documents. He liked doing research at a library. He liked the feeling of accumulating knowledge in his brain. It was something he had enjoyed ever since he was a child.

Once he had finished at the library, he went to Aomame's apartment in Jiyugaoka, to make sure once more that it was unoccupied. The mailbox still had her name on it, but no one seemed to be living there. He stopped by the office of the real estate agent who handled the rental.

"I heard that there was a vacant apartment in the building," Ushikawa said, "and I was wondering if I could rent it."

"It is vacant, yes," the agent told him, "but no one can move in until the beginning of February. The rental contract with the present occupant doesn't expire until the end of next January. They are going to be paying the monthly rent the same as always until then. They have moved everything out and the electricity and water have been shut off. But the lease remains intact."

"So until the end of January, they're paying rent for an empty apartment?"

"Correct," the real estate agent said. "They said they will pay the entire amount owed on the lease so they would like us to keep the apartment as it is. As long as they pay the rent, we can't object."

"It's a strange thing – wasting money to pay for an empty apartment."

"Well, I was concerned myself, so I had the owner accompany me and let me in to take a look at the place. I wouldn't want there to be a mummified body in the closet or anything. But nothing was there. The place had been nicely cleaned. It was simply empty. I have no idea, though, what the circumstances are."

Aomame was obviously no longer living there. But for some reason they still wanted her listed as nominally renting the place, which is why they were paying four months' rent for an empty apartment. Whoever *they* were, they were cautious, and not hurting for money.

Precisely ten days later, in the early afternoon, Bat called Ushikawa's office in Kojimachi.

"Mr. Ushikawa," the hoarse voice said. In the background, there was the usual emptiness – a complete lack of any sound.

"Speaking."

"Do you mind if we talk now?"

"That would be fine," Ushikawa said.

"The Witnesses had very tight security. But I was expecting that. I was able to get the information related to Aomame okay."

"No homing missile?"

"Nothing so far."

"Glad to hear it."

"Mr. Ushikawa," the man said, and he cleared his throat a few times. "I'm really sorry, but could you put out the cigarette?"

"Cigarette?" he asked, glancing at the Seven Stars between his fingers. Smoke silently swirled up toward the ceiling. "You're right, I am smoking, but how can you tell?"

"Obviously I can't smell it. Just hearing your breathing makes it hard for me to breathe. I have terrible allergies, you see."

"I see. I hadn't noticed. My apologies."

The man cleared his throat a few times. "I'm not blaming you, Mr. Ushikawa. I wouldn't expect you to notice."

Ushikawa crushed the cigarette out in the ashtray and poured some tea he had been drinking over it. He stood up and opened the window wide.

"I put out the cigarette, opened the window, and let in some fresh air. Not that the air outside is all that clean."

"Sorry for the trouble."

Silence continued for about ten seconds. A total, absolute quiet.

"So, you were able to get the information from the Witnesses?" Ushikawa asked.

"Yes. Quite a lot, actually. The Aomame family are devout, long-time members, so there was plenty of material related to them. It is probably easiest if I give you the whole file, and then at your end you decide what is important material and what isn't."

Ushikawa agreed. That was what he had been hoping for.

"The sports club wasn't much of a problem – just open the door, go in, do your job, shut the door, that's it. Time was kind of limited, so I grabbed everything I could. There's a lot of material here too. I'll send over a folder with both sets of material. As usual, in exchange for the fee."

Ushikawa wrote down the fee that Bat gave him. It was about twenty percent higher than the estimate. Not that he had a choice.

"I don't want to use the mail this time, so a messenger will bring it over to your place tomorrow. Please have the fee ready. And as usual, don't expect a receipt."

"All right," Ushikawa replied.

"I mentioned this before, but I will repeat it just to make sure. I was able to get all the available information on the topic you asked me to look into. So even if you aren't satisfied with it, I take no responsibility. I did everything that was technically possible. Compensation was for the time and effort involved, not the results. So please don't ask me to give your money back if you don't find the information you're looking for. I would like you to acknowledge this point."

"I do," Ushikawa replied.

"Another thing is that I wasn't able to obtain a photograph of Miss Aomame, no matter how much I tried," Bat said. "All photos of her have been carefully removed."

"Understood. That's okay," Ushikawa said.

"Her face may be different by now," Bat commented.

"Maybe so," Ushikawa said.

Bat cleared his throat several times. "Well, that's it," he said, and hung up.

Ushikawa put the phone back in its cradle, sighed, and placed a new cigarette between his lips. He lit it with his lighter, and slowly exhaled smoke in the direction of the phone.

The next afternoon, a young woman visited his office. She was probably not yet twenty. She had on a short white dress that revealed the curves of her body, matching white high heels, and pearl earrings. Her earlobes were large for her small face. She was barely five feet tall. She wore her hair long and straight, and her eyes were big and bright. She looked like a fairy in training. The woman looked straight at Ushikawa and smiled a cheerful, intimate smile, as if she were viewing something precious she would never forget. Neatly aligned white teeth peeked out happily from between her tiny lips. Perhaps it was just her business smile. Very few people did not flinch when they came face-to-face with Ushikawa for the first time.

"I have brought the materials that you requested," the woman said, and extracted two large, thick manila envelopes from the cloth bag hanging from her shoulders. As if she were a shamaness transporting an ancient stone lithograph, she held up the envelopes in front of her, then carefully placed them on Ushikawa's desk.

From a drawer Ushikawa took out the envelope he had ready and passed it over to her. She opened the envelope, extracted the sheaf of ten-thousand-yen bills, and counted them as she stood there. She was very adept at counting, her beautiful, slim fingers moving swiftly. She finished counting, returned the bills to the envelope, and put the envelope in her cloth bag. She showed Ushikawa an even bigger, warmer smile than before, as if nothing could have made her happier than to meet him.

Ushikawa tried to imagine what connection this woman could have with Bat. Passing along the material, receiving payment. That was perhaps the only role she played.

After the small woman had left, Ushikawa stared at the door for the longest time. She had shut the door behind her, but there was still a strong sense of her in the room. Maybe in exchange for leaving a trace of herself behind, she had taken away a part of Ushikawa's soul. He could feel that new void within his chest. *Why did this happen?* he wondered, finding it odd. *And what could it possibly mean?*

After about ten minutes, he finally took the materials out of the envelopes, which had been sealed with several layers of adhesive tape. The inside was stuffed with a jumble of printouts, photocopies, and original documents. Ushikawa didn't know how Bat had accomplished it, but he had certainly come up with a lot of material in such a short time. As always, the man did an impressive job. Still, faced with that bundle of documents, Ushikawa was hit by a deep sense of impotence. No matter how much he might rustle around in it, would he ever arrive anywhere? Or would he spend a small fortune just to wind up with a stack of wastepaper? The sense of powerlessness he experienced was so deep that he could stare as much as he wanted into the well and never get a glimpse of its bottom. Everything Ushikawa could see was covered in a gloomy twilight, like an intimation of death. *Perhaps this was due to something that woman left behind,* he thought. *Or perhaps due to something she took away with her.*

Somehow, though, Ushikawa recovered his strength. He patiently went through the stack of materials until evening, copying the information he felt was important into a notebook, organizing it under different categories. By concentrating on this, he was able to dispel the mysterious listlessness that had grabbed hold of him. And by the time it grew dark and he switched on his desk lamp, Ushikawa was thinking that the information had been worth every yen he had paid for it.

*   *   *

He began by reading through the material from the sports club. Aomame was a highly skilled trainer, popular with the members. Along with teaching general classes, she was also a personal trainer. Looking through the copies of the daily schedule he could figure out when, where, and how she trained these private clients. Sometimes she trained them individually at the club, sometimes she went to their homes. Among the names of her clients was a well-known entertainer, and a politician. The dowager of the Willow House, Shizue Ogata, was her oldest client.

Her connection with Shizue Ogata began not long after Aomame started working at the club four years earlier, and continued until just before she disappeared. This was exactly the same period during which the two-story apartment building at the Willow House became a safe house for victims of domestic violence. Maybe it was a coincidence, but maybe not. At any rate, according to the records, their relationship appeared to have deepened over time.

Perhaps a personal bond had grown between Aomame and the old dowager. Ushikawa's intuition sensed this. At first it started out as the relationship between a sports club instructor and a client, but at a certain point, the nature of this relationship changed. As Ushikawa went through the businesslike descriptions in chronological order, he tried to pinpoint that moment. Something happened that transformed their relationship beyond that of mere instructor and client. They formed a close personal relationship that transcended the difference in age and status. This may even have led to some secret emotional understanding between the two, a secret understanding that eventually led Aomame down the path to murder Leader at the Hotel Okura. Ushikawa's sense of smell told him so.

But what *was* that path? And what secret understanding did they have?

That was as far as Ushikawa's conjectures could take him.

Most likely, domestic violence was one factor in it. At first glance this seemed to be a critical theme for the older woman. According to the records, the first time Shizue Ogata came in contact with Aomame was at a self-defense class. It wasn't very common for a woman in her seventies to take a self-defense class. Something connected with violence must have brought the old lady and Aomame together.

Or maybe Aomame herself had been the victim of domestic violence. And Leader had committed domestic violence. Perhaps they found out about this and decided to punish him. But these were all simply hypotheses, and these hypotheses didn't square with the image Ushikawa had of Leader. Certainly people, no matter who they are, have something hidden deep down inside, and Leader was a deeper person than most. He was, after all, the driving force behind a major religious organization. Wise and intelligent, he also had depths no one else could access. But say he really had committed domestic violence? Would these acts have been so significant to these women that, when they learned of them, they planned out a meticulous assassination – one of them giving up her identity, the other risking her social standing?

One thing was for sure: the murder of Leader was not carried out on a whim. Behind it stood an unwavering will, a clear-cut, unclouded motivation, and an elaborate system – a system that had been meticulously crafted using a great deal of time and money.

The problem was that there was no concrete proof to back up his conjectures. What Ushikawa had before him was nothing more than circumstantial evidence based on theories. Something that Occam's razor could easily prune away. At this stage he couldn't report anything to Sakigake. Still, he knew he was on to something. There was a certain smell to it, a distinctive texture. All the elements pointed in a single direction. Something to do with domestic violence made the dowager direct Aomame to kill Leader and then hide her away. Indirectly, all the information Bat had provided him supported this conclusion.

Plowing through the materials dealing with the Witnesses took a long time. There were an enormous number of documents, most of them useless to Ushikawa. The majority of the materials were reports on what Aomame's family had contributed to the activities of the Witnesses. As far as these documents were concerned, Aomame's family were earnest, devout followers. They had spent the better part of their lives propagating the religion's message. Her parents presently resided in Ichikawa, in Chiba Prefecture. In thirty-five years they had moved twice, both times within Ichikawa. Her father, Takayuki Aomame (58), worked in an engineering firm, while her mother, Yasuko (56), wasn't employed. The couple's eldest son, Keiichi Aomame (34), had worked in a small printing company in Tokyo after graduating from a prefectural high school in Ichikawa, but after three years he quit the company and began working at the Witnesses' headquarters in Odawara. There he also worked in printing, making pamphlets for the religion, and was now a supervisor. Five years earlier he had married a woman who was also a member of the Witnesses. They had two children and rented an apartment in Odawara.

The record for the eldest daughter, Masami Aomame, ended when she was eleven. That was when she abandoned the faith. And the Witnesses seemed to have no interest at all in anyone who had left the faith. To the Witnesses, it was the same as if Masami Aomame had died at age eleven. After this, there wasn't a single detail about what sort of life she led – not even whether or not she was alive.

In this case, Ushikawa thought, *the only thing to do is visit the parents or the brother and ask them. Maybe they will provide me with some hint.* From what he gathered from the documentary evidence, he didn't imagine they would be too pleased to answer his questions. Aomame's family – as far as Ushikawa could see it, that is – were narrow-minded in their thinking, narrow-minded in the way they lived. They were people who had no doubt whatsoever that the more narrow-minded they became, the closer they got to heaven. To them, anyone who abandoned the faith, even a relative, was traveling down a wicked, defiled path. Who knows, maybe they didn't even think of them as relatives anymore.

Had Aomame been the victim of domestic violence as a girl?

Maybe she had, maybe she hadn't. Even if she had, her parents most likely would not have seen this as abuse. Ushikawa knew very well how strict members of the Witnesses were with their children. In many cases this included corporal punishment.

But would a childhood experience like that form such a deep wound that it would lead a person, after she grew up, to commit murder? This wasn't out of the realm of possibility, but Ushikawa thought it was pushing the limits of conjecture to an extreme. Carrying out a premeditated murder on one's own wasn't easy. It was dangerous, to begin with, and the emotional toll was enormous. If you got caught, the punishment was stiff. There had to be a stronger motivation behind it.

Ushikawa picked up the sheaf of documents and carefully reread the details about Masami Aomame's background, up to age eleven. Almost as soon as she could walk, she began accompanying her mother to proselytize. They went from door to door handing out pamphlets, telling people about the judgment to come at the end of the world and urging them to join the faith. Joining meant you could survive the end of the world. After that, the heavenly kingdom would appear. A church member had knocked on Ushikawa's door any number of times. Usually it was a middle-aged woman, wearing a hat or holding a parasol. Most wore glasses and stared fixedly at him with eyes like those of a clever fish. Often she had a child along. Ushikawa pictured little Aomame trundling around from door to door with her mother.

Aomame didn't attend kindergarten, but went into the local neighborhood municipal public elementary school in Ichikawa. And when she was in fifth grade she withdrew from the Witnesses. It was unclear why she left. The Witnesses didn't record each and every reason a member renounced the faith. Whoever fell into the clutches of the devil could very well stay there. Talking about paradise and the path to get there kept members busy enough. The righteous had their own work to do, and the devil, his – a spiritual division of labor.

In Ushikawa's brain someone was knocking on a cheaply made, plywood partition. "Mr. Ushikawa! Mr. Ushikawa!" the voice was yelling. Ushikawa closed his eyes and listened carefully. The voice was faint, but persistent. *I must have overlooked something,* he thought. *A critical fact must be written here, somewhere, in these very documents. But I can't see it. The knock must be telling me this.*

Ushikawa turned again to the thick stack of documents, not just following what was written, but trying to imagine actual scenes in his mind. Three-year-old Aomame going with her mother as she spread the gospel door to door. Most of the time people slammed the door in their faces. Next she's in elementary school. She continues proselytizing. Her weekends are taken up entirely with propagating their faith. She doesn't have any time to play with friends. She might not even have had any friends. Most children in the Witnesses were bullied and shunned at school. Ushikawa had read a book on the Witnesses and was well aware of this. And at age eleven she left the religion. That must have taken a great deal of determination. Aomame had been raised in the faith, had had it drummed into her since she was born. The faith had seeped into every fiber of her being, so she couldn't easily slough it off, like changing clothes. That would mean she was isolated within the home. They wouldn't easily accept a daughter who had renounced the faith. For Aomame, abandoning the faith was the same as abandoning her family.

When Aomame was eleven, what in the world had happened to her? What could have made her come to that decision?

The Ichikawa Municipal ** Elementary School. Ushikawa tried saying the name aloud. *Something had happened there. Something had most definitely happened . . .* He inhaled sharply. *I've heard the name of that school before,* he realized.

But where? Ushikawa had no ties to Chiba Prefecture. He had been born in Urawa, a city in Saitama, and ever since he came to Tokyo to go to college – except for the time he lived in Chuorinkan, in Kanagawa Prefecture – he had lived entirely within the twenty-three wards of

Tokyo. He had barely set foot in Chiba Prefecture. Only once, as he recalled, when he went to the beach at Futtsu. So why did the name of an elementary school in Ichikawa ring a bell?

It took him a while to remember. He rubbed his misshapen head as he concentrated. He fumbled through the dark recesses of memory, as if sticking his hand deep down into mud. It wasn't so long ago that he first heard that name. Very recently, in fact. Chiba Prefecture . . . Ichikawa Municipal ** Elementary School. Finally he grabbed onto one end of a thin rope.

Tengo Kawana. That's it – Tengo Kawana was from Ichikawa! And I think he attended a municipal public elementary school in town, too.

Ushikawa pulled down from his document shelf the file on Tengo. This was material he had compiled a few months back, at the request of Sakigake. He flipped through the pages to confirm Tengo's school record. His plump finger came to rest on Tengo's name. It was just as he had thought: Masami Aomame had attended the same elementary school as Tengo Kawana. Based on their birthdates, they were probably in the same year in school. Whether they were in the same class or not would require further investigation. But there was a high probability they knew each other.

Ushikawa put a Seven Stars cigarette in his mouth and lit up with his lighter. He had the distinct feeling that things were starting to fall into place. He was connecting the dots, and though he was unsure of what sort of picture would emerge, before long he should be able to see the outlines.

Miss Aomame, can you hear my footsteps? Probably not, since I'm walking as quietly as I can. But step by step I'm getting closer. I'm a dull, silly tortoise, but I'm definitely making progress. Pretty soon I'll catch sight of the rabbit's back. You can count on it.

Ushikawa leaned back from his desk, looked up at the ceiling, and slowly let the smoke rise up from his mouth.

8

AOMAME

Not Such a Bad Door

EXCEPT FOR THE SILENT MEN WHO brought supplies every Tuesday afternoon, for the next two weeks no one else visited Aomame's apartment. The man who claimed to be an NHK fee collector had insisted that he would be back. He had been determined, or at least that was the way it sounded to Aomame. But there hadn't been a knock on the door since. Maybe he was busy with another route.

On the surface, these were quiet, peaceful days. Nothing happened, nobody came by, the phone didn't ring. To be on the safe side, Tamaru called as little as possible. Aomame always kept the curtains closed, living as quietly as she could so as not to attract attention. After dark, she turned on the bare minimum number of lights.

Trying to stay as quiet as possible, she did strenuous workouts, mopped the floor every day, and spent a lot of time preparing meals. She asked for some Spanish-language tapes and went over the lessons aloud. Not speaking for a long time makes the muscles around the mouth grow slack. She had to focus on moving her mouth as much as she could, and foreign language drills were good for that. Plus Aomame had long fantasized about South America. If she could go anywhere, she would like to live in a small, peaceful country in South America, like Costa Rica. She would rent a small villa on the coast and spend the days swimming and reading. With the money she had stuffed in her bag she should be able to live for ten years there, if she watched her expenses. She couldn't see them chasing her all the way to Costa Rica.

As she practiced Spanish conversation Aomame imagined a quiet, peaceful life on the Costa Rican beach. Could Tengo be a part of her life there? She closed her eyes and pictured the two of them sunbathing on a Caribbean beach. She wore a small, black bikini and sunglasses and was holding Tengo's hand. But a sense of reality, the kind that would move her, was missing from the picture. It was nothing more than an ordinary tourist brochure photo.

When she ran out of things to do, she cleaned the pistol. She followed the manual and disassembled the Heckler & Koch, cleaned each part with a cloth and brush, oiled them, and then reassembled it. She made sure the action was smooth. By now she had mastered the operation and the pistol felt like a part of her body.

She would go to bed at ten, read a few pages in her book, and fall asleep. Aomame had never had trouble falling asleep. As she read, she would get sleepy. She would switch off the bedside lamp, rest her head on the pillow, and shut her eyes. With few exceptions, when she opened her eyes again it was morning.

Ordinarily she didn't tend to dream much. Even if she did, she usually had forgotten most of the dream by the time she woke up. Sometimes faint scraps of her dream would get caught on the wall of her consciousness, but she couldn't retrace these fragments back to any coherent narrative. All that remained were small, random images. She slept deeply, and the dreams she did have came from a very deep place. Like fish that live at the bottom of the ocean, most of her dreams weren't able to float to the surface. Even if they did, the difference in water pressure would force a change in their appearance.

But after coming to live in this hiding place, she dreamed every night. And these were clear, realistic dreams. She would be dreaming and wake up in the middle of a dream, unable to distinguish whether she was in the real world or the dream world. Aomame couldn't remember ever having had this experience before. She would look over at the digital clock beside her bed. The numbers would say 1:15, 2:37, or 4:07. She would close her eyes and try to fall asleep again, but it wasn't easy. The two different worlds were silently at odds within her, fighting over her consciousness, like the mouth of a river where the seawater and the fresh water flow in.

Not much I can do about it, she told herself. *I'm not even sure if this world with two moons in the sky is the* real *reality or not. So it shouldn't be so strange, should it? That in a world like this, if I fall asleep and dream, I find it hard to distinguish dream from reality? And let's not forget that I've killed a few men with my own hands. I'm being chased by fanatics who aren't about to give up, and I'm hiding out. How could I not be tense, and afraid? I can still feel the sensation, in my hands, of having murdered somebody. Maybe I'll never be able to sleep soundly the rest of my life. Maybe that's the responsibility I have to bear, the price I have to pay.*

The dreams she had – at least the ones she could recall – fell into three set categories.

The first was a dream about thunder. She is in a dark room, with thunder roaring continuously. But there is no lightning, just like the night she murdered Leader. There is something in the room. Aomame is lying in bed, naked, and something is wandering about around her, slowly, deliberately. The carpet is thick, and the air lies heavy and still. The windowpane rattles slightly in the thunder. She is afraid. She doesn't know what is there in the room. It might be a person. Maybe it's an animal. Maybe it's neither one. Finally, though, whatever it is leaves the room. Not through the door, nor by the window. But still its presence fades away until it has completely disappeared. She is alone now in the room.

She fumbles for the light near her bed. She gets out of bed, still naked, and looks around the room. There is a hole in the wall opposite her bed, a hole big enough for one person to barely make it through. The hole isn't in a set spot. It changes shape and moves around. It shakes, it moves, it grows bigger, it shrinks – as if it's alive. *Something* left through that hole. She stares into the hole. It seems to be connected to something else, but it's too dark inside to see, a darkness so thick that it's as if you could cut it out and hold it in your hand. She is curious, but at the same time afraid. Her heart pounds, a cold, distant beat. The dream ends there.

The second dream took place on the shoulder of the Metropolitan Expressway. And here, too, she is totally nude. Caught in the traffic jam, people leer at her from their cars, shamelessly ogling her naked body. Most are men, but there are a few women, too. The people are staring at her less-than-ample breasts and her pubic hair and the strange way it grows, all of them evaluating her body. Some are frowning, some smiling wryly, others yawning. Others are staring intently at her, their faces blank. She wants to cover herself up – at least her breasts and groin, if she can. A scrap of cloth would do the trick, or a sheet of newspaper. But there is nothing around her she can pick up. And for some reason (she has no idea why) she can't move her arms. From time to time the wind blows, stimulating her nipples, rustling her pubic hair.

On top of this – as if things couldn't get any worse – it feels like she is about to get her period. Her back feels dull and heavy, her abdomen hot. What should she do if, in front of all these people, she starts bleeding?

Just then the driver's-side door of a silver Mercedes coupe opens and a very refined middle-aged woman steps out. She's wearing bright-colored high heels, sunglasses, and silver earrings. She's slim, about the same height as Aomame. She wends her way through the backed-up cars, and when she comes over she takes off her coat and puts it on Aomame. It's an eggshell-colored spring coat that comes down to her knees. It's light as a feather. It's simple, but obviously expensive. The coat fits her perfectly, like it was made for her. The woman buttons it up for her, all the way to the top.

"I don't know when I can return it to you. I'm afraid I might bleed on it," Aomame says.

Without a word, the woman shakes her head, then weaves her way back through the cars to the Mercedes coupe. From the driver's side it looks like she lifts her hand in a small wave to Aomame, but it may be an illusion. Wrapped in the light, soft spring coat, Aomame knows she is protected. Her body is no longer exposed to anyone's view. And right then, as if it could barely wait, a line of blood drips down her thigh. Hot, thick, heavy blood. But as she looks at it she realizes it isn't blood. It's colorless.

The third dream was hard to put into words. It was a rambling, incoherent dream without any setting. All that was there was a feeling of being in motion. Aomame was ceaselessly moving through time and space. It didn't matter when or where this was. All that mattered was this movement. Everything was fluid, and a specific meaning was born of that fluidity. But as she gave herself up to it, she found her body growing transparent. She could see through her hands to the other side. Her bones, organs, and womb became visible. At this rate she might very well no longer exist. After she could no longer see herself, Aomame wondered what could possibly come then. She had no answer.

At two p.m. the phone rang and Aomame, dozing on the sofa, leapt to her feet.

"Is everything going okay?" Tamaru asked.

"Yes, fine," Aomame replied.

"How about the NHK fee collector?"

"I haven't seen him at all. Maybe he was just threatening me, saying he would be back."

"Could be," Tamaru said. "We set it up so the NHK subscription fee is automatically paid from a bank account, and an up-to-date sticker is on the door. Any fee collector would be bound to see it. We called NHK and they said the same thing. It must be some kind of clerical error."

"I just hope I don't have to deal with him."

"Yes, we need to avoid any kind of attention. And I don't like it when there are mistakes."

"But the world is full of mistakes."

"The world can be that way, but I have my own way of doing things," Tamaru said. "If there is anything that bothers you – anything at all – make sure you get in touch."

"Is there anything new with Sakigake?"

"Everything has been quiet. I imagine something is going on below the surface, but we can't tell from the outside."

"I heard you had an informant within the organization."

"We've gotten some reports, but they're focused on details, not the big picture. It does seem as if they are tightening up control of the faith. The faucet has been shut."

"But they are definitely still after me."

"Since Leader's death, there has clearly been a large gap left in the organization. They haven't decided yet who is going to succeed him, or what sort of policies Sakigake should take. But when it comes to pursuing you, opinion is unwavering and unanimous. Those are the facts we have been able to find out."

"Not very heartwarming facts, are they."

"Well, with facts what's important is their weight and accuracy. Warmth is secondary."

"Anyway," Aomame said, "if they capture me and the truth comes to light, that will be a problem for you as well."

"That is why we want to get you to a place they can't reach, as soon as we can."

"I know. But I need you to wait a little longer."

"*She* said that we would wait until the end of the year. So of course that's what I'll do."

"I appreciate it."

"I'm not the one you should be thanking."

"Be that as it may," Aomame said. "There is one item I'd like to add to the list the next time you bring over supplies. It's hard to say this to a man, though."

"I'm like a rock wall," Tamaru said. "Plus, when it comes to being gay, I'm in the big leagues."

"I would like a home pregnancy test."

There was silence. Finally Tamaru spoke. "You believe there's a need for that kind of test."

It wasn't a question, so Aomame didn't reply.

"Do you think you might be pregnant?" Tamaru asked.

"No, that isn't the reason."

Tamaru quickly turned this over in his mind. If you were quiet, you could actually hear the wheels turning.

"You don't think you're pregnant. Yet you need a pregnancy test."

"That's right."

"Sounds like a riddle to me."

"All I can tell you is that I would like to have the test. The kind of simple home test you can pick up in a drugstore is fine. I'd also appreciate a handbook on the female body and menstruation."

Tamaru was silent once more – a hard, concentrated silence.

"I think it would be better if I called you back," he said. "Is that okay?"

"Of course."

He made a small sound in the back of his throat, and hung up the phone.

* * *

The phone rang again fifteen minutes later. It had been a long while since Aomame had heard the dowager's voice. She felt like she was back in the greenhouse. That humid, warm space where rare butterflies flutter about, and time passes slowly.

"Are you doing all right there?"

"I'm trying to keep to a daily routine," Aomame replied. Since the dowager wanted to know, Aomame gave her a summary of her daily schedule, her exercising and meals.

"It must be hard for you," the dowager said, "not being able to go outside. But you have a strong will, so I'm not worried about you. I know you will be able to get through it. I would like to have you leave there as soon as possible and get you to a safer place, but if you want to stay there longer, I will do what I can to honor your wishes."

"I am grateful for that."

"No, I'm the one who should be grateful to you. You have done a wonderful thing for us." A short silence followed, and then the dowager continued. "Now, I understand you have requested a pregnancy test."

"My period is nearly three weeks late."

"Are your periods usually regular?"

"Since they began when I was ten, I have had a period every twenty-nine days, almost without fail. Like the waxing and waning of the moon. I've never skipped one."

"You are in an unusual situation right now. Your emotional balance and physical rhythm will be thrown off. It's possible your period might stop, or the timing may be off."

"It has never happened before, but I understand how it could."

"According to Tamaru you don't see how you could be pregnant."

"The last time I had sexual relations with a man was the middle of June. After that, nothing at all."

"Still, you suspect you might be pregnant. Is there any evidence for that? Other than your period being late?"

"I just have a feeling about it."

"A feeling?"

"A feeling inside me."

"A feeling that you have conceived?"

"Once we talked about eggs, remember? The evening we went to see Tsubasa. About how women have a set number of them?"

"I remember. The average woman has about four hundred eggs. Each month, she releases one of them."

"Well, I have the distinct sensation that one of those eggs has been fertilized. I don't know if *sensation* is the right word, though."

The dowager pondered this. "I have had two children, so I think I have a very good idea of what you mean by *sensation*. But you're saying you've been impregnated without having had sex with a man. That is a little difficult to accept."

"I know. I feel the same way."

"I'm sorry to have to ask this, but is it possible you've had sexual relations with someone while you weren't conscious?"

"That is not possible. My mind is always clear."

The dowager chose her words carefully. "I have always thought of you as a very calm, logical person."

"I've always tried to be," Aomame said.

"In spite of that, you think you are pregnant without having had sex."

"I think that *possibility exists*. To put it more accurately," Aomame replied. "Of course, it might not make any sense even to consider it."

"I understand," the dowager said. "Let's wait and see what happens. The pregnancy kit will be there tomorrow. It will come at the same time and in the same way as the rest of the supplies. We will include several types of tests, just to be sure."

"I really appreciate it," Aomame said.

"If it does turn out that you are pregnant, when do you think it happened?"

"I think it was that night when I went to the Hotel Okura. The night there was a storm."

The dowager gave a short sigh. "You can pinpoint it that clearly?"

116

"I calculated it, and that night just happened to be the day when I was most fertile."

"Which would mean that you are two months along."

"That's right," Aomame said.

"Do you have any morning sickness? This would normally be when you would have the worst time of it."

"No, I don't feel nauseous at all. I don't know why, though."

The dowager took her time, and carefully chose her next words. "If you do the test and it does turn out you're pregnant, how do you think you'll react?"

"I suppose I'll try to figure out who the child's biological father could be. This would be very important to me."

"But you have no idea."

"Not at the moment, no."

"I understand," the dowager said, calmly. "At any rate, whatever does happen, I will always be with you. I'll do everything in my power to protect you. I want you to remember that."

"I'm sorry to cause so much trouble at a time like this," Aomame said.

"It's no trouble at all," the dowager said. "This is the most important thing for a woman. Let's wait for the test results, and then decide what we'll do. Just relax."

And she quietly hung up.

Someone knocked at the door. Aomame was in the bedroom doing yoga, and she stopped and listened carefully. The knock was hard and insistent. She remembered that sound.

She took the automatic pistol from the drawer and switched off the safety. She pulled back the slide to send a round into the chamber. She stuck the pistol in the back of her sweatpants and softly padded out to the dining room. She gripped the softball bat in both hands and stared at the door.

"Miss Takai," a thick, hoarse voice called out. "Are you there, Miss Takai? NHK here, come to collect the subscription fee."

Plastic tape was wrapped around the handle of the bat so it wouldn't slip.

"Miss Takai, to repeat myself, I know you're in there. So please stop playing this silly game of hide-and-seek. You're inside, and you're listening to my voice."

The man was saying almost exactly the same things he had said the previous time, like a tape being replayed.

"I told you I would be back, but you probably thought that was just an empty threat. You should know that I always keep my promises. And if there are fees to collect, I most definitely will collect them. You're in there, Miss Takai, and you're listening. And you're thinking this: If I just stay patient, the collector will give up and go away."

He knocked on the door again for some time. Twenty, maybe twenty-five times. *What sort of hands does this man have?* Aomame wondered. *And why doesn't he use the doorbell?*

"And I know you're thinking this, too," the fee collector said, as if reading her mind. "You are thinking that this man must have pretty tough hands. And that his hands must hurt, pounding on the door like this so many times. And there is another thing you are thinking: Why in the world is he knocking, anyway? There's a doorbell, so why not ring that?"

Aomame grimaced.

The fee collector continued. "No, I don't want to ring the bell. If I do, all you hear is the bell ringing, that's all. No matter who pushes the bell, it makes the same harmless little sound. Now, a knock – *that* has personality. You use your physical body to knock on something and there's a flesh-and-blood emotion behind it. Of course my hand does hurt. I'm not Superman, after all. But it can't be helped. This is my profession. And every profession, no matter high or low, deserves respect. Don't you agree, Miss Takai?"

Knocks pounded on the door again. Twenty-seven in all, powerful knocks with a fixed pause between each one. Aomame's hands grew sweaty as they gripped the bat.

"Miss Takai, people who receive the NHK TV signal have to pay the fee – it's the law. There are no two ways about it. It is a rule we have to follow. So why don't you just cheerfully pay the fee? I'm not pounding on your door because I want to, and I know you don't want this unpleasantness to go on forever. You must be thinking, Why do I have to go through this? So just cheerfully pay up. Then you can go back to your quiet life again."

The man's voice echoed loudly down the hallway. *This man is enjoying the sound of his own voice,* Aomame thought. *He's getting a kick out of insulting people, making fun of them and abusing them.* She could sense the perverse pleasure he was getting from this.

"You're quite the stubborn lady, aren't you, Miss Takai. I'm impressed. You're like a shellfish at the bottom of a deep ocean, maintaining a strict silence. But I know you're in there. You're there, glaring at me through the door. The tension is making your underarms sweat. Do I have that right?"

Thirteen more knocks. Then he stopped. Aomame realized she was, indeed, sweating under her arms.

"All right. That's enough for today. But I'll be back soon. I'm starting to grow fond of this door. There are lots of doors in the world, and this one is not bad at all. It is definitely a door worth knocking on. At this rate I won't be able to relax unless I drop by here regularly to give it a few good knocks. Good-bye, Miss Takai. I'll be back."

Silence reigned. The fee collector had apparently left for good, but she hadn't heard any footsteps. Maybe he was pretending to have left and was waiting outside the door. Aomame gripped the bat even tighter and waited a couple of minutes.

"I'm still here," the fee collector suddenly announced. "Ha! You thought I left, didn't you? But I'm still here. I lied. Sorry about that, Miss Takai. That's the sort of person I am."

She heard him cough. An intentionally grating cough.

"I've been at this job for a long time. And over the years I've become able to picture the people on the other side of the door. This is the truth. Quite a few people hide behind their door and try to get away with not paying the NHK fee. I've been dealing with them for decades. Listen, Miss Takai."

He knocked three times, louder than he ever had.

"Listen, Miss Takai. You're very clever at hiding, like a flounder on the sea floor covered in sand. *Mimicry*, they call it. But in the end you won't be able to escape. Someone will come and open this door. You can count on it. As a veteran NHK fee collector, I guarantee it. You can hide as cleverly as you like, but in the final analysis mimicry is deception, pure and simple. It doesn't solve a thing. It's true, Miss Takai. I'll be on my way soon. Don't worry, this time for real. But I'll be back soon. When you hear a knock, you'll know it's me. Well, see you, Miss Takai. Take care!"

She couldn't hear any footsteps this time, either. She waited five minutes, then went up to the door and listened carefully. She squinted through the peephole. No one was outside. This time the fee collector really had left, it seemed.

Aomame leaned the metal bat up against the kitchen counter. She slid the round out of the pistol's chamber, set the safety, wrapped it back up in a pair of thick tights, and returned it to the drawer. She lay down on the sofa and closed her eyes. The man's voice still rang in her ears.

But in the end you won't be able to escape. Someone will come and open this door.

At least this man wasn't from Sakigake. They would take a quieter, more indirect approach. They would never yell in an apartment hallway, insinuate things like that, putting their target on guard. That was not their MO. Aomame pictured Buzzcut and Ponytail. They would sneak up on you without making a sound. And before you knew it, they would be standing right behind you.

Aomame shook her head, and breathed quietly.

Maybe he really was an NHK fee collector. If so, it was strange that he didn't notice the sticker that said they paid the subscription fee automatically. Aomame had checked that the sticker was pasted to the side of the door. Maybe the man was a mental patient. But the things he said had a bit too much reality to them for that. *The man certainly did seem to sense my presence on the other side of the door. As if he had sniffed out my secret, or a part of it.* But he did not have the power to open the door and come in. The door had to be opened from inside. *And I'm not planning on opening it.*

No, she thought, *it's hard to say that for sure. Someday I might open the door. If Tengo were to show up at the playground, I wouldn't hesitate to open the door and rush outside. It doesn't matter what might be waiting for me.*

Aomame sank down into the garden chair on the balcony and gazed as usual through the cracks in the screen at the playground. A high school couple were sitting on the bench underneath the zelkova tree, discussing something, serious expressions on their faces. Two young mothers were watching their children, not yet old enough for kindergarten, playing in the sandbox. They were deep in conversation yet kept their eyes glued to their children. A typical afternoon scene in a park. Aomame stared at the top of the slide for a long time.

She brought her hand down to her abdomen, shut her eyes, and listened carefully, trying to pick up the voice. Something was definitely alive inside her. A small, living something. She knew it.

Dohta, she whispered.

Maza, something replied.

9

TENGO

Before the Exit Is Blocked

THE FOUR OF THEM HAD *yakiniku,* then went to another place where they sang karaoke and polished off a bottle of whiskey. It was nearly ten p.m. when their cozy but boisterous little party broke up. After they left the bar, Tengo took Nurse Adachi back to her apartment. The other two women could catch a bus near the station, and they casually let things work out that way. Tengo and the young nurse walked down the deserted streets, side by side, for a quarter of an hour.

"Tengo, Tengo, Tengo," she sang out. "Such a nice name. *Tengo.* It's so easy to say."

Nurse Adachi had drunk a lot, but her cheeks were normally rosy so it was hard to tell, just by looking at her face, how drunk she really was. Her words weren't slurred and her footsteps were solid. She didn't seem drunk. Though people had their own ways of being drunk.

"I always thought it was a weird name," Tengo said.

"It isn't at all. *Tengo.* It has a nice ring to it and it's easy to remember. It's a wonderful name."

"Speaking of which, I don't know your first name. Everybody calls you Ku."

"That's my nickname. My real name is Kumi. Kind of a nothing name."

"*Kumi Adachi*," Tengo said aloud. "Not bad. Compact and simple."

"Thank you," Kumi Adachi said. "But putting it like that makes me feel like a Honda Civic or something."

"I meant it as a compliment."

"I know. I get good mileage, too," she said, and took Tengo's hand. "Do you mind if I hold your hand? It makes it more fun to walk together, and more relaxed."

"I don't mind," Tengo replied. Holding hands like this with Kumi Adachi, he remembered Aomame and the classroom in elementary school. It felt different now, but there was something in common.

"I must be a little drunk," Kumi said.

"You think so?"

"Yup."

Tengo looked at the young nurse's face again. "You don't look drunk."

"I don't show it on the outside. That's just the way I am. But I'm wasted."

"Well, you were knocking them back pretty steadily."

"I know. I haven't drunk this much in a long time."

"You just have to get out like this sometimes," Tengo said, quoting Mrs. Tamura.

"Of course," Kumi said, nodding vigorously. "People have to get out sometimes – have something good to eat, have some drinks, belt out some songs, talk about nothing in particular. But I wonder if you ever have times like that. Where you just get it out of your system, to clear your head? You always seem so cool and composed, Tengo."

Tengo thought about it. Had he done anything lately to unwind? He couldn't recall. If he couldn't recall, that probably meant he hadn't. The whole concept of *getting something out of his system* was something he might be lacking.

"Not so much, I guess," Tengo admitted.

"Everybody's different."

"There are all sorts of ways of thinking and feeling."

"Just like there are lots of ways of being drunk," the nurse said, and giggled. "But it's important, Tengo."

"You may be right," he said.

They walked on in silence for a while, hand in hand. Tengo felt uneasy about the change in the way she spoke. When she had on her nurse's uniform, Kumi was invariably polite. But now in civilian clothes, she was more outspoken, probably partly due to the alcohol. That informal way of talking reminded him of someone. Somebody had spoken the same way. Someone he had met fairly recently.

"Tengo, have you ever tried hashish?"

"Hashish?"

"Cannabis resin."

Tengo breathed in the night air and exhaled. "No, I never have."

"How about trying some?" Kumi Adachi asked. "Let's try it together. I have some at home."

"You have hashish?"

"Looks can be deceiving."

"They certainly can," Tengo said vaguely. So a healthy young nurse living in a little seaside town on the Boso Peninsula had hashish in her apartment. And she was inviting him to smoke some.

"How did you get ahold of it?" Tengo asked.

"A girlfriend from high school gave it to me for a birthday present last month. She had gone to India and brought it back." Kumi began swinging Tengo's hand with her own in a wide arc.

"But there's a stiff penalty if you're caught smuggling pot into the country. The Japanese police are really strict about it. They have pot-sniffing dogs at the airports."

"She's not the type to worry about little details," Kumi said. "Anyhow, she got through customs okay. Would you like to try it? It's high-quality stuff, very potent. I checked into it, and medically speaking there's nothing dangerous about it. I'm not saying it isn't habit forming, but it's much milder than tobacco, alcohol, or cocaine. Law enforcement says it's addictive, but that's ridiculous. If you believe that, then pachinko is far more dangerous. You don't get a hangover, so I think it would be good for you to try it to blow off some steam."

"Have you tried it yourself?"

"Of course. It was fun."

"Fun," Tengo repeated.

"You'll understand if you try it," Kumi said, and giggled. "Say, did you know? When Queen Victoria had menstrual cramps she used to smoke marijuana to lessen the pain. Her court doctor actually prescribed it to her."

"You're kidding."

"It's true. I read it in a book."

Which book? Tengo was about to ask, but decided it was too much trouble. That was as far as he wanted to go picturing Queen Victoria having menstrual cramps.

"So how old were you on your birthday last month?" Tengo asked, changing subjects.

"Twenty-three. A full-fledged adult."

"Of course," Tengo said. He was already thirty, but yet to have a sense of himself as an adult. It just felt to him like he had spent thirty years in the world.

"My older sister is staying over tonight at her boyfriend's, so I'm by myself. So come on over. Don't be shy. I'm off duty tomorrow so I can take it easy."

Tengo searched for a reply. He liked this young nurse. And she seemed to like him, too. But she was inviting him to her place. He looked up at the sky, but it was covered with thick gray clouds and he couldn't see the moons.

"The other day when my girlfriend and I smoked hashish," Kumi began, "that was my first time, but it felt like my body was floating in the air. Not very high, just a couple of inches. You know, floating at that height felt really good. Like it was just right."

"Plus you won't hurt yourself if you fall."

"Yeah, it's just the right height, so you can feel safe. Like you're being protected. Like you're wrapped in an air chrysalis. I'm the *dohta*, completely enveloped in the air chrysalis, and outside I can just make out *maza*."

"*Dohta?*" Tengo asked. His voice was surprisingly hard. "*Maza?*"

The young nurse was humming a tune, swinging their clasped hands as they walked down the deserted streets. She was much shorter than Tengo, but it didn't seem to bother her at all. An occasional car passed by.

"*Maza* and *dohta*. It's from the book *Air Chrysalis*. Do you know it?" she asked.

"I do."

"Have you read it?"

Tengo silently nodded.

"Great. That makes things easier. I *love* that book. I bought it in the summer and read it three times. I hardly ever read a book three times. And as I was smoking hashish for the first time in my life I thought it felt like I was inside an air chrysalis myself. Like I was enveloped in something and waiting to be born. With my *maza* watching over me."

"You saw your *maza*?" Tengo asked.

"Yes, I did. From inside the air chrysalis you can see outside, to a certain extent. Though you can't see in from outside. That's how it's structured. But I couldn't make out her expression. She was a vague outline. But I knew it was my *maza*. I could feel it very clearly. That this person was my *maza*."

"So an air chrysalis is actually a kind of womb."

"I guess you could say that. I don't remember anything from when I was in the womb, so I can't make an exact comparison," Kumi Adachi said, and giggled again.

* * *

It was the kind of cheaply made two-story apartment building you often find in the suburbs of provincial cities. It looked fairly new, yet it was already starting to fall apart. The outside stairway creaked, and the doors didn't quite hang right. Whenever a large truck rolled by outside, the windows rattled. The walls were thin, and if anyone were to practice a bass guitar in one of the apartments, the whole building would end up being one large sound box.

Tengo wasn't all that drawn to the idea of smoking hashish. He had a sane mind, yet he lived in a world with two moons. There was no need to distort the world any more than that. He also didn't have any sexual desire for Kumi Adachi. Certainly he did feel friendly toward this young twenty-three-year-old nurse. But friendliness and sexual desire were two different things, at least for Tengo. So if she hadn't mentioned *maza* and *dohta*, most likely he would have made up an excuse and not gone inside. He would have taken a bus back, or, if there weren't any buses, he would have had her call a cab, and then returned to the inn. This was, after all, the cat town. It was best to avoid any dangerous spots. But once Kumi mentioned the words *maza* and *dohta*, Tengo couldn't turn down her invitation. Maybe she could give him a hint as to why the young Aomame had appeared in the air chrysalis in the hospital room.

The apartment was a typical place for two sisters in their twenties living together. There were two small bedrooms, plus a combined kitchen and dining room that connected to a tiny living room. The furniture looked thrown together from all over, with no unifying style. Above the laminated dining table there hung a tacky imitation Tiffany lamp, quite out of place. If you were to open the curtain, with its tiny floral pattern, outside there was a cultivated field, and beyond that, a thick, dark grove of various trees. The view was nice, with nothing to obstruct it, but far from heartwarming.

Kumi sat Tengo down on the love seat in the living room – a gaudy, red love seat – facing the TV. She took out a can of Sapporo beer from the fridge and set it down, with a glass, in front of him.

"I'm going to change into something more comfortable, so wait here. I'll be right back."

But she didn't come back for a long time. He could hear the occasional sound from behind the door across the narrow corridor – the sound of drawers that didn't slide well, opening and closing, the thud of things clunking to the ground. With each thud, Tengo couldn't help but look in that direction. Maybe she really was drunker than she looked. He could hear a TV through the thin walls of the apartment. He couldn't make out what the people were saying, but it appeared to be a comedy show, and every ten or fifteen seconds there was a burst of laughter from the audience. Tengo regretted not having turned down her invitation. At the same time, though, in a corner of his mind he felt it was inevitable that he had come here.

The love seat was cheap, and the fabric itched whenever his skin touched it. Something bothered him, too, about the shape of it, and he couldn't get comfortable no matter how he shifted around. This only amplified his sense of unease. Tengo took a sip of beer and picked up the TV remote from the table. He stared at it for a time, as if it were some odd object, and then hit the on button. He surfed through a few channels, finally settling on an NHK documentary about railroads in Australia. He chose this program simply because it was quieter than the others. While an oboe piece played in the background, a woman announcer was calmly introducing the elegant sleeper cars in the line that ran across the whole of Australia.

Tengo sat there in the uncomfortable love seat, unenthusiastically following the images on the screen, but his mind was on *Air Chrysalis*. Kumi Adachi had no idea that he was the one who had really written the book. Not that it mattered – what did matter was that while he had written such a detailed description of the air chrysalis, Tengo knew next to nothing about it. What *was* an air chrysalis? And what did *maza* and *dohta* signify? He had no idea what they meant when he wrote *Air Chrysalis*, and he still didn't. Still, Kumi liked the book and had read it three times. How could such a thing be possible?

Kumi came back out as the show was discussing the dining-car menu. She plunked down on the love seat next to Tengo. It was so narrow their shoulders touched. She had changed into an oversized long-sleeved shirt and faded cotton pants. The shirt had a large smiley face on it. The last time Tengo had seen a smiley face was the beginning of the 1970s, back when Grand Funk Railroad rattled the jukeboxes with their crazy loud songs. But the shirt didn't look that old. Somewhere, were people still manufacturing smiley-face shirts?

Kumi took a fresh beer from the fridge, loudly popped it open, poured it in her glass, and chugged down a third of it. She narrowed her eyes like a satisfied cat and pointed at the TV screen. In between red cliffs the train was traveling down an endlessly straight line.

"Where is this?"

"Australia," Tengo said.

"Australia," Kumi Adachi said, as if searching the recesses of memory. "The Australia in the Southern Hemisphere?"

"Right. The Australia with the kangaroos."

"I have a friend who went to Australia," Kumi said, scratching next to her eye. "It was right during the kangaroo mating season. He went to one town and the kangaroos were doing it all over the place. In the parks, in the streets. Everywhere."

Tengo thought he should make a comment, but he couldn't think of anything. Instead he took the remote and turned off the TV. With the TV off, the room suddenly grew still. The sound of the TV next door, too, was gone. The occasional car would pass by on the road outside, but other than that it was a quiet night. If you listened carefully, though, there was a muffled, far-off sound. It was steady and rhythmic, but Tengo had no idea what it was. It would stop for a time, then start up again.

"It's an owl," the nurse explained. "He lives in the woods nearby. He hoots at night."

"An owl," Tengo repeated vaguely.

Kumi rested her head on his shoulder and held his hand. Her hair tickled his neck. The love seat was still uncomfortable. The owl continued hooting knowingly off in the woods. That voice sounded encouraging to Tengo, but at the same time like a warning. Or maybe a warning that contained a note of encouragement. It was a very ambiguous sound.

"Tell me, do you think I'm too forward?" Kumi Adachi asked.

Tengo didn't reply. "Don't you have a boyfriend?"

"That's a perplexing question," she said, indeed looking a bit perplexed. "Most of the smart young men head off to Tokyo as soon as they graduate from high school. There are no good colleges here, and not enough decent jobs, either. They have no other choice."

"But you're here."

"Yes. Considering the lousy pay they give us, the work is pretty hard. But I kind of like living here. The problem is finding a boyfriend. I'm open to it if I find someone, but there aren't so many chances."

The hands of the clock on the wall pointed to just before eleven. If he didn't go back to the inn by the eleven o'clock curfew, he wouldn't be able to get in. But Tengo couldn't rouse himself from the cramped love seat. His body just wouldn't listen. Maybe it was the shape of the chair, or maybe he was drunker than he thought. He listened vaguely to the owl's hooting, felt Kumi's hair tickle his neck, and gazed at the faux Tiffany lamp.

Kumi Adachi whistled cheerfully as she prepared the hashish. She used a safety razor to slice thin slices off a black ball of hash, stuffed the shavings into a small, flat pipe, and then, with a serious look on her face, lit a match. A unique, sweetly smoky smell soon filled the room. Kumi took the first hit. She inhaled deeply, held it in her lungs for a long time, then slowly exhaled. She motioned to Tengo to do the same. Tengo took the pipe and followed her example. He tried to hold the smoke in his lungs as long as possible, and then let it out ever so slowly.

They leisurely passed the pipe back and forth, never exchanging a word. The neighbor next door switched on his TV and they could hear the comedy show again. The volume was a bit louder than before. The happy laughter of the studio audience swelled up, the laughter only stopping during the commercials.

They took turns smoking for about five minutes, but nothing happened. The world around Tengo was unchanged – colors, shapes, and smells were the same as before. The owl kept on hooting in the woods, Kumi Adachi's hair on his neck still itched. The two-person love seat remained uncomfortable. The second hand on the clock ticked away at the same speed and the people on TV kept on laughing out loud when someone said something funny, the kind of laugh that you could laugh forever but never end up happy.

"Nothing's happening," Tengo said. "Maybe it doesn't work on me."

Kumi lightly tapped his knee twice. "Don't worry. It takes time."

And she was right. Finally it hit him. He heard a click, like a secret switch being turned on, and then something inside his head sloshed thickly. It felt like tipping a bowl of rice porridge sideways. *My brain is vibrating,* Tengo thought. This was a new experience for him – considering his brain as an object apart from the rest of him, physically experiencing the viscosity of it. The deep hoot of the owl came in through his ears, mixed with the porridge inside, and melted into it.

"The owl is inside me," Tengo commented. The owl had become a part of his consciousness, a vital part that couldn't be separated out.

"The owl is the guardian deity of the woods. He knows all and gives us the wisdom of the night," Kumi said.

But where and how should he seek this wisdom? The owl was everywhere, and nowhere. "I can't think of a question to ask him," Tengo said.

Kumi Adachi held his hand. "There's no need for questions. All you need to do is go into the woods yourself. That way is much simpler."

He could hear laughter again from the comedy next door. Applause as well. The show's assistant, off camera, was probably holding up cue cards to the audience that said *Laugh* and *Applaud*. Tengo closed his eyes and thought of the woods, of himself going into the woods. Deep in the dark forest was the realm of the Little People. But the owl was still there too. The owl knows all and gives us the wisdom of the night.

Suddenly all sound vanished, as if someone had come up behind him stealthily and stuck corks in his ears. Someone had closed one lid, while someone else, somewhere, had opened another lid. Entrance and exit had switched.

Tengo found himself in an elementary school classroom.

The window was wide open and children's voices filtered in from the schoolyard. The wind blew, almost as an afterthought, and the white curtains waved in the breeze. Aomame was beside him, holding his hand tightly. It was the same scene as always – but something was different. Everything he could see was crystal clear, almost painfully clear, fresh and focused down to the texture. He could make out each and every detail of the forms and shapes of things around him. If he reached out his hand, he could actually touch them. The smell of the early-winter afternoon hit him strongly, as if what had been covering up those smells until then had been yanked away. Real smells. The set smells of the season: of the blackboard erasers, the floor cleaner, the fallen leaves burning in the incinerator in a corner of the schoolyard – all these were mixed inseparably together. When he breathed in these scents, he felt them spread out deep and wide within his mind. The structure of his body was being reassembled. His heartbeat was no longer just a heartbeat.

For an instant, he could push the door of time inward. Old light mixed with the new light, the two becoming one. The old air mixed in with the new to become one. *It is this light, and this air,* Tengo thought. He understood everything now. Almost everything. *Why couldn't I remember this smell until now? It's so simple. It's such a straightforward world, yet I didn't get it.*

"I wanted to see you," Tengo said to Aomame. His voice was far away and faltering, but it was definitely his voice.

"I wanted to see you, too," the girl said. The voice sounded like Kumi Adachi's. He couldn't make out the boundary between reality and imagination. If he tried to pin it down, the bowl slipped sideways and his brains sloshed around.

Tengo spoke. "I should have started searching for you long ago. But I couldn't."

"It's not too late. You can still find me," the girl said.

"But how can I find you?"

No response. The answer was not put into words.

"But I know I can find you," Tengo said.

The girl spoke. "Because I could find *you*."

"You found me?"

"Find me," the girl said. "While there's still time."

Like a departed soul that had failed to leave in time, the white curtain soundlessly and gently wavered. That was the last thing Tengo saw.

When he came to, he was lying in a narrow bed. The lights were out, the room faintly lit by the streetlights filtering in through a gap in the curtains. He was wearing a T-shirt and boxers. Kumi wore only her smiley-face shirt. Underneath the long shirt, she was nude. Her soft breasts lay against his arm. The owl was still hooting in Tengo's head. The woods lingered inside him – he was still clinging to the nighttime woods.

Even in bed like this with the young nurse, he felt no desire. Kumi seemed to feel the same way. She wrapped her arms around his body and giggled. What was so funny? Tengo had no idea. Maybe somebody, somewhere, was holding out a sign that said *Laugh*.

What time could it be? He lifted his head to look for a clock but couldn't see any. Kumi suddenly stopped laughing and wrapped her arms around his neck.

"I was reborn," she said, her hot breath brushing his ear.

"You were reborn," Tengo said.

"Because I died once."

"You died once," Tengo repeated.

"On a night when there was a cold rain falling," she said.

"Why did you die?"

"So I would be reborn like this."

"You would be reborn," Tengo said.

"More or less," she whispered very quietly. "In all sorts of forms."

Tengo pondered this statement. What did it mean to *be reborn more or less, in all sorts of forms*? His brain was heavy, and was brimming with the germs of life, like some primeval sea. Not that these led him anywhere.

"Where do air chrysalises come from, anyway?"

"That's the wrong question," Kumi said, and chuckled.

She twisted her body on top of his and Tengo could feel her pubic hair against his thighs. Thick, rich hair. It was like her pubic hair was a part of her thinking process.

"What is necessary in order to be reborn?" Tengo asked.

"The biggest problem when it comes to being reborn," the small nurse said, as if revealing a secret, "is that people aren't reborn for their own sakes. They can only do it for someone else."

"Which is what you mean by *more or less, in all sorts of forms.*"

"When morning comes you will be leaving here, Tengo. Before the exit is blocked."

"When morning comes I'll be leaving here," Tengo repeated the nurse's words.

Once more she rubbed her rich pubic hair against his thigh, as if to leave behind some sort of *sign.* "Air chrysalises don't come from somewhere. They won't come no matter how long you wait."

"You know that."

"Because I died once," she said. "It's painful to die. Much more painful than you imagine, Tengo. You are utterly lonely. It's amazing how completely lonely a person can be. You had better remember that. But you know, unless you die once, you won't be reborn."

"Unless you die once, you won't be reborn," Tengo confirmed.

"But people face death while they're still alive."

"People face death while they're still alive," Tengo repeated, unsure of what it meant.

The white curtain continued to flutter in the breeze. The air in the classroom smelled of a mixture of blackboard erasers and cleaner. There was the scent of burning leaves. Someone was practicing the recorder. The girl was squeezing his hand tightly. In his lower half he felt a sweet ache, but he didn't have an erection. That would come later on. The words *later on* promised him eternity. Eternity was a single long pole that stretched out without end. The bowl tipped a bit again, and again his brains sloshed to one side.

When he woke up, it took Tengo a while to figure out where he was, and to piece together the events of the previous night. Bright sunlight shone in through the gap between the flowery curtains, while birds whistled away noisily outside. He had been sleeping in an uncomfortable, cramped position in the narrow bed. He found it hard to believe he could have slept the whole night in such a position. Kumi was lying beside him, her face pressed into the pillow, sound asleep. Her hair was plastered against her cheeks, like lush summer grass wet with dew. *Kumi Adachi,* Tengo thought. A young nurse who just turned twenty-three. His wristwatch had fallen to the floor. The hands showed 7:20 – 7:20 in the morning.

Tengo slipped quietly out of bed, careful not to wake Kumi, and looked out the window through a crack in the curtains. There was a cabbage field. Rows of cabbages crouched stolidly on the dark soil. Beyond the field was the woods. Tengo remembered the hoot of the owl. Last night it had definitely been hooting. The wisdom of the night. Tengo and the nurse had listened to it as they smoked hashish. He could still feel her stiff pubic hair on his thigh.

Tengo went to the kitchen, scooped up water from the faucet with his hands, and drank. He was so thirsty he drank and drank, and still wanted more. Other than that, nothing else had changed. His head didn't hurt, and his body wasn't listless. His mind was clear. But somehow, inside him, things seemed to flow a bit too well – as if pipes had been carefully, and professionally, cleaned. In his T-shirt and boxers he padded over to the toilet and took a good long pee. In the unfamiliar mirror, his face didn't look like his own. Tufts of hair stood up here and there on his head, and he needed a shave.

He went back to the bedroom and gathered up his clothes. His discarded clothes lay mixed in with Kumi's, scattered on the floor. He had no memory of when, or how, he had undressed. He located both socks, tugged on his jeans, buttoned up his shirt. As he did, he stepped on a large, cheap ring. He picked it up and put it on the nightstand next to the bed. He tugged on his crew-neck sweater and picked up his windbreaker. He checked that his wallet and keys were in his pocket. The young nurse was sleeping soundly, the blanket pulled up to just below her ears. Her breathing was quiet. Should he wake her up? Even though they hadn't – he was pretty sure – *done* anything, they had spent the night in bed together. It seemed rude to leave without saying good-bye. But she was sleeping so soundly, and she had said this was her day off. Even if he did wake her, what were they supposed to do then?

He found a memo pad and ballpoint pen next to the telephone. *Thanks for last night,* he wrote. *I had a good time. I'm going back to my inn. Tengo.* He wrote down the time. He placed the memo on the nightstand, and put the ring he had picked up on top, as a paperweight. He then slipped on his worn-out sneakers and left.

He walked down the road for a while, until he came across a bus stop. He waited there for five minutes and soon a bus heading for the station arrived. The bus was full of noisy high school boys and girls, and he rode with them to the end of the line. The people at the inn took his unshaven eight a.m. arrival in stride. It didn't seem to be that out of the ordinary for them. Without a word, they briskly prepared his breakfast.

As he ate his hot breakfast and drank tea, Tengo went over the events of the previous night. The three nurses had invited him out and they went to have *yakiniku*. Then on to a bar, where they sang karaoke. Then he went to Kumi Adachi's apartment, where they smoked Indian hashish, while an owl hooted outside. Then his brain felt like it had changed into hot, thick porridge. And suddenly he was in his elementary school classroom in winter, he could smell the air, and he was talking with Aomame. Then Kumi, in bed, was talking about death and resurrection. There were wrong questions, ambiguous answers. The owl in the woods went on hooting, people on a TV show went on laughing.

His memory was patchy and there were definitely several *gaps*. But the parts he did recall were amazingly vivid and clear. He could retrace each and every word they spoke. Tengo recalled the last thing Kumi said. It was both advice and a warning.

When morning comes you will be leaving here, Tengo. Before the exit is blocked.

Maybe this was the right time to leave. He had taken off from his job and come to this town hoping to see ten-year-old Aomame inside the air chrysalis once more. And he had spent nearly two weeks going every day to the sanatorium, reading aloud to his father. But the air chrysalis had never appeared. Instead, when he was about to give up, Kumi Adachi had prepared a different kind of vision just for him. And in it he was able once more to see Aomame as a girl, and speak with her. *Find me*, Aomame had said. *While there's still time.* Actually, it may have been Kumi who said that. Tengo couldn't tell. Not that it mattered. Kumi had died once, and been reborn. Not for herself, but for someone else. For the time being, Tengo decided to believe what he had heard from her. It was important to do so. At least, he was pretty sure it was.

This was the cat town. There was something specific that could only be found here. That's why he had taken the train all the way to this far-off place. But everything he found here held an inherent risk.

137

If he believed Kumi's hints, these risks could be fatal. *By the pricking of my thumbs, something wicked this way comes.*

It was time to go back to Tokyo – before the exit was blocked, while the train still stopped at this station. But before that he needed to go to the sanatorium again, and say good-bye to his father. There were things he still needed to clarify.

10

USHIKAWA

Gathering Solid Leads

USHIKAWA TRAVELED TO ICHIKAWA. IT FELT like quite a long excursion, but actually Ichikawa was just over the river in Chiba Prefecture, not far from downtown Tokyo. At the station he boarded a cab and gave the driver the name of the elementary school. It was after one p.m. when he arrived at the school. Lunch break was over and classes had just begun for the afternoon. He heard a chorus singing in the music room and a gym class was playing soccer outside. Children were yelling as they chased after the ball.

Ushikawa didn't have good memories of his own days in elementary school. He wasn't good at sports, particularly any kind that involved a ball. He was short, a slow runner, had astigmatism, and was unco-ordinated. Gym class was a nightmare. His grades in other classes were excellent, though. He was pretty bright and applied himself to his schoolwork (which led to passing the difficult bar exam when he was only twenty-five). But nobody liked him, or respected him. Not being good at sports may have been one reason. And then there was his face.

Since he was a child, he had had this big, ugly face, with a misshapen head. His thick lips sagged at the corners and looked as if they were about to drool at any moment, though they never actually did. His hair was frizzy and unruly. These were not the sort of looks to attract others.

In elementary school he hardly ever spoke. He knew he could be eloquent if necessary, but he didn't have any close friends and never had the opportunity to show others how well spoken he could be. So he always kept his mouth shut. He kept his ears open and listened closely to whatever anyone else had to say, aiming to learn something from everything he heard. This habit eventually became a useful tool. Through this, he discovered a number of important realities, including this one: most people in the world don't really use their brains to think. And people who don't think are the ones who don't listen to others.

At any rate, his elementary school days were not a page of his life that Ushikawa enjoyed reminiscing over. Just thinking that he was about to visit an elementary school depressed him. Despite any differences between Saitama and Chiba prefectures, elementary schools were pretty much alike anywhere you went in Japan. They looked the same and operated on the same principles. Still, Ushikawa insisted on going all the way to visit this school in Ichikawa himself. This was important, something he couldn't leave up to anyone else. He had called the school's front office and already had an appointment for one thirty.

The vice principal was a petite woman in her mid-forties, slim, attractive, and nicely dressed. *Vice principal?* Ushikawa was puzzled. He had never heard that term before. But it was ages ago when he graduated from elementary school. Lots of things must have changed since then. The woman must have dealt with many people over the years, for she didn't blink an eye when faced with Ushikawa's extraordinary features. Or perhaps she was just a very well-mannered person. She showed Ushikawa to a tidy reception room and invited him to take a seat. She sat down in the chair across from him and smiled broadly, as if wondering what sort of enjoyable conversation they were about to have.

She reminded Ushikawa of a girl who had been in his class in school. The girl had been pretty, got good grades, was kind and responsible. She was well brought up and good at piano. She was one of the teacher's favorites. During class Ushikawa spent a lot of time gazing at her, mainly at her back. But he never once talked with her.

"I understand that you're looking into one of the graduates of our school?" the vice principal asked.

"I'm sorry, I should have given you this before," Ushikawa said, and passed her his business card. It was the same card he had given Tengo, the one with his title on it: Full-time Director, New Japan Foundation for the Advancement of Scholarship and the Arts. What he told the woman was the same fabricated story he had told Tengo. Tengo Kawana, who had graduated from this school, had become a writer and was on a short list to receive a grant from the foundation. Ushikawa was just running an ordinary background check on him.

"That's wonderful news," the vice principal said, beaming. "It's a great honor for our school, and we will do everything we can to help you."

"I was hoping to meet and speak directly with the teacher who taught Mr. Kawana," Ushikawa said.

"I'll check into that. It's more than twenty years ago, so she may be retired already."

"I appreciate that," Ushikawa said. "If it's all right, there's one other thing I would like you to look into, if you would."

"And what would that be?"

"There was a girl in the same year, I believe, as Mr. Kawana, a Miss Masami Aomame. Would you be able to check into whether she was in the same class as Mr. Kawana?"

The vice principal looked a bit dubious. "Is this Miss Aomame in some way connected with the question of funding for Mr. Kawana?"

"No, it's not that. In one of the works by Mr. Kawana, there is a character who seems to be modeled on someone like Miss Aomame, and I have a few questions of my own on this topic that I need to clear up. It's nothing very involved. Basically a formality."

"I see," the vice principal said, the corners of her lips rising ever so slightly. "I am sure you understand, however, that in some cases we may not be able to give you information that might touch on a person's privacy. Grades, for instance, or reports on a pupil's home environment."

"Of course, I'm fully aware of that. All we are after is information on whether or not she was actually in the same class as Mr. Kawana. And if she was, I would appreciate it very much if you could give me the name and contact information for the teacher in charge of their class at the time."

"I understand. That shouldn't be a problem. Miss Aomame, was it?"

"Correct. It's written with the characters for green and peas. An uncommon name."

Ushikawa wrote the name "Masami Aomame" in pen on a page on his pocket notebook and passed the page to the vice principal. She looked at it for a few seconds, then placed it in the pocket of a folder on her desk.

"Could you please wait here for a few minutes? I'll go check our staff records. I'll have the person in charge photocopy whatever can be made public."

"I'm sorry to bother you with this when you are obviously so busy," Ushikawa said.

The vice principal's flared skirt swished prettily as she exited the room. She had beautiful posture, and she moved elegantly. Her hairstyle was attractive too. She was clearly aging gracefully. Ushikawa shifted in his seat and killed time by reading a paperback book he had brought along.

* * *

The vice principal came back fifteen minutes later, a brown business envelope clutched to her breast.

"It turns out that Mr. Kawana was quite the student. He was always at the top of his class as well as a very successful athlete. He was especially good at arithmetic and mathematics, and even in elementary school he was able to solve high-school-level problems. He won a math contest and was written up in the newspaper as a child prodigy."

"That's amazing," Ushikawa said.

"It's odd that while he was touted as a math prodigy, today he has distinguished himself in literature."

"Abundant talent is like a rich vein of water underground that finds all sorts of places to gush forth. Presently he is teaching math while writing novels."

"I see," the vice principal said, raising her eyebrows at a lovely angle. "Unlike Tengo, there wasn't much on Masami Aomame. She transferred to another school in fifth grade. She was taken in by relatives in Adachi Ward in Tokyo and transferred to a school there. She and Tengo Kawana were classmates in third and fourth grades."

Just as I suspected, Ushikawa thought. *There* was *some connection between the two of them.*

"A Miss Ota was in charge of their class then. Toshie Ota. Now she's teaching at a municipal elementary school in Narashino."

"If I contact that school, perhaps I will be able to get in touch with her?"

"We have already made the call," the vice principal said, smiling faintly. "When we explained the situation, she said she would be very pleased to meet with you."

"I really appreciate that," Ushikawa said. *She wasn't just a pretty face,* he thought, *but an efficient administrator, too.*

On the back of her business card, the vice principal wrote down the teacher's name and the phone number of the school, the Tsudanuma elementary school, and handed it to Ushikawa. Ushikawa carefully stashed the card in his billfold.

"I heard that Miss Aomame was raised with some sort of religious background," Ushikawa said. "We are a bit concerned about this."

The vice principal frowned, tiny lines forming at the corners of her eyes. The kind of subtle, charming, intelligent lines acquired only by middle-aged women who have taken great care to train themselves.

"I'm sorry, but that is not a subject we can discuss here," she said.

"It touches on areas of personal privacy, doesn't it," Ushikawa asked.

"That's correct. Especially issues dealing with religion."

"But if I meet with this Miss Ota, I might be able to ask her about this."

The vice principal inclined her slender jaw slightly to the left and smiled meaningfully. "If Miss Ota wishes to speak as a private individual, that is no concern of ours."

Ushikawa stood up and politely thanked her. She handed him the brown business envelope. "The materials we could copy are inside. Documents pertaining to Mr. Kawana. There's a little bit, too, concerning Miss Aomame. I hope it's helpful to you."

"I'm sure it will be. Thank you very much for all you have done. You've been very kind."

"When the results of that grant are decided, you'll be sure to let us know, won't you? This will be a great honor for our school."

"I'm positive there will be a good outcome," Ushikawa said. "I have met him a number of times and he is a talented young man with a promising future."

Ushikawa stopped at a diner in front of Ichikawa Station, ate a simple lunch, and looked through the material in the envelope. There was a basic record of attendance at the school for both Tengo and Aomame, as well as records of awards given to Tengo for his achievements in academics and sports. He did indeed seem to be an extraordinary student. He probably never once thought of school as a nightmare. There was also a copy of a newspaper article about the math contest he had won. It was an old article and the photo wasn't very clear, but it was obviously Tengo as a boy.

After lunch Ushikawa phoned the Tsudanuma elementary school. He spoke with Miss Ota, the teacher, and made an appointment to meet her at four at her school. *After four I'm free to talk,* she had said.

I know it's my job, Ushikawa sighed, *but two elementary schools in one day is a bit much.* Just thinking about it made him depressed. But so far it had been worth the effort. He now had proof that Tengo and Aomame were classmates for two years – a huge step forward.

Tengo had helped Eriko Fukada to revise *Air Chrysalis* into a decent novel, and make it a bestseller. Aomame had secretly murdered Eriko's father, Tamotsu Fukada, in a suite at the Hotel Okura. It would appear that they shared the goal of attacking, in their own ways, the religious organization Sakigake. Perhaps they were working together. That's what most people would conclude.

But it wouldn't do to tell that duo from Sakigake about this – not yet. Ushikawa didn't like to reveal information in fits and starts. He much preferred gathering as much information as he could, making absolutely sure of all the facts, and then, when he had solid proof, revealing the results with a flourish. It was a theatrical gesture he still retained from his days as a lawyer. He would act self-deprecating so that other people would let down their guard. Then, just when things were drawing to a conclusion, he would bring forth his irrefutable evidence and turn the tables.

As he rode the train to Tsudanuma, Ushikawa mentally assembled a number of hypotheses.

Tengo and Aomame might be lovers. They wouldn't have been lovers when they were ten, of course, but it was possible to see them, after they graduated from elementary school, running into each other and growing intimate. And for some reason – the reason was still unclear – they decided to work together to destroy Sakigake. This was one hypothesis.

As far as Ushikawa could tell, however, there was no evidence of Tengo and Aomame having a relationship. Tengo had maintained an ongoing affair with a married woman ten years older than himself. If Tengo had been deeply involved with Aomame, he would not then regularly cheat on her with another woman – he wasn't adroit enough to pull that off. Ushikawa had previously investigated Tengo's habits over a two-week period. He taught math at a cram school three days a week, and on the other days he was mostly alone in his apartment. Writing novels, most likely. Other than occasionally shopping or going for a walk, he seldom left his place. It was a very monotonous, simple lifestyle, easy to fathom. There was nothing mysterious about it. Somehow Ushikawa just couldn't picture him involved in a plot that involved murdering someone.

Personally, Ushikawa liked Tengo. Tengo was an unaffected, straight-forward young man, independent and self-reliant. As is often the case with physically large people, he tended to be a bit slow on the uptake at times, but he wasn't sly or cunning in the least. He was the kind of guy who, once he decided on a course of action, never deviated from it. The kind who would never make it as a lawyer or a stockbroker. Rather, he was more likely to get tripped up and stumble at the most critical juncture. He would make a good math teacher and novelist, though. He wasn't particularly sociable or eloquent, but he did appeal to a certain type of woman. In a nutshell, he was the polar opposite of Ushikawa.

In contrast to what he knew about Tengo, Ushikawa knew next to nothing about Aomame – other than her background with the Witnesses and that she had later been a star softball player. When it came to her personality – her way of thinking, her strong points and weaknesses, what sort of private life she led – he was clueless. The facts that he had assembled were nothing more than what you would find on a résumé.

But while comparing the backgrounds of Tengo and Aomame, some similarities came to light. First of all, both of them must have had unhappy childhoods. Aomame was dragged all over town by her mother to proselytize, slogging from house to house, ringing doorbells. All the Witness children were made to do that. In Tengo's case, his father was an NHK fee collector. This was another job that involved making the rounds from one house to the next. Had Tengo been dragged along with him? Maybe he had. If Ushikawa had been Tengo's father, he probably would have taken Tengo with him on his rounds. Having a child with you helped you collect more fees, and you saved on babysitting money – two birds with one stone. For Tengo this couldn't have been much fun. Perhaps these two children even passed each other on the streets of Ichikawa.

Second, as they grew older, Tengo and Aomame worked hard to win athletic scholarships so they could get far away from home as quickly as possible. And both of them turned out to be superb athletes. They both must have been pretty talented to begin with. But there was also a reason they *had to be superb*. Being an athlete was a way to be recognized by others, and having outstanding records in sports was just about the only way they could win their independence. This was the valuable ticket they needed to survive. They thought differently from average teenagers. They confronted the world differently.

When he thought about it, Ushikawa realized his own situation somewhat resembled theirs.

I'm from an affluent family and had no need to get a scholarship. I always had plenty of spending money. But in order to get into a top university, and pass the bar exam, I had to study like mad, just like Tengo and Aomame. I had no time to have fun like my classmates. I had to abstain from all worldly pleasures – not that I had much chance of obtaining them to begin with – and focus solely on my studies. I was always stuck between feelings of inferiority and superiority. I often used to think I was like Raskolnikov, except I never met Sonia.

Enough about me. Thinking about that won't change anything. I have to get back to Tengo and Aomame.

Say Tengo and Aomame did happen to run across each other

sometime in their twenties and started talking. They would have been so amazed at all the things they had in common. And there would be so many things they had to talk about. Maybe they found themselves attracted to each other, as a man and a woman. Ushikawa had a vivid mental image of this scene – a fateful meeting, the ultimate romantic moment.

But had such a meeting actually taken place? Had a romance blossomed? Ushikawa didn't know. But it would make sense if they had actually met. That would explain how they joined forces to attack Sakigake, each of them from a different angle – Tengo with his pen, Aomame no doubt with some special skill she had. Somehow, though, Ushikawa couldn't warm to this hypothesis. On one level it all made sense, but he wasn't convinced.

If indeed Tengo and Aomame did have such a deep relationship, there would be evidence. This fateful meeting would have had fateful results, and this would not have passed unnoticed by Ushikawa's observant eyes. Aomame might have been able to hide it, but not Tengo.

In general, Ushikawa saw things logically. Without proof, he couldn't go forward. However, he also trusted his natural intuition. When it came to a scenario where Tengo and Aomame had conspired together, his intuition shook its head no. It was just a little shake, but insistent nonetheless. Maybe the two of them weren't even aware of each other's existence. Maybe it *just turned out* that they were both simultaneously involved with Sakigake.

Even if it was hard to picture such a coincidence, Ushikawa's intuition told him that this hypothesis felt more likely than the conspiracy theory. The two of them, driven by different motives, and approaching things from different angles, just happened to simultaneously shake Sakigake to the core. Two story lines at work, with different starting points but running parallel to each other.

The question was, would the Sakigake twosome accept such a convenient hypothesis? *No way,* Ushikawa concluded. Instead, they would jump at the conspiracy theory, for they loved anything that hinted of sinister plots. Before he handed over any raw information, he needed solid proof. Otherwise they would be misled and it might wind up hurting him.

As Ushikawa rode the train from Ichikawa to Tsudanuma, he pondered all this. Without realizing it, he must have been frowning, sighing, and glaring into space, because an elementary-school girl in the seat across from him was looking at him oddly. To cover his embarrassment, he relaxed his expression and rubbed his balding head. But this gesture only ended up making the little girl frightened, and just before Nishi-Funabashi Station, she leapt to her feet and rushed away.

He spoke with Toshie Ota in her classroom after school. She looked to be in her mid-fifties. Her appearance was the polar opposite of the refined vice principal back at the Ichikawa elementary school. Miss Ota was short and stocky and, from behind, had a weird sort of gait, like a crustacean. She wore tiny metal-framed glasses, but the space between her eyebrows was flat and broad and you could clearly see the downy hair growing there. She had on a wool suit of indeterminate age, though no doubt it was already out of fashion by the time it was manufactured, and it carried with it a faint odor of mothballs. The suit was pink, but an odd sort of pink, like some other color had been accidentally mixed in. They had probably been aiming for a classy, subdued sort of hue, but because they didn't get it right, the pink of her suit sank deeply back into diffidence, concealment, and resignation. Thanks to this, the brand-new white blouse peeking out of the collar looked like some indiscreet person who had wandered into a wake. Her dry hair, with some white strands mixed in, was pinned back with a plastic clip, probably the nearest thing she had had on hand. Her limbs were on the beefy side, and she wore no rings on her stubby fingers. There were three thin wrinkles at her neckline, sharply etched, like notches on the road of life. Or maybe they were marks to commemorate when three wishes had come true – though Ushikawa had serious doubts that this had ever happened.

The woman had been Tengo Kawana's homeroom teacher from third grade until he graduated from elementary school. Teachers changed classes every two years, but in this case she had happened to be in charge of his class for all four. Aomame was in her class in only third and fourth grades.

"I remember Mr. Kawana very well," she said.

In contrast to her gentle-looking exterior, her voice was strikingly clear and youthful. It was the kind of voice that would pierce the farthest reaches of a noisy classroom. *Your profession really molds you,* Ushikawa thought, impressed, sure that she must be a most capable teacher.

"Mr. Kawana was an outstanding pupil in every area of school. I have taught countless students in a number of schools, for over twenty-five years, yet I have never run across a student as brilliant as he was. He outdid everyone in anything he tried. He was quite personable and had strong leadership qualities. I knew he could make it in any field he chose. In elementary school he particularly stood out in arithmetic and math, but I wasn't so surprised to hear that he has been a success in literature."

"I understand that his father was an NHK fee collector."

"Yes, that's right," the teacher said.

"Mr. Kawana told me that his father was quite strict," Ushikawa said. This was just a shot in the dark.

"Exactly so," she said, without hesitating. "His father did have a strict way about him. He was proud of his work – a wonderful thing – but this seemed to be a burden at times for Tengo."

Ushikawa had skillfully tied topics together and teased out the details from her. This was his forte – to let the other person do the talking, as much as possible. Tengo hated having to tag along with his father on his rounds on the weekend, she told him, and in fifth grade he ran away from home. "It was more like he was kicked out rather than ran away," she explained. So Tengo *had* been forced to go with his father to collect the fees, Ushikawa mused. And – just as he thought – this must have taken an emotional toll on the boy.

Miss Ota had taken the temporarily homeless Tengo into her home for the night. She prepared a bed for him, and made sure he ate breakfast the next morning. That evening she went to Tengo's house and convinced his father to take him back. From the way she talked about this event, you would have thought it was the highlight of her entire life. She told him too about how they happened to run into each other again at a concert when Tengo was in high school. Tengo had played the timpani, wonderfully, she added.

"It was Janáček's *Sinfonietta*. Not an easy piece, by any means. Tengo had first taken up the timpani only a few weeks before. But even with such little preparation he played his part beautifully. It was miraculous."

This lady has deep feelings for Tengo, Ushikawa thought admiringly. *Almost a kind of unconditional love. What would it feel like to be loved that deeply by someone else?*

"Do you remember Masami Aomame?" Ushikawa asked.

"I remember her very well," the teacher replied. But her voice wasn't as happy as when she had talked about Tengo. The tone of her voice had dropped two notches on the scale.

"Quite an unusual name, isn't it?" Ushikawa said.

"Yes, very unusual. But I don't remember her just because of her name."

A short silence followed.

"I heard her family were devout members of the Witnesses," Ushikawa said, sounding her out.

"Could you keep this between just the two of us?" the teacher asked.

"Of course. I won't repeat it to anyone."

The woman nodded. "There is a large branch office of the religion in Ichikawa, so I have had several children from the Witnesses in my class over the years. As a teacher this led to some delicate problems I had to address. But no one was as devout as Miss Aomame's parents."

"In other words, they were uncompromising."

As if recalling the time, the teacher bit her lip. "Exactly. When it came to their principles they were extremely firm, and I think they sought the same strict obedience from their children. This made Miss Aomame quite isolated in the class."

"So in a sense she was someone rather special."

"She was," the teacher admitted. "But you can't blame the child for this. Responsibility for it lies in the intolerance that can take over a person's mind."

The teacher explained more about Aomame. Generally the other children just ignored her. They tried to treat her as if she *wasn't there.* She was a foreign element, brandishing strange principles that bothered others. The class was all in agreement on this. Aomame reacted by keeping a low profile.

"I tried to do my best, but children's unity is stronger than you might think, and the way Miss Aomame reacted to this was to transform herself into something close to a ghost. Nowadays we would have referred her to counseling, but such a system wasn't in place back then. I was still young, and it took all I had to get everybody in the class on the same page. Though I'm sure that sounds like I'm trying to excuse myself."

Ushikawa could understand what she was getting at. Being an elementary school teacher was hard work. To a certain extent, you had to let the children figure out things on their own.

"There is always just a thin line separating deep faith from intolerance," Ushikawa said. "And it's very hard for people to do anything about it."

"Absolutely," the woman said. "But still, at a different level there should have been something I could do. I tried talking with Miss Aomame any number of times, but she would barely respond. She had a very strong will, and once she was set on something she wouldn't change her mind. She was quite bright, very quick-witted, with a strong desire to learn. But she tried hard to suppress any of that, to keep it from showing. Probably *not standing out* was her only way of protecting herself. I'm sure if she had been living in a normal environment she would have been an outstanding pupil. I feel really bad looking back on it now."

"Did you ever speak with her parents?"

The teacher nodded. "Many times. Her parents came to school to complain about religious persecution. When they did, I asked them to try to make more of an effort to help their daughter fit in to the class. I asked if they could bend their principles just a little. They refused point-blank. Their top priority was keeping true to the rules of their faith. To them the highest happiness lay in going to heaven, and life in this profane world was merely transient. But this was the logic of an adult worldview. Unfortunately, I could never get them to see how much pain it was causing their young daughter to be ignored in class, shunned by the other children – how this would lead to an emotional wound that might never heal."

Ushikawa told her how Aomame was a leading softball player on teams in college and in a company, and how she was working as a very capable fitness instructor in a high-class sports club. Or rather, *had been working* until recently, he should have said, but he didn't insist on making the distinction.

"I'm very glad to hear that," the woman said. She blushed slightly. "I'm so relieved to hear that she grew up all right, and is healthy and independent now."

"There was one thing, though, that I wasn't able to find out," Ushikawa said, a seemingly innocent smile rising to his lips. "Do you think it was possible that Tengo Kawana and Miss Aomame had a close personal relationship?"

The woman teacher linked her fingers together and thought about this. "That may have been possible. But I never saw it myself, or heard about it. I find it hard to picture any child in that class ever being really friendly with Miss Aomame. Perhaps Tengo did reach out to her. He was a very kind, responsible sort of boy. But even supposing it did happen, Miss Aomame wouldn't have opened up that easily. She was like an oyster stuck on a rock. It can't easily be pried open."

The teacher stopped for a moment, and then added, "It pains me to have to put it this way, but there was nothing I could do at the time. As I said before, I was inexperienced and not very effective."

"If Mr. Kawana and Miss Aomame did have a close relationship, that would have caused quite a sensation in class, and you would have heard of it. Am I right?"

The teacher nodded. "There was intolerance on both sides."

"It has been very helpful to be able to talk with you," Ushikawa said, thanking her.

"I hope what I've said about Miss Aomame won't become an obstacle in awarding the grant," the teacher said worriedly. "As the teacher in charge of the class I had ultimate responsibility for problems like that arising in the classroom. It wasn't the fault of either Tengo or Miss Aomame."

Ushikawa shook his head. "Please don't worry about that. I'm merely checking the background behind a work of fiction. Religious issues, as I'm sure you know, can be very complicated. Mr. Kawana is a major talent, and I know he will soon make a name for himself."

Hearing this, the teacher gave a satisfied smile. Something in her small eyes caught the sunlight and glistened, like a glacier on the faraway face of a mountain. She is remembering Tengo when he was a boy, Ushikawa surmised. It was twenty-some years ago, but for her it was like yesterday.

As he waited near the main gate of the school for the bus back to Tsudanuma Station, Ushikawa thought about his own teachers in elementary school. Did they still remember him? Even if they did, it wouldn't make their eyes sparkle with a friendly glimmer.

What he had verified was very close to his hypothesis. Tengo was the top student in his class, and he was popular. Aomame had no friends and was ignored by everyone. There was little possibility that the two of them would have gotten close. They were simply too unalike. Plus, when she was in fifth grade Aomame moved out of Ichikawa and went to another school. Any connection was severed then.

If he had to list one thing they had in common in elementary school, it would be this: they had both unwillingly had to obey their parents. Their parents' goals might have been different – proselytizing and fee collection – but both Tengo and Aomame were required to traipse all over town with their parents. In class they were in totally different positions, yet both of them must have been equally lonely, searching desperately for *something*. Something that would accept them unconditionally and hold them close. Ushikawa could imagine their feelings. In a sense, these were feelings that he shared.

Okay, Ushikawa said to himself. He was seated in an express train from Tsudanuma back to Tokyo, arms folded. *Okay, now what? I was able to find some connections between Tengo and Aomame. Very interesting connections. Unfortunately, however, this doesn't prove anything.*

There's a tall stone wall towering in front of me. It has three doors, and I have to choose one. Each door is labeled. One says Tengo, *one says* Aomame, *and the third says* the Dowager from Azabu. *Aomame vanished, as they say, like smoke. Without a trace. And the Azabu Willow House is locked up tight as a bank vault. Nothing I can do to get in. Which leaves only one door.*

It looks like I'll be sticking with Tengo for the time being, Ushikawa decided. *There's no other choice – a perfect example of the process of elimination. So perfect an example, it makes me want to print it up in a pamphlet and hand it out to people on the street. Hi, how are you? Check out the process of elimination.*

Tengo, always the nice young man. Mathematician and novelist. Judo champion and teacher's pet. Right now he's the only way to unravel this knotty tangle. The more I think about it, the less I seem to understand, like my brain is a tub of tofu past its expiration date.

So what about Tengo? Did he see the whole picture here? Probably not. As far as Ushikawa could make out, Tengo was doing things through trial and error, taking detours where he found the need. *He must be confused himself, trying out various hypotheses. Still, he was a born mathematician. A master at fitting together the pieces of a puzzle. And he probably has a lot more pieces of the puzzle than I do.*

For the time being I'll keep watch over Tengo Kawana. I'm sure he'll lead me somewhere – *if I get lucky, right to Aomame's hideout.* Ushikawa was a master at sticking to somebody, like a remora to a shark. Once he made up his mind to latch onto someone, there was no way they could shake free of him.

Once he had decided, Ushikawa closed his eyes and switched off his thinking process. *Time to get a little shut-eye,* he thought. It had been a rough day, given that he had had to visit two elementary schools out in crummy old Chiba Prefecture and listen to two female schoolteachers, a beautiful vice principal and a teacher who walked like a crab. After that you need to relax. Soon his huge misshapen head began to bob up and down in time to the movement of the train, like a life-sized sideshow doll that spat out unlucky fortunes.

The train was crowded, but no one dared sit down beside him.

11

AOMAME

A Serious Shortage of Both Logic and Kindness

ON TUESDAY MORNING AOMAME WROTE A memo to Tamaru explaining how the man calling himself an NHK fee collector had come again – how he had banged on the door and yelled, insulting Aomame (or a person named Takai who lived there), berating her. The whole thing was too much, too bizarre. She needed to remain vigilant.

Aomame placed the memo in an envelope, sealed it, and put it on the kitchen table. She wrote the initial *T* on the envelope. The men who delivered supplies would make sure it got to Tamaru.

Just before one p.m. she went into her bedroom, locked the door, lay down in bed, and continued where she had left off with Proust. At one o'clock on the dot the doorbell rang once. After a pause the door was unlocked and the supply team came inside. As always, they briskly resupplied the fridge, got the garbage together, and checked the supplies on the shelves. In fifteen minutes they had finished their appointed tasks, left the apartment, shut the door, and locked it from the outside. Then the doorbell rang once again as a signal – the same procedure as usual.

Just to be on the safe side, Aomame waited until the clock showed 1:30 before she came out of her bedroom and went to the kitchen. The memo to Tamaru was gone, replaced by a paper bag on the table with the name of a pharmacy printed on it. There was also a thick book Tamaru had gotten for her, *The Women's Anatomical Encyclopedia*. Inside the paper bag there were three different home pregnancy tests. She opened the boxes one by one and read over the instructions, comparing them. They were all the same. You could use the tests if your period was a week or more late. The tests were 95 percent accurate, but if they were positive, the instructions said – in other words, if they did show you were pregnant – then you should be examined by a medical specialist as soon as possible. You should not jump to conclusions. The tests indicated merely the *possibility* that one was pregnant.

The test itself was simple. Just urinate into a clean container and then dip the indicator stick into it. Or, alternately, urinate directly onto the stick. Then wait a few minutes. If the color changes to blue you're pregnant, if it doesn't change color, you're not. In one version, if two vertical lines appear in the little window, you're pregnant. One line, and you're not. The details might vary but the principle was the same. The presence or absence of human chorionic gonadotropin in urine indicated whether or not you were pregnant.

Human chorionic gonadotropin? Aomame frowned. She had been a female for thirty years and had never once heard that term. *All this time, some crazy substance was stimulating her sex glands?*

Aomame opened up *The Women's Anatomical Encyclopedia*.

Human chorionic gonadotropin is secreted during the early stages of pregnancy, the book said, *and helps maintain the corpus luteum. The corpus luteum secretes progestogens and estrogen to preserve the inner lining of the womb and prevent menstruation. In this way the placenta gradually takes form. In seven to nine weeks, once the placenta is complete, there is no more need for the corpus luteum and the role of the human chorionic gonadotropin is over.*

In other words, this hormone was secreted from the time of implantation for seven to nine weeks. The timing was a little tricky in her case. One thing she could say was that if the test came back positive, she was without a doubt pregnant. If it was negative, then the conclusion wouldn't be so clear-cut. It was possible that she had passed the time when she was secreting the hormone.

She didn't feel the need to urinate. She went to the fridge, took out a bottle of mineral water, and had two glasses. But she still didn't feel the need to go. *Well, no need to rush it,* she thought. She forgot about the pregnancy kits for a while and sat down on the sofa and concentrated on Proust.

It was after three when she felt the need to urinate. She peed into a container she found and stuck the test strip in it. As she watched, the strip changed color, until it was a vivid blue. A lovely shade of blue that would work well as the color of a car. A small blue convertible with a tan top. How great it would feel to drive along the coast in a car like that, racing through the summer breeze. But in the bathroom of an apartment in the middle of the city, in the deepening autumn, what this blue told her was the fact that she was pregnant – or, at least, that there was a 95 percent chance of it. Aomame stood in front of the mirror and gazed at the thin strip of paper, now blue. No matter how long she stared, the color wasn't about to change.

Just to be sure, she tried another test. This one instructed you to "urinate directly onto the tip of the stick." But since she wouldn't feel the need to pee for a while she dipped the stick into the container of urine. Freshly collected urine. Pee directly on it or dip it in pee – what is the difference? You would get the same result. Two vertical lines clearly appeared in the little plastic window. This, too, told Aomame she *might be pregnant.*

Aomame poured the urine into the toilet and flushed it down. She wrapped the test strip in a wad of tissue and threw it in the trash, and rinsed the container in the bath. She went to the kitchen and drank two more glasses of water. *Tomorrow I will try again and do the third test,* she thought. *Three is a good number to stop at. Strike one, strike two.* Waiting, with bated breath, for the final pitch.

Aomame boiled some water and made hot tea, sat down on the sofa, and continued reading Proust. She laid out some cheese biscuits on one of a set of matching plates and munched on them as she sipped her tea. A quiet afternoon, perfect for reading. Her eyes followed the printed words, but nothing stayed with her. She had to reread the same spot several times. She gave up, shut her eyes, and she was driving a blue convertible, the top down, speeding along the shore. The light breeze, fragrant with the smell of the sea, rustled her hair. A sign along the road had two vertical lines. These meant *Warning: You May Be Pregnant.*

Aomame sighed and tossed her book aside.

She knew very well there was no need to try the third test. She could do it a hundred times and the result would be the same. It would be a waste of time. *My human chorionic gonadotropin would still maintain the same attitude toward my womb – keeping the corpus luteum intact, obstructing my period from coming, helping form the placenta. Face it: I'm pregnant. The human chorionic gonadotropin knows that. And so do I. I can feel it as a pinpoint in my lower abdomen. It's still tiny – nothing more than* a hint of something. *But eventually it will have a placenta, and grow bigger. It will take nutrition from me and, in the dark, heavy liquid, grow – steadily, unceasingly.*

This was the first time she had been pregnant. She was always a very careful person, and only trusted what she could see with her own eyes. When she had sex she made absolutely sure her partner used a condom. Even when she was drunk, she never failed to check. As she had told the dowager, ever since her first menstruation at age ten, she had never missed a period. Her periods were regular, never more than a day late. Her cramps were light. She merely bled for a few days, that was all. It never got in the way of her exercising or playing sports.

She got her first period a few months after holding Tengo's hand in the elementary school classroom. Somehow, she felt that the two events were connected. The feel of Tengo's hand may have stirred something inside her. When she told her mother she got her period, her mother made a face, like it was one more burden to add to all the others she carried. It's a little early, her mother commented. But that didn't bother Aomame. It was her problem, not her mother's or anybody else's. She had stepped into a brand-new world.

And now she was pregnant.

She thought about her eggs. *Of my allotted four hundred or so, one of them (near the middle of the bunch, she imagined) went and got herself fertilized. Most likely on that September night, during the terrible storm. In a dark room when I murdered a man. When I stuck a sharp needle from the base of his neck into the lower part of his brain. But that man was completely different from the men I had killed before. He knew he was about to be murdered, and he wanted it to happen. I actually gave him what he* wanted. *Not as punishment, but more as an act of mercy. In exchange for which, he gave me what I was seeking. An act of negotiation carried out in a deep, dark place. Very quietly, fertilization took place that night. I know it,* she thought.

With these hands I took a man's life, and almost simultaneously, a new life began inside me. Was this part of the transaction?

Aomame shut her eyes and stopped thinking. Her head empty, something silently flowed inside. And before she knew it, she was praying.

O Lord in Heaven, may Thy name be praised in utmost purity for ever and ever, and may Thy kingdom come to us. Please forgive our many sins, and bestow Thy blessings upon our humble pathways. Amen.

Why would a prayer come to my lips at a time like this? I don't believe in things like heaven or paradise or the Lord, yet the words are chiseled into my brain. Ever since I was three or four and didn't even know what they meant, I could recite this prayer from memory. If I made the slightest mistake, I got the back of my hands smacked with a ruler. Though you couldn't normally see it, when something happened it would rise to the surface, like a secret tattoo.

What would my mother say if I told her I got pregnant without having had sex? She might see it as a terrible sacrilege against her faith. In any case, it was a kind of immaculate conception – though Aomame was certainly not a virgin. But still. Or maybe her mother wouldn't be bothered to even deal with it, not even listen to her. *Because she sees me as a failure, someone who long ago had fallen from her world.*

Let me think about it in a different way, Aomame thought. *I won't try to force an explanation on the inexplicable, but instead I'll examine the phenomenon from a different angle, as the riddle that it is.*

Am I seeing this pregnancy as something good, something to be welcomed? Or as something unwelcome, something inappropriate?

I can't reach a conclusion no matter how hard I think about it. I'm still in a state of shock. I'm mixed up, confused. In certain ways I feel split in two. And understandably I'm having trouble swallowing this new reality.

Yet Aomame also had to recognize that she was watching this little heat source with a positive sense of anticipation. She simply had to see what happened to this thing growing inside her. Obviously she was anxious and scared. *It* might be more than she could imagine. It might be a hostile foreign entity that greedily devoured her from the inside. She could imagine all sorts of negative possibilities. But she was in thrall to a healthy curiosity. Like a sudden flash of light in the dark, a thought abruptly sprang to her mind.

Maybe this is Tengo's child inside my womb.

Aomame frowned a bit and considered this. *Why do I have to be pregnant with Tengo's child?*

How about looking at it like this? she thought. *On that chaotic night, when so much took place, some process was at work in this world and Tengo sent his semen into my womb. Somehow, through a gap in the thunder and rain, the darkness and the murder, a special kind of passageway opened, through some logic I can't understand. Just for an instant. And in that instant we took advantage of the passageway. I took that opportunity to greedily accept Tengo into me. I became pregnant. Egg 201 – or was it 202? – grabbed onto one of his millions of spermatozoa, a single sperm cell that was as healthy and clever and straightforward as the one who produced it.*

That's a pretty wild idea. It doesn't make any sense. I could try to explain it until I went hoarse and nobody would ever believe me. But the whole notion of me being pregnant itself doesn't make any sense. But remember – this is the year 1Q84. A strange world where anything can happen.

What if this really is Tengo's child? she wondered.

That morning at the turnout on Metropolitan Expressway No. 3 through Tokyo, I didn't pull the trigger. I really went there, and stuck the muzzle in my mouth, planning to die. I wasn't afraid of death, because I was dying to save Tengo. But some higher power acted on me and snatched me away from death. From far away I heard a voice calling my name. Maybe it called me because I was pregnant? Was something trying to tell me of this new life inside me?

Aomame recalled the dream, and the refined older woman who put her coat on her to cover her nakedness. *She got out of her silver Mercedes and gave me her light, soft eggshell-colored coat. She knew then that I was pregnant, and she gently protected me from people's stares, the cold wind, and other vicious things.*

This was a good sign.

Aomame's tight face relaxed, her expression returned to normal. *Someone is watching over me, protecting me,* she believed. *Even in this 1Q84 world, I'm not alone. Probably.*

*   *   *

Aomame took her now cold tea over to the window. She went out to the balcony and sank into the garden chair so no one could spot her, and gazed out through the gaps in the screen at the playground. She tried to think of Tengo. For some reason, though, today her thoughts just wouldn't go to him. What she saw instead was the face of Ayumi Nakano. Ayumi was smiling cheerfully, a totally natural, unreserved smile. The two of them were at a restaurant seated across from each other, drinking wine. They were both pretty drunk. The excellent Burgundy in their blood gently coursed through their bodies, giving the world around them a faint purplish tinge.

"But still," Ayumi said, "it seems to me that this world has a serious shortage of both logic and kindness."

"Oh well, no problem," Aomame said. "The world's going to end before we know it."

"Sounds like fun."

"And the kingdom is going to come."

"I can hardly wait," Ayumi said.

Why did I talk about the kingdom then, I wonder? Aomame found it odd. *Why would I suddenly bring up a kingdom that I don't even believe in? And not long after that Ayumi died.*

I think when I mentioned the kingdom, the mental image I had was different from the kingdom the Witnesses believe in. Probably it was a more personal kind of kingdom, which is why the term could slip out so naturally. But what sort of kingdom do I believe in? What sort of kingdom do I think will appear after the world has been destroyed?

She gently laid her hands on her stomach and listened carefully. No matter how hard she listened, she didn't hear a thing.

Ayumi Nakano was cast off by this world. Her hands were tightly bound with cold handcuffs, and she was choked to death with a rope (and, as far as Aomame knew, the murderer had yet to be caught). An official autopsy was conducted, then she was sewn back up, taken to a crematorium, and burned. The person known as Ayumi Nakano no longer existed in this world. Her flesh and her blood were lost forever. She only remained in the realm of documents and memory.

No, maybe that's not entirely true. Maybe she was still alive and well in 1984. Still grumbling that she wasn't allowed to carry a pistol, still sticking parking tickets under the wipers of illegally parked cars. Still going around to high schools to teach girls about contraception. "If he doesn't have on a condom, girls, then there shouldn't be any penetration."

Aomame desperately wanted to see Ayumi. If she could climb back up that emergency stairway on the Metropolitan Expressway No. 3 and return to the world of 1984, then maybe she would see her again. *Maybe there Ayumi is still alive, and I'm not being chased by these Sakigake freaks. Maybe we could stop by that restaurant on Nogizaka again and enjoy another glass of Burgundy. Or perhaps –*

Climb back up that emergency stairway?

Like rewinding a cassette tape, Aomame retraced her thoughts. *Why haven't I thought of that before? I tried to go down that emergency stairway again but couldn't find the entrance. The stairway, which should have been across from the Esso billboard, had vanished. But maybe if I took it from the opposite direction it would work out – not climb down the stairway but go up. Slip into that storage area under the expressway and go the opposite direction, back up to the Metropolitan Expressway No. 3. Go back up the passage. Maybe that's the answer.*

Aomame wanted to race out that very minute to Sangenjaya and see if it was possible. *It might actually work out. Or maybe it wouldn't. But it was worth trying. Wear the same suit, the same high heels, and climb back up that spiderweb-infested stairway.*

But she suppressed the impulse.

No, it won't work. I can't do that. It was because I came to the 1Q84 world that I was able to see Tengo again, and to be pregnant with what is most likely his child. I have to see him one more time in this new

*world. I have to meet him again. Face-to-face. I can't leave this world
until that happens.*

Tamaru called her the following afternoon.

"First, about the NHK fee collector," Tamaru began. "I called the
NHK business office and checked into it. The fee collector who covers
the Koenji District said he had no memory of knocking on the door
of apartment 303. He said he checked beforehand that there was a
sticker on the door indicating that the fee was paid automatically from
the account. Plus he said there was a doorbell, so he wouldn't have
knocked. He said that would only make his hand hurt. And on the
day the fee collector was at your place, this man was making the rounds
in another district. I don't think he's lying. He's a fifteen-year veteran,
and he has a reputation as a very patient, courteous person."

"Which means –" Aomame said.

"Which means that there's a strong possibility that the fee collector
who came to your place was a fake – someone pretending to be from
NHK. The person I talked to on the phone was concerned about this
too. The last thing they want are phony NHK collectors popping up.
The person in charge asked to see me and get more details. As you
can imagine, I turned him down. There was no actual harm done,
and I don't want it to get all blown out of proportion."

"Maybe he was a mental patient? Or someone who's after me?"

"I don't think anyone pursuing you would act like that. It wouldn't
do any good, and would actually put you on your guard."

"If the man was crazy, I wonder why he would choose this particular door. There are lots of other doors around. I'm always careful to
make sure no light leaks out, and I'm very quiet. I always keep the
curtains closed and never hang laundry outside to dry. But still that
guy picked this door to bang on. He knows I'm hiding inside here – or
at least he insists he knows that – and he tries whatever he can to get
me to open up."

"Do you think he's going to come back?"

"I don't know. But if he's really serious about getting me to open up, I'm betting he'll keep coming back until I do."

"And that unsettles you."

"I wouldn't say it unsettles me, exactly," Aomame replied. "I just don't like it."

"I don't like it either, not one little bit. But even if that phony collector comes back again, we can't call NHK or the police. And if you call me and I race over, he will probably have vanished by the time I get there."

"I think I can handle it myself," Aomame said. "He can be as intimidating as he wants, but all I have to do is keep the door shut."

"I'm sure he will use whatever means he can to intimidate you."

"No doubt," Aomame said.

Tamaru cleared his throat for a moment and changed the subject. "Did you get the test kits all right?"

"It was positive," Aomame said straight out.

"A hit, in other words."

"Exactly. I tried two tests and the results were identical."

There was silence. Like a lithograph with no words carved on it yet.

"No room for doubt?" Tamaru asked.

"I knew it from the start. The tests merely confirmed it."

Tamaru silently rubbed the lithograph for a time with the pads of his fingers.

"I have to ask a pretty forward question," he said. "Do you plan to have the baby? Or are you going to deal with it?"

"I'm not going to *deal with* it."

"Which means you will give birth."

"If things go smoothly, the due date will be between June and July of next year."

Tamaru did the math in his head. "Which means we will have to make some changes in our plans."

"I'm sorry about that."

"No need to apologize," Tamaru said. "All women have the right to give birth. We have to protect that right as much as we can."

"Sounds like a Declaration of Human Rights," Aomame said.

"I'm asking this again just to make sure, but you have no idea who the father is?"

"Since June I haven't had a sexual relationship with anyone."

"So this is a kind of immaculate conception?"

"I imagine religious people would get upset if you put it that way."

"If you do anything out of the ordinary, you can be sure someone, somewhere, will get upset," Tamaru said. "But when you're dealing with a pregnancy, it's important to get a specialist to check you over. You can't just stay shut up in that room waiting it out."

Aomame sighed. "Let me stay here until the end of the year. I promise I won't be any trouble."

Tamaru was silent for a while. Then he spoke. "You can stay there until the end of the year, like we promised. But once the new year comes, we have to move you to a less dangerous place, where you can easily get medical attention. You understand this, right?"

"I do," Aomame said. She wasn't fully convinced, though. *If I don't see Tengo,* she thought, *will I really be able to leave here?*

"I got a woman pregnant once," Tamaru said.

Aomame didn't say anything for a time. "You? But I thought you were –"

"Gay? I am. A card-carrying homosexual. I have always been that way, and I imagine I always will be."

"But still you got a woman pregnant."

"Everybody makes mistakes," Tamaru said, with no hint of humor. "I don't want to go into the details, but it was when I was young. I did it once, but *bang*! A bull's-eye."

"What happened to the woman?"

"I don't know," Tamaru said.

"You don't know?"

"I know how she was up to her sixth month. But after that I have no idea."

"If you get to the sixth month, abortion is not an option."

"That's my understanding."

"So there's a high possibility she had the baby," Aomame said.

"Most likely."

"If she really did have the baby, don't you want to see it?"

"I'm not that interested," Tamaru said without missing a beat. "That's not the kind of life I lead. What about you? Would you want to see your child?"

Aomame gave it some thought. "I am someone whose parents threw her away when she was small, so it's hard for me to imagine what it would be like to have my own child. I have no good model to follow."

"Still, you're going to be bringing that child into the world – into this violent, mixed-up world."

"It's because I'm looking for love," Aomame said. "Not love between me and the child, though. I haven't reached that stage yet."

"But the child is part of that love."

"I think so, in one way or another."

"But if things don't turn out like you expect, and that child isn't part of the love you're looking for, then he'll end up hurt. Just like the two of us."

"It's possible. But I don't sense that will happen. Call it intuition."

"I respect intuition," Tamaru said. "But once the ego is born into this world, it has to shoulder morality. You would do well to remember that."

"Who said that?"

"Wittgenstein."

"I'll keep it in mind," Aomame said. "If your child was born, how old would it be?"

Tamaru did the math in his head. "Seventeen."

"Seventeen." Aomame imagined a seventeen-year-old boy, or girl, shouldering morality.

"I'll let Madame know about this," Tamaru said. "She has been wanting to talk with you directly. As I have said a number of times, however, from a security standpoint I am none too happy about the idea. On a technical level I'm taking all necessary precautions, but the telephone is still a risky means of communication."

"Understood."

"But she is very concerned about what has happened, and is worried about you."

"I understand that, too. And I'm grateful for her concern."

"It would be the smart thing to trust her, and follow her advice. She is a very wise person."

"Of course," Aomame said.

But apart from that, Aomame told herself, *I need to hone my own mind and protect myself. The dowager is certainly a very wise person. And she wields a considerable amount of power. But there are some things she has no way of knowing. I doubt she knows what principles the year 1Q84 is operating on. I mean – has she even noticed that there are two moons in the sky?*

After she hung up, Aomame lay on the sofa and dozed for a half hour. It was a short, deep sleep. She dreamed, but her dream was like a big, blank space. Inside that space she was thinking about things. And she was writing, with invisible ink, in that pure white notebook. When she woke up, she had an indistinct yet strangely clear image in her mind. *I will give birth to this child. This little life will be safely born into the world.* Like Tamaru had put it, as an unavoidable bearer of morality.

She laid her palm on her abdomen and listened. She couldn't hear a thing. For now.

12

TENGO

The Rules of the World Are Loosening Up

AFTER HE FINISHED BREAKFAST, TENGO TOOK a shower. He washed his hair and shaved at the sink, then changed into the clothes he had washed and dried. He left the inn, bought the morning edition of the paper at a kiosk at the station, and went to a coffee shop nearby and had a cup of hot black coffee.

There wasn't much of interest in the newspaper. At least as far as this particular morning's paper was concerned, the world was a dull, boring place. It felt like he was rereading a paper from a week ago, not today. Tengo folded up the paper and glanced at his watch. It was nine thirty. Visiting hours at the sanatorium began at ten.

It didn't take long to pack for the trip back home. He didn't have much luggage, just a few changes of clothes, toiletries, a few books, and a sheaf of manuscript paper. He stuffed it all inside his canvas shoulder bag. He slung the bag over his shoulder, paid his bill for the inn, and took a bus from the station to the sanatorium. It was the beginning of winter, and there were few people this morning heading to the beach. Tengo was the only one getting out at the stop in front of the sanatorium.

At the reception desk he wrote his name and the time in the visitors' log. A young nurse he had never seen before was stationed at the reception desk. Her arms and legs were terribly long and thin, and a smile played around the corners of her lips. She made him think of a kindly spider guiding people along the path through a forest. Usually it was Nurse Tamura, the middle-aged woman with glasses, who sat at the reception desk, but today she wasn't there. Tengo felt a bit relieved. He had been dreading any suggestive comments she might make because he had accompanied Kumi Adachi back to her apartment the night before. Nurse Omura, too, was nowhere to be seen. They might have been sucked into the earth without a trace. Like the three witches in *Macbeth*.

But that was impossible. Kumi Adachi was off duty today, but the other two nurses said they were working as usual. They must just be working somewhere else in the facility right now.

Tengo went upstairs to his father's room, knocked lightly, twice, and opened the door. His father was lying on the bed, sleeping as always. An IV tube came out of his arm, a catheter snaked out of his groin. There was no change from the day before. The window was closed, as were the curtains. The air in the room was heavy and stagnant. All sorts of smells were mixed together – a medicinal smell, the smell of the flowers in the vase, the breath of a sick person, the smell of excreta – all the smells that life brings with it. Even if the life force here was weak, and his father was unconscious, metabolism went on unchanged. His father was still on this side of the great divide. Being alive, if you had to define it, meant emitting a variety of smells.

The first thing Tengo did when he entered the sickroom was go straight to the far wall, where he drew the curtains and flung open the window. It was a refreshing morning, and the room was in desperate need of fresh air. It was chilly outside, but not what you would call cold. Sunlight streamed in and the curtain rustled in the sea breeze. A single seagull, legs tucked neatly underneath, caught a draft of wind and glided over the pine trees. A ragged line of sparrows sat on an electrical line, constantly switching positions like musical notes being rewritten. A crow with a large beak came to rest on top of a mercury-vapor lamp, cautiously surveying his surroundings as he mulled over his next move. A few streaks of clouds floated off high in the sky, so high and far away that they were like abstract concepts unrelated to the affairs of man.

With his back to the patient, Tengo gazed for a while at this scene outside. Things that are living and things that are not. Things that move and things that don't. What he saw out the window was the usual scenery. There was nothing new about it. The world has to move forward. Like a cheap alarm clock, it does a halfway decent job of fulfilling its assigned role. Tengo gazed blankly at the scenery, trying to postpone facing his father even by a moment, but he couldn't keep delaying forever.

Finally Tengo made up his mind, turned, and sat down on the stool next to the bed. His father was lying on his back, facing the ceiling, his eyes shut. The quilt that was tucked up to his neck was neat and undisturbed. His eyes were deeply sunken. It was like some piece was missing, and his eye sockets couldn't support his eyeballs, which had quietly caved in. Even if he were to open his eyes, what he would see would be like the world viewed from the bottom of a hole.

"Father," Tengo began.

His father didn't answer. The breeze blowing in the room suddenly stopped and the curtains hung limply, like a worker in the midst of a task suddenly remembering something else he had to do. And then, after a while, as if gathering itself together, the wind began to blow again.

"I'm going back to Tokyo today," Tengo said. "I can't stay here forever. I can't take any more time off from work. It's not much of a life, but I do have a life to get back to."

There was a two- to three-day growth of whiskers on his father's cheeks. A nurse shaved him with an electric razor, but not every day. His whiskers were salt-and-pepper. He was only sixty-four, but he looked much older, like someone had mistakenly fast-forwarded the film of his life.

"You didn't wake up the whole time I was here. The doctor says your physical condition is still not so bad. The strange thing is, you're almost as healthy as you used to be."

Tengo paused, letting the words sink in.

"I don't know if you can hear what I'm saying or not. Even if the words are vibrating your eardrums, the circuit beyond that might be shot. Or maybe the words I speak are actually reaching you but you're unable to respond. I don't really know. But I have been talking to you, and reading to you, on the assumption that you can hear me. Unless I assume that, there's no point in me speaking to you, and if I can't speak to you, then there's no point in me being here. I can't explain it well, but I'm sensing something tangible, as if the main points of what I'm saying are, at least, getting across."

No response.

"What I'm about to say may sound pretty stupid. But I'm going back to Tokyo today and I don't know when I might be back here. So I'm just going to say what's in my mind. If you find it dumb, then just go ahead and laugh. If you *can* laugh, I mean."

Tengo paused and observed his father's face. Again, there was no response.

"Your body is in a coma. You have lost consciousness and feeling, and you are being kept alive by life-support machines. The doctor said you're like a living corpse – though he put it a bit more euphemistically. Medically speaking, that's what it probably is. But isn't that just a sham? I have the feeling your consciousness isn't lost at all. You have put your body in a coma, but your consciousness is off somewhere else, alive. I've felt that for a long time. It's just a feeling, though."

Silence.

"I can understand if you think this is a crazy idea. If I told anybody else, they would say I was hallucinating. But I have to believe it's true. I think you lost all interest in this world. You were disappointed and discouraged, and lost interest in everything. So you abandoned your physical body. You went to a world apart and you're living a different kind of life there. In a world that's inside you."

Again more silence.

"I took time off from my job, came to this town, rented a room at an inn, and have been coming here every day and talking to you – for almost two weeks now. But I wasn't just doing it to see how you were doing or to take care of you. I wanted to see where I came from, what sort of bloodline I have. None of that matters anymore. I am who I am, no matter who or what I'm connected with – or not connected with. Though I do know that you are the one who is my father. And that's fine. Is this what you call a reconciliation? I don't know. Maybe I just reconciled with myself."

Tengo took a deep breath. He spoke in a softer tone.

"During the summer, you were still conscious. Your mind was muddled, but your consciousness was still functioning. At that time I met a girl here, in this room, again. After they took you to the examination room she *appeared*. I think it must have been something like her alter ego. I came to this town again and have stayed here this long because I have been hoping I could see her one more time. Honestly, that's why I came."

Tengo sighed and brought his hands together on his lap.

"But she didn't come. What brought her here last time was a thing called an air chrysalis, a capsule she was encased in. It would take too long to explain the whole thing, but an air chrysalis is a product of the imagination, a fictitious object. But it's not fictitious anymore. The boundary between the real world and the imaginary one has grown obscure. There are two moons in the sky now. These, too, were brought over from the world of fiction."

175

Tengo looked at his father's face. Could he follow what Tengo was saying?

"In that context, saying your consciousness has broken away from your body and is freely moving about some other world doesn't sound so farfetched. It's like the rules that govern the world have begun to loosen up around us. As I said before, I have this strange sense that you are *actually doing that.* Like you have gone to my apartment in Koenji and are knocking on the door. You know what I mean? You announce you're an NHK fee collector, bang hard on the door, and yell out a threat in a loud voice. Just like you used to do all the time when we made the rounds in Ichikawa."

He felt a change in the air pressure in the room. The window was open, but there was barely any sound coming in. There was just the occasional burst of chirping sparrows.

"There is a girl staying in my apartment in Tokyo. Not a girlfriend or anything – something happened and she's taking shelter there temporarily. A few days ago she told me on the phone about an NHK collector who came by, how he knocked on the door, and what he did and said out in the corridor. It was strange how closely it resembled the methods you used to use. The words she heard were exactly the same lines I remember, the expressions I was hoping I could totally erase from my memory. And I'm thinking now that that fee collector might actually have been you. Am I wrong?"

Tengo waited thirty seconds. His father didn't twitch a single eyelash.

"There's just one thing I want: for you to never knock on my door again. I don't have a TV. And those days when we went around together collecting fees are long gone. I think we already agreed on that, that time in front of my teacher – I don't remember her name, the one who was in charge of my class. A short lady, with glasses. You remember that, right? So don't knock on my door ever again, okay? And not just my place. Don't knock on any more doors anywhere. You're not an NHK fee collector anymore, and you don't have the right to scare people like that."

Tengo stood up, went to the window, and looked outside. An old man in a bulky sweater, clutching a cane, was walking in front of the woods. He was probably just taking a stroll. He was tall, with white hair, and excellent posture. But his steps were awkward, as if he had forgotten how to walk, as if with each step forward he was remembering how to do it. Tengo watched him for a while. The old man slowly made his way across the garden, then turned the corner of the building and disappeared. It didn't look like he had recalled the art of walking. Tengo turned to face his father.

"I'm not blaming you. You have the right to send your consciousness wherever you want. It's your life, and your consciousness. You have your own idea of what is right, and you're putting it into practice. Maybe I don't have the right to say these things. But you need to understand: *you are not an NHK fee collector anymore.* So you shouldn't pretend to be one. It's pointless."

Tengo sat down on the windowsill and searched for his next words in the air of the cramped hospital room.

"I don't know what kind of life you had, what sorts of joys and sorrows you experienced. But even if there was something that left you unfulfilled, you can't go around seeking it at other people's doors. Even if it is at the place you're most familiar with, and the sort of act that is your forte."

Tengo gazed silently at his father's face.

"I don't want you to knock on anybody's door anymore. That's all I ask of you, Father. I have to be going. I came here every day talking to you in your coma, reading to you. And I think at least a part of us has reconciled, and I think that reconciliation has actually taken place in the real world. Maybe you won't like it, but you need to come back here again, to *this* side. This is where you belong."

Tengo lifted his shoulder bag and slung it across his shoulder. "Well, I'll be off, then."

His father said nothing. He didn't stir and his eyes remained shut – the same as always. But somehow it seemed like he was thinking about something. Tengo was quiet and paid careful attention. It felt to him like his father might pop open his eyes at any moment and abruptly sit up in bed. But none of that happened.

The nurse with the spidery limbs was still at the reception desk as he left. A plastic name tag on her chest said *Tamaki*.

"I'm going back to Tokyo now," Tengo told her.

"It's too bad your father didn't regain consciousness while you were here," she said, consolingly. "But I'm sure he was happy you could stay so long."

Tengo couldn't think of a decent response. "Please tell the other nurses good-bye for me. You have all been so helpful."

He never did see bespectacled Nurse Tamura or busty Nurse Omura and her ever-present ballpoint pen. It made him a little sad. They were outstanding nurses, and had always been kind to him. But perhaps it was for the best that he didn't see them. After all, he was slipping out of the cat town alone.

As the train pulled out of Chikura Station, he recalled spending the night at Kumi Adachi's apartment. It had only just happened yesterday. The gaudy Tiffany lamp, the uncomfortable love seat, the TV comedy show he could hear from next door. The hooting of the owl in the woods. The hashish smoke, the smiley-face shirt, the thick pubic hair pressed against his leg. It had been less than a day, but it felt like long ago. His mind felt unstable. Like an unbalanced set of scales, the core of his memories wouldn't settle down in one spot.

Suddenly anxious, Tengo looked around him. Was this reality actually real? Or had he once again boarded the wrong reality? He asked a passenger nearby and made sure this train was indeed headed to Tateyama. *It's okay, don't worry,* he told himself. *At Tateyama I can change to the express train to Tokyo.* He was drawing farther and farther away from the cat town by the sea.

As soon as he changed trains and took his seat, as if it could barely wait, sleep claimed him. A deep sleep, like he had lost his footing and fallen into a bottomless hole. His eyelids closed, and in the next instant his consciousness had vanished. When he opened his eyes again, the train had passed Makuhari. The train wasn't particularly hot inside, yet he was sweating under his arms and down his back. His mouth had an awful smell, like the stagnant air he had breathed in his father's sick room. He took a stick of gum out of his pocket and popped it in his mouth.

Tengo was sure he would never visit that town again – at least not while his father was alive. While there was nothing in this world that he could state with one hundred percent certainty, he knew there was probably nothing more he could do in that seaside town.

When he got back to the apartment, Fuka-Eri wasn't there. He knocked on the door three times, paused, then knocked two more times. Then he unlocked the door. Inside, the apartment was dead silent. He was immediately struck by how neat and clean everything was. The dishes were neatly stacked away in the cupboard, everything on the table and desk was neatly arranged, and the trash can had been emptied. There were signs that the place had been vacuumed as well. The bed was made, and no books or records lay scattered about. Dried laundry lay neatly folded on top of the bed.

The oversized shoulder bag that Fuka-Eri used was also gone. It didn't appear, however, that she had remembered something she had to do or that something had suddenly come up and she had hurriedly left. Nor did it look like she had just gone out for a short time. Instead, all indications were that she had decided to leave for good, that she had taken her time cleaning the apartment and then left. Tengo tried picturing her pushing around the vacuum cleaner and wiping here and there with a wet cloth. It just didn't fit her image at all.

He opened the mail slot inside the front door and found the spare key. From the amount of mail, she must have left yesterday or the day before. The last time he had called her had been in the morning two days earlier, and she had still been in the apartment. Last night he had had dinner with the three nurses and had gone back to Kumi's place. What with one thing and another, he had forgotten to call her.

Normally she would have left a note behind in her unique cuneiform-like script, but there was no sign of one. She had left without a word. Tengo wasn't particularly surprised or disappointed. No one could predict what the girl was thinking or what she would do. She just showed up when she wanted to, and left when she felt like it – like a capricious, independent-minded cat. In fact, it was unusual for her to have stayed put this long in one place.

The refrigerator was more full of food than he had expected. He guessed that a few days earlier, Fuka-Eri must have gone out and done some shopping on her own. There was a pile of steamed cauliflower as well, which seemed to have been cooked recently. Had she known that Tengo would be back in Tokyo in a day or two? Tengo was hungry, so he fried some eggs and ate them with the cauliflower. He made some toast and drank two mugs of coffee.

Next he phoned his friend who had covered for him at school and told him he expected to be back at work at the beginning of the week. His friend updated him on how much they had covered in the textbook.

"You really helped me out. I owe you one."

"I don't mind teaching," the friend said. "I even enjoy it at times. But I found that the longer you teach, the more you feel like a total stranger to yourself."

Tengo had often had an inkling of the same thing.

"Anything out of the ordinary happen while I was gone?"

"Not really. Oh, you did get a letter. I put it in a drawer in your desk."

"A letter?" Tengo asked. "From whom?"

"A thin young girl brought it by. She had straight hair down to her shoulders. She came up to me and said she had a letter to give to you. She spoke sort of strangely. I think she might be a foreigner."

"Did she have a large shoulder bag?"

"She did. A green shoulder bag. Stuffed full of things."

Fuka-Eri may have been afraid to leave the letter behind in his apartment, scared that someone else might read it, or take it away. So she went directly to the cram school and gave it to his friend.

Tengo thanked his friend again and hung up. It was already evening, and he didn't feel like taking the train all the way to Yoyogi to pick up the letter. He would leave it for tomorrow.

Right afterward he realized he had forgotten to ask his friend about the moon. He started to dial again but decided against it. Most likely his friend had forgotten all about it. This was something he would have to resolve on his own.

Tengo went out and aimlessly sauntered down the twilight streets. With Fuka-Eri gone, his apartment was too quiet and he couldn't settle down. When they had been living together he didn't really sense her presence all that much. He followed his daily routine, and she followed hers. But without her there, Tengo noticed a human-shaped void she had left behind.

It wasn't because he was attracted to her. She was a beautiful, attractive young girl, for sure, but since Tengo first met her he had never felt anything like desire for her. Even after sharing the same apartment for so long, he never felt anything stirring within his heart. *How come? Is there some reason I shouldn't feel sexual desire for her?* he wondered. It was true that on that stormy night they had had intercourse. But it wasn't what he had wanted. It had all been *her* doing.

Intercourse was exactly the right word to describe the act. She had climbed on top of Tengo, who had been numb and unable to move, and inserted his penis inside her. Fuka-Eri had seemed to be in some transcendent state then, like a fairy in the throes of a lewd dream.

Afterward they lived together in the tiny apartment as if nothing had happened. The storm had stopped, morning came, and Fuka-Eri acted like she had completely forgotten the incident. And Tengo didn't bring it up. He felt that if she really had forgotten, it was better to let her stay that way. It might be best if he himself forgot it too. Still, the question remained – why had she suddenly done such a thing? Was there some objective behind it all? Or had she been temporarily possessed?

There was only one thing Tengo knew for sure: *it wasn't an act of love*. Fuka-Eri had a natural affinity for Tengo – that seemed certain. But it was farfetched to believe that she loved him, or desired him, or felt anything even close to these emotions. *She felt no sexual desire for anyone*. Tengo wasn't confident in his powers of observation when it came to people, but still he couldn't quite imagine Fuka-Eri passionately making love with a man, her breath hot and heavy. Or even engaged in not-so-passionate sex. That just wasn't her.

These thoughts ran through his head as he walked the streets of Koenji. The sun had set and a cold wind had picked up, but he didn't mind. He liked to think while he walked, then sit down at his desk and give form to his thoughts. That was his way of doing things. That was why he walked a lot. It might rain, it might be windy, he didn't care. As he walked he found himself in front of a bar called Mugiatama – "Ears of Wheat." Tengo couldn't think of anything better to do, so he popped inside and ordered a Carlsberg draft beer. The bar had just opened and he was the only customer. He stopped thinking for a while, kept his mind a blank, and slowly sipped his beer.

But just like nature abhors a vacuum, Tengo wasn't afforded the leisure of keeping his mind blank for long. He couldn't help thinking of Fuka-Eri. Like a scrap of a dream, she wended her way into his mind.

That person may be very close. Somewhere you can walk to from here.

Fuka-Eri had said this. Which is why I went out to look for her. And came inside this bar. What other things did she say?

Do not worry. Even if you cannot find that person, that person will find you.

Just as Tengo was searching for Aomame, Aomame was searching for him. Tengo hadn't really grasped that. He had been caught up in *himself* searching for her. It had never occurred to him that Aomame might be looking for *him* too.

I perceive and you receive.

This was also something Fuka-Eri had said. She perceives it, and Tengo receives it. But Fuka-Eri only made clear what she perceived when she felt like it. Whether she was operating on some principle or theory, or merely acting on a whim, Tengo couldn't tell.

Again Tengo remembered the time they had intercourse. The beautiful seventeen-year-old climbed on top of him and put his penis inside her. Her ample breasts moved lithely in the air, like ripe fruit. She closed her eyes in rapture, her nostrils flaring with desire. Her lips formed something that didn't come together as actual words. He could see her white teeth, her pink tongue darting out from between them every now and then. Tengo had a vivid memory of that scene. His body may have been numb, but his mind was clear. And he had a rock-hard erection.

But no matter how clearly he relived the scene in his head, Tengo didn't feel any stir of sexual excitement. And it didn't cross his mind to want to have sex with her again. He hadn't had sex for the nearly three months since that encounter. More than that, he hadn't even come once. For him this was quite unusual. He was a healthy, thirty-year-old single guy, with a normal sex drive, the sort of desire that had to be taken care of one way or another.

Still, when he was in Kumi Adachi's apartment, in bed with her, her pubic hair pressing against his leg, he had felt no desire at all. His penis had remained flaccid the whole time. Maybe it was the hashish. But that wasn't the reason, he decided. On that stormy night when he had had sex with Fuka-Eri, she had taken *something* important away, from his heart. Like moving furniture out of a room. He was convinced of it.

Like what, for instance?

Tengo shook his head.

When he had polished off the beer, he ordered a Four Roses on the rocks and some mixed nuts. Just like the last time.

Most likely his erection on that stormy night was *too* perfect. It was far harder, and bigger, than he had ever experienced. It didn't look like his own penis. Smooth and shiny, it seemed less an actual penis than some conceptual symbol, and when he ejaculated it was powerful, heroic even, the semen copious and thick. This must have reached her womb, or even beyond. It was the perfect orgasm.

But when something is so complete, there has to be a reaction. That's the way things go. *What kind of erections have I had since?* Tengo wondered. He couldn't recall. Maybe he hadn't even had one. Or if he had, it was obviously not very memorable, a subpar hard-on. If his erection had been a movie, it would have been low budget, straight to video. Not an erection even worth discussing. Most likely.

Maybe I'm fated to drift through life with nothing but second-rate erections, he asked himself, *or not even second-rate ones? That would be a sad sort of life, like a prolonged twilight. But depending on how you look at it, it might be unavoidable.* At least once in his life he had had the perfect erection, and the perfect orgasm. It was like the author of *Gone With the Wind*. Once you have achieved something so magnificent, you have to be content with it.

*   *   *

He finished his whiskey, paid the bill, and continued wandering the streets. The wind had picked up and the air was chillier than before. *Before the world's rules loosen up too much,* he thought, *and all logic is lost, I have to find Aomame.* Nearly the only hope he could cling to now was the thought that he might run across her. *If I don't find her, then what value is there to my life?* he wondered. She had been here, in Koenji, in September. If he were lucky, she was still in the same place. Not that he could prove it – but all he could do right now was pursue that possibility. *Aomame is somewhere around here. And she is searching for me, too. Like two halves of a coin, each seeking the other.*

He looked up at the sky, but he couldn't see the moons. *I have to go someplace where I can see the moons,* Tengo decided.

13

USHIKAWA

Is This What They Mean by Back to Square One?

USHIKAWA'S APPEARANCE MADE HIM STAND OUT. He did not have the sort of looks suited for stakeouts or tailing people. As much as he might try to lose himself in a crowd, he was as inconspicuous as a centipede in a cup of yogurt.

His family wasn't like that at all. Ushikawa's family consisted of his parents, an older and younger brother, and a younger sister. His father ran a health clinic, where his mother was the bookkeeper. Both brothers were outstanding students, attended medical school, and became doctors. His older brother worked in a hospital in Tokyo, while his younger brother was a research doctor at a university. When his father retired, his older brother was due to take over the family clinic in Urawa, a suburb of Tokyo. Both brothers were married and had one child. Ushikawa's sister had studied at a college in the United States and was now back in Japan, working as an interpreter. She was in her mid-thirties but still single. All his siblings were slim and tall, with pleasantly oval features.

In almost every respect, particularly in looks, Ushikawa was the exception in his family. He was short, with a large, misshapen head and unkempt, frizzy hair. His legs were stumpy and bent like cucumbers. His popping eyes always looked startled, and he had a thick layer of flesh around his neck. His eyebrows were bushy and large and nearly came together in the middle. They looked like two hairy caterpillars reaching out to each other. In school he had generally gotten excellent grades, but his performance in some subjects was erratic and he was particularly hopeless at sports.

In this affluent, self-satisfied, elite family, he was the foreign element, the sour, dissonant note that ruined the familial harmony. In family photos he looked like the odd man out, the insensitive outsider who had pushed his way into the group and had his picture taken with them.

The other members of his family couldn't understand how someone who didn't resemble them in the least could be one of them. But there was no mistaking the fact that his mother had given birth to him, with all the attendant labor pains (her recollection was how particularly painful that birth had been). No one had laid him at their doorstep in a basket. Eventually, someone recalled that there was a relative who also had an oversized, misshapen head – Ushikawa's grandfather's cousin. During the war he had worked in a metal shop in Koto Ward in Tokyo, but he died in the massive air raid in the spring of 1945. His father had never met the man, though he had a photo of him in an old album. When the family saw the photo, they exclaimed, "It all makes sense now!" Ushikawa and his uncle were such peas in a pod that you would think that Ushikawa was the man reincarnated. The genetic traits of this uncle had, for whatever reason, surfaced once more.

The Ushikawa family of Urawa, Saitama Prefecture, would have been the perfect family – in both looks and academic and career achievements – if only Ushikawa hadn't existed. They would have been the kind of memorable, photogenic family that anyone would envy. But with Ushikawa in the mix, people tended to frown and shake their heads. People might begin to think that somewhere along the line a joker or two had tripped up the goddess of beauty. No, they *definitely* must think this, his parents decided, which is why they tried their hardest to keep him out of the public eye or at least make sure he didn't stand out (though the attempt was always pointless).

Being put in this situation, however, never made Ushikawa feel dissatisfied, sad, or lonely. He wasn't sociable to begin with and usually preferred to stay in the shadows. He wasn't particularly fond of his brothers and sister. From Ushikawa's perspective, they were irretrievably shallow. To him, their minds were dull, their vision narrow and devoid of imagination, and all they cared about was what other people thought. More than anything, they were completely lacking in the sort of healthy skepticism needed to attain any degree of wisdom.

Ushikawa's father was a moderately successful doctor of internal medicine in the countryside, but he was so utterly boring that talking with him gave you chest pains. Like the king whose touch turned everything to gold, every single word he uttered turned into insipid grains of sand. But as a man of few words he was able – probably unintentionally – to conceal how boring and ignorant he really was. In contrast, his mother was a real talker, a hopeless snob. Money was everything to her, and she was self-centered and proud, loved anything gaudy and showy, and could always be counted on to bad-mouth other people in a shrill voice. Ushikawa's older brother had inherited his father's disposition; his younger brother had his mother's. His sister was very independent. She was irresponsible and had no consideration for others. As the baby of the family, she had been totally pampered and spoiled by her parents.

All of which explained why, since he was a boy, Ushikawa had kept to himself. When he came home from school, he had shut himself in his room and gotten lost in books. He had no friends other than his dog, so he never had the chance to talk with someone about what he had learned, or debate anyone. Still, he was convinced that he was a clear, eloquent, logical thinker, and he patiently honed these abilities all by himself. For instance, he would propose an idea for discussion and debate it, taking both sides. He would passionately argue in support of the proposition, then argue – just as vigorously – against it. He could identify equally with either of the two positions and was completely and sincerely absorbed by whatever position he happened to be supporting at the moment. Before he had realized it, these exercises had given him the talent to be skeptical about his own self, and he had come to the recognition that most of what is generally considered the truth is entirely relative. Subject and object are not as distinct as most people think. If the boundary separating the two isn't clear-cut to begin with, it is not such a difficult task to intentionally shift back and forth from one to the other.

In order to use logic and rhetoric more clearly and effectively, he filled his mind with whatever knowledge he could find – both what he thought would be useful and what he was pretty sure was the opposite. He chose things he agreed with, and things that, initially, he opposed. It wasn't cultivation and learning in the usual sense that he was after, but more tangible information – something you could actually handle, something with a real shape and heft.

That huge, misshapen head of his turned out to be the perfect container for these quantities of accumulated information. Thanks to all this, he was far more erudite than any of his contemporaries. If he felt like it, he knew he could shoot down anybody in an argument – not just his siblings or classmates, but his teachers and parents as well. But he didn't want to attract any kind of attention if he could avoid it, so he kept this ability hidden. Knowledge and ability were tools, not things to show off.

Ushikawa began to think of himself as a nocturnal creature, concealed in a dark forest, waiting for prey to wander by. He waited patiently for an opportunity, and when it came he would leap out and grab it. But until that point, he couldn't let his opponent know he was there. It was critical to keep a low profile and catch the other person off guard. Even as an elementary school pupil, he had thought this way. He never depended on others or readily revealed his emotions.

Sometimes he imagined how his life would be if he had been born a little better-looking. He didn't need to be handsome. There was no need to look that impressive. He just needed to be normal-looking, or enough so that people wouldn't turn and stare. *If only I had been born like that,* he wondered, *what sort of life would I have led?* But this was a supposition that exceeded his powers of imagination. Ushikawa was too Ushikawa-like, and there was no room in his brain for such hypotheses. It was precisely because of his large, misshapen head, his bulging eyes, and his short, bandy legs that he was who he was, a skeptical young boy, full of intellectual curiosity, quiet but eloquent.

As the years passed the ugly boy grew up into an ugly youth, and before he knew it, into an ugly middle-aged man. At every stage of his life, people continued to turn and stare. Children would stare unabashedly at him. *When I become an ugly old man,* Ushikawa sometimes thought, *then maybe I won't attract so much attention.* But he wouldn't know for sure. Maybe he would end up the ugliest old man the world had ever seen.

At any rate, he was not equipped with the skills needed to blend into the background. And to make matters worse, Tengo knew what he looked like. If he was discovered hanging around outside Tengo's building, the whole operation would come crashing down.

In situations like this, Ushikawa normally hired someone from a PI agency. Ever since he was a lawyer, he had made use of these sorts of organizations, which mostly employed former policemen who were adept at digging up information, shadowing people, and conducting surveillance. But in this case, he didn't want to involve any outsiders. Things were too touchy, and a serious crime – murder – was involved.

Besides, Ushikawa wasn't even sure what he might gain by putting Tengo under surveillance.

What Ushikawa wanted was to make clear the *connection* between Tengo and Aomame, but he wasn't even sure what Aomame looked like. He had tried all sorts of methods but had yet to come up with a decent photo. Even Bat hadn't been able to obtain one. Ushikawa had looked at her high school graduation album, but in the class photo her face was tiny and somehow unnatural-looking, like a mask. In the photo of her company softball team she had on a wide-brimmed cap and her face was in shadow. So even if Aomame were to pass him on the street, he would have no way of knowing if it was really her. He knew she was nearly five feet six inches tall and had a trim body and good posture. Her eyes and cheekbones were distinctive, and she wore her hair down to her shoulders. But there were plenty of women in the world who fit that description.

So it looked like Ushikawa would have to undertake the surveillance by himself. He would have to keep his eyes open, patiently waiting for something to happen, and, when it did, instantly react. He couldn't ask someone else to handle such a delicate undertaking.

Tengo was living on the third floor of an old, three-story concrete apartment building. At the entrance was a row of mailboxes for all the residents, one of them with a name tag on it that said *Kawana*. Some of the mailboxes were rusty, the paint peeling off. They all had locks, but most of the residents left them unlatched. The front door of the building was unlocked, and anyone could go inside.

The dark corridor inside had that special odor you find in older apartment buildings. It is a peculiar mix of smells – of unrepaired leaks, old sheets washed in cheap detergent, stale tempura oil, a dried-up poinsettia, cat urine from the weed-filled front yard. Live there long enough and you would probably get used to the smell. But no matter how used to it you got, the fact remained that this was not a heartwarming odor.

Tengo's apartment faced the main road. It wasn't all that noisy, but there was a fair amount of foot traffic. An elementary school was nearby and at certain times of day there were large groups of children outside. Across from the building was a clump of small single-family homes, two-story houses with no garden. Just down the road were a liquor store and a stationery store catering to elementary school children. And two blocks farther down was a small police substation. There was nowhere to hide, and if he were to stand by the road and look up at Tengo's apartment – even if Tengo didn't discover him – the neighbors would be sure to cast a suspicious eye his way. And since he was such an *unusual*-looking character, the locals' alert level would be ratcheted up a couple of levels. He might be mistaken for a pervert waiting for the kids to get out of school, and neighbors might call the police.

In surveillance the first requirement is finding a suitable place from which to watch, a place to track your target's movements and maintain a steady supply of water and food. The ideal situation would be to have a room from which Ushikawa could see Tengo's apartment. He could set up a camera with a telephoto lens on a tripod and keep watch over movement in the apartment and who came in and out. Since he was alone on the assignment, twenty-four-hour coverage was impossible, but Ushikawa figured he could cover it for ten hours a day. Needless to say, however, finding a suitable place was going to be tricky.

Even so, Ushikawa walked the neighborhood, searching. He wasn't the type to give up easily. Tenaciousness was, after all, his forte. But after pounding the pavement of every nook and cranny of the neighborhood, Ushikawa called it quits. Koenji was a densely populated residential area, flat with no tall buildings. The number of places from which Tengo's apartment was visible was very limited, and there was not a single one he thought he could use.

Whenever Ushikawa had trouble coming up with a good idea, he liked to take a long, lukewarm soak in the tub, so he went back home and drew a bath. As he lay in the acrylic bathtub, he listened to Sibelius's violin concerto on the radio. He didn't particularly want to listen to Sibelius – and Sibelius's concerto wasn't exactly the right music to listen to at the end of a long day as you soaked in the tub. Perhaps, he mused, Finnish people liked to listen to Sibelius while in a sauna during their long nights. But in a tiny, one-unit bathroom of a two-bedroom condo in Kohinata, Bunkyo Ward, Sibelius's music was too emotional, too tense. Not that this bothered him – as long as there was some background music, he was fine. A concerto by Rameau would do just as well, nor would he have complained if it had been Schumann's *Carnaval*. The radio station just happened to be broadcasting Sibelius's violin concerto. That was all there was to it.

As usual, Ushikawa let half his mind go blank and thought with the other half. David Oistrakh's performance of Sibelius went through the blank half of his mind, like a gentle breeze wafting in through a wide-open entrance and out through a wide-open exit. Maybe it was not the most laudable way of appreciating music. If Sibelius knew his music was being treated this way, it was easy to imagine how those large eyebrows would frown, the folds of his thick neck coming together. But Sibelius had died long ago, and even Oistrakh had long since gone to his grave. So Ushikawa could do as he pleased and let the music filter from right to left, as the unblank half of his brain toyed with random thoughts.

In times like these, Ushikawa didn't like to have a set objective. He let his thoughts run free, as if he were releasing dogs on a broad plain. He would tell them to go wherever they wanted and do whatever they liked, and then he would just let them go. He sank down in the bathwater up to his neck, closed his eyes, and, half listening to the music, let his mind wander. The dogs frolicked around, rolled down slopes, gamboled after each other tirelessly, chased pointlessly after squirrels, then came back, covered in mud and grass, and Ushikawa patted their heads and fastened their collars back on. The music came to an end. Sibelius's violin concerto was a roughly thirty-minute piece – just the right length. The next piece, the announcer intoned, is Janáček's *Sinfonietta*. Ushikawa had a vague memory of hearing the name of the piece before, but he couldn't remember exactly. When he tried to recall, his vision turned strangely cloudy and indistinct, as if a cream-colored mist had settled over his eyeballs. He must have stayed too long in the bath, he decided. He gave up, switched off the radio, got out of the bathtub, wrapped a towel around his waist, and got a beer from the fridge.

Ushikawa lived by himself. He used to have a wife and two small daughters. They had bought a house in the Chuorinkan District in Yamato, in Kanagawa Prefecture. It was a small house, but they had a garden and a dog. His wife was good-looking enough, and his daughters were even pretty. Neither daughter had inherited anything of Ushikawa's looks, which was a great relief.

Then, like a sudden blackout on the stage between acts, he was alone. He found it hard to believe that there had ever been a time when he had a family and lived with them in a house in the suburbs. Sometimes he was even sure the whole thing must be a misunderstanding, that he had unconsciously fabricated this past for himself. But it had actually happened. He had actually had a wife he shared a bed with and two children who shared his bloodline. In his desk drawer, he had a family photo of the four of them. They were all smiling happily. Even the dog seemed to be grinning.

There was no likelihood that they would ever be a family again. His wife and daughters lived in Nagoya now. The girls had a new father, the kind of father with normal looks who wouldn't embarrass them when he showed up at parent-teacher conference day. The girls hadn't seen Ushikawa for nearly four years, but they didn't seem to regret this. They never even wrote to him. It didn't bother Ushikawa much either that he couldn't see his daughters. This didn't mean that his daughters weren't important to him. It was just that now his top priority was simply keeping himself secure, so for the time being he had to switch off any unnecessary emotional circuits and focus on the tasks at hand.

Plus, he knew this: that no matter how far away his daughters went from him, his blood still flowed inside them. His daughters might forget all about him, but that blood would not lose its way. Blood had a frighteningly long memory. And the sign of that large head would, sometime, somewhere in the future, reappear, in an unexpected time and unexpected place. When it did, people would sigh and remember that Ushikawa had once existed.

Ushikawa might be alive to witness this eruption, or perhaps not. It didn't really matter. He was satisfied just to know that it was *possible*. It wasn't like he was hoping for revenge. Rather, he felt content to know that he was, unavoidably, an inherent part of the world's structure.

He sat down on his sofa, plopped his stubby legs up on the table, and, as he sipped his beer, a thought suddenly came to him. *It might not work out,* he thought, *but it was worth trying. It's so simple – why hadn't it occurred to me?* he wondered, finding it odd. *Maybe the easiest things are the hardest to come up with. Like they say, people miss what's going on right under their noses.*

The next morning Ushikawa went to Koenji again. He saw a real estate agency, went inside, and asked if there were any apartments available for rent in Tengo's building. But this agency didn't handle that building. All rentals in that apartment building were handled by an agency in front of the station.

"I sort of doubt there are any units available," the agent said. "The rent is reasonable, and it's a convenient location, so few people move out."

"Well, I'll ask anyway, just to make sure," Ushikawa said.

He stopped by the agency in front of the station. A young man in his early twenties was the one who dealt with him. The man had jet-black hair, hardened with gel to the consistency of a bird's nest. He wore a bright white shirt and a brand-new tie. He probably hadn't been working there long. He still had marks from pimples on his cheeks. The man flinched a bit when he looked at Ushikawa, but soon recovered and gave him a pleasant, professional smile.

"You're in luck, sir," the young man said. "The couple on the first floor had some family issues that arose and they had to move out quickly, so one of the units has been vacant for a week. We finished cleaning it yesterday but haven't advertised it yet. It's on the first floor so it might be a bit noisy, and it doesn't get a lot of sun, but it's a wonderful location. There is one condition of the contract, however: in five or six years the owner plans to completely rebuild the place, so when you receive notice of that renovation six months ahead of time, you'll need to move out, with no complaints. Plus, there's no parking lot there."

"Not a problem," Ushikawa replied. He didn't plan to stay there that long, and he didn't have a car.

"Excellent. If you agree to those conditions, then you can move in at once. I imagine you would like to see the apartment first?"

"Yes, of course," Ushikawa replied. The young man took a key out of a desk drawer and passed it to him.

"I'm very sorry, but I have an errand to run, so if you don't mind, could you check out the place by yourself? The apartment is empty, and all you need to do is drop off the key on your way back."

"That sounds fine," Ushikawa said, "but what if I'm some evil man who never gives the key back, or makes a copy and sneaks in later to ransack the place? What would you do then?"

The young man stared in surprise at Ushikawa for a time. "Yes, good point. I see. Just to be on the safe side, could you give me a card?"

Ushikawa took out one of his New Japan Foundation for the Advancement of Scholarship and the Arts business cards and handed it to him.

"Mr. Ushikawa," the young man frowned as he read the name. But then he looked relieved. "You don't look to me like someone who would do something bad."

"Much appreciated," Ushikawa replied. And he smiled, a smile as meaningless as the title listed on his card.

No one had ever told him this before. Maybe it meant his looks were too unusual for him to ever do anything bad. It would be too easy for anyone to describe him, and a simple matter to draw a police sketch. If a warrant were issued for his arrest, he wouldn't last three days.

The apartment was nicer than he had imagined. Tengo's third-floor apartment was two stories directly above, so it was impossible to observe his place. But the front entrance was visible from his window so he could see when Tengo entered and exited the building, and spot anyone visiting him. He could just camouflage a telephoto lens and take pictures of each person's face.

In order to rent this apartment he had to pay two months' security deposit: one month's rent up front, plus a fee equivalent to the second month's rent. The rent itself wasn't that high, and the security deposit would be returned when the lease was up, but still, this all came to a hefty sum. Having just paid Bat, his resources were severely depleted, but he knew he had to rent that apartment. There was no other choice. Ushikawa went back to the real estate agency, took out the cash he had already prepared in an envelope, and signed the lease. The lease was with the New Japan Foundation for the Advancement of Scholarship and the Arts. He told them he would mail them a certified copy of the foundation's registry later. This didn't seem to faze the young real estate agent. Once the lease was signed, the agent again handed him the keys.

"Mr. Ushikawa, the apartment is ready for you to move in today. The electricity and water are on, but you will have to be present when they turn on the gas, so please contact Tokyo Gas yourself. What will you do about a phone?"

"I'll handle that myself," Ushikawa said. It took a lot of time and effort to get a contract with the phone company, and a workman would have to come to the apartment to install it. It was easier to use a nearby pay phone.

Ushikawa went back to the apartment and drew up a list of items he would be needing. Thankfully the previous resident had left the curtains up. They were old, flowery curtains, but as long as they were curtains, he felt lucky to have them. Curtains of some kind were indispensable to a stakeout.

The list of necessary items wasn't all that long. The main things he would need were food and drinking water, a camera with a telephoto lens, and a tripod. The rest of his list included toilet paper, a heavy-duty sleeping bag, portable kerosene containers, a camping stove, a sharp knife, a can opener, garbage bags, basic toiletries, and an electric razor, several towels, a flashlight, and a transistor radio. The minimal amount of clothes and a carton of cigarettes. That was about it. No need for a fridge, a table, or bedding. As long as he had a place to keep out of the weather, he considered himself lucky. Ushikawa returned to his own house and put a single reflex and a telephoto lens in a camera bag, as well as an ample amount of film. He then stuffed all the items on his list into a travel bag. He bought the additional things he still needed in the shopping district in front of Koenji Station.

He set up his tripod next to the window, attached the latest Minolta automatic camera to it, screwed on the telephoto lens, aimed it at the level of the faces of anyone who came in or exited the building, and set the camera to manual. He made it so he could use a remote control to work the shutter and set the motor drive. He fashioned a cardboard cone to go around the lens so that light wouldn't reflect off the lens. From the outside, part of a paper tube was visible at one end of the slightly raised curtain, but no one would ever notice it. No one would ever imagine that someone was secretly photographing the entrance of such a nondescript apartment building.

Ushikawa took a few test shots of people coming in and out of the building. Because of the motor drive he was able to get three quick shots of each person. As a precaution he wrapped a towel around the body of the camera to muffle any noise. As soon as he finished the first roll, he took it to the photo store next to the station. The clerk placed it in a machine that would automatically develop and print the photos. It handled great numbers of photos at high speed, so no one ever noticed or cared about the images printed on them.

The photos came out fine – not very artistic, to be sure, but service-able. The faces of the people entering and exiting the building were clear enough to distinguish one from another. On the way back from the photo shop, Ushikawa bought some mineral water and several cans of food. And he bought a carton of Seven Stars at a smoke shop. Holding his bags of purchases in front of him to hide his face, he returned to the apartment and sat down again in front of the camera. As he kept watch over the entrance he drank some water, ate canned peaches, and smoked a couple of cigarettes. The electricity was on, but for some reason not the water. When he turned on the tap there was a rumbling sound in the wall, but nothing came out. Something had to be holding them up from turning on the water. He thought of contacting the real estate agent, but, wanting to limit his trips in and out of the building, he decided to wait and see. No running water meant he couldn't use the toilet, so instead he peed into an old bucket the cleaning company had conveniently forgotten to take away.

The impatient early-winter twilight came quickly and the room grew totally dark, but still he didn't turn on the lights. Ushikawa rather welcomed the darkness. The light came on at the entrance and he continued to survey the faces that passed by under the yellowish light.

As evening came, the foot traffic into and out of the building increased a bit, though the number of people was still not that great. It was, after all, a small apartment building. Tengo was not among them, and neither was anyone who could possibly be Aomame. Tengo was scheduled to teach at the cram school today. He would be coming back in the evening. He didn't usually stop off anywhere on the way home after work. He preferred to make his own dinner rather than eat out, and he liked to eat alone while reading. Ushikawa knew all this. But Tengo didn't come home. Perhaps he was meeting someone after work.

A variety of people lived in the building, everyone from young, single working people, to college students, to couples with small children, to elderly people living alone – people from all walks of life. But all of them entered the frame of the lens, unaware they were under surveillance. Despite some differences in age and circumstances, every one of them looked worn out, tired of life. They appeared hopeless, abandoned by ambition, their emotions worn away, with only resignation and numbness filling the void left behind. As if they had just had a tooth pulled, their faces were dark, their steps heavy.

But he may have been mistaken. Some of them may have actually been enjoying life to the fullest. Once they opened their doors, there was some breathtaking little paradise waiting just for them. Perhaps some of them were pretending to live a Spartan life to avoid getting audited by the Tax Bureau. This was possible. But through the telephoto lens, they all looked like dead-end city dwellers not going anywhere in life, clinging to a cheap apartment scheduled to be torn down.

That night Tengo didn't make an appearance and Ushikawa saw no one who could be connected to him. When ten thirty rolled around, he decided to call it a day. He hadn't quite settled into a routine and didn't want to push it. *There will be many days to come,* he decided, *so this is enough for now.* He did a variety of stretches to loosen his stiff muscles, then ate a sweet *anpan* bun, poured coffee from his thermos into the cap, and drank it. He tried the faucet in the sink, and now the water was running. He washed his face with soap, brushed his teeth, and took a good, long pee. He leaned back against the wall and smoked a cigarette. He longed for a sip of whiskey, but he had decided that as long as he was here, he wouldn't touch a drop of alcohol.

He stripped to his underwear and snuggled into the sleeping bag. The cold made him tremble slightly. At night the empty apartment was unexpectedly chilly. He thought he might need a small electric space heater.

As he lay shivering, alone in the sleeping bag, he recalled the days when he had been surrounded by his family. He didn't particularly miss those days. His life now was so completely different that these memories merely popped up to illustrate that fact. Even when he was living with his family, Ushikawa had felt lonely. He never opened up to anyone and thought that his ordinary life would never last. Deep down he was convinced that one day it would all too easily fall apart – his busy days as a lawyer, his generous income, his nice house in Chuorinkan, his not-bad-looking wife, his cute daughters, both attending private elementary school, his pedigreed dog. So when his life steadily fell apart bit by bit and he was left all alone, he was actually relieved. *Thank God,* he thought. *Nothing to worry about now. I'm back right where I started.*

Is this what it means to go back to square one?

He curled up like a maggot in the sleeping bag and stared at the dark ceiling. He had sat in the same position for too long and his joints ached. Shivering in the cold, making do with a cold bun for dinner, standing watch over the entrance of a cheap apartment that was ready to be torn down, watching the unattractive people coming in and out, peeing into a wash bucket. *Is this what it means to go back to square one?* he asked again. He remembered something he had forgotten to do. He crawled out of the sleeping bag, poured the urine in the bucket into the toilet, pushed the wobbly handle, and flushed it down. The sleeping bag had just started to warm up, and he had hesitated to get out. *Just leave it,* he had thought – but if he happened to slip in the dark he would regret it. Afterward he crawled back into the sleeping bag and shivered in the cold again.

Is this what it means to go back to square one?

Most likely. He had nothing left to lose, other than his life. It was all very clear-cut. In the darkness, a razor-thin smile came to Ushikawa's lips.

14

AOMAME

This Little One of Mine

FOR THE MOST PART, AOMAME'S LIFE had become filled with confusion. She felt as though she were blindly groping around in the dark. Ordinary logic and reason didn't function in this 1Q84 world, and she couldn't predict what was going to happen to her next. She felt sure, though, that she would survive the next few months and give birth to the baby. This was nothing more than a hunch, though a strong one. Everything was proceeding on the premise that she would give birth to this child. She could just sense it.

She remembered the last words that Leader had spoken. "You are fated to pass through great hardships and trials," he had said. "Once you have done that, you should be able to see things as they are supposed to be."

He *knew* something. Something vital. *And he had tried – in vague and ambiguous terms – to give me this message,* Aomame thought. *The hardship he spoke of may have been when I took myself to the brink of death, when I took the pistol to that spot in front of the Esso sign, meaning*

*to kill myself. But I came back, without dying, and discovered I was
pregnant. This, too, might have been preordained.*

As they entered December, the winds grew fierce for a few days.
The fallen zelkova leaves whipped against the plastic screen on the
balcony with a dry, biting sound. The cold wind let out a warning as
it whistled between the bare branches of the trees. The caws of the
crows grew sharper, keener. Winter had arrived.

Every day, she became even more convinced that the baby growing in
her womb was Tengo's child, until this theory became an established
fact. It wasn't logical enough to convince a third party, but it made
sense to her. It was obvious.

**If I'm pregnant without having had sex, who could the man
possibly be other than Tengo?**

In November she had begun putting on weight. She couldn't go
outside, but she more than made up for it by continuing to work out
and strictly watching her diet. After age twenty she never weighed
more than 115 pounds. But one day the scale showed she weighed 119,
and after that her weight never dropped below it. She felt like her face,
too, had rounded out. No doubt this *little one* wanted its mother to
plump up.

Together with this *little one* she continued to keep watch over the
playground at night, hoping to spot the silhouette of a large young
man sitting alone on the slide. As she gazed at the two moons, lined
up side by side in the early-winter sky, Aomame rubbed her belly
through the blanket. Occasionally tears would well up for no reason.
She would find a tear rolling down her cheek and falling to the blanket
on her lap. Maybe it was because she was lonely, or because she was
anxious. Or maybe pregnancy had made her more sensitive. Or maybe
it was merely the cold wind stimulating the tear ducts to produce
tears. Whatever the reason, Aomame let the tears flow without wiping
them away.

Once she had cried for a while, at a certain point the tears would stop, and she would continue her lonely vigil. *No,* she thought, *I'm not that lonely. I have this* little one *with me. There are two of us – two of us looking up at the two moons, waiting for Tengo to appear.* From time to time she would pick up her binoculars and focus on the deserted slide. Then she would pick up the automatic pistol to check its heft and what it felt like. *Protecting myself, searching for Tengo, and providing this* little one *with nourishment. Those are my duties now.*

One time, as the cold wind blew and she kept watch over the playground, Aomame realized she believed in God. It was a sudden discovery, like finding, with the soles of your feet, solid ground beneath the mud. It was a mysterious sensation, an unexpected awareness. Ever since she could remember, she had always hated this thing called God. More precisely, she rejected the people and the system that intervened between her and God. For years she had equated those people and that system with God. Hating them meant hating God.

Since the moment she was born *they* had been near her, controlling her, ordering her around, all in the name of God, driving her into a corner. In the name of God, they stole her time and her freedom, putting shackles on her heart. They preached about God's kindness, but preached twice as much about his wrath and intolerance. At age eleven, Aomame made up her mind and was ultimately able to break free from that world. In doing so, though, much had been sacrificed.

If God didn't exist, then how much brighter my life would be, how much richer. Aomame often thought this. Then she should be able to share all the beautiful memories that normal children had, without the constant anger and fear that tormented her. And then how much more positive, peaceful, and fulfilling her life might be.

Despite all this, as she sat there, her palm resting on her belly, peeking through the slats of the plastic boards at the deserted playground, she couldn't help but come to the realization that she believed in God. When she had mechanically repeated the words of the prayer, when she brought her hands together, she had believed in a God outside the conscious realm. It was a feeling that had seeped into her marrow, something that could not be driven away by logic or emotion. Even hatred and anger couldn't erase it.

But this isn't their God, she decided. *It's my God. This is a God I have found through sacrificing my own life, through my flesh being cut, my skin ripped off, my blood sucked away, my nails torn, all my time and hopes and memories being stolen from me. This is not a God with a form. No white clothes, no long beard. This God has no doctrine, no scripture, no precepts. No reward, no punishment. This God doesn't give, and doesn't take away. There is no heaven up in the sky, no hell down below. When it's hot, and when it's cold, God is simply* there.

From time to time, she would recall Leader's final words before he died. She could never forget his rich baritone. Just like she could never forget the feeling of stabbing a needle into the back of his neck.

Where there is light, there must be shadow, where there is shadow, there must be light. There is no shadow without light and no light without shadow. . . . We do not know if the so-called Little People are good or evil. This is, in a sense, something that surpasses our understanding and our definitions. We have lived with them since long, long ago – from a time before good and evil even existed, when people's minds were still benighted.

Are God and the Little People opposites? Or two sides of the same thing?
Aomame had no idea. What she did know was that she had to protect this *little one* inside her. And to do so it became necessary to somehow believe in God. Or to recognize the fact that she believed in God.

Aomame pondered the idea of God. God has no form, yet is able to take on any form. The image she had was of a streamlined Mercedes coupe, a brand-new car just delivered from the dealer. An elegant, middle-aged woman coming out of that car, in the middle of an expressway running through the city, offering her beautiful spring coat to the naked Aomame. To protect her from the chilly wind, and people's rude stares. And then, without a word, getting back in her silver coupe. The woman knew – that Aomame had a baby within her. That Aomame had to be protected.

She began to have a new dream. In the dream she is imprisoned in a white room. A small, cube-shaped room, no windows, a single door. A plain bed, no frills, on which she lies sleeping, faceup. A light hanging over the bed illuminates her hugely swollen belly. It doesn't look like her own body, but it is definitely a part of Aomame's flesh. It is getting close to the time for the baby's delivery.

The room is guarded by Buzzcut and Ponytail. The duo is dead set against making any more errors. They made a mistake once and they need to recover their reputation. Their assignment is to make sure that Aomame does not leave this room, and that no one enters. They wait for the birth of the *little one*. It seems they plan to snatch it away from Aomame the moment it is born.

Aomame calls out, desperately seeking help. But this room is built of special material. The walls, floor, and ceiling immediately absorb any sound. She can't even hear her own scream. Aomame prays that the woman in the Mercedes coupe will come and rescue her – her and the *little one*. But her voice is sucked, in vain, into the walls of that white room.

The *little one* absorbs nourishment through its umbilical cord, and is growing larger by the minute. Hoping to break out of that lukewarm darkness, it kicks against the walls of her womb. Hoping for light, and freedom.

Tall Ponytail sits in a chair beside the door, hands in his lap, staring at a point in space. Perhaps a small, dense cloud is floating there. Buzzcut stands next to the bed. They wear the same dark suits as before. Buzzcut raises his arm from time to time to glance at his watch, like somebody waiting for an important train to pull into the station.

Aomame can't move her arms and legs. It doesn't feel like she is tied down, but still she can't move. There is no feeling in her fingers. She has a premonition that her labor pains are about to begin. Like that fateful train drawing nearer to the station, exactly on schedule. She can hear the slight vibration of the rails as it gets closer.

And then she wakes up.

She took a shower to wash off the sweat and changed clothes. She tossed her sweaty clothes into the washer. There was no way she wanted to have this dream, but it came upon her anyway. The details sometimes changed, but the place and outcome were always the same: the cube-shaped white room, the approaching labor pains, the duo in their bland, dark suits.

The two men knew she was pregnant with the *little one* – or they were going to find out. Aomame was prepared. If need be, she would have no problem pumping all the 9mm bullets she had into Ponytail and Buzzcut. The God that protected her was also, at times, a bloody God.

A knock came at the door. Aomame sat down on a stool in the kitchen and gripped the automatic pistol tight, the safety off. Outside a cold rain had been falling since morning. The world was enveloped in the smell of winter rain.

The knocks stopped. "Hello, Miss Takai," a man's voice said on the other side of the door. "It's me, your friendly NHK collector. Sorry to bother you again, but I'm back to collect the subscription fee. I know you're there, Miss Takai."

Aomame faced the door and silently spoke. We called NHK and asked about this. You're nothing but someone posing as an NHK man. Who *are* you? And what do you want here?

"When people receive things, they have to pay for them. That's the way the world works. You receive a TV signal, so you have to pay the fee. Receiving without paying isn't fair. It's the same as stealing."

His voice echoed loudly in the hallway. A hoarse, but piercing voice.

"My personal feelings are not involved in this at all. I don't hate you, and I'm not trying to punish you whatsoever. It's just that I can't stand when things are unfair. People have to pay for what they receive. Miss Takai, as long as you don't open up, I'll be back again and again to bang on your door. And I don't think that's what you want. I'm not some unreasonable old coot. If we talk, I'm sure we can come to an understanding. So would you be kind enough to open the door?"

The knocking continued.

Aomame gripped the pistol tighter. *This man must know I'm having a baby.* A thin sheen of sweat formed under her arms and on the tip of her nose. *I am never going to open this door. He can try to use a duplicate key, or try to force it open, but if he does I'm going to empty this entire clip into his belly – NHK collector or not.*

No, that probably wouldn't happen. And she knew it. He couldn't open the door. As long as she didn't open it from the inside, the door was set up so it couldn't be opened. Which is why the man got so irritated and voluble, using every verbal trick in the book trying to make her tense and on edge.

Ten minutes later, the man left. But only after he had, in a thunderous voice, threatened and ridiculed her, slyly tried to win her over to his side, denounced her in no uncertain terms, and finally announced he would be back to pay her another visit.

"You can't escape, Miss Takai. As long as you get the TV signal I will be back. I'm not the kind of man who gives up so easily. That's just my personality. Well, we will be seeing each other again very soon."

She didn't hear his footsteps, but he was no longer standing outside the door. Aomame peeked through the peephole to make sure. She set the safety on the pistol and washed her face in the sink. Her armpits were soaked. As she changed to a fresh shirt she stood, naked, in front of the mirror. Her stomach still wasn't showing enough to notice, but she knew an important secret lay hidden within.

She spoke to the dowager on the phone. After Tamaru had gone over a few points with her, he handed the phone to the dowager without a word. They used a roundabout way of speaking, avoiding any clear-cut terms. At least at first.

"We have already secured a new place for you," the dowager said. "There you can perform the *task you've been planning on.* It's a safe place and you can get checked out regularly by a specialist. If you're willing, you can move there as soon as you would like."

Should she tell the dowager about the people who were after her little one? *How in her dreams the guys from Sakigake were trying to get hold of her child? How the phony NHK collector using all his wiles to get her to open the door was probably after the same thing?* But Aomame gave up the idea. She trusted the dowager, and respected her deeply. But that wasn't the issue. *Which world was she living in?* For the time being, that was the point.

"How have you been feeling?" the dowager asked.

"Everything seems to be going well so far," Aomame replied.

"I'm very glad to hear it," the dowager said. "But your voice seems different somehow. Maybe I'm just imagining things, but you sound a little tense and guarded. If there's anything that's bothering you, anything at all, please don't hesitate to tell us. We might be able to help you."

"I think being in one place for so long has made me anxious, maybe, without my even realizing it. But I'm taking good care of myself. That's my field, after all," Aomame replied, careful with her tone of voice.

"Of course," the dowager responded. She paused again. "A little while ago a suspicious man was hanging around our place for a couple of days. He seemed mainly interested in checking out the safe house. I asked the three women staying there to look at the pictures on our security cameras, but none of them recognized him. It might be somebody who's after you."

Aomame frowned slightly. "You mean they've figured out our connection?"

"I'm not sure about that. We're at the point where we *need to consider* that possibility, though. This man looks quite unusual. He has a big, misshapen head. The top is flat, and he's balding. He's short, with stubby arms and legs, and stocky. Does that sound at all familiar?"

A misshapen head? "From the balcony I keep a close eye on the people walking down the street, but I've never seen anyone that fits that description. He sounds like the kind of person you couldn't miss."

"Exactly. He sounds like a colorful circus clown. If he's the one *they* selected and sent to check us out, I would say it's an odd choice."

Aomame agreed. Sakigake wouldn't deliberately send a person who stood out like that to reconnoiter. They couldn't be that desperate for help. Which meant that the man probably had nothing to do with the religion, and that Sakigake still didn't know about her relationship with the dowager. But then who was this man, and what was he doing checking out the safe house? Maybe he was the same man who pretended to be an NHK fee collector and kept on bothering her? She had no proof. She had just mentally linked the fee collector's eccentric manner and the description of this other weird man.

"If you see him, please get in touch. We may have to take steps."

"Of course I will get in touch right away," Aomame replied.

The dowager was silent again. This was rather unusual, for usually when they talked on the phone she was quite no-nonsense, and hated to waste any time.

"Are you well?" Aomame asked casually.

"The same as always. I have no complaints," the dowager said. But Aomame could hear a faint hesitation in her voice – something else that was unusual.

Aomame waited for her to continue.

Finally, as if resigned to it, the dowager spoke. "It's just that recently I feel old more often than I used to. Especially after you left."

"I never left," Aomame said brightly. "I'm still here."

"I know. You're there and we can still speak on the phone. It's just that when we were able to meet regularly and exercise together, some of your vitality rubbed off on me."

"You have a lot of your own vitality to begin with. All I did was help bring it out. Even if I'm not there, you should be able to make it on your own."

"To tell you the truth, I thought the same thing until a while ago," the dowager said, giving a laugh that was best characterized as dry. "I was confident that I was a special person. But time slowly chips away at life. People don't just die when their time comes. They gradually die away, from the inside. And finally the day comes when you have to settle accounts. Nobody can escape it. People have to pay the price for what they've received. I have only just learned that truth."

You have to pay the price for what you've received. Aomame frowned. It was the same line that the NHK collector had spoken.

"On that night in September, when there was the huge thunderstorm, this thought suddenly came to me," the dowager said. "I was in my house, alone in the living room, anxious about you, watching the flashes of lightning. And a flash of lightning lit up this truth for me, right in front of my eyes. That night I lost you, I also lost something inside me. Or perhaps several things. Something central to my existence, the very support for who I am as a person."

"Was anger a part of this?" Aomame ventured.

There was a silence, like after the tide had gone out. Finally the dowager spoke. "You mean was my anger among the things I lost then? Is that what you're asking?"

"Yes."

The dowager slowly breathed in. "The answer to your question is – yes. That's what happened. In the midst of that tremendous lightning, the seething anger I had had was suddenly gone – at least, it had retreated far away. It was no longer the blazing anger I used to have. It had transformed into something more like a faintly colored sorrow. I thought such an intense anger would last forever. . . . But how do you know this?"

"Because the same thing happened to me," Aomame said, "that night when there was all that thunder."

"You're talking about your own anger?"

"That's right. I can't feel the pure, intense anger I used to have anymore. It hasn't completely disappeared, but like you said, it has withdrawn to someplace far away. For years this anger has occupied a large part of me. It's been what has driven me."

"Like a merciless coachman who never rests," the dowager said. "But it has lost power, and now you are pregnant. Instead of being angry."

Aomame calmed her breathing. "Exactly. Instead of anger, there's a *little one* inside me. Something that has nothing to do with anger. And day by day it is growing inside me."

"I know I don't need to say this," the dowager said, "but you need to take every precaution with it. That is another reason you need to move as soon as possible to a more secure location."

"I agree, but before that happens, there's something I need to take care of."

After she hung up, Aomame went out to the balcony, looked down through the plastic slats at the afternoon road below, and gazed at the playground. Twilight was fast approaching. *Before 1Q84 is over,* she thought, *before they find me, I have to find Tengo.*

No matter what it takes.

15

TENGO

Not Something
He's Allowed to Talk About

TENGO LEFT THE BAR, MUGIATAMA, AND wandered the streets, lost in thought. Eventually, he made up his mind and headed toward the small children's playground – the place where he had first discovered two moons in the sky. *I will climb the slide like last time,* he thought, *and look up at the sky once more.* He might be able to see the moons from there again. And they might tell him something.

As he walked, he wondered when exactly he had last visited the playground. He couldn't recall. The flow of time wasn't uniform anymore, the sense of distance uncertain. But it probably had been in the early autumn. He remembered wearing a long-sleeved T-shirt. And now it was December.

A cold wind was blowing the mass of clouds off toward Tokyo Bay. The free-form clouds looked stiff and hard, as if made of putty. The two moons were visible, occasionally hiding behind the clouds. The familiar yellow moon, and the new, smaller green moon, both of them past full, about two-thirds size. The smaller moon was like a child hiding in its mother's skirts. The moons were in almost the same location as the time he saw them before, as if they had been patiently waiting for Tengo's return.

There was no one else in the playground. The mercury-vapor lamp shone brighter than before, a cold, harsh light. The bare branches of the zelkova tree reminded him of ancient white bones. It was the sort of night when you would expect to hear an owl. But there were no owls to be found in the city's parks. Tengo tugged the hood of his yacht parka over his head and stuck his hands in the pockets of his leather jacket. He climbed up the slide, leaned against the handrail, and gazed up at the two moons as they appeared, then disappeared, among the clouds. Beyond that, the stars twinkled silently. The amorphous filth that hangs over the city was blown away in the wind, leaving the air pure and clear.

Right now, how many people besides me have noticed these two moons? Tengo considered this. Fuka-Eri knew about it, because this was something that she initiated. Most likely. Other than her, though, nobody he knew had mentioned that the number of moons had increased. Have people not noticed? Or they don't dare to bring it up in conversation? Is it just common knowledge? Either way, other than the friend who filled in for him at the cram school, Tengo hadn't asked anybody about the moons. Actually, he had been careful not to bring it up in conversation, like it was some morally inappropriate subject.

Why?

Perhaps the moons wanted it that way, Tengo thought. *Maybe these two moons are a special message meant just for me, and I am not permitted to share this information with anyone else.*

But this was a strange way to see it. Why would the number of moons be a personal message? And what could they be trying to tell him? To Tengo it seemed less a message than a kind of complicated riddle. And if it's a riddle, then who made it? Who's *not permitting* things?

The wind rushed between the branches of the zelkova tree, making a piercing howl, like the coldhearted breath leaking out between the teeth of a person who has lost all hope. Tengo gazed at the moons, not paying much attention to the sound of the wind, sitting there until his whole body was chilled to the bone. It must have been around fifteen minutes. No, maybe more. His sense of time had left him. His body, initially warmed by the whiskey, now felt hard and cold, like a lonely boulder at the bottom of the sea.

The clouds continued to scud off toward the south. No matter how many were blown away, others appeared to take their place. There was an inexhaustible source of clouds in some land far to the north. Decisive people, minds fixed on the task, clothed in thick, gray uniforms, working silently from morning to night to make clouds, like bees make honey, spiders make webs, and war makes widows.

Tengo looked at his watch. It was almost eight. The playground was still deserted. Occasionally people would walk by quickly on the street in front. People who have finished work and are on the way home all walk the same way. In the new six-story apartment building on the other side of the street the lights were on in half the units. On windy winter nights, a window with a light shining in it acquires a gentle warmth. Tengo looked from one lit window to the next, in order, like looking up at a huge luxury cruise liner from a tiny fishing boat bobbing in the night sea. As if by prearrangement, all the curtains at the windows were closed. Seen from a freezing-cold slide in a park at night, they looked like a totally different world – a world founded on different principles, a world that ran by different rules. Beyond those curtains there must be people living their quite ordinary lives, peaceful and content.

Quite ordinary lives?

The only image that Tengo had of *quite ordinary lives* was stereotypical, lacking depth and color. A married couple, probably with two kids. The mother has on an apron. Steam rising from a bubbling pot, voices around the dining table – that's as far as his imagination took him before plowing into a solid wall. What would a *quite ordinary* family talk about around the dinner table? He had no memory himself of ever talking with his father at the dinner table. They each just stuffed food into their mouths, silently, whenever they felt like it. And what they ate was hard to call a real meal.

After checking out all the illuminated windows in the building, Tengo again looked up at the pair of moons. But no matter how long he waited, neither moon said anything to him. Their faces were expressionless as they floated in the sky beside each other, like a precarious couplet in need of reworking. Today there was no message. That was the only thing they conveyed to Tengo.

The clouds swept tirelessly toward the south. All sizes and shapes of clouds appeared, then disappeared. Some of them had very unusual shapes, as if they had their own unique thoughts – small, hard, clearly etched thoughts. But Tengo wanted to know what the moons were thinking, not the clouds.

He finally gave up and stood, stretching his arms and legs, then climbed down from the slide. *That's all I can do. I was able to see that the number of moons hasn't changed, and I will leave it at that for now.* He stuck his hands in the pockets of his leather jacket, left the playground, and strode back to his apartment. As he walked he suddenly thought of Komatsu. It was about time for them to talk. He had to sort out, even if just barely, what had transpired between them. And Komatsu, too, had some things he must need to talk to Tengo about. Tengo had left the number of the sanatorium in Chikura with Komatsu's office, but he had never heard from him. He would give Komatsu a call tomorrow. Before that, though, he needed to go to the cram school and read the letter that Fuka-Eri had left for him.

Fuka-Eri's letter was in his desk drawer, unopened. For such a tightly sealed envelope, it was a short letter. On a page and a half of notebook paper, in blue ink, was her writing, that distinctive cuneiform-like script, the kind of writing that would be more appropriate on a clay tablet than notebook paper. Tengo knew it must have taken her a long time to write like that.

Tengo read the letter over and over. She *had to get out of* his place. *Right this minute,* she had written, because they were being *watched.* She had underlined these three places with a soft, thick pencil. Terribly eloquent underlining.

Who was watching us, and *how* she knew this – about this she said nothing. In the world that Fuka-Eri lived in, it seemed that facts were not conveyed directly. Like a map showing buried pirate treasure, things had to be connected through hints and riddles, ellipses and variations. He had grown used to it and, for the time being, provisionally, accepted whatever Fuka-Eri announced. When she said that they were being *watched,* no doubt they actually were being watched. When she felt that she *had to get out,* that meant the time had come for her to leave. The first thing to do was to accept all those statements as one comprehensive fact. Later on he could discover, or surmise, the background, the details, the basis for these hypotheses – or else just give up on it from the very beginning.

We're being watched.

Did this mean people from Sakigake had found Fuka-Eri? They knew about his relationship with her. They had uncovered the fact that he was the one, at Komatsu's request, who rewrote *Air Chrysalis,* which would explain why Ushikawa tried to get closer to Tengo. And if that was true, then there was a distinct possibility his apartment was under surveillance.

If this was true, though, they were really taking their time. Fuka-Eri had settled down in his apartment for nearly three months. These were organized people, people with real power and influence. If they had wanted to, they could have grabbed her anytime. There was no need to go to all the trouble of putting his apartment under surveillance. And if they really were watching her, they wouldn't let her just leave.

The more Tengo tried to follow the logic of it, the more confused he got. All he concluded was that *they weren't trying to grab Fuka-Eri*. Maybe at a certain point they had changed objectives. They weren't after Fuka-Eri, but someone connected to her. For some reason they no longer viewed Fuka-Eri as a threat to Sakigake. If you accept that, though, then why go to the trouble of putting Tengo's apartment under surveillance?

Tengo used the pay phone at the cram school to call Komatsu's office. It was Sunday, but Tengo knew that he liked to come in and work on the weekend. The office could be a nice place, he liked to say, if there was nobody else there. But no one answered. Tengo glanced at his watch. It was eleven a.m., too early for Komatsu to show up at work. He started his day, and it didn't matter what day of the week it was, after the sun had reached its zenith. Tengo, on a chair in the cafeteria, sipped the weak coffee and reread the letter from Fuka-Eri. As always she used hardly any kanji at all, and no paragraphs or punctuation.

Tengo you are back from the cat town and are reading this letter that's good but we're being *watched* so I *have to get out* of this place *right this minute* do not worry about me but I can't stay here any longer as I said before the person you are looking for is within walking distance of here but be careful not to let somebody see you

Tengo read this telegram-like letter again three times, then folded it and put it in his pocket. As before, the more he read it, the more believable her words became. He was being watched by someone. Now he accepted this as a certainty. He looked up and scanned the cram school cafeteria. Class was in session so the cafeteria was nearly deserted. A handful of students were there, studying textbooks or writing in their notebooks. But he didn't spot anyone in the shadows stealthily spying on him.

A basic question remained: If they weren't watching Fuka-Eri, then why would there be surveillance here? Were they interested in Tengo himself, or was it his apartment? Tengo considered this. This was all at the level of conjecture. Somehow, he didn't feel he was the object of their interest. His role in *Air Chrysalis* was long past.

Fuka-Eri had barely taken a step out of his apartment, so her sense that she was being *watched* meant that his apartment was under surveillance. But where could somebody keep his place under watch? The area where he lived was a crowded urban neighborhood, but Tengo's third-floor apartment was, oddly enough, situated so that it was almost out of anyone's line of sight. That was one of the reasons he liked the place and had lived there so long. His older girlfriend had liked the apartment for the same reason. "Putting aside how the place looks," she often said, "it's amazingly tranquil. Much like the person who lives here."

Just before the sun set each day, a large crow would fly over to his window. This was the crow Fuka-Eri had talked about on the phone. It settled in the window box and rubbed its large, jet-black wings against the glass. This was part of the crow's daily routine, to rest for a spell outside his apartment before homing back to its nest. This crow seemed to be curious about the interior of Tengo's apartment. The large, inky eyes on either side of its head shifted swiftly, gathering information through a gap in the curtain. Crows are highly intelligent animals, and extremely curious. Fuka-Eri claimed to be able to talk with this crow. Still, it was ridiculous to think that a crow could be somebody's tool to reconnoiter Tengo's apartment.

So how were they watching him?

On the way home from the station Tengo stopped by a supermarket and bought some vegetables, eggs, milk, and fish. Standing at the entrance to his building, paper bag in hand, he glanced all around just to make sure. Nothing looked suspicious, the same scene as always – the electric lines hanging in the air like dark entrails; the small front yard, its lawn withered in the winter cold; the rusty mailboxes. He listened carefully, but all he could hear was the distinctive, incessant background noise of the city, like the faint hum of wings.

He went into his apartment, put away the food, then went over to the window, drew back the curtains, and inspected the scene outside. Across the road were three old houses, two-story homes built on minuscule lots. The owners were all long-term, elderly residents, people with crabby expressions who loathed any kind of change, so they weren't about to welcome a newcomer to their second floor. Plus, even if someone was on the second floor and leaned way out the window, all they would be able to see was a glimpse of his ceiling.

Tengo closed the window, boiled water, and made coffee. As he sat at the dining table and drank it, he considered every scenario he could think of. Someone nearby was keeping him under watch. And Aomame was (or *had been*) within walking distance. Was there some connection between the two? Or was it all mere coincidence? He thought long and hard, but he couldn't reach a conclusion. His thoughts went around and around, like a poor mouse stuck in an exitless maze allowed only to smell the cheese.

He gave up thinking about it and glanced through the newspaper he had bought at the station kiosk. Ronald Reagan, just reelected president that fall, had taken to calling Prime Minister Yasuhiro Nakasone *Yasu*, and Nakasone was calling him *Ron*. It might have been the way the photo was taken, but the two of them looked like a couple of men in the construction industry discussing how they were going to switch to cheap, shoddy building material. Riots in India following the assassination of Indira Gandhi were still ongoing, with Sikhs being butchered throughout the country. In Japan there was an unprecedented bumper crop of apples. But nothing in the paper aroused Tengo's interest.

He waited until the clock showed two and then called Komatsu's office once more.

As always, it took twelve rings before Komatsu picked up. Tengo wasn't sure why, but it always seemed hard for him to get to the phone.

"Tengo, it's been a while," Komatsu said. His voice sounded like the old Komatsu. Smooth, a bit forced, difficult to pin down.

"I took two weeks off from work and was in Chiba. I just got back last night."

"You said your father wasn't doing so well. It must have been hard on you."

"Not really. He's in a deep coma, so I just spent time with him, gazing at his sleeping face. The rest of the time I was at the inn, writing."

"Still, you're talking about a life-or-death situation, so it couldn't have been easy for you."

Tengo changed the subject. "When we talked last, quite a while ago, you mentioned having to talk with me about something."

"I remember," Komatsu said. "I would like to have a nice long talk with you, if you're free?"

"If it's something important, maybe the sooner the better?"

"Yes, sooner is better."

"Tonight could work for me."

"That would be fine. I'm free tonight, too. Say, seven?"

"Seven it is," Tengo said.

Komatsu told him to meet him in a small bar near his office, a place Tengo had been to a number of times. "It's open on Sundays," Komatsu added, "but there are hardly any people there then. So we can have a nice, quiet talk."

"Is this going to be a long story?"

Komatsu thought about this. "I'm not sure. Until I actually tell it to you, I have no idea how long it will be."

"That's all right. I'll be happy to listen. Because we're in the same boat together, right? Or have you changed to another?"

"No, not at all," Komatsu said, his tone more serious. "We're still in the same boat. Anyway, I'll see you at seven. I'll tell you everything then."

After he hung up, Tengo sat down at his desk, switched on his word processor, and typed up the story he had written out in fountain pen at the inn in Chikura. As he reread the story, he pictured the town in his mind: the sanatorium, the faces of the three nurses; the wind from the sea rustling through the pine trees, the pure white seagulls floating up above. Tengo stood up, pulled back the curtains, opened the sliding glass door, and deeply inhaled the cold air.

Tengo you are back from the cat town and are reading this letter that's good

So wrote Fuka-Eri in her letter. But this apartment he had returned to was under surveillance. There could even be a hidden camera right here in the room. Anxious now that he had thought of this, Tengo scoured every corner of the apartment. But he found no hidden camera, no electronic bugs. This was, after all, an old, tiny, one-room unit, and anything like that would be next to impossible to keep hidden.

Tengo kept typing his manuscript until it grew dark. It took him much longer than he expected because he rewrote parts as he typed. He stopped for a moment to turn on the desk lamp and realized that the crow hadn't come by today. He could tell when it came by from the sound, the large wings rubbing against the window. It left behind faint smudge marks on the glass, like a code waiting to be deciphered.

At five thirty he made a simple dinner. He wasn't that hungry, but he had barely eaten anything for lunch. *Best to get something in my stomach,* he figured. He made a tomato and wakame salad and ate a slice of toast. At six fifteen he pulled on a black, high-neck sweater and an olive-green corduroy blazer and left the apartment. As he exited the front door he stopped and looked around again, but nothing caught his eye – no man hiding in the shadows of a telephone pole, no suspicious-looking car parked nearby. Even the crow wasn't there. But this made Tengo all the more uneasy. All the seemingly benign things around him seemed to be watching him. Who knew if the people around – the housewife with her shopping basket; the silent old man taking his dog for a walk; the high school students, tennis rackets slung over their shoulders, pedaling by, ignoring him – might be part of a cleverly disguised Sakigake surveillance team.

I'm being paranoid, Tengo told himself. *I need to be careful, but it's no good to get overly jumpy.* He hurried on toward the station, shooting an occasional glance behind him to make sure he wasn't being followed. If he was being shadowed, Tengo was sure he would know it. His peripheral vision was better than most people's, and he had excellent eyesight. After glancing back three times, he was certain that there was no one tailing him.

He arrived at the bar at five minutes before seven. Komatsu was not there yet, and Tengo was the first customer of the evening. A lush arrangement of bright flowers was in a large vase on the counter and the smell of freshly cut greenery wafted toward him. Tengo sat in a booth in the back and ordered a draft beer. He took a paperback out of the pocket of his jacket and began reading.

Komatsu came at seven fifteen. He had on a tweed jacket, a light cashmere sweater, a cashmere muffler, wool trousers, and suede shoes. His *usual outfit.* High-quality, tasteful clothes, nicely worn out. When he wore these, the clothes looked like he had been born in them. Maybe any new clothes he bought he then slept in and rolled around in. Maybe he washed them over and over and laid them out to dry in the shade. Only once they were broken in and faded would he wear them in front of others. At any rate, the clothes did make him look like a veteran editor. From the way he was dressed, that was the only possible thing he *could* be. Komatsu sat down across from Tengo and also ordered a draft beer.

"You seem the same as ever," Komatsu commented. "How is the new novel coming?"

"I'm getting there, slowly but surely."

"I'm glad to hear it. Writers have to keep on writing if they want to mature, like caterpillars endlessly chewing on leaves. It's like I told you – taking on the rewrite of *Air Chrysalis* would have a good influence on your own writing. Was I right?"

Tengo nodded. "You were. Doing that rewrite helped me learn a lot about fiction writing. I started noticing things I had never noticed before."

"Not to brag or anything, but I know exactly what you mean. You just needed the right *opportunity*."

"But I also had a lot of hard experiences because of it. As you are aware."

Komatsu's mouth curled up neatly in a smile, like a crescent moon in winter. It was the kind of smile that was hard to read.

"To get something important, people have to pay a price. That's the rule the world operates by."

"You may be right. But I can't tell the difference between what's important and the price you have to pay. It has all gotten too complicated."

"Complicated it definitely is. It's like trying to carry on a phone conversation when the wires are crossed. Absolutely," Komatsu said, frowning. "By the way, do you know where Fuka-Eri is now?"

"I don't know where she is at present, no," Tengo said, choosing his words carefully.

"*At present*," Komatsu repeated meaningfully.

Tengo said nothing.

"But until a short while ago she was living in your apartment," Komatsu said. "At least, that's what I hear."

Tengo nodded. "That's right. She was at my place for about three months."

"Three months is a long time," said Komatsu. "And you never told anybody."

"She told me not to tell anyone, so I didn't. Including you."

"But now she isn't there anymore."

"Right. She took off when I was in Chikura, and left behind a letter. I don't know where she is now."

Komatsu took out a cigarette, stuck it in his mouth, and lit a match. He narrowed his eyes and looked at Tengo.

"After she left your place Fuka-Eri went back to Professor Ebisuno's house, on top of the mountain in Futamatao," he said. "Professor Ebisuno contacted the police and withdrew the missing person's report, since she had just gone off on her own and hadn't been kidnapped. The police must have interviewed her about what happened. She is a minor, after all. I wouldn't be surprised if there's an article in the paper about it before long, though I doubt it will say much. Since nothing criminal was involved, apparently."

"Will it come out that she stayed with me?"

Komatsu shook his head. "I don't think Fuka-Eri will mention your name. You know how she is. It can be the cops she's talking to, the military police, a revolutionary council, or Mother Teresa – once she has decided not to say something, then mum's the word. So I wouldn't let that worry you."

"I'm not worried. I would just like to know how things are going to work out."

"Whatever happens, your name won't be made public. Rest assured," Komatsu said. His expression turned serious. "But there is something I need to ask you. I hesitate to bring it up."

"How come?"

"Well, it's very – personal."

Tengo took a sip of beer and put the glass back on the table. "No problem. If it's something I can answer, I will."

"Did you and Fuka-Eri have a sexual relationship? While she was staying at your place, I mean. Just a simple yes or no is fine."

Tengo paused for a moment and slowly shook his head. "The answer is no. I didn't have that kind of relationship with her."

Tengo made an instinctive decision that he shouldn't reveal what had taken place between them on that stormy night. Besides, it wasn't really what you would call a sex act. There was no sexual desire involved, not in the normal sense. On either side.

"So you didn't have a sexual relationship."

"We didn't," Tengo said, his voice dry.

Komatsu scrunched up his nose. "Tengo, I'm not doubting you. But you did hesitate before you replied. Maybe something close to sex happened? I'm not blaming you. I'm just trying to ascertain certain facts."

Tengo looked straight into Komatsu's eyes. "I wasn't hesitating. I just felt weird, wondering why in the world you were so concerned about whether Fuka-Eri and I had a sexual relationship. You're usually not the type to stick your head into other people's private lives. You avoid that."

"I suppose," Komatsu said.

"Then why are you bringing something like that up now?"

"Who you sleep with or what Fuka-Eri does is basically none of my business." Komatsu scratched the side of his nose. "As you have pointed out. But as you are well aware, Fuka-Eri isn't just some ordinary girl. How should I put it? Every action she takes is significant."

"Significant," Tengo repeated.

"Logically speaking, all the actions that everybody takes have a certain significance," Komatsu said. "But in Fuka-Eri's case they have a *deeper meaning*. Something about her is different that way. So we need to be certain of whatever facts we can."

"By *we*, who do you mean, exactly?" Tengo asked.

Komatsu looked uncharacteristically nonplussed. "Truth be told, it's not me who wants to know whether the two of you had a sexual relationship, but Professor Ebisuno."

"So Professor Ebisuno knows that Fuka-Eri stayed at my apartment?"

"Of course. He knew that the first day she showed up at your place. Fuka-Eri told him where she was."

"I had no idea," Tengo said, surprised. She had told him she hadn't revealed to anyone where she was. Not that it mattered much now. "There's one thing I just don't get. Professor Ebisuno is her legal guardian and protector, so you would expect him to pay attention to things like that. But in the crazy situation we're in now you would think his top priority would be to make sure she's safe – not whether she's staying chaste or not."

Komatsu raised one corner of his lips. "I don't really know the background. He just asked me to find out – to see you and ask whether the two of you had a physical relationship. That is why I asked you this, and the answer was no."

"That's correct. Fuka-Eri and I did not have a physical relationship," Tengo said firmly, gazing steadily into Komatsu's eyes. Tengo didn't feel like he was lying.

"Good, then," Komatsu said. He put another Marlboro between his lips, and lit a match. "That's all I need to know."

"Fuka-Eri is an attractive girl, no question about it," Tengo said. "But as you are well aware, I have gotten mixed up in something quite serious, unwillingly. I don't want things to get any more complicated than they are. Besides, I was seeing somebody."

"I understand perfectly," Komatsu said. "I know you're a very clever person when it comes to things like that, with a very mature way of thinking. I will tell Professor Ebisuno what you said. I'm sorry I had to ask you. Don't let it bother you."

"It doesn't especially bother me. I just thought it was strange, why such a thing like that would come up at this point." Tengo paused for a moment. "What was it you wanted to tell me?"

Komatsu had finished his beer and ordered a Scotch highball from the bartender.

"What's your pleasure?" he asked Tengo.

"I'll have the same," Tengo said.

Two highballs in tall glasses were brought over to their table.

"Well, first of all," Komatsu began after a long silence, "I think that as much as possible we need to unravel some things about the situation that we've gotten entangled in. After all, we're all in the same boat. By *we* I mean the four of us – you, me, Fuka-Eri, and Professor Ebisuno."

"A very interesting group," Tengo said, but his sarcasm didn't seem to register with Komatsu.

Komatsu went on. "I think each of the four of us had his own expectation regarding this plan, and we're not all on the same level, or moving in the same direction. To put it another way, we weren't all rowing our oars at the same rhythm and at the same angle."

"This isn't the sort of group you would expect to be able to work well together."

"That might be true."

"And our boat was headed down the rapids toward a waterfall."

"Our boat was indeed headed down the rapids toward a waterfall," Komatsu admitted. "I'm not trying to make excuses, but from the start this was an extremely simple plan. We fool everybody, we make a bit of money. Half for laughs, half for profit. That was our goal. But ever since Professor Ebisuno got involved, the plot has thickened. A number of complicated subplots lie just below the surface of the water, and the water is picking up speed. Your reworking of the novel far exceeded my expectations, thanks to which the book got great reviews and had amazing sales. And then this took our boat off to an unexpected place – a somewhat perilous place."

Tengo shook his head slightly. "It's not a somewhat perilous place. It's an *extremely dangerous place*."

"You could be right."

"Don't act like this doesn't concern you. You're the one who came up with this idea in the first place."

"Granted. I'm the one who had the idea and pushed the start button. Things went well at first, but unfortunately as it progressed I lost control. I do feel responsible for it, believe me. Especially about getting you involved, since I basically forced you into it. But it's time for us to stop, take stock of where we are, and come up with a plan of action."

After getting all this out, Komatsu took a breath and drank his highball. He picked up the glass ashtray and, like a blind man feeling an object all over to understand what it is, carefully ran his long fingers over the surface.

"To tell you the truth," he finally said, "I was imprisoned for seventeen or eighteen days somewhere. From the end of August to the middle of September. The day it happened I was in my neighborhood, in the early afternoon, on my way to work. I was on the road to the Gotokuji Station. This large black car stopped beside me and the window slid down and someone called my name. I went over, wondering who it could be, when two men leapt out of the car and dragged me inside. Both of them were extremely powerful. One pinned my arms back, and the other put chloroform or something up to my nose. Just like in a movie, huh? But that stuff really does the trick, believe me. When I came to, I was being held in a tiny, windowless room. The walls were white, and it was like a cube. There was a small bed and a small wooden desk, but no chair. I was lying on the bed."

"You were kidnapped?" Tengo asked.

Komatsu finished his inspection of the ashtray, returned it to the table, and looked up at Tengo. "That's right. A real kidnapping. Like in that old movie, *The Collector*. I don't imagine most people in the world ever think they will end up kidnapped. The idea never occurs to them. Right? But when they kidnap you, believe me, you're kidnapped. It's kind of – how shall I put it? – surreal. You can't believe you are *actually* being kidnapped by someone. Could you believe it?"

Komatsu stared at Tengo, as if looking for a reply. But it was a rhetorical question. Tengo was silent, waiting for him to continue. He hadn't touched his highball. Beads of moisture had formed on the outside, wetting the coaster.

16

USHIKAWA

A Capable, Patient, Unfeeling Machine

THE NEXT MORNING USHIKAWA AGAIN TOOK a seat by the window and continued his surveillance through a gap in the curtain. Nearly the same lineup of people who had come back to the apartment building the night before, or at least people who looked the same, were now exiting. Their faces were still grim, their shoulders hunched over. A new day had barely begun and yet they already looked fed up and exhausted. Tengo wasn't among them, but Ushikawa went ahead and snapped photos of each and every face that passed by. He had plenty of film and it was good practice so he could be more efficient at stealthily taking photos.

When the morning rush had passed and he saw that everyone who was going out had done so, he left the apartment and slipped into a nearby phone booth. He dialed the Yoyogi cram school and asked to speak with Tengo.

"Mr. Kawana has been on leave for the last ten days," said the woman who answered the phone.

"I hope he's not ill?"

"No, someone in his family is, so he went to Chiba."

"Do you know when he will be back?"

"I'm afraid I haven't asked him that," the woman said.

Ushikawa thanked her and hung up.

Tengo's family, as far as Ushikawa knew, meant just his father – the father who used to be an NHK fee collector. Tengo still didn't know anything about his mother. And as far as Ushikawa was aware, Tengo and his father had always had a bad relationship. Yet Tengo had taken more than ten days off from work in order to take care of his sick father. Ushikawa found this hard to swallow. How could Tengo's antagonism for his father soften so quickly? What sort of illness did his father have, and where in Chiba was he in the hospital? There should be ways of finding out, though it would take at least a half a day to do so. And he would have to put his surveillance on hold while he did.

Ushikawa wasn't sure what to do. If Tengo was away from Tokyo, then it was pointless to stake out this building. It might be smarter to take a break from surveillance and search in another direction. He should find out where Tengo's father was a patient, or investigate Aomame's background. He could meet her classmates and colleagues from her college days and from the company she used to work for, and gather more personal information. Who knows but this might provide some new clues.

But after mulling it over, he decided to stay put and continue watching the apartment building. First, if he suspended his surveillance at this point, it would put a crimp in the daily rhythm he had established, and he would have to start again from scratch. Second, even if he located Tengo's father, and learned more about Aomame's friend-ships, the payoff might not be worth the trouble. Pounding the pave-ment on an investigation can be productive up to a point, but oddly, once you pass that point, nothing much comes of it. He knew this through experience. Third, his intuition told him, in no uncertain terms, to *stay put* – to stay right where he was, watch all the faces that passed by, and let nothing get by him.

So he decided that, with or without Tengo, he would continue to stake out the building. If he stayed put, by the time Tengo came back Ushikawa would know each and every face. Once he knew all the residents, then he would know in a glance if someone was new to the building. *I'm a carnivore,* Ushikawa thought. *And carnivores have to be forever patient. They have to blend in with their surroundings and know everything about their prey.*

Just before noon, when the foot traffic in and out of the building was at its most sparse, Ushikawa left the apartment. He tried to disguise himself a bit, wearing a knit cap and a muffler pulled up to his nose, but still he couldn't help but draw attention to himself. The beige knit cap perched on top of his huge head like a mushroom cap. The green muffler looked like a big snake coiled around him. Trying a disguise didn't work. Besides, the cap and muffler clashed horribly.

Ushikawa stopped by the film lab near the station and dropped off two rolls of film to be developed. Then he went to a soba noodle shop and ordered a bowl of soba noodles with tempura. It had been a while since he had had a hot meal. He savored the tempura noodles and drank down the last drop of broth. By the time he finished he was so hot he had started to perspire. He put on his knit cap, wrapped the muffler around his neck again, and walked back to the apartment. As he smoked a cigarette, he lined up all the photos that he had had printed on the floor. He collated the photos of people going out in the morning and the ones of people coming back, and if any matched he put them together. In order to easily distinguish them, he made up names for each person, and wrote the names on the photos with a felt-tip pen.

Once the morning rush hour was over, hardly any residents left the building. One young man – a college student, by the looks of him – hurried out around ten a.m., a bag slung over his shoulder. An old woman around seventy and a woman in her mid-thirties also went out but then returned lugging bags of groceries from a supermarket. Ushikawa took their photos as well. During the morning the mailman came and sorted the mail into the various mailboxes at the entrance. A deliveryman with a cardboard box came in and left, empty-handed, five minutes later.

Once an hour Ushikawa left his camera and did some stretching for five minutes. During that interval his surveillance was put on hold, but he knew from the start that total coverage by one person was impossible. It was more important to make sure his body didn't get numb. His muscles would start to atrophy and then he wouldn't be able to react quickly if need be. Like Gregor Samsa when he turned into a beetle, he deftly stretched his rotund, misshapen body on the floor, working the kinks out of his tight muscles.

He listened to AM radio with an earphone to keep from getting bored. Most of the daytime programs appealed to housewives and elderly listeners. The people who appeared on the programs told jokes that fell flat, pointlessly burst out laughing, gave their moronic, hackneyed opinions, and played music so awful you felt like covering your ears. Periodically they gave blaring sales pitches for products no one could possibly want. At least this is how it all sounded to Ushikawa. But he wanted to hear people's voices, so he endured listening to the inane programs, wondering all the while why people would produce such idiotic shows and go to the trouble of using the airwaves to disseminate them.

Not that Ushikawa himself was involved in an operation that was so lofty and productive – hiding behind the curtains in a cheap one-room apartment, secretly snapping photos of people. He couldn't very well criticize the actions of others.

It was not just now, either. Back when he was a lawyer it was the same. He couldn't remember having done anything that helped society. His biggest clients ran small and medium-sized financial firms and had ties to organized crime. Ushikawa created the most efficient ways to disperse their profits and made all the arrangements. Basically, it was money laundering. He was also involved in land sharking: when investors had their eyes on an area, he helped drive out longtime residents so they could knock down their houses and sell the remaining large lot to condo builders. Huge amounts of money rolled in. The same type of people were involved in this as well. He also specialized in defending people brought up on tax-evasion charges. Most of the clients were suspicious characters that an ordinary lawyer would hesitate to have anything to do with. But as long as a client wanted him to represent him – and as long as a certain amount of money changed hands – Ushikawa never hesitated. He was a skilled lawyer, with a decent track record, so he never hurt for business. His relationship with Sakigake began in the same way. For whatever reason, Leader took a personal liking to him.

If he had followed the path that ordinary lawyers take, Ushikawa would probably have found it hard to earn a living. He had passed the bar exam not long after he left college, and he had become a lawyer, but he had no connections or influential backers. With his looks, no prestigious law firm would ever hire him, so if he had stayed on a straight and narrow path he would have had very few clients. There can't be many people in the world who would go out of their way to hire a lawyer who looked as unappealing as Ushikawa, plus pay the high fees involved. The blame might lie with TV law dramas, which have conditioned people to expect lawyers to be both bright and attractive.

So as time went on, Ushikawa became linked with the underworld. People in the underworld didn't care about his looks. In fact, his peculiar appearance was one element that helped them trust and accept him, since neither of them were accepted by the ordinary world. They recognized his quick mind, his practical abilities, his eloquence. They put him in charge of moving vast sums of money (a task they couldn't openly undertake), and compensated him generously. Ushikawa quickly learned the ropes – how to evade the authorities while still doing what was barely legal. His intuitiveness and strong will were a big help. Unfortunately, though, he got too greedy, made some assumptions he shouldn't have, and went over the line. He avoided criminal punishment – barely – but was expelled from the Tokyo Bar Association.

Ushikawa switched off the radio and smoked a Seven Stars. He breathed the smoke deep into his lungs, then leisurely exhaled. He used an empty can of peaches as an ashtray. If he went on like this, he would probably die a miserable death. Before long he would make a false step and fall alone in some dark place. *Even if I left this world, I doubt anyone would notice. I would shout out from the dark, but no one would hear me. Still, I have to keep soldiering on until I die, the only way I know how. Not a laudable sort of life, but the only life I know how to live.* And when it came to *not very laudable things,* Ushikawa was more capable than almost anyone.

At two thirty a young woman wearing a baseball cap exited the building. She had no bags with her and quickly strode across Ushikawa's line of sight. He hurriedly pushed the motor drive switch in his hand and got off three quick shots. It was the first time he had seen her. She was a beautiful young girl, thin and long limbed with wonderful posture, like a ballerina. She looked about sixteen or seventeen and had on faded jeans, white sneakers, and a man's leather jacket. Her hair was tucked into the collar of the jacket. After leaving the building the girl took a couple of steps, then stopped, frowned, and looked intently up above the electric pole in front. She then lowered her gaze to the ground and started off again. She turned left and disappeared from Ushikawa's sight.

That girl looks like somebody, he thought. Somebody he knew, that he had seen recently. With her looks she might be a TV personality. Ushikawa never watched anything on TV but news, and had never been interested in cute girl TV stars.

Ushikawa pushed his memory accelerator to the floor and shifted his brain into high gear. He narrowed his eyes and squeezed his brain cells hard, like wringing out a dishrag. His nerves ached painfully with the effort. And suddenly it came to him: that *somebody* was none other than Eriko Fukada. He had never seen her in person, only a photo of her in the literary column of the papers. But the sense of aloof transparency that hung over her was exactly the same impression he had gotten from the tiny black-and-white photo of her in the paper. She and Tengo must have met each other during the rewriting of *Air Chrysalis*. It was entirely possible that she had grown fond of Tengo and was lying low in his apartment.

Almost without thinking, Ushikawa grabbed his knit cap, yanked on his navy-blue pea coat, and wrapped his muffler around his neck. He left the building and trotted off in the direction he had last seen her.

She was a very fast walker. *It might be impossible to catch up with her,* he thought. But she was carrying nothing, which meant she wasn't going far. Instead of shadowing her and risking drawing her attention, wouldn't it make more sense to wait patiently for her to return? Ushikawa pondered this, but couldn't stop following her. The girl had a certain illogical something that shook him. The same feeling as the moment at twilight when a mysteriously colored beam of light conjures up a special memory.

After a while he spotted her. Fuka-Eri had stopped in front of a tiny stationery store and was peering intently inside, where something had undoubtedly caught her interest. Ushikawa casually turned his back on her and stood in front of a vending machine. He took some coins out and bought a can of hot coffee.

Finally the girl took off again. Ushikawa laid the half-finished can of coffee at his feet and followed her at a safe distance. The girl seemed to be concentrating very hard on the act of walking, as if she were gliding across the surface of a placid lake. Walk in this special way, and you won't sink or get your shoes wet. It was as if she had grasped the key to doing this.

There was something different about this girl. She had a special something most people didn't. Ushikawa didn't know a lot about Eriko Fukada. From what he had gathered, she was Leader's only daughter, had run away from Sakigake at age ten, had grown up in the household of a well-known scholar named Professor Ebisuno, and had written a novel entitled *Air Chrysalis,* which was reworked by Tengo Kawana and became a bestseller. But she was supposedly missing now – a missing person's report had been filed with the police, and the police had searched Sakigake headquarters not long ago.

The contents of *Air Chrysalis* were problematic for Sakigake, it appeared. Ushikawa had bought the novel and read through it carefully, though which parts were troublesome, and for what reason, he had no idea. He found the novel fascinating and well written. But to him, it seemed a harmless work of fantasy and he was sure the rest of the world must agree. Little People emerge from a goat's mouth, create an air chrysalis, the main character splits into *maza* and *dohta,* and there are two moons. So where in the midst of this fantastical story are there elements that would damage Sakigake if they came out?

But when Eriko Fukada was in the public eye, it would have been too risky to take any action against her. Which is why, Ushikawa surmised, they wanted him to approach Tengo. In Ushikawa's view Tengo was a mere bit player in the bigger scheme of things. Ushikawa still couldn't grasp why they were so fixated on Tengo. But as Ushikawa was just a foot soldier in these operations, he had to unquestioningly follow orders. The problem was, Tengo had quickly rejected the generous proposal that Ushikawa had worked hard to create, and the plan he had made to forge a connection with Tengo had come to a screeching halt. Right when he had been trying to think of another approach, Eriko Fukada's father, Leader, had died, and things were left as they were.

So Ushikawa was in the dark regarding Sakigake's focus. He didn't even know who was in charge now that they had lost Leader. In any case, they were trying to locate Aomame, find out why Leader had been murdered, and who was behind it. No doubt they would mete out some pretty harsh punishment on whoever had done it. And they were determined not to get the law involved.

So what about Eriko Fukada? What was Sakigake's take now on *Air Chrysalis*? Did they still view the book as a threat?

Eriko Fukada didn't slow down or turn around, like a homing pigeon heading straight to her goal. He soon determined that that *goal* was a midsized supermarket, the Marusho. Shopping basket in hand, Fuka-Eri went from one aisle to another, selecting various canned and fresh foods. Just selecting a single head of lettuce took time, as she examined it from every possible angle. *This is going to take a while,* Ushikawa thought. He left the supermarket, went across the street to a bus stop, and pretended to be waiting for a bus while he kept an eye on the store's entrance.

But no matter how long he waited, the girl didn't emerge. Ushikawa started to get worried. Maybe she had left by another exit? As far as he could tell, though, the market had only the one door, facing the main street. Probably shopping was just taking time for her. Ushikawa recalled the serious, strangely depthless eyes of the girl as she contemplated heads of lettuce and decided to sit tight. Three buses came and went. Each time Ushikawa was the only one left behind. He regretted not having brought a newspaper. He could have hidden behind it. When you are shadowing someone a newspaper or magazine is an absolute must. But there was nothing he could do – he had dropped everything and rushed out of the apartment empty-handed.

When Fuka-Eri finally emerged, his watch showed 3:35. The girl didn't glance his way but marched off in the direction from which she had come. Ushikawa let some time pass and then set off in pursuit. The two shopping bags she carried looked heavy, but she carried them lightly, tripping down the street like a water skipper skimming across a puddle.

What an odd young woman, Ushikawa thought again as he kept her in sight. *It's like watching some rare exotic butterfly. Pleasant to watch, but you can't touch it, for as soon as you do, it dies, its brilliance gone.* That would put an end to his exotic dream.

Ushikawa quickly calculated whether it made sense to let the Sakigake duo know he had discovered Fuka-Eri's whereabouts. It was a tough decision. If he did tell them he had located her, he would definitely score some points. At the very least, it wouldn't hurt his standing with them – he could show them he was making decent progress. But if he got too involved with Fuka-Eri, he might very well miss the chance to find the real object of his search, Aomame. That would be a disaster. So what should he do? He stuffed his hands deep into the pockets of his pea coat, pulled the muffler up to his nose, and continued following her, keeping a longer distance between them than before.

Maybe I'm only following her because I wanted to see her. The thought suddenly occurred to him. Just watching her stride along the road, bags of groceries clutched to her, made his chest grow tight. Like a person hemmed in between two walls, he could go neither forward nor back. His breathing turned ragged and forced, and he found it almost impossible to breathe, like he was caught up in a tepid blast of wind. A thoroughly strange feeling he had never experienced.

At any rate, I'll let her go for a while. I'll stick to the original plan and focus on Aomame. Aomame is a murderer. It doesn't matter what reason she may have had for doing it – she deserves to be punished. Turning her over to Sakigake didn't bother him. But this young girl was different. She was a quiet little creature living deep in the woods, with pale wings like the shadow of a spirit. *Just observe her from a distance,* he decided.

Ushikawa waited a while after Fuka-Eri had disappeared into the entrance of the apartment, grocery bags in hand, before he went in. He went to his room, took off his muffler and cap, and plopped back down in front of the camera. His cheeks were cold from the wind. He smoked a cigarette and drank some mineral water. His throat felt parched, as if he had eaten something very spicy.

Twilight fell, streetlights snapped on, and it was getting near the time people would be coming home. Still wearing his pea coat, Ushikawa held the remote control for the shutter and intently watched the entrance to the building. As the memory of the afternoon sunlight faded, his empty room rapidly grew chilly. It looked like tonight would be much colder than last night. Ushikawa considered going to the discount electrical goods store in front of the station and buying an electric space heater or electric blanket.

Eriko Fukada came out of the entrance again at four forty-five. She had on the same black turtleneck sweater and jeans, but no leather jacket. The tight sweater revealed the swell of her breasts. She had generous breasts for such a slim girl. Ushikawa watched this lovely swelling through his viewfinder, and as he did again he felt the same tightness and difficulty breathing.

Since she wasn't wearing a jacket, she couldn't be going far. As before, she stopped at the entrance, narrowed her eyes, and looked up above the electric pole in front. It was getting dark, but if you squinted you could make out the outlines of things. She stood there for a while as if searching for something. But she apparently didn't find what she was looking for. She gave up looking above the pole and, like a bird, twisted her head and gazed at her surroundings. Ushikawa pushed the remote button and snapped photos of her.

As if she had heard the sound of the shutter, Fuka-Eri turned to look right in the direction of the camera. Through the viewfinder Ushikawa and Fuka-Eri were face-to-face. Ushikawa could see her face quite clearly. He was looking through a telephoto lens, after all. On the other end of the lens, though, Fuka-Eri was staring steadily right at him. Deep within the lens, she could see him. Ushikawa's face was clearly reflected within those soft, jet-black eyes. He found it strange that they were directly in touch like this. He swallowed. *This can't be real. From where she is, she can't see anything. The telephoto lens is camouflaged, the sound of the shutter dampened by the towel wrapped around it, so there's no way she could hear it from where she is.* Still, there she stood at the entrance, staring right at where he was hiding. That emotionless gaze of hers was unwavering as it stared straight at Ushikawa, like starlight shining on a nameless, massive rock.

For a long time – Ushikawa had no idea just how long – the two of them stared at each other. Suddenly Fuka-Eri twisted around and strode through the entrance, as if she had seen all that she needed to see. After she disappeared, Ushikawa let all the air out of his lungs, waited a moment, then breathed fresh air in deeply. The chilled air became countless thorns, stinging his lungs.

People were coming back, just like last night, passing under the light at the entrance, one after another. Ushikawa, though, was no longer gazing through his viewfinder. His hand was no longer holding the shutter remote. The girl's open, unreserved gaze had plucked the strength right out of him – as if a long steel needle had been stabbed right into his chest, so deep it felt like it was coming out the other side.

The girl *knew* that he was secretly watching her, that she was being photographed by a hidden camera. He couldn't say how, but Fuka-Eri knew this. Maybe she understood it through some special tactile sense she possessed.

He really needed a drink, to fill a glass of whiskey to the brim and drink it down in one gulp. He considered going out to buy a bottle. There was a liquor store right nearby. But he gave it up – drinking wouldn't change anything. On the other side of the viewfinder, she had seen him. *That beautiful girl saw me, my misshapen head and dirty spirit, hiding here, secretly snapping photos.* Nothing could change that fact.

Ushikawa left his camera, leaned back against the wall, and looked up at the stained ceiling. Soon everything struck him as empty. He had never felt so utterly alone, never felt the dark to be this intense. He remembered his house back in Chuorinkan, his lawn and his dog, his wife and two daughters, the sunlight shining there. And he thought of the DNA he had given to his daughters, the DNA for a misshapen head and a twisted soul.

Everything he had done seemed pointless. He had used up all the cards he'd been dealt – not that great a hand to begin with. He had taken that lousy hand and used it as best he could to make some clever bets. For a time things looked like they were going to work out, but now he had run out of cards. The light at the table was switched off, and all the players had filed out of the room.

That evening he didn't take a single photo. Leaning against the wall, he smoked Seven Stars, and opened another can of peaches and ate it. At nine he went to the bathroom, brushed his teeth, tugged off his clothes, slipped into the sleeping bag, and, shivering, tried to sleep. The night was cold, but his shivering wasn't just brought on by the cold alone. The chill seemed to be arising from inside his body. *Where in the world did I come from?* he asked himself in the dark. *And where the hell am I going?*

The pain of her gaze still stabbed at him. Maybe it would never go away. *Or was it always there,* he wondered, *and I just didn't notice it?*

The next morning, after a breakfast of cheese and crackers washed down by instant coffee, he pulled himself together and sat back down in front of the camera. As he did the day before, he observed the people coming and going and took a few photos. Tengo and Fuka-Eri, though, were not among them. Instead it was more hunched-over people, carried by force of habit into the new day. The weather was fine, the wind strong. People's white breath swirled away in the air.

I'm not going to think of anything superfluous, Ushikawa decided. *Be thick-skinned, have a hard shell around my heart, take one day at a time, go by the book. I'm just a machine. A capable, patient, unfeeling machine. A machine that draws in new time through one end, then spits out old time from the other end. It exists in order to exist.* He needed to revert back again to that pure, unsullied cycle – that perpetual motion that would one day come to an end. He pumped up his will-power and put a cap on his emotions, trying to rid his mind of the image of Fuka-Eri. The pain in his chest from her sharp gaze felt better now, little more than an occasional dull ache. *Good. Can't ask for more. I'm a simple system again,* he told himself, *a simple system with complex details.*

Before noon he went to the discount store near the station and bought a small electric space heater. He then went to the same noodle place he had been to before, opened his newspaper, and ate an order of hot tempura soba. Before going back to his apartment he stood at the entrance and gazed above the electric pole at the spot Fuka-Eri had been so focused on yesterday, but he found nothing to draw his attention. All that was there were a transformer and thick black electric lines entwined like snakes. What could she have been looking at? Or was she looking *for* something?

Back in his room, he switched on the space heater. An orange light flickered into life and he felt an intimate warmth on his skin. It was not enough to fully heat the place, but it was much better than nothing. Ushikawa leaned against the wall, folded his arms, and took a short nap in a tiny spot of sunlight. A dreamless sleep, a pure blank in time.

He was pulled out of this happy, deep sleep by the sound of a knock. Someone was knocking on his door. He bolted awake and gazed around him, unsure for a moment of his surroundings. He spotted the Minolta single-lens reflex camera on a tripod and remembered he was in a room in an apartment in Koenji. Someone was pounding with his fist on the door. As he hurriedly scraped together his consciousness, Ushikawa thought it was odd that someone would knock on the door. There was a doorbell – all you had to do was push the button. It was simple enough. Still this person insisted on knocking – pounding it for all he was worth, actually. Ushikawa frowned and checked his watch. One forty-five. One forty-five p.m., obviously. It was still light outside.

He didn't answer the door. Nobody knew he was here, and he wasn't expecting any visitors. It must be a salesman, or someone selling newspaper subscriptions. Whoever it was might need him, but he certainly didn't need them. Leaning against the wall, he glared at the door and maintained his silence. The person would surely give up after a time and go away.

But he didn't. He would pause, then start knocking once more. A barrage of knocks, nothing for ten or fifteen seconds, then a new round. These were firm knocks, nothing hesitant about them, each knock almost unnaturally the same as the next. From start to finish they were demanding a response from Ushikawa. He grew uneasy. Was the person on the other side of the door maybe – Eriko Fukada? Coming to complain to him about his despicable behavior, secretly photographing people? His heart started to pound. He licked his lips with his thick tongue. But the banging against this steel door could only be that of a grown man's fist, not that of a girl's.

Or had she informed somebody else of what Ushikawa was up to, and that person was outside the door? Somebody from the rental agency, or maybe the police? That couldn't be good. But the rental agent would have a master key and could let himself in, and the police would announce themselves. And neither one would bang on the door like this. They would simply ring the bell.

"Mr. Kozu," a man called out. "Mr. Kozu!"

Ushikawa remembered that Kozu was the name of the previous resident of the apartment. His name remained on the mailbox. Ushikawa preferred it that way. The man outside must think Mr. Kozu still lived here.

"Mr. Kozu," the man intoned. "I know you're in there. I can sense you're holed up inside, trying to stay perfectly quiet."

A middle-aged man's voice, not all that loud, but slightly hoarse. At the core his voice had a hardness to it, the hardness of a brick fired in a kiln and carefully allowed to dry. Perhaps because of this, his voice echoed throughout the building.

"Mr. Kozu, I'm from NHK. I've come to collect your monthly subscription fee. So I would appreciate it if you'd open the door."

Ushikawa wasn't planning to pay any NHK subscription fee. *It might be faster,* he thought, *to just let the man in and show him the place. Tell him, look, no TV, right?* But if he saw Ushikawa, with his odd features, shut up alone in an apartment in the middle of the day without a stick of furniture, he couldn't help but be suspicious.

"Mr. Kozu, people who have TVs have to pay the subscription fee. That's the law. Some people say they never watch NHK, so they're not going to pay. But that argument doesn't hold water. Whether you watch NHK or not, if you have a TV you have to pay."

So it's just a fee collector. Let him get it out of his system. Don't respond, and he'll go away. But how could he be so sure there's someone in this apartment? After he came back an hour or so ago, Ushikawa hadn't been out again. He hardly made a sound, and he always kept the curtains closed.

"Mr. Kozu, I know very well that you are in there," the man said, as if reading Ushikawa's thoughts. "You must think it strange that I know that. But I do know it – that you're in there. You don't want to pay the NHK fee, so you're trying to not make a sound. I'm perfectly aware of this."

The homogeneous knocks started up again. There would be a slight pause, like a wind instrument player pausing to take a breath, then once more the pounding would start, the rhythm unchanged.

"I get it, Mr. Kozu. You have decided to ignore me. Fine. I'll leave today. I have other things to do. But I'll be back. Mark my words. If I say I'll be back, you can count on it. I'm not your average fee collector. I never give up until I get what is coming to me. I never waver from that. It's like the phases of the moon, or life and death. There is no escape."

A long silence followed. Just when Ushikawa thought he might be gone, the collector spoke up again.

"I'll be back soon, Mr. Kozu. Look forward to it. When you're least expecting it, there will be a knock on the door. *Bang bang!* And that will be me."

No more knocks now. Ushikawa listened intently. He thought he heard footsteps fading down the corridor. He quickly went over to his camera and fixed his gaze on the entrance to the apartment. The fee collector should finish his business in the building soon and be leaving. He had to check and see what sort of man he was. NHK collectors wear uniforms, so he should be able to spot him right away. But maybe he wasn't really from NHK. Maybe he was pretending to be one to try to get Ushikawa to open the door. Either way, he had to be someone Ushikawa had never seen before. The remote for the shutter in his right hand, he waited expectantly for a likely-looking person to appear.

For the next thirty minutes, though, no one came into or out of the building. Eventually a middle-aged woman he had seen a number of times emerged and pedaled off on her bike. Ushikawa had dubbed her "Chin Lady" because of the ample flesh dangling below her chin. A half an hour later Chin Lady returned, a shopping bag in the basket of her bike. She parked her bike in the bike parking area and went into the building, bag in hand. After this, a boy in elementary school came home. Ushikawa's name for him was "Fox," since his eyes slanted upward. But no one who could have been the fee collector appeared. Ushikawa was puzzled. The building had only one way in and out, and he had kept his eyes glued to the entrance every second. If the collector hadn't come out, that could only mean he was *still inside*.

He continued to watch the entrance without a break. He didn't go to the bathroom. The sun set, it grew dark, and the light at the entrance came on. But still no fee collector. After six, Ushikawa gave up. He went to the bathroom and let out all the pee he had been holding in. The man was definitely still in the building. Why, he didn't know. It didn't make any sense. But that weird fee collector had decided to stay put.

The wind, colder now, whined through the frozen electric lines. Ushikawa turned on the space heater, and as he smoked a cigarette he tried to make sense of it all. *Why did the man have to speak in such an aggressive, challenging tone? Why was he so positive that someone was inside the apartment? And why hadn't he left the building? If he hasn't left here, then where is he?*

Ushikawa left the camera, leaned against the wall, and stared for the longest time at the orange filament of the space heater.

17

AOMAME

I Only Have One Pair of Eyes

IT WAS A WINDY SATURDAY, NEARLY eight p.m., when the phone rang. Aomame was wearing a down jacket, a blanket on her lap, sitting on the balcony. Through a gap in the screen, she kept an eye on the slide in the playground, which was illuminated by the mercury-vapor lamp. Her hands were under the blanket so they wouldn't get numb. The deserted slide looked like the skeleton of some huge animal that had died in the Ice Age.

Sitting outside on a cold night might not be good for the baby, but Aomame decided it wasn't cold enough to present a problem. No matter how cold you may be on the outside, amniotic fluid maintained nearly the same temperature as blood. There are plenty of places in the world way colder and harsher, she concluded. And women keep on having babies, even there. But above all, this cold was something she felt she had to endure if she wanted to see Tengo again.

As always, the large yellow moon and its smaller green companion floated in the winter sky. Clouds of assorted sizes and shapes scudded swiftly across the sky. The clouds were white and dense, their outlines sharply etched, and they looked to her like hard blocks of ice floating down a snowmelt river to the sea. As she watched the clouds, appearing from somewhere only to disappear again, Aomame felt she had been transported to a spot near the edge of the world. This was the northern frontier of reason. There was nothing north of here – only the chaos of nothingness.

The sliding glass door was open just a crack, so the ringing phone sounded faint, and Aomame was lost in thought, but she didn't miss the sound. The phone rang three times, stopped, then twenty seconds later rang one more time. It had to be Tamaru. She threw aside the blanket, slid open the cloudy glass door, and went inside. It was dark inside and the heat was at a comfortable level. Her fingers still cold, she lifted the receiver.

"Still reading Proust?"

"But not making much progress," Aomame replied. It was like an exchange of passwords.

"You don't like it?"

"It's not that. How should I put it – it's a story about a different place, somewhere totally unlike here."

Tamaru was silent, waiting for her to go on. He was in no hurry.

"By different place, I mean it's like reading a detailed report from a small planet light-years away from *this world* I'm living in. I can picture all the scenes described and understand them. It's described very vividly, minutely, even. But I can't connect the scenes in that book with where I am now. We are physically too far apart. I'll be reading it, and I find myself having to go back and reread the same passage over again."

Aomame searched for the next words. Tamaru waited as she did.

"It's not boring, though," she said. "It's so detailed and beautifully written, and I feel like I can grasp the structure of that lonely little planet. But I can't seem to go forward. It's like I'm in a boat, paddling upstream. I row for a while, but then when I take a rest and am thinking about something, I find myself back where I started. Maybe that way of reading suits me now, rather than the kind of reading where you forge ahead to find out what happens. I don't know how to put it exactly, but there is a sense of time wavering irregularly when you try to forge ahead. If what is in front is behind, and what is behind is in front, it doesn't really matter, does it. Either way is fine."

Aomame searched for a more precise way of expressing herself.

"It feels like I'm experiencing someone else's dream. Like we're simultaneously sharing feelings. But I can't really grasp what it means to be simultaneous. Our feelings seem extremely close, but in reality there's a considerable gap between us."

"I wonder if Proust was aiming for that sort of sensation."

Aomame had no idea.

"Still, on the other hand," Tamaru said, "time in this real world goes ever onward. It never stands still, and never reverses course."

"Of course. In the real world time goes forward."

As she said this Aomame glanced at the glass door. But was it really true? That time was always flowing forward?

"The seasons have changed, and we are getting close to the end of 1984," Tamaru said.

"I doubt I'll finish *In Search of Lost Time* by the end of the year."

"It doesn't matter," Tamaru said. "Take your time. It was written over fifty years ago. It's not like it's crammed with hot-off-the-press information or anything."

You might be right, Aomame thought. *But maybe not.* She no longer had much trust in time.

"Is that *thing inside you* doing all right?" Tamaru asked.

"So far, so good."

"I'm glad to hear it," Tamaru said. "By the way, you heard about the short balding guy who has been loitering outside the Willow House, right?"

"I did. Is he still hanging around?"

"No. Not recently. He did for a couple of days and then he

disappeared. But he went to the rental agencies in the area, pretending to be looking for an apartment, gathering information about the safe house. This guy really stands out. As if that weren't bad enough, his clothes are awful. So everyone who talked with him remembers him. It was easy to track his movements."

"He doesn't sound like the right type to be doing investigations or reconnaissance."

"Exactly. With looks like those, he's definitely not cut out for that kind of work. He has a huge head, too, like one of those Fukusuke good-luck dolls. But he does seem to be good at what he does. He knows how to pound the pavement and dig up information. And he seems quite sharp. He doesn't skip what is important, and he ignores what isn't."

"And he was able to gather a certain amount of information on the safe house."

"He knows it's a refuge for women fleeing domestic violence, and that the dowager has provided it free of charge. I think he must also have discovered that the dowager is a member of the sports club where you worked, and that you often visited her mansion to do private training sessions with her. If I were him, I would have been able to find out that much."

"You're saying he's as good as you are?"

"As long as you don't mind the effort involved, you can learn how to best gather information and train yourself to think logically. Anyone can do that much."

"I can't believe there would be that many people like that in the world."

"Well, there are a few. Professionals."

Aomame sat down and touched the tip of her nose. It was still cold from being outside.

"And that man isn't hanging around outside the mansion anymore?" Aomame asked.

"I think he recognizes that he stands out too much. And he knows about the security cameras. So he gathered as much information as he could in a short time and then moved on."

"So he knows about the connection between me and the dowager, that this is more than just a relationship between a sports club trainer and a wealthy client, and that the safe house is connected, too. And that we were involved in some sort of project together."

"Most likely," Tamaru said. "As far as I can tell, the guy is getting close to the heart of things. Step by step."

"From what you're saying, though, it sounds like he's working on his own, not as part of some larger organization."

"I had the same impression. Unless they had some special ulterior motive, a large organization would never hire a conspicuous man like that to undertake a secret investigation."

"So why is he doing this investigation – and for whom?"

"You got me," Tamaru said. "All I know is he's good at what he does and he's dangerous. Anything beyond that is just speculation. Though my own modest speculation leads me to believe that, in some form or another, Sakigake is involved."

Aomame considered this prospect. "And the man has moved on."

"Right. I don't know where he has gone, though. But if I had to make a logical guess I would say that he is trying to track you down."

"But you told me it was next to impossible to find this place."

"Correct. A person could investigate all he wanted and never discover anything that linked the dowager to the apartment. Any possible connection has been erased. But I'm talking about the short term. If it's long term, chinks in the armor will appear, just where you least expect them. You might wander outside, for instance, and be spotted. That's just one possibility."

"I don't go outside," Aomame insisted. But this wasn't entirely true. She had left the apartment twice: once when she ran over to the playground in search of Tengo, the other time when she took the taxi to the turnout on the Metropolitan Expressway No. 3, near Sangenjaya, in search of an exit. But she couldn't reveal this to Tamaru.

"Then how is he going to locate this place?"

"If I were him, I would take another look at your personal information. Consider what kind of person you are, where you came from, what kind of life you have led up till now, what you're thinking, what you're hoping for in life, what you're not hoping for. I would take all the information I could get my hands on, lay it all out on a table, verify it, and dissect it from top to bottom."

"Expose me, in other words."

"That's right. Expose you under a cold, harsh light. Use tweezers and a magnifying glass to check out every nook and cranny, to discover patterns in the way you act."

"I don't get it. Would an analysis like that really turn up where I am now?"

"I don't know," Tamaru said. "It might, and it might not. It depends. I'm just saying *that's what I would do*. Because I can't think of anything else. Every person has his set routines when it comes to thinking and acting, and where there's a routine, there's a weak point."

"It sounds like a scientific investigation."

"People need routines. It's like a theme in music. But it also restricts your thoughts and actions and limits your freedom. It structures your priorities and in some cases distorts your logic. In the present situation, you don't want to move from where you are now. At least until the end of the year you have refused to move to a safer location – because you're searching for *something* there. And until you find that something you can't leave. Or you don't want to leave."

Aomame was silent.

"What that might be, or how much you really want it, I have no idea. And I don't plan to ask. But from my perspective that *something* constitutes your personal weak point."

"You may be right," Aomame admitted.

"And Bobblehead's going to follow that. He will mercilessly trace that personal element that's restraining you. He thinks it will lead to a breakthrough – provided he is as skilled as I imagine and is able to trace fragmentary clues to arrive at that point."

"I don't think he will be able to," Aomame said. "He won't be able to find a path. Because it's something that is found only in my heart."

"You're a hundred percent sure of that?"

Aomame thought about it. "Not a hundred percent. Call it ninety-eight."

"Well, then you had better be very concerned about that two percent. As I said, this guy is a professional. He is very smart, and very persistent."

Aomame didn't reply.

"A professional is like a hunting dog," Tamaru said. "He can sniff out what normal people can't smell, hear what they can't pick up. If you do the same things everyone else does, in the same way, then you're no professional. Even if you are, you're not going to survive for long. So you need to be vigilant. I know you are a very cautious person, but you have to be much more careful than you have been up till now. The most important things aren't decided by percentages."

"There's something I would like to ask you," Aomame said.

"What would that be?"

"What do you plan to do if Bobblehead shows up there again?"

Tamaru was silent for a moment. The question seemed to have caught him by surprise. "I probably won't do anything. I'll just leave him be. There's nothing he can do around here."

"But what if he starts to do something that bothers you?"

"Like what, for instance?"

"I don't know. Something that's a nuisance."

Tamaru made a small sound in the back of his throat. "I think I would send him a message."

"As a fellow professional?"

"I suppose. But before I actually did anything, I would need to find out who he's working with. If he has backup, I could be the one in danger instead of him. I would want to make sure of that before I did anything."

"Like checking the depth of the water before jumping in a pool."

"That is one way of putting it."

"But you believe he is acting on his own. You said he probably doesn't have any backup."

"I did, but sometimes my intuition is off," Tamaru said. "And unfortunately, I don't have eyes in the back of my head. At any rate, I would like you to keep an eye out, all right? See if there's anyone suspicious around, any change in the scenery outside, anything out of the ordinary. If you notice anything unusual, no matter how small, make sure you let me know."

"I understand. I will be careful," Aomame said. She didn't need to be told. *I'm looking for Tengo, so I won't miss the most trivial detail. Still, like Tamaru said, I only have one pair of eyes.*

"That's about it from me," he said.

"How is the dowager?" Aomame asked.

"She is well," Tamaru replied. Then he added, "Though she seems kind of quiet these days."

"She never was one to talk much."

Tamaru gave a low growl in the back of his throat, as if his throat were equipped with an organ to express special emotions. "She is even quieter than usual."

Aomame pictured the dowager, alone on her chair, a large watering can at her feet, endlessly watching butterflies. Aomame knew very well how quietly the old lady breathed.

"I will include a box of madeleines with the next supplies," Tamaru said as he wound up the conversation. "That might have a positive effect on the flow of time."

"Thank you," Aomame said.

Aomame stood in the kitchen and made cocoa. Before going back outside to resume her watch, she needed to warm up. She boiled milk in a pan and dissolved cocoa powder in it. She poured this into an oversized cup and added a cap of whipped cream she had made ahead of time. She sat down at the dining table and slowly sipped her cocoa as she reviewed her conversation with Tamaru. The man with the large, misshapen head is laying me out bare under a cold, harsh light. He's a skilled professional, and dangerous.

She put on the down jacket, wrapped the muffler around her, and, the cup of half-drunk cocoa in hand, went out again to the balcony. She sat down on the garden chair and spread the blanket on her lap. The slide was deserted, as usual. But just then she spotted a child leaving the playground. It was strange for a child to be visiting the playground alone at this hour. A stocky child wearing a knit cap. She was looking at him from well above, through a gap in the screen on the balcony, and the child quickly cut across her field of vision and disappeared into the shadows of the building. His head seemed too big for a child, but it might just have been her imagination.

It certainly wasn't Tengo, so Aomame gave it no more thought and turned back to the slide. She sipped her cocoa, warming her hands with the cup, and watched one bank of clouds after another scud across the sky.

Of course, it wasn't a child that Aomame saw for a moment, but Ushikawa. If the light had been better, or if she had seen him a little longer, she would have noticed that his large head wasn't that of a child. It would have dawned on her that that dwarfish, huge-headed person was none other than the man Tamaru had described. But Aomame had only glimpsed him for a few seconds, and at less than the ideal angle. Luckily, for the same reasons, Ushikawa hadn't spotted Aomame out on the balcony.

At this point, a number of "if"s came to mind. *If* Tamaru had hung up a little earlier, *if* Aomame hadn't made cocoa while mulling over things, she would have seen Tengo, on top of the slide, gazing up at the sky. She would have raced out of the room, and they would have been reunited after twenty years.

If that had happened, however, Ushikawa, who had been tailing Tengo, would have noticed that this was Aomame, would have figured out where she lived, and would have immediately informed the duo from Sakigake.

So it's hard to say if Aomame's not seeing Tengo at this point was an unfortunate or fortunate occurrence. Either way, as he had done before, Tengo climbed up to the top of the slide and gazed steadily at the two moons floating in the sky and the clouds crossing in front. Ushikawa watched Tengo from the shadows. In the interim Aomame left the balcony, talked with Tamaru on the phone, and made her cocoa. In this way, twenty-five minutes elapsed. A fateful twenty-five minutes. By the time Aomame had put on her down jacket and returned to the balcony, Tengo had left the playground. Ushikawa didn't immediately follow after him. Instead, he stayed at the playground, checking on something he needed to make sure of. When he had finished, he quickly left the playground. It was during those few seconds that Aomame spotted him from the balcony.

The clouds were still racing across the sky, moving south, over Tokyo Bay and then out to the broad Pacific. After that, who knows what fate awaited them, just as no one knows what happens to the soul after death.

At any rate, the circle was drawing in tighter. But Tengo and Aomame weren't aware that the circle around them was closing in. Ushikawa sensed what was happening, since he was actively taking steps to tighten it, but even he couldn't see the big picture. He didn't know the most important point: that the distance between him and Aomame was now no more than a couple dozen meters. And unusually for Ushikawa, when he left the playground his mind was incomprehensibly confused.

By ten it was too cold to stay outside, so Aomame reluctantly got up and went back into the warm apartment. She undressed and climbed into a hot bath. As she soaked in the water, letting the heat take away the lingering cold, she rested a hand on her belly. She could feel the slight swelling there. She closed her eyes and tried to feel the *little one* that was inside. There wasn't much time left. Somehow she had to let Tengo know: that she was carrying his child. And that she would fight desperately to protect it.

She dressed, got into bed, lay on her side in the dark, and fell asleep. Before she fell into a deep sleep she had a short dream about the dowager.

Aomame is in the greenhouse at the Willow House as they watch butterflies together. The greenhouse is like a womb, dim and warm. The rubber tree she left behind in her old apartment is there. It has been well taken care of and is so green that she hardly recognizes it. A butterfly from a southern land that she has never seen before is resting on one of its thick leaves. The butterfly has folded its brightly colored wings and seems to be sleeping peacefully. Aomame is happy about this.

In the dream her belly is hugely swollen. It seems near her due date. She can make out the heartbeat of the *little one*. Her heartbeat and that of the *little one* blend together into a pleasant, joint rhythm.

The dowager is seated beside her, her back ramrod straight as always, her lips a straight line, quietly breathing. The two of them don't talk, in order not to wake the sleeping butterfly. The dowager is detached, as if she doesn't notice that Aomame is next to her. Aomame of course knows how closely the dowager protects her, but even so, she can't shake a sense of unease. The dowager's hands in her lap are too thin and fragile. Aomame's hands unconsciously feel for the pistol, but can't find it.

She is swallowed up by the dream, yet at the same time aware it is a dream. Sometimes Aomame has those kinds of dreams, where she is in a distinct, vivid reality but knows it isn't real. It is a detailed scene from a small planet somewhere else.

In the dream, someone opens the door to the greenhouse. An ominous cold wind blows in. The large butterfly opens its eyes, spreads its wings, and flutters off, away from the rubber tree. Who is it? She twists her head to look in that direction. But before she can see who it is, the dream is over.

She was sweating when she woke up, an unpleasant, clammy sweat. She stripped off her damp pajamas, dried herself with a towel, and put on a new T-shirt. She sat up in bed for a time. *Something bad might be about to happen. Somebody might be trying to get the* little one. *And whoever that is might be very close by.* She had to find Tengo – there was not a moment to lose. But other than watching the playground every night, there wasn't a thing she could do. Nothing other than what she was already doing – carefully, patiently, dutifully, keeping her eyes open, trained on this one tiny section of the world, that single point at the top of the slide. Even with such focus, though, a person can overlook things. Because she only has one pair of eyes.

Aomame wanted to cry, but the tears wouldn't come. She lay down again in bed, rested her palms on her stomach, and quietly waited for sleep to overtake her.

18

TENGO

When You Prick a Person with a Needle,
Red Blood Comes Out

"NOTHING HAPPENED FOR THREE DAYS AFTER that," Komatsu said. "I ate the food they gave me, slept at night in the narrow little bed, woke up when morning came, and used the small toilet in one corner of the room. The toilet had a partition for privacy, but no lock on it. There was still a lot of residual summer heat at the time, but the ventilator shaft seemed to be connected to an AC, so it didn't feel hot."

Tengo listened to Komatsu's story without comment.

"They brought food three times a day. At what time, I don't know. They took my watch away, and the room didn't have a window, so I didn't even know if it was day or night. I listened carefully but couldn't hear a sound. I doubt anyone could hear any sound from me. I had no idea where they had taken me, though I did have a vague sense that we were somewhere off the beaten track. Anyhow, I was there for three days, and nothing happened. I'm not actually certain it was three days. They brought me nine meals altogether, and I ate them when they brought them. The lights in the room were turned out three times, and I slept three times. Usually I'm a light, irregular sleeper, but for some reason I slept like a log. It's kind of strange, if you think about it. Do you follow me so far?"

Tengo silently nodded.

"I didn't say a word for the entire three days. A young man brought my meals. He was thin and had on a baseball cap and a white medical face mask. He wore a kind of sweatshirt and sweatpants, and dirty sneakers. He brought my meals on a tray and then took them away when I was finished. They used paper plates and flimsy plastic knives, forks, and spoons. The food they brought was ordinary prepared food in silver foil packages – not very good, but not so bad you wouldn't eat it. They didn't bring much each meal, and I was hungry, so I ate every bite. This was kind of weird, too. Usually I don't have much of an appetite, and if I'm not careful, sometimes I even forget to eat. They gave me milk and mineral water to drink. They didn't provide coffee or tea. No single-malt whiskey or draft beer. No smokes, either. But what're you going to do? It wasn't like I was lounging around some nice hotel."

As if he had just remembered that now he could smoke at his leisure, Komatsu pulled out a red Marlboro pack, stuck a cigarette between his lips, and lit it with a paper match. He sucked the smoke deep into his lungs, exhaled, and then frowned.

"The man who brought the meals never said a word. He must have been ordered by his superiors not to say anything. I'm sure he was at the bottom of the totem pole, a kind of all-purpose gofer. I think he must have been trained in one of the martial arts, though. He had a sort of focus to the way he carried himself."

"You didn't ask him anything?"

"I knew that if I spoke to him, he wouldn't respond, so I just kept quiet and let things be. I ate the food they brought me, drank my milk, went to bed when they turned out the lights, woke up when they turned them back on. In the morning the young guy would come and bring me an electric razor and toothbrush, and I would shave and brush my teeth. When I was done he would take them back. Other than toilet paper, there was nothing else to speak of in the room. They didn't let me take a shower or change my clothes, but I never felt like taking a shower or changing. There was no mirror in the room, but that didn't bother me. The worst thing was definitely the boredom. I mean, from the time I woke up till the time I went to sleep, I had to sit there alone, not speaking to anyone, in this white, completely square, dice-like room. I was bored to tears. I'm kind of a print junkie, I always need to have something to read with me – a room-service menu, you name it. But I didn't have any books, newspapers, or magazines. No TV or radio, no games. No one to talk to. Nothing to do but sit in the chair and stare at the floor, the walls, the ceiling. It was a totally absurd feeling. I mean, you're walking down the road when some people jump out of nowhere, grab you, put chloroform or something over your nose, drag you off somewhere, and hold you in a strange, windowless little room. A weird situation no matter how you cut it. And you get so bored you think you're going to lose your mind."

Komatsu stared with deep feeling at the cigarette between his fingers, the smoke curling up, then flicked the ash into the ashtray.

"I think they must have thrown me into that tiny room for three days, with nothing to do, trying to get me to break down. They seemed to know what they were doing when it came to breaking a person's spirit, pushing someone to the edge. On the fourth day – after I had my fourth breakfast, in other words – two other men came in. I figured this was the pair that had kidnapped me. I was attacked so suddenly that I didn't get a good look at their faces. But when I saw them on the fourth day, it started to come back to me – how they had pulled me into the car so roughly that I thought they were going to twist my arm off, how they had stuffed a cloth soaked with some kind of drug on my nose and mouth. The two of them didn't say a word the whole time, and it was over in an instant."

Remembering the events, Komatsu frowned.

"One of them wasn't very tall, but he was solidly built, with a buzz cut. He had a deep tan and prominent cheekbones. The other one was tall, with long limbs, sunken cheeks, his hair tied up behind him in a ponytail. Put them side by side and they looked like a comedy team. You've got your tall, thin one, and your short, stocky one with a goatee. But I could tell at a glance these were no comedians. They were a dangerous pair. They would never hesitate to do whatever had to be done, without making a big scene. They acted very relaxed, which made them all the more scary, and their eyes were frighteningly cold. They both wore black cotton trousers and white short-sleeved shirts. They were probably in their mid- to late twenties, the one with the buzz cut maybe a little older than the other one. Neither one wore a watch."

Tengo was silent, waiting for him to go on.

"Buzzcut did all the talking. Ponytail just stood there in front of the door, ramrod straight, without moving a muscle. It seemed like he was listening to our conversation, but then again, maybe not. Buzzcut sat down right across from me in a folding metal chair he had brought, and talked. There were no other chairs, so I sat on the bed. The guy had no facial expression at all. His mouth moved when he spoke, but other than that, his face was frozen, like a ventriloquist's dummy."

The first thing Buzzcut said when he sat down across from Komatsu was this: "Are you able to guess who we are, and why we brought you here?"

"No, I can't," Komatsu replied.

Buzzcut stared at Komatsu for a while with his depthless eyes. "But say you had to make a guess," he went on, "what would you say?" His words were polite enough, but his tone was forceful, his voice as hard and cold as a metal ruler left for a long time in a fridge.

Komatsu hesitated, but then said, honestly, that if he were forced to make a guess, he would say it had something to do with the *Air Chrysalis* affair. Nothing else came to mind. "That would mean you two are probably from Sakigake," he continued, "and we are in your compound."

Buzzcut neither confirmed nor denied what Komatsu had said. He just stared at him. Komatsu kept silent as well.

"Let's talk, then, based on that hypothesis," Buzzcut quietly began. "What we're going to say from now on is an extension of that hypothesis of yours, all based on the assumption that this is indeed the case. Is that acceptable?"

"That would be fine," Komatsu replied. They were going to talk about this as indirectly as they could. This was not a bad sign. If they were planning not to let him out of here alive, they wouldn't go to the trouble.

"As an editor at a publishing house, you were in charge of publishing Eriko Fukada's *Air Chrysalis*. Am I correct?"

"You are," Komatsu admitted. This was common knowledge.

"Based on our understanding, there was some fraud involved in the publication. *Air Chrysalis* received a literary prize for debut novelists from a literary journal. But before the selection committee received the manuscript, a third party rewrote it considerably at your direction. After the work was secretly revised, it won the prize, was published as a book, and became a bestseller. Do I have my facts correct?"

"It depends on how you look at it," Komatsu said. "There are times when a submitted manuscript is rewritten, on advice of the editor –"

Buzzcut put his hand up to cut him off. "There's nothing dishonest about the author revising parts of the novel based on the editor's advice. You're right. But having a third party rewrite the work is unscrupulous. Not only that, but forming a phony company to distribute royalties – I don't know how this would be interpreted from a legal standpoint, but morally speaking these actions would be roundly condemned. It's inexcusable. Newspapers and magazines would have

264

a field day over it, and your company's reputation would suffer. I'm sure you understand this very well, Mr. Komatsu. We know all the facts, and have incontrovertible proof we can reveal to the world. So it's best not to try to talk your way out of it. It's a waste of time, for both of us."

Komatsu nodded.

"If it did come to that, obviously you would have to resign from the company. Plus, you know that you would be blackballed from the field. There would be no place left for you in publishing. For legitimate work, at least."

"I imagine not," Komatsu said.

"But at this point only a limited number of people know the truth," Buzzcut said. "You, Eriko Fukada, Professor Ebisuno, and Tengo Kawana, who rewrote the book. And just a handful of others."

Komatsu chose his words carefully. "According to our working hypothesis, this *handful of others* would be members of Sakigake."

Buzzcut nodded, barely. "Yes. According to our hypothesis, that would be the case."

Buzzcut paused, allowing the hypothesis to sink in. And then he went on.

"And if that hypothesis is indeed true, then *they* can do whatever they want to you. They can keep you here as their guest of honor for as long as they like. No problem at all. Or, if they wanted to shorten the length of your stay, there are any number of other choices they can make – including ones that would be unpleasant for both sides. Either way, they have the power and the means. I believe you already have a pretty good grasp of that."

"I think I do," Komatsu replied.

"Good," Buzzcut said.

Buzzcut raised a finger, and Ponytail left the room. He soon returned with a phone. He plugged it into a jack on the wall and handed the phone to Komatsu. Buzzcut directed him to call his company.

"You have had a terrible cold and a fever and have been in bed for a few days. It doesn't look like you'll be able to come in to work for a while. Tell them that and then hang up."

Komatsu asked for one of his colleagues, briefly explained what he had to say, and hung up without responding to his questions. Buzzcut nodded and Ponytail unplugged the phone from the jack and took the phone and left the room. Buzzcut intently studied the back of his hands, then turned to Komatsu. There was a faint tinge of kindness in his voice.

"That's it for today," he said. "We'll talk again another day. Until then, please consider carefully what we have discussed."

The two of them left, and Komatsu spent the next ten days in silence, in that room. Three times a day the masked young man would bring in the mediocre meals. After the fourth day, Komatsu was given a change of clothes – a cotton pajama-like top and bottom – but until the very end, they didn't let him take a shower. The most he could do was wash his face in the tiny sink attached to the toilet. His sense of time's passage grew more uncertain.

Komatsu thought that he had been taken to the cult's headquarters in Yamanashi. He had seen it on TV. It was deep in the mountains, surrounded by a tall fence, like some independent realm. Escape, or finding help, was out of the question. If they did end up killing him (which must be what they had meant by an *unpleasant choice*), his body would never be found. He had never felt death so real, or so close.

Ten days after he had made that forced call to his company (most likely ten days, though he wouldn't bet on it), the same duo made another appearance. Buzzcut seemed thinner than before, which made his cheekbones all the more prominent. His cold eyes were now blood-shot. As before, he sat down on the folding chair he had brought, across the table from Komatsu. He didn't say a word for a long time. He simply stared at Komatsu with his red eyes.

* * *

Ponytail looked the same. Again he stood, ramrod straight, in front of the door, his emotionless eyes fixed on an imaginary point in space. They were again dressed in black trousers and white shirts, most likely a sort of uniform.

"Let's pick up where we left off last time," Buzzcut finally said. "We were saying that we can do whatever we like with you."

Komatsu nodded. "Including choices that wouldn't be pleasant for either side."

"You really do have a great memory," Buzzcut said. "You are correct. An unpleasant outcome is looming."

Komatsu was silent. Buzzcut went on.

"*In theory*, that is. Practically speaking, *they* would much prefer not to make an extreme choice. If you were suddenly to disappear now, Mr. Komatsu, that would lead to unwanted complications. Just like it did when Eriko Fukada disappeared. There aren't many people who would be sad if you were gone, but you're a respected editor, prominent in your field. And I'm sure that if you fall behind in your alimony payments, your wife will have something to say about it. For *them*, this would not be a very favorable development."

Komatsu gave a dry cough and swallowed.

"They're not criticizing you personally, or trying to punish you. They understand that in publishing *Air Chrysalis* you weren't intending to attack a specific religious organization. At first you didn't even know the connection between the novel and that organization. You perpetrated this fraud for fun and out of ambition. And money became a factor, too, as things developed. It's very hard for a mere company employee to pay alimony and child support, isn't it? And you brought Tengo Kawana – an aspiring novelist and cram school instructor who didn't know anything about the circumstances – into the mix. The plan itself was smart, but your choice of the novel and the writer? Not so much. And things got more complicated than you imagined. You were like ordinary citizens who had wandered across the front lines and stepped into a minefield. You can't go forward, and can't go back. Am I correct in this, Mr. Komatsu?"

"That might sum it up, I suppose," Komatsu replied.

"There still seem to be some things you don't entirely understand," Buzzcut said, his eyes narrowing a fraction. "If you did, you wouldn't pretend that this has nothing to do with you. Let's make things crystal clear. You are, frankly, in the middle of a minefield."

Komatsu silently nodded.

Buzzcut closed his eyes, and ten seconds later opened them. "This situation has put you in a bind, but understand that it has created some real problems for *them* as well."

Komatsu took the plunge and spoke. "Do you mind if I ask you a question?"

"If it's something I can answer."

"By publishing *Air Chrysalis* we created a little trouble for the religious organization. Is that what you're saying?"

"More than a *little* trouble," Buzzcut said. He grimaced slightly. "The voice no longer speaks to them. Do you have any idea what that means?"

"No," Komatsu croaked, his voice dry.

"Fine. I can't explain any more to you than that. And it's better for you not to know. *The voice no longer speaks to them.* That's all I can tell you now." Buzzcut paused. "And this unhappy turn of events was brought about by the publication of *Air Chrysalis.*"

Komatsu posed a question. "And did Eriko Fukada and Professor Ebisuno expect that by making *Air Chrysalis* public, they would bring about this *unhappy turn of events*?"

Buzzcut shook his head. "No, I don't think Professor Ebisuno knew things would turn out this way. It's unclear what Eriko Fukada's intentions were. Saying it was unintentional is just conjecture. But even if you assume it was intentional, I don't believe it was her intention."

"People read *Air Chrysalis* as a fantasy novel," Komatsu said. "A harmless, dreamy little tale written by a high school girl. Actually the novel was criticized quite a lot for being a bit too surreal. No one ever suspected that some great secret, or concrete information, was exposed in the pages of the book."

"I imagine you're right," Buzzcut said. "The vast majority of people would never notice. But that's not the issue. Those secrets should never have been made public. *In any form whatsoever.*"

Ponytail stood rooted to a spot in front of the door, staring at the wall, at some prospect that no one else could see.

"What *they* want is to get the voice back," Buzzcut said, choosing his words. "The well hasn't run dry. It has just sunk down deeper, where it can't be seen. It will be quite difficult to restore, but it can be done."

Buzzcut looked deep into Komatsu's eyes. He looked like he was measuring the depths of something inside, like eyeballing a room to see if a piece of furniture would fit.

"As I said earlier, all of you have wandered into a minefield. You can't go forward, and you can't go back. What *they* can do is show you the path, so you can get out safely. If they do, you'll have a narrow escape, and they'll peacefully manage to get rid of some bothersome intruders."

Buzzcut folded his arms.

"We would like you to quietly withdraw from all this. They aren't really concerned if you leave here in one piece. But it will present problems if we make a lot of noise here right now. So, Mr. Komatsu, I will show you the way to retreat. I will guide you back to a safe place. What I ask for in return is the following: You must stop publishing *Air Chrysalis.* You won't print any more copies, or reprint it in paperback. And all advertising for the book will cease. And you will sever all connections with Eriko Fukada. What do you say? You have enough influence to handle that."

"It won't be easy, but maybe I can manage it," Komatsu said.

"Mr. Komatsu, we didn't bring you all the way here to talk about *maybe*s." Buzzcut's eyes grew even redder and sharper. "We're not asking you to collect all the copies of the book that are out there. Do that, and the media would jump on the story. And we know your influence doesn't extend that far. We would just like you to quietly take care of things. We can't undo what has already happened. Once something's ruined, it can't go back to the way it was. What *they* would like is to remove this from the spotlight. Do you follow me?"

Komatsu nodded.

"Mr. Komatsu, as I have explained, there are several facts here that must not come to light. If they did, all those involved would suffer repercussions. So for the sake of both parties, we would like to conclude a truce. They will not hold you responsible beyond this point. Peace will be guaranteed. You will have nothing further to do with *Air Chrysalis*. This isn't such a bad deal, you know."

Komatsu thought it over. "All right. I will begin by making sure *Air Chrysalis* is no longer published. It may take some time, but I'll find a way. And speaking personally, I can put this entire matter out of my mind. I think Tengo Kawana can do the same. He wasn't enthusiastic about it from the very beginning. I got him involved against his will. His role in this is long past. And I don't think Eriko Fukada will be a problem. She said that she doesn't plan to write any more novels. Professor Ebisuno is the only one whose reaction I can't gauge. Ultimately he wanted to determine if his friend, Tamotsu Fukada, was all right. He wants to know where he is now and what he's doing. Whatever I might tell him, he may continue to pursue information on Mr. Fukada."

"Tamotsu Fukada is dead," Buzzcut said. His voice was quiet, uninflected, but there was something terribly heavy within.

"*Dead?*" Komatsu asked.

"It happened recently," Buzzcut said. He took a deep breath and slowly exhaled. "He died of a heart attack. It was over in a moment, and he didn't suffer. Due to the circumstances, we didn't submit a notification of death, and we held the funeral secretly at our compound. For religious reasons the body was incinerated, the bones crushed and sprinkled in the nearby mountains. Legally, this constitutes desecration of a body, but it would be difficult to make a formal case against us. But this is the truth. We never lie when it comes to matters of life and death. I would like you to let Professor Ebisuno know about this."

"A natural death."

Buzzcut nodded deeply. "Mr. Fukada was a very important person for us. No – important is too trite a term to express what he was. He was a giant. His death has only been reported to a limited number of people. They grieved deeply for the loss. His wife – Eriko Fukada's mother – died several years ago of stomach cancer. She refused chemotherapy, and passed away within our treatment facility. Her husband, Tamotsu, cared for her to the end."

"Even so, you didn't file a notification of her death," Komatsu asked.

No words of denial came.

"And Tamotsu Fukada passed away recently."

"Correct," Buzzcut said.

"Was this after *Air Chrysalis* was published?"

Buzzcut's gaze went down to the table for a moment, then he raised his head and looked at Komatsu.

"That's right. Mr. Fukada passed away after *Air Chrysalis* was published."

"Are the two events related?" Komatsu dared to ask.

Buzzcut didn't say anything for a while, pondering how he should respond. Finally, as if he had made up his mind, he spoke. "Fine. I think it might be best to let Professor Ebisuno know all the facts, so he will understand. Mr. Tamotsu Fukada was the real Leader, the *one who hears the voice*. When his daughter, Eriko Fukada, published *Air Chrysalis*, the voice stopped speaking to him, and at that point Mr. Fukada himself put an end to his existence. It was a natural death. More precisely, he put an end to his own existence naturally."

"Eriko Fukada was the daughter of Leader," Komatsu murmured.

Buzzcut gave a concise, abbreviated nod.

"And Eriko Fukada ended up driving her father to his death," Komatsu continued.

Buzzcut nodded once more. "That is correct."

"But the religion still continues to exist."

"The religion does still exist," Buzzcut replied, and he stared at Komatsu with eyes like ancient pebbles frozen deep within a glacier. "Mr. Komatsu, the publication of *Air Chrysalis* has done more than a little damage to Sakigake. However, *they* are not thinking to punish you for this. There is nothing to be gained from punishing you at this point. They have a mission they must accomplish, and in order to do so, quiet isolation is required."

"So you want everyone to take a step back and forget it all happened."

"In a word, yes."

"Was it absolutely necessary to kidnap me in order to get this message across?"

Something akin to an expression crossed Buzzcut's face for the first time, a superficial emotion, located somewhere in the interstice between humor and sympathy. "They went to the trouble of bringing you here because *they* wanted you to understand the seriousness of the situation. They didn't want to do anything drastic, but if something is necessary, they don't hesitate. They wanted you to really feel this, viscerally. If all of you do not keep your promise, then something quite unpleasant will occur. Do you follow me?"

"I do," Komatsu replied.

"To tell you the truth, Mr. Komatsu, you were very fortunate. Because of all the heavy fog you may not have noticed this, but you were just a few inches from the edge of a cliff. It would be best if you remember this. At the moment *they* do not have the freedom to deal with you. There are many more pressing matters at hand. And in that sense, too, you are quite fortunate. So while this good fortune still continues . . ."

As he said this he turned his palms faceup, like someone checking to see if it was raining. Komatsu waited for his next words, but there weren't any. Now that he had finished speaking, Buzzcut looked exhausted. He slowly rose from his chair, folded it, and exited the cube-shaped room without so much as a glance back. The heavy door closed, the lock clicking shut. Komatsu was left all alone.

"They kept me locked away in that square little room for four more days. We had already discussed what was important. They had told me what they wanted to say and we had come to an agreement. So I couldn't see the point of keeping me there any longer. That duo never appeared again, and the young man in charge of me never uttered a word. I ate the same monotonous food, shaved with the electric razor, and spent my time staring at the ceiling and the walls. I slept when they turned off the lights, woke up when they switched them on. And I pondered what Buzzcut had told me. What really struck me most was the fact that he said *we were fortunate.* Buzzcut was right. If these guys wanted to, they could do anything they wanted. They could be as cold-blooded as they liked. While I was locked up in there, I really came to believe this. I think they must have kept me locked up for four more days knowing that would be the result. They don't miss a beat – they're very meticulous."

Komatsu picked up his glass and took a sip of the highball.

"They drugged me again with chloroform or whatever, and when I woke up it was daybreak and I was lying on a bench in Jingu Gaien. It was the end of September, and the mornings were cold. Thanks to this I actually did wind up with a cold and a fever and I really was in bed for the next three days. But I guess I should consider myself fortunate if that's the worst that happened to me."

Komatsu seemed to be finished with his story. "Did you tell this to Professor Ebisuno?" Tengo asked.

"Yes, after I was released, and a few days after my fever broke, I went to his house on the mountain. I told him pretty much what I told you."

"What was his reaction?"

Komatsu drained the last drop of his highball and ordered a refill. He urged Tengo to do the same, but Tengo shook his head.

"Professor Ebisuno had me repeat the story over and over and asked a lot of detailed questions. I answered whatever I could. I could repeat the same story as many times as he wished. I mean, after I last spoke with Buzzcut, I was locked up alone for four days in that room. I had nobody to talk to, and plenty of time on my hands. So I went over what he had told me and was able to accurately remember all the details. Like I was a human tape recorder."

"But the part about Fuka-Eri's parents dying was just something they claimed happened. Right?" Tengo asked.

"That's right. They insisted it happened, but there's no way to verify it. They didn't file a death notice. Still, considering the way Buzzcut sounded, it didn't seem like he was making it up. As he said, Sakigake considers people's lives and deaths a sacred thing. After I finished my story, Professor Ebisuno was silent for a time, thinking it over. He really thinks about things deeply, for a long time. Without a word, he stood up, left the room, and didn't come back for quite a while. I think he was trying to accept his friends' deaths, trying to understand them as inevitable. He may have already half expected that they were no longer of the world and had resigned himself to that fact. Still, actually being told that two close friends have died has got to hurt."

Tengo remembered the bare, spartan living room, the chilly, deep silence, the occasional sharp call of a bird outside the window. "So," he asked, "have we actually backed our way out of the minefield?"

A fresh highball was brought over. Komatsu took a sip.

"No conclusion was reached right then. Professor Ebisuno said he needed time to think. But what other choice do we have than to do what they told us? I got things rolling right away. At work I did everything I could and stopped them from printing additional copies of *Air Chrysalis,* so in effect it's out of print. There will be no paperback edition, either. The book already sold a lot of copies and made the company plenty of money, so they won't suffer a loss. In a large company like this you have to have meetings about it, the president has to sign off on it – but when I dangled before them the prospect of a scandal connected with a ghostwriter, the higher-ups were terrified and in the end did what I wanted. It looks like I'll be given the silent treatment from now on, but it's okay. I'm used to it."

"Did Professor Ebisuno accept what they said about Fuka-Eri's parents being dead?"

"I think so," Komatsu said. "But I imagine it will take some time for it to really sink in, for him to fully accept it. As far as I could tell, those guys were serious. They would make a few concessions, but I think they're hoping to avoid any more trouble. Which is why they resorted to kidnapping – they wanted to make absolutely sure we got the message. And they didn't need to tell me about how they secretly incinerated the bodies of Mr. and Mrs. Fukada. Even though it would be hard to prove, desecration of bodies is a major crime. But still they brought it up. They laid their cards on the table. That's why I think most of what Buzzcut told me was the truth. Maybe not every detail, but the overall picture, at least."

Tengo went over what Komatsu had told him. "Fuka-Eri's father was *the one who heard the voice.* A prophet, in other words. But when his daughter published *Air Chrysalis* and it became a bestseller, the voice stopped speaking to him, and as a result the father died a natural death."

"Or rather he put an end to his own existence *naturally,*" Komatsu said.

"And so it's critical for Sakigake to gain a new prophet. If the voice stops speaking, then the religion's whole reason for existence is lost. So they don't have the time to worry about the likes of us. In a nutshell, that's the story, right?"

"I think so."

"*Air Chrysalis* contains information of critical importance to them. When it was published and became widely read, the voice went silent. But what critical information could the book be pointing toward?"

"During those last four days of my confinement I thought a lot about that," Komatsu said. "*Air Chrysalis* is a pretty short novel. In the story the world is filled with Little People. The ten-year-old girl who is the protagonist lives in an isolated community. The Little People secretly come out at night and create an air chrysalis. The girl's alter ego is inside the chrysalis and a mother-daughter relationship is formed – the *maza* and the *dohta*. There are two moons in that world, a large one and a small one, probably symbolizing the *maza* and the *dohta*. In the novel the protagonist – based on Fuka-Eri herself, I think – rejects being a *maza* and runs away from the community. The *dohta* is left behind. The novel doesn't tell us what happened to the *dohta* after that."

Tengo stared for a time at the ice melting in his glass.

"I wonder if the *one who hears the voice* needs the *dohta* as an intermediary," Tengo said. "It's through her that he can hear the voice for the first time, or perhaps through her that the voice is translated into comprehensible language. Both of them have to be there for the message of the voice to take its proper form. To borrow Fuka-Eri's terms, there's a Receiver and a Perceiver. But first of all the air chrysalis has to be created, because the *dohta* can only be born through it. And to create a *dohta*, the *proper maza* must be there."

"That's your opinion, Tengo."

Tengo shook his head. "I wouldn't call it an opinion. As I listened to you summarize the plot, I just thought that must be the way it is."

As he rewrote the novel, and afterward, Tengo had pondered the meaning of the *maza* and the *dohta*, but he was never quite able to grasp the overall picture. But now, as he talked with Komatsu, the pieces gradually fell into place. Though he still had questions: Why did an air chrysalis materialize above his father's bed in the hospital? And why was Aomame, as a young girl, inside?

"It's a fascinating system," Komatsu said. "But isn't it a problem for the *maza* to be separated from the *dohta*?"

"Without the *dohta*, it's hard to see the *maza* as a complete entity. As we saw with Fuka-Eri, it's difficult to pinpoint exactly what that means, but there is something missing – like a person who has lost his shadow. What the *dohta* is like without the *maza,* I have no idea. Probably they're both incomplete, because, ultimately, the *dohta* is nothing more than an alter ego. But in Fuka-Eri's case, even without the *maza* by her side, the *dohta* may have been able to fulfill her role as a kind of medium."

Komatsu's lips were stretched in a tight line for a while, then turned up slightly. "Are you thinking that everything in *Air Chrysalis* really took place?"

"I'm not saying that. I'm just making an assumption – hypothesizing that it's all real, and going from there."

"All right," Komatsu said. "So even if Fuka-Eri's alter ego goes far away from her body, she can still function as a medium."

"Which explains why Sakigake isn't forcing her to return, even if they know her whereabouts. Because in her case, even if the *maza* isn't nearby, the *dohta* can still fulfill her duties. Maybe their connection is that strong, even if they're far apart."

"Okay . . ."

Tengo continued, "I imagine that they have multiple *dohta*s. The Little People must use the chance to create many air chrysalises. They would be anxious if all they had was one Perceiver. Or the number of *dohta*s who can function correctly might be limited. Maybe there is one powerful, main *dohta,* and several weaker auxiliary *dohta*s, and they function collectively."

"So the *dohta* that Fuka-Eri left behind was the main *dohta,* the one who functions properly?"

"That seems possible. Throughout everything that has happened, Fuka-Eri has always been at the center, like the eye of a hurricane."

Komatsu narrowed his eyes and folded his hands together on the table. When he wanted to, he could really focus on an issue.

"You know, Tengo, I was thinking about this. Couldn't you hypothesize that the Fuka-Eri we met is actually the *dohta* and what was left behind at Sakigake was the *maza*?"

This came as a bit of a shock. The idea had never occurred to Tengo. For him, Fuka-Eri was an actual person. But put it that way, and it started to sound possible. I have no *periods*. So there's no chance I'll get *pregnant*. Fuka-Eri had announced this, after they had had intercourse that night. If she was nothing more than an alter ego, her inability to get pregnant would make sense. An alter ego can't reproduce itself – only the *maza* can do it. Still, Tengo couldn't accept that hypothesis – that it was possible he had had intercourse with her alter ego, not the real Fuka-Eri.

"Fuka-Eri has a distinct personality. And her own code of conduct. I sort of doubt an alter ego could have those."

"Exactly," Komatsu agreed. "If she has nothing else, Fuka-Eri does have her own distinct personality and code of conduct. I would have to agree with you on that one."

Still, Fuka-Eri was hiding a secret, a critical code hidden away inside this lovely girl, a code he had to crack. Tengo sensed this. Which one was the real person and which one the alter ego? Or was the whole notion of classifying into "real" and "alter ego" a mistake? Maybe Fuka-Eri was able, depending on the situation, to manipulate both her real self and her alter ego?

"There are several things I still don't understand," Komatsu said, resting his hands on the table and staring at them. For a middle-aged man, his fingers were long and slender.

"The voice has stopped speaking, the water in the well has dried up, the prophet has died. What will happen to the *dohta* after that? She won't follow him in death like widows do in India."

"When there's no more Receiver, there's no need for a Perceiver."

"If we take your hypothesis a step further, that is," Komatsu said. "Did Fuka-Eri know that would be the result when she wrote *Air Chrysalis*? That Sakigake man told me it wasn't intentional. At least it wasn't *her* intention. But how could he know this?"

"I don't know," Tengo said. "But I just can't see Fuka-Eri intentionally driving her father to his death. I think her father was facing death for some other reason. Maybe that's why she left in the first place. Or maybe she was hoping that her father would be freed from the voice. I'm just speculating, though, and I have nothing to back it up."

Komatsu considered this for a long time, wrinkles forming on either side of his nose. Finally he sighed and glanced around. "What a strange world. With each passing day, it's getting harder to know how much is just hypothetical and how much is real. Tell me, Tengo, as a novelist, what is your definition of reality?"

"When you prick a person with a needle, red blood comes out – that's the real world," Tengo replied.

"Then this is most definitely the real world," Komatsu said, and he rubbed his inner forearm. Pale veins rose to the surface. They were not very healthy-looking blood vessels – blood vessels damaged by years of drinking, smoking, an unhealthy lifestyle, and various literary intrigues. Komatsu drained the last of his highball and clinked the ice around in the empty glass.

"Could you go on with your hypothesis? It's getting more interesting."

"They are looking for a successor to the *one who hears the voice*," Tengo said. "But they also have to find a new, *properly functional dohta*. A new Receiver will need a new Perceiver."

"In other words, they need to find a new *maza* as well. And in order to do so, they have to make a new air chrysalis. That sounds like a pretty large-scale operation."

"Which is why they're so deadly serious."

"Exactly."

"But they can't be going about this blind," Tengo said. "They've got to have somebody in mind."

Komatsu nodded. "I got that impression, too. That's why they wanted to get rid of us as fast as they could – so we don't bother them anymore. I think we were quite a blot on their personal landscape."

"How so?"

Komatsu shook his head. He didn't know either.

"I wonder what message the voice told them until now. And what connection there is between the voice and the Little People."

Komatsu shook his head listlessly again. This, too, went beyond anything the two of them could imagine.

"Did you see the movie *2001: A Space Odyssey*?"

"I did," Tengo said.

"We're like the apes in the movie," Komatsu said. "The ones with shaggy black fur, screeching out some nonsense as they dance around the monolith."

A new pair of customers came into the bar, sat down at the counter like they were regulars, and ordered cocktails.

"There's one thing we can say for sure," Komatsu said, sounding like he wanted to wind things down. "Your hypothesis is convincing. It makes sense. I always really enjoy having these talks with you. But we're going to back out of this scary minefield, and probably never see Fuka-Eri or Professor Ebisuno again. *Air Chrysalis* is nothing more than a harmless fantasy novel, with not a single piece of concrete information in it. And what that voice is, and what message it's transmitting, have nothing to do with us. We need to leave it that way."

"Get off the boat and get back to life onshore."

Komatsu nodded. "You got it. I'll go to work every day, gathering manuscripts that don't make a difference one way or another in order to publish them in a literary journal. You will go to cram school and teach math to promising young people, and in between teaching, you'll write novels. We'll each go back to our own peaceful, mundane lives. No rapids, no waterfalls. We'll quietly grow old. Any objection?"

"We don't have any other choice, do we?"

Komatsu stretched out the wrinkles next to his nose with his finger. "That's right. We have no other choice. I can tell you this – I don't want to ever be kidnapped again. Being locked up in that room once is more than enough. If there were a next time, I might not see the light of day. Just the thought of meeting that duo again makes my heart quake. They only need to glare at you and you would keel over."

Komatsu turned to face the bar and signaled with his glass for a third highball. He stuck a fresh cigarette in his mouth.

"But why haven't you told me this until now? It has been quite some time since the kidnapping, over two months. You should have told me earlier."

"I don't know," Komatsu said, slightly inclining his head. "You're right. I was thinking I should tell you, but I kept putting it off. I'm not sure why. Maybe I had a guilty conscience."

"Guilty conscience?" Tengo said, surprised. He had never expected to hear Komatsu say that.

"Even I can have a guilty conscience," Komatsu said.

"About what?"

Komatsu didn't reply. He narrowed his eyes and rolled the unlit cigarette around between his lips.

"Does Fuka-Eri know her parents have died?" Tengo asked.

"I think she probably does. I imagine at some point Professor Ebisuno told her about it."

Tengo nodded. Fuka-Eri must have known about it a long time ago. He had a distinct feeling she did. He was the only one who hadn't been told.

"So we get out of the boat and return to our lives onshore," Tengo repeated.

"That's right. We edge away from the minefield."

"But even if we want to do that, do you think we can go back to our old lives that easily?"

"All we can do is try," Komatsu said. He struck a match and lit the cigarette. "What specifically bothers you?"

"Lots of things around us are already starting to fall into strange patterns. Some things have already been transformed, and it may not be easy for them to go back the way they were."

"Even if our lives are on the line?"

Tengo gave an ambiguous shake of his head. He had been feeling for some time that he was caught up in a strong current, one that never wavered. And that current was dragging him off to some unknown place. But he couldn't really explain it to Komatsu.

Tengo didn't reveal to Komatsu that the novel he was writing now carried on the world in *Air Chrysalis*. Komatsu probably wouldn't welcome the news. And Sakigake would certainly be less than pleased. If he wasn't careful, he might step into a different minefield, or get the people around him mixed up in it. But a narrative takes its own direction, and continues on, almost automatically. And whether he liked it or not, Tengo was a part of that world. To him, this was no longer a fictional world. This was the real world, where red blood spurts out when you slice open your skin with a knife. And in the sky in this world, there were two moons, side by side.

19

USHIKAWA

What He Can Do
That Most People Can't

IT WAS A QUIET, WINDLESS THURSDAY morning. Ushikawa woke as usual before six and washed his face with cold water. He brushed his teeth as he listened to the NHK news on the radio, and he shaved with the electric razor. He boiled water in a pot, made instant ramen, and, after he finished eating, drank a cup of instant coffee. He rolled up his sleeping bag, stowed it in the closet, and sat down at the window in front of his camera. The eastern sky was beginning to grow light. It looked like it was going to be a warm day.

The faces of all the people who left for work in the morning were etched in his mind. There was no need to take any more photos. From seven to eight thirty they hurried out of the apartment building to the station – the usual suspects. Ushikawa heard the lively voices of a group of elementary school pupils heading off for school. The children's voices reminded him of when his daughters were little. His daughters had thoroughly enjoyed elementary school. They took piano and ballet lessons, and had lots of friends. To the very end, Ushikawa had found it hard to accept that he had these ordinary, happy kids. How could someone like him possibly be the father of children like these?

After the morning rush, almost no one came in or out of the building. The children's lively voices had disappeared. Ushikawa laid aside the remote control for the shutter, leaned against the wall, smoked a cigarette, and kept an eye on the entrance through a gap in the curtain. As always, just after ten a.m., the mailman came on his small red motorcycle and adeptly sorted the mail into all the boxes. From what Ushikawa could make out, half of it was junk mail, stuff that would be tossed away, unopened. As the sun rose higher, the temperature went up, and most of the people along the street took off their coats.

It was after eleven when Fuka-Eri appeared at the entrance to the building. She wore the same black turtleneck as before, a gray short coat, jeans, sneakers, and dark sunglasses. And an oversized green shoulder bag slung diagonally across her shoulder. The bag was bulging with, no doubt, all sorts of things. Ushikawa left the wall he was leaning against, went over to the camera on the tripod, and squinted through the viewfinder.

The girl was leaving there, that much he understood. She had stuffed all her belongings in that bag and was setting off for somewhere else. She would never be back there again. He could sense it. *Maybe she decided to leave here,* he thought, *because she noticed I was staking out the place.* The thought made his heart race.

As she stepped out of the entrance, she came to a halt and stared up at the sky like she had done before, searching for something among the tangle of electric lines and the transformers. Her sunglasses caught the light and glittered. Had she found what she was looking for? Or maybe not? He couldn't read her expression through the sunglasses. She must have stood there, frozen, for a good thirty seconds, gazing up at the sky. Then, almost as an afterthought, she turned her head and looked straight at the window behind which Ushikawa was hiding. She took off her sunglasses and stuck them in a coat pocket. She frowned and focused her gaze right on the camouflaged telephoto lens. *She knows,* Ushikawa thought once again. *The girl knows I'm hiding in here, that she's being secretly watched.* And she was looking at him in the opposite direction, watching Ushikawa through the lens and back through the viewfinder. Like water flowing backward through a curved pipe. Ushikawa felt the flesh crawl on both his arms.

Fuka-Eri blinked every few moments. Like independent, silent living creatures, her eyelids slowly went up and down in a studied way. Nothing else moved. She stood there like some lofty bird with neck twisted, staring straight at Ushikawa. He couldn't pull his eyes away from her. It felt as if the entire world had come to a momentary halt. There was no wind, and sounds no longer made the air vibrate.

Finally Fuka-Eri stopped looking at him. She raised her head again and gazed up at the sky, as she had done a moment before. This time, though, she stopped after a couple of seconds. Her expression was unchanged. She took the dark sunglasses out of her pocket, put them on again, and headed toward the street. She walked with a smooth, unhesitant stride.

I should go out and follow her. Tengo isn't back yet, and I have the time to find out where she's going. It couldn't hurt to find out where she's moving to. But somehow Ushikawa couldn't stand up from the floor. His body was numb. That sharp gaze she had sent through the viewfinder had robbed him of the strength he needed to take action.

It's okay, Ushikawa told himself as he sat there on the floor. *Aomame is the one I have to locate. Eriko Fukada is a fascinating girl, but she's not my main priority here. She's just a supporting actress. If she's leaving, why not just let her go?*

Once on the main street, Fuka-Eri hurried off toward the station. She didn't look back. Through the gap in the sun-bleached curtains, Ushikawa watched as she went. Once the green shoulder bag, swinging back and forth, disappeared from view, he practically crawled away from the camera and leaned against the wall again, waiting for his strength to return. He took out a Seven Stars, lit it, and inhaled the smoke deeply. But the cigarette was tasteless.

His strength didn't return. His arms and legs still felt numb. He suddenly realized a strange space had formed inside him, a kind of pure hollow. This space signified a simple lack, a nothingness. Ushikawa sat there in the midst of this unknown void, unable to rise. He felt a dull pain in his chest – not exactly pain, but more like the difference in air pressure at the point where the material and the immaterial meet.

He sat for a long time at the bottom of that void, leaning against the wall, smoking tasteless cigarettes. *When that girl left, she left behind this void. No, maybe not. Maybe she just showed me something that was already there, inside me.*

Ushikawa knew that Eriko Fukada had literally shaken him to his core. Her unwavering, pointed gaze shook him not only physically, but to the center of his being, like someone who had fallen passionately in love. He had never felt this way before in his life.

No, that can't be right, he thought. *Why should I be in love with that girl? We have to be the most ill-matched pair one could possibly imagine.* He didn't need to check himself out in the mirror to confirm this. But it wasn't just about looks. *In every possible aspect,* he decided, *no one is further removed from her than me.* Sexually, he wasn't attracted to her. As far as sexual desire was concerned, a couple of times a month Ushikawa called a prostitute he knew, and that was enough. Call her up, have her over to a hotel room, and have sex – like going to the barber.

It had to be something on a more spiritual level, Ushikawa concluded. It was hard to accept, but Ushikawa and that lovely girl had – while staring at each other through opposite ends of the camouflaged telephoto lens – reached a kind of understanding that emanated from the deepest, darkest recesses of their beings. It had happened in an instant, yet they had laid bare their very souls. And then she had gone off, leaving Ushikawa behind, alone in this void.

The girl knew I was secretly observing her through this telephoto lens, and she must have known, too, that I followed her to the supermarket near the station. She never looked back even once then, but she definitely knew I was there. But he hadn't seen any criticism in her eyes. Ushikawa felt that somehow, in some far-off, deep place, she had understood him.

The girl had shown up, then left. *We came from different directions, our paths happened to cross, our eyes met for an instant, then we moved off in different directions once more. I probably won't ever run across Eriko Fukada again.*

Leaning against the wall, Ushikawa looked through the gap in the curtain and watched people coming and going. Maybe Fuka-Eri would come back. Maybe she would remember something important she had left back in the apartment. But she didn't. She had made up her mind to move on to somewhere else, and she would never return.

Ushikawa spent the afternoon feeling deeply powerless. This sense of impotence was formless, weightless. His blood moved slowly, sluggishly, through his veins. It was as if his vision were covered by a fine mist, while the joints in his arms and legs felt creaky and dull. When he shut his eyes, the ache of her gaze stabbed at his ribs, the ache rolling in and out like gentle waves at the shore, rolling in again, then receding. Sometimes the pain was so great it made him wince. At the same time, though, Ushikawa realized it gave him a warm feeling, like nothing he had ever experienced.

His wife and two daughters, his snug little house with a lawn in Chuorinkan – they had never made him feel this warm. He had always had something like a clod of frozen dirt stuck in his heart – a hard, cold core he had always lived with. He had never even felt it as cold. For him this was the *normal temperature*. Even so, Fuka-Eri's gaze had, if even for a moment, melted that icy core. And it brought on the dull ache. The warmth and the pain came as a pair, and unless he accepted the pain, he wouldn't feel the warmth. It was a kind of trade-off.

In a little sunny spot, Ushikawa experienced the pain and the warmth simultaneously. Quietly, without moving a muscle. It was a calm, peaceful winter's day. People on the street passed through the delicate sunshine as they strolled by, but the sun was steadily moving west, hidden in the shadow of the building, and the little pool of sunlight he was in soon disappeared. The warmth of the afternoon was gone, and the cold of the night was gathering around him.

Ushikawa sighed deeply and reluctantly peeled himself away from the wall. His body still had a lingering numbness, but not enough to stop him from moving about the room. He finally rose to his feet, stretched his limbs, and moved his short, thick neck around to work out the kinks. He balled his fists, then stretched out his fingers, again and again. Then he got down on the tatami and did his usual stretching exercises. All his joints crackled dully, and his muscles slowly regained their normal suppleness.

It was now the time of day when people came back from work and school. *I need to continue to keep a watch over them,* he told himself. *This isn't a question of whether I want to or not, or whether it's the right thing to do. Once I start something, I have to see it through.*

Ushikawa sat down again behind the camera. It was completely dark outside now, and the light at the entrance had come on. *It must be on a timer,* he thought. Like nameless birds returning to their shabby nests, people stepped into the entrance. Tengo Kawana wasn't among them, but Ushikawa figured he would be back before long. He couldn't take care of his sick father forever. Most likely he would be back in Tokyo before the new week started, so he could return to work. Within a few days – or maybe even today or tomorrow.

I may well be just a cheerless, grubby little creature, a bug on the damp underside of a rock. So be it – I'll be the first to admit it. But I'm a relentlessly capable, patient, tenacious bug. I don't give up easily. Once I get ahold of a clue, I pursue it to the bitter end. I'll climb up the highest wall you've got. I have to get back that cold core inside me. Right now, that's exactly what I need.

Ushikawa rubbed his hands together in front of the camera, and checked to make sure all ten fingers were working properly.

There are lots of things ordinary people can do that I can't. That's for sure. Playing tennis, skiing, for instance. Working in a company, having a happy family. On the other hand, there are a few things I can do that most other people can't. And I do these few things very, very well. I'm not expecting applause or for people to shower me with coins. But I do need to show the world what I'm capable of.

At nine thirty Ushikawa ended his surveillance for the day. He heated a can of chicken soup over the portable stove and carefully sipped it with a spoon. He ate two cold rolls, then polished off an apple, peel and all. He peed, brushed his teeth, spread out his sleeping bag, stripped down to his underwear, and snuggled inside. He zipped the bag up to his neck and curled up like a bug.

And thus Ushikawa's day was over. It hadn't been a very productive day. All he had been able to do was watch Fuka-Eri exit the building with all her belongings. He didn't know where she had gone. *Somewhere,* but *where?* Inside the sleeping bag he shook his head. Wherever she went, it didn't concern him. After a time his frozen body warmed up, his mind faded, and he fell into a deep sleep. Once more, the tiny frozen core occupied a solid place in his soul.

Nothing much happened the next day. Two days later was Saturday, another warm, peaceful day. Most people slept in during the morning. Ushikawa, though, sat by the window, listening to a tiny radio – the news, traffic updates, the weather report.

Just before ten a large crow flew up and stood at the empty front steps of the building. The crow looked around meticulously, moving its head a few times like it was nodding. It bobbed its thick large beak up and down, its brilliant black feathers glistening in the sunlight. The mailman pulled up on his small red motorcycle and the crow reluctantly spread its wings wide and flew off. As it flew away it squawked once. After the mailman had sorted all the mail into the mailboxes and left, a flock of sparrows twittered over. They bustled around the entrance but found nothing worthwhile and flew away. Next it was a striped cat's turn. He had on a flea collar and probably belonged to a neighbor. Ushikawa had never seen the cat before. The cat peed in the dried-up flower bed, sniffed the result, and – apparently displeased with what it found – twitched its whiskers, as if it were bored. Tail up, it disappeared behind the building.

In the morning several residents exited the building. From the way they were dressed, it looked like they were going out for a relaxed day, or going shopping in the neighborhood – one or the other. Ushikawa knew almost all their faces by now, but he had not a speck of interest in their personalities or private lives. He never even tried to imagine them.

Your own lives are surely very important to each one of you. Very precious to you. I get it. But to me they don't matter one way or the other. To me, you're just flimsy paper dolls walking across a stage. There's only one thing I'm asking of all of you – remain paper dolls and don't interfere with my job here.

"Isn't that right, Mrs. Pear?" He had given the woman currently passing this nickname, because she was pear shaped with a huge rear end. "You're just a cutout paper doll. You're not real. Do you realize that? Though you are a bit on the chunky side for a paper doll."

As he thought this, though, everything in the scene before him began to seem meaningless, to *not matter one way or the other*. Maybe the scene in front of him didn't exist in the first place. Maybe *he* was the one being deceived, by cutout people who didn't really exist. Ushikawa grew uneasy. Being locked up in this empty apartment, day after day, spying on people, must be getting to him – something that would definitely get on a person's nerves. He decided to verbalize his thoughts, to pull himself out of this funk.

"G'morning, there, Long Ears," he said, looking through the view-finder and addressing a tall, thin old man. The tips of the old man's ears stuck out like horns from beneath his white hair. "Out for a walk? Walking's good for you. It's nice out today, so have a good time. I would love to take a walk and stretch my limbs a bit, but I'm stuck here keeping watch over this crummy entrance day after day."

The old man had on a cardigan and wool trousers, and had excellent posture. He would look perfect taking a faithful white dog out for a walk, but pets weren't allowed in the building. Once the old man was gone, Ushikawa was suddenly struck by a sense of impotence. *This surveillance is going to end up being a waste of time,* he decided. *My intuition is worthless, and all the hours I've spent in this vacant room are leading me exactly nowhere. All I have to show for it is a set of frayed nerves, worn away like the bald head of a Jizo statue that passing children rub for good luck.*

After twelve Ushikawa ate an apple and some cheese and crackers, and a rice ball with pickled plum inside. He then leaned back against the wall and fell asleep. It was a short, dreamless sleep, yet when he awoke he couldn't remember where he was. His memory was a perfectly square, perfectly empty box. The only thing in the box was empty space. Ushikawa gazed around the space. He found it wasn't just a void, but a dim room – empty, cold, without a stick of furniture. He didn't recognize the place. There was an apple core on an unfolded newspaper next to him. Ushikawa felt confused. *Why am I in such a weird place?*

Finally it came to him, and he remembered what he had been doing: staking out the entrance to Tengo's apartment. *That's right. That's why I have this single-lens reflex Minolta with a telephoto lens.* He remembered the old man with white hair and long ears out for a walk alone. Like birds flying home to their nests at twilight, memories gradually returned to the empty box. And two solid facts emerged:

1 Eriko Fukada has left.

2 Tengo Kawana hasn't come back yet.

No one was in Tengo Kawana's third-floor apartment. The curtains were drawn, and silence enveloped the deserted space. Other than the compressor of the fridge switching on from time to time, nothing disturbed the silence. Ushikawa let his imagination wander over the scene. Imagining a deserted room was a lot like imagining the world after death. Suddenly he remembered the NHK fee collector and his obsessive knocking. He had kept constant watch but never saw any trace that this mysterious man had left the building. *Could he be a resident here? Or was it someone who lived here who liked to pretend to be a fee collector to harass the other residents? If the latter, what would possibly be the point?* This was a very morbid theory, but what else could explain such a strange situation? Ushikawa had no idea.

Tengo Kawana showed up at the entrance to the apartment building just before four that afternoon. He wore an old windbreaker with the collar turned up, a navy-blue baseball cap, and a travel bag slung over his shoulder. He didn't pause at the entrance, didn't glance around, and went straight inside. Ushikawa's mind was still a bit foggy, but he couldn't miss that large figure.

"Welcome back, Mr. Kawana," Ushikawa muttered aloud, and snapped three photos with the motor-drive camera. "How's your father doing? You must be exhausted. Please rest up. Nice to come home, isn't it, even to a miserable place like this. By the way, Eriko Fukada moved out, with all her belongings, while you were gone."

But his voice didn't reach Tengo. He was just muttering to himself. Ushikawa glanced at his watch and wrote a memo in his notebook. *3:56 p.m., Tengo Kawana back home from trip.*

At the same moment that Tengo appeared at the entrance, a door somewhere opened wide and Ushikawa felt reality returning. Like air rushing into a vacuum, his nerves were instantly sharp, his body filled with a fresh vitality. He was again a useful part of the outside world. There was a satisfying click as things fell into place. His circulation sped up, and just the right amount of adrenaline surged through his body. *Good, this is how it should be. This is the way I'm supposed to be, the way the world is supposed to be.*

It was after seven p.m. when Tengo appeared at the entrance again. The wind had picked up after sunset, and the temperature had dropped. Tengo wore a sweater under a windbreaker with faded jeans. He stepped outside and stood there, looking around, but he didn't see anything. He glanced at where Ushikawa was hiding, but didn't pick out the observer. *He's different from Eriko Fukada,* Ushikawa thought. *She's special. She can see what others can't. But you, Tengo – for better or worse you're an ordinary person. You can't see me sitting here.*

Seeing that nothing had changed outside, Tengo zipped his jacket up to his neck, stuck his hands in his pockets, and walked out onto the main road. Ushikawa hurriedly put on his knit cap, wrapped the muffler around his neck, slipped on his shoes, and went out to follow Tengo.

Tengo strolled slowly down the street and turned around to look behind him a few times, but Ushikawa was careful and Tengo didn't see him. Tengo seemed to have something on his mind. Perhaps he was thinking about Fuka-Eri being gone. He was apparently heading toward the station. Maybe he was going to take a train somewhere? That would make tailing him difficult. The station was well lit, and on a Saturday night there wouldn't be many passengers. Ushikawa would be extremely conspicuous. In that case, it would be smarter to give up.

But Tengo wasn't heading toward the station. He walked for a while and then turned down a nearly deserted street and came to a halt in front of a bar named Mugiatama. It was a bar for young people, by the look of it. Tengo glanced at his watch to check the time, stood there pondering for a few seconds, then went inside. *Mugiatama,* Ushikawa thought. He shook his head. *What a stupid name for a bar.*

Ushikawa hid in the shadow of a telephone pole and checked out his surroundings. Tengo was probably going to have a couple of drinks there and a bite to eat, so it would take at least a half hour. Worst-case scenario, Ushikawa would have to stay put for an hour. He looked around for a good place nearby to kill time while he watched the people going in and out of the bar. Unfortunately, though, there was just a milk distributor, a small Tenrikyo meeting hall, and a rice wholesaler, and all of them were closed. *Man, I never get a break,* he thought. The strong northwest wind blew the clouds swiftly by. The warmth of the daytime seemed like a dream now. Ushikawa wasn't relishing the idea of standing in the freezing cold for thirty minutes to an hour, doing nothing.

Maybe I should give it up. Tengo's just having a meal here. There is no need to go to all the trouble of shadowing him. Ushikawa considered popping in to some place himself, having a hot meal, then going home. Tengo would come back home before long. That was a very attractive choice. Ushikawa pictured himself in a cozy little restaurant, enjoying a piping hot bowl of *oyakodon* – rice topped with chicken and eggs. These last few days he hadn't eaten anything worth mentioning. Some hot sake would hit the spot too. In this cold, one step outside and you'll sober up quick.

But another scenario came to him. Tengo might be meeting somebody at Mugiatama. When Tengo left his apartment, he went straight there, and he checked his watch just before he went in. Someone might be waiting for him inside, or might be on his way. If that was the case, Ushikawa had to know who this person was. His ears might freeze off, but he had to stand watch and see who went into the bar. He resigned himself to this, wiping the picture of *oyakodon* and hot sake from his mind.

The person he's meeting might be Fuka-Eri. Or Aomame. Ushikawa pulled himself together. *After all, perseverance is my strong point.* If there was a glimmer of hope, he clung to it desperately. The rain could pelt him, the wind could blow, he could be burned by the sun and beaten with a stick, but he would never let go. Once you let go, you never know when you will get ahold of it again. He knew full well there were more painful things than this in the world – a thought that helped him endure his own suffering.

He leaned against the wall, in the shadows of the telephone pole and a sign advertising the Japanese Communist Party, and kept a sharp watch over the front door of Mugiatama. He wrapped the green muffler up to his nose and stuck his hands inside the pockets of his pea coat. Other than occasionally extracting a tissue from his pocket to blow his nose, he didn't move an inch. Announcements over the PA system at Koenji Station would filter over, on the wind, from time to time. Some pedestrians looked nervous when they saw Ushikawa huddled in the shadows, and hurried past. Since it was dark, though, they couldn't make out his features. His stocky frame loomed in the shadows like some ominous ornament and sent people scurrying away in fright.

What could Tengo be drinking and eating in there? The more he thought about it, the hungrier, and colder, he got. But he couldn't help imagining it. *Anything's fine – doesn't have to be hot sake or* oyakodon. *I just want to go someplace warm and have a regular meal. But if I can stand being out here in the cold, I can take anything.*

Ushikawa had no choice. There was no other path for him to take than this one, freezing in the cold wind until Tengo finished his meal. Ushikawa thought about his home in Chuorinkan, and the dining table there. There must have been hot meals on that table every day, but he couldn't recall them. *What in the world did I eat back then?* It was like something out of antiquity. Long, long ago, a fifteen-minute walk from Chuorinkan Station on the Odakyu Line, there had been a newly built house and a warm, inviting dinner table. Two little girls played piano, and a small pedigreed puppy scampered about the tiny garden and lawn.

Tengo came out of the bar thirty-five minutes later. Not bad. It could have been a lot worse, Ushikawa reassured himself. The thirty-five minutes had been terrible, but it was certainly better than an awful hour and a half. His body was chilled, but at least his ears hadn't frozen. While Tengo was in the bar, there was no one going in or out of Mugiatama who caught Ushikawa's attention. Just one couple went inside, and no one came out. Tengo must have just had a few drinks and a light meal. Keeping the same distance as before, Ushikawa followed behind him. Tengo walked down the same street, most likely headed back to his apartment.

But Tengo turned off this street and headed down a road that Ushikawa had never been on before. It looked like Tengo was not on his way home after all. Ushikawa was convinced that he was still lost in thought, maybe even more so than before. He didn't glance back this time. Ushikawa kept track of the scenery passing by, checked the street signs, trying to memorize the route so he could retrace it later on. Ushikawa wasn't familiar with this area, but from the increasing buzz of traffic, like the rushing of a river, he surmised they must be getting closer to the Ring Road. Before long Tengo picked up the pace. Getting closer to his destination, perhaps.

Not bad. So this guy is heading somewhere. It was worth tailing him after all.

Tengo quickly cut through a residential street. It was a Saturday night, with a cold wind blowing, so everyone else was inside, in front of the TV, enjoying a hot drink. The street was practically deserted. Ushikawa followed behind Tengo, making sure to keep enough distance between them. Tengo was an easy type of person to shadow. He was tall and big-boned, and wouldn't get lost in a crowd. He just forged on ahead and didn't get sidetracked. He was always looking slightly down, thinking. He was essentially a straightforward, honest man, not the type to hide anything. *Totally different from me*, Ushikawa thought.

Ushikawa's wife had also liked to hide things. No – it wasn't that she liked to hide things, she couldn't help it. Ask her what time it was, and she probably wouldn't tell you the correct time. Ushikawa wasn't like this. He only hid things when it was necessary, only when it pertained to work. If someone asked him the time and there was no reason for him to be dishonest, he would tell them, and be nice about it. Not like his wife. She even lied about her age, shaving four years off. When they submitted the documents for their marriage license he found out how old she really was, but pretended not to notice. Ushikawa couldn't fathom why she had to lie about something that was going to come out anyway. Who cared if his wife happened to be seven years older?

As they got even farther from the station, there were fewer people on the street. Eventually Tengo turned into a little park, a nothing little playground in one corner of a residential district. The park was deserted. *Of course it is,* Ushikawa thought. *Who feels like spending time in a playground on a cold, windy December night?* Tengo passed under the cold light of a mercury-vapor lamp and headed straight toward the slide. He stepped onto it and climbed to the top.

Ushikawa hid behind a phone booth and kept an eye on Tengo. A *slide*? Ushikawa frowned. Why does a grown man have to climb to the top of a slide on a freezing cold night like this? This wasn't near Tengo's apartment. There must be some reason he would go out of his way to come here. It wasn't exactly the most appealing playground. It was cramped and shabby. In addition to the slide there were two swings, a small jungle gym, and a sandbox. A single mercury-vapor lamp that looked like it had illuminated the end of the world more than a few times, a single crude, leafless zelkova tree. A locked-up public toilet was the perfect canvas for graffiti. There was not a thing in this park to warm people's hearts, or to stimulate the imagination. Perhaps on a bracing May afternoon there might be something. But on a windy December night? Forget it.

Was Tengo meeting up with somebody here? Waiting for somebody to show? Ushikawa didn't think so. Tengo didn't give any signs to indicate that he was looking for someone. When he entered the park, he ignored all the other equipment. The only thing on his mind seemed to be the slide. *Tengo came here to climb up that slide.*

Maybe he had always liked to sit on top of slides when he needed to think. Maybe the top of a slide in a park at night was the perfect place to think about the plot of the novel he was writing, or mathematical formulas. Maybe the darker it was, the colder the wind blew, the shabbier the park, the better he could think. What or how novelists (or mathematicians) thought was way beyond anything Ushikawa could imagine. His practical mind told him that he had to stay put, patiently keeping an eye on Tengo. His watch showed exactly eight p.m.

Tengo sat down on top of the slide, as if folding his large frame. He looked up at the sky. He moved his head back and forth, then settled on a single spot, and gazed upward, his head still.

Ushikawa recalled a sentimental old pop song by Kyu Sakamoto. It began: *Look up at the night sky / see the little stars.* He didn't know how the rest of it went and he really didn't care to know. Sentiment and a sense of justice were Ushikawa's two weakest areas. Up on top of the slide, was Tengo feeling sentimental as he gazed at the stars?

Ushikawa tried looking up at the sky himself, but he couldn't see any stars. Koenji, Suginami Ward, Tokyo, was not the best place to observe the night sky. Neon signs and lights along the street dyed the whole sky a weird color. Some people, if they squinted hard, might be able to make out a few stars, but that would require extraordinary vision and concentration. On top of that, the clouds tonight were blowing hard across the sky. Still, Tengo sat motionless on top of the slide, his eyes on a fixed point in the sky.

What a pain in the butt this guy is, Ushikawa decided. What possible reason could there be to sit on a slide, gaze up at the sky, and ponder things on a windy winter night like this? Not that he had any right to criticize Tengo. Ushikawa had taken it upon himself, after all, to secretly observe Tengo, and shadow him. Tengo was a free citizen and had every right to look at what he wanted, where he wanted, the whole year round.

Still, it's damn cold. He had needed to pee for some time, but had held it in. The public toilet was locked, though, and even in a deserted place like this he couldn't very well just pee next to a phone booth. *Come on,* he thought, stamping his feet, *can't you just get up and leave already? You might be lost in thought, overtaken by sentiment, deep into your astronomical observations, but Tengo – you gotta be freezing too. Time to go back to your place and warm up, don't you think? Neither of us has anyone waiting for us, but it's still a hell of a lot better than hanging out here and freezing our rear ends off.*

Tengo didn't seem about to get up, though. He finally stopped gazing at the sky, and he turned his attention to the apartment building across the way. It was a new condo, six stories tall, with lights on in about half the windows. Tengo stared at the building. Ushikawa did the same but found nothing that caught his attention. It was just an ordinary condo. It was not an exclusive building, but fairly high-class nonetheless. High-quality design, expensive tile exterior. The entrance was beautiful and well lit. It was a different animal entirely from the cheap, slated-to-be-torn-down place that Tengo called home.

As he gazed up at the condo, was Tengo wishing he could live in a place like that? Ushikawa didn't think so. As far as Ushikawa knew, Tengo wasn't the type to care about where he lived. Just like he didn't care much about clothes. Most likely he was happy with his shabby apartment. A roof over your head and a place to keep out of the cold – that was enough for him. Whatever was running through his head up there on the slide must be something else.

After Tengo had looked at all the windows in the condo, he turned his gaze once more to the sky. Ushikawa followed suit. From where he was hidden, the branches of the zelkova tree, the electric lines, and the other buildings got in the way. He could only see half the sky. What particular point in the sky Tengo was looking at wasn't at all clear. Countless clouds ceaselessly scudded across the sky like some overwhelming army bearing down on them.

Eventually, Tengo stood up and silently climbed down from the slide, like a pilot having just landed after a rough solo flight at night.

He cut across the playground and left. Ushikawa hesitated, then decided not to follow him. Most likely Tengo was on his way back to his place. Plus Ushikawa had to pee like crazy. After he saw Tengo disappear, he went into the playground, hustled behind the public toilet, and in the darkness where no one could see him, he peed into a bush. His bladder was ready to burst.

He finally finished peeing – the operation taking as long as it would take a long freight train to cross a bridge – zipped up his pants, shut his eyes, and gave a deep sigh of relief. His watch showed 8:17. Tengo had been on top of the slide for about fifteen minutes. Ushikawa checked again that Tengo wasn't around and headed toward the slide. He clambered up the ladder with his short, bandy legs, sat down on the very top of the freezing slide, and looked up. What could he have been staring at so intently?

Ushikawa had pretty good eyesight. Astigmatism made his eyes a bit out of balance, but generally he could get by every day without glasses. Still, no matter how hard he looked, he couldn't make out a single star. What caught his attention instead was the large moon in the sky, about two-thirds full. Its dark, bruised exterior was clearly exposed between the clouds. Your typical winter moon. Cold, pale, full of ancient mysteries and inklings. Unblinking like the eyes of the dead, it hung there, silent, in the sky.

Ushikawa gulped. For a while, he forgot to breathe. Through a break in the clouds, there was another moon, a little way apart from the first one. This was much smaller than the original moon, slightly warped in shape, and green, like it had moss growing on it. But it was undoubtedly a moon. No star was that big. And it couldn't be a satellite. Yet there it was, pasted onto the night sky.

Ushikawa shut his eyes, then a few seconds later opened them again. This must be an illusion. *That kind of thing can't be there.* But no matter how many times he opened and closed his eyes, the little moon was still in the sky. Passing clouds hid it occasionally, but once they passed by, there it was, in the same exact spot.

This is what Tengo was looking at. Tengo Kawana had come to this playground to see this scene, or perhaps to check that it still existed. He has known for some time that there are two moons. No doubt about it. He didn't look at all surprised to see it. On top of the slide, Ushikawa sighed deeply. *What kind of crazy world is this?* he asked himself. *What sort of world have I gotten myself into?* But no answer came. Swept by countless clouds racing by, the two moons – one big, one small – hung in the sky like a riddle.

There's one thing I can say for sure, he decided. *This isn't the world I came from. The earth I know has only one moon. That is an undeniable fact. And now it has increased to two.*

Ushikawa began to have a sense of déjà vu. *I've seen the same thing before somewhere,* he thought. He focused, desperately searching his memory. He frowned, grit his teeth, dredging the dark sea bottom of his mind. And it finally hit him. *Air Chrysalis.*

He looked around, but all he saw was the same world as always. White lace curtains were drawn in windows in the condo across the street, peaceful lights on behind them. Nothing out of the ordinary. *Only the number of moons was different.*

He carefully climbed down from the slide, and hurriedly left the playground as if running from the eyes of the moons. *Am I going nuts?* he wondered. *No, that can't be it. I'm not going crazy. My mind is like a brand-new steel nail – hard, sober, straight. Hammered at just the right angle, into the core of reality. There's nothing wrong with me. I'm completely sane.*

It's the world around me that's gone crazy.

And I have to find out why.

20

AOMAME

One Aspect of My Transformation

ON SUNDAY THE WIND HAD DIED down. It was a warm, calm day, totally different from the night before. People took off their heavy coats and enjoyed the sunshine. Aomame, however, did not enjoy the nice weather – she spent the day as always, shut away in her room, the curtains closed.

As she listened to Janáček's *Sinfonietta,* the sound down low, she stretched and then turned to her exercise machine to do some resistance training. She was gradually adding routines to her training workout and it now took nearly two hours to complete. Afterward she cooked, cleaned the apartment, and lay on the sofa to read *In Search of Lost Time.* She had finally begun volume three, *The Guermantes Way.* She tried her best to keep busy. She only watched TV twice a day – the NHK news broadcasts at noon and seven p.m. As always, nothing big was going on – no, actually, lots of big events were happening in the world. People all around the world had lost their lives, many of them in tragic ways – train wrecks, ferry boats sinking, plane crashes. A civil war went on with no end in sight, an assassination, a terrible ethnic massacre. Weather shifts had brought on drought, floods, famine. Aomame deeply sympathized with the people caught up in these tragedies and disasters, but even so, not a single thing had occurred that had a direct bearing on her.

Neighborhood children were playing in the playground across the street, shouting something. She could hear the crows gathered on the roof, cawing out the latest gossip. The air had that early-winter city smell.

It suddenly hit her that ever since she had been living in this condo she had never once felt any sexual desire. Not once had she felt like having sex. She hadn't even masturbated. Maybe it was due to her pregnancy and her body's hormonal changes. Still, Aomame was relieved. This wasn't exactly the place to find a sexual outlet, should she decide she had to sleep with someone. She was happy, too, to not have any more periods. Her periods had never been heavy, but still she felt as if she had set down a load she had been carrying forever. It was one less thing to have to think about.

In the three months that she had been here, her hair had grown long. In September it had barely touched her shoulders, but now it was down to her shoulder blades. When she was a child her mother had always trimmed it short, and from junior high onward, because sports had been her life, she had never let it grow out. It felt a bit too long now, but she couldn't very well cut it herself. She trimmed her bangs, but that was all. She kept her hair up during the day and let it down at night. And then, while listening to music, she brushed it a hundred strokes, something you can only do if you have plenty of time on your hands.

Normally she wore almost no makeup, and now especially there was no need for it. But she wanted to keep a set daily routine as much as she could, so she made sure to take good care of her skin. She massaged her skin with creams and lotions, put on a face mask before bedtime. She was basically a very healthy person, and just a little extra care was all it took for her skin to be beautiful and lustrous. Or maybe this, too, was a by-product of being pregnant? She had heard that pregnant women had beautiful skin. Either way, when she sat at her mirror, let down her hair, and examined her face, she did feel she looked prettier than ever before. Or at least she was taking on the composure of a mature woman. Probably.

Aomame had never once felt beautiful. No one had ever told her that she was. Her mother treated her like she was an ugly child. "If only you were prettier," her mother always said – meaning if she were prettier, a cuter child, they could recruit more converts. So Aomame had always avoided looking at herself in mirrors. When she absolutely had to, she quickly, efficiently, checked out her reflection.

Tamaki Otsuka had told her she liked her features. *Not bad at all,* she had said. *They are actually very nice. You should have more confidence.* That had made Aomame happy. She was just entering puberty, and her friend's warm words calmed her. *Maybe I'm not as ugly as my mother said I was,* she began to think. But even Tamaki had never called her *beautiful.*

Now, however, for the first time in her life, Aomame saw something beautiful in her face. She was able to sit in front of the mirror longer than ever before and examine her face more thoroughly. She wasn't being narcissistic. She inspected her face from a number of angles, as if it were somebody else's. Had she really become beautiful? Or was it her way of appreciating everything that had changed, not her face itself? Aomame couldn't decide.

Occasionally she would put on a big frown in the mirror. Her frowning face looked the same as it always had. The muscles in her face stretched in all directions, her features unraveled, each distinct from the other. All possible emotions in the world gushed out from her face. It was neither beautiful nor ugly. From one angle she looked demonic, from a different angle comic. And from yet another angle her face was a chaotic jumble. When she stopped frowning her facial muscles gradually relaxed, like ripples vanishing on the surface of water, and her usual features returned. And then Aomame discovered a new, slightly different version of herself.

"You should smile more naturally," Tamaki had often told her. "Your features are gentle when you smile, so it's a shame that you don't do so more often." But Aomame could never smile easily, or casually, in front of people. When she forced it, she ended up with a tight sneer, which made others even more tense and uncomfortable. Tamaki was different: she had a natural, cheerful smile. People meeting her for the first time immediately felt friendly toward her. In the end, though, disappointment and despair drove Tamaki to take her own life, leaving Aomame – who couldn't manage a decent smile – behind.

It was a quiet Sunday. The warm sunshine had led many people to the playground across the road. Parents stood around, their children playing in the sandbox or on the swings. Some kids were playing on the slide. Elderly people sat on the benches, intently watching the children at play. Aomame went out on her balcony, sat on her garden chair, and half-heartedly watched through a gap in the screen. It was a peaceful scene. Time was marching on in the world. Nobody there was under threat of death, nobody there was on the trail of a killer. Nobody there had a fully loaded 9mm automatic pistol wrapped in tights in her dresser drawer.

Will I ever be able to participate in that quiet, normal world again? Aomame asked herself. *Will there ever come a day when I can lead this* little one *by the hand, go to the park, and let it play on the swings, on the slides? Lead my daily life without thinking about who I will kill next, or who will kill me? Is that possible in this 1Q84 world? Or is it only possible in some other world? And most important of all – will Tengo be beside me?*

Aomame stopped looking at the park and went back inside. She closed the sliding glass door and shut the curtains. She couldn't hear the children's voices now and a sadness tugged at her. She was cut off from everything, stuck in a place that was locked from the inside. *I'll stop watching the playground during the day. Tengo won't come in the daytime.* What he was looking for was a clear view of the two moons.

After she had a simple dinner and washed the dishes, Aomame dressed warmly and went out on the balcony once more. She lay the blanket on her lap and sank back in the chair. It was a windless night. The kind of clouds that watercolor artists like lingered faintly in the sky, a test of the artist's delicate brushstrokes. The larger moon, which was not blocked by the clouds, was two-thirds full and shone bright, distinct light down on the earth below. At this time of evening, from where she sat Aomame couldn't see the second, smaller moon. It was just behind a building, but Aomame knew *it was there.* She could feel its presence. No doubt it would soon appear before her.

Ever since she had gone into hiding, she had been able to intentionally shut thoughts out of her mind. Especially when she was on the balcony like this, gazing at the playground, she could make her mind a complete blank. She kept her eyes focused on the playground, especially on the slide, but she wasn't thinking of anything – no, her mind might have been thinking of something, but this was mostly below the surface. What her mind was doing below the surface, she had no idea. At regular intervals something would float up, like sea turtles and porpoises poking their faces through the surface of the water to breathe. When that happened, she knew that indeed she *had been thinking of something* up till then. Then her consciousness, lungs full of fresh oxygen, sank back below the surface. It was gone again, and Aomame no longer thought of anything. She was a surveillance device, wrapped in a soft cocoon, her gaze absorbed in the slide.

She was seeing the park, but at the same time she was seeing nothing. If anything new came across her line of vision, her mind would react immediately. But right now nothing new was happening. There was no wind. The dark branches of the zelkova tree stuck out, unmoving, like sharp probes pointed toward the sky. The whole world was still. She looked at her watch. It was after eight. Today might end as always, with nothing out of the ordinary. A Sunday night, as quiet as could be.

The world stopped being still at exactly 8:23.

She suddenly noticed a man on top of the slide. He sat down and looked up at one part of the sky. Aomame's heart shrunk to the size of a child's fist, and stayed that size so long she was afraid it would never start pumping again. But it just as quickly swelled up to normal size and started beating again. With a dull sound it began furiously pumping fresh blood throughout her body. Aomame's mind quickly broke through to the surface of the water, shook itself, and stood by, ready to take action.

It's Tengo, she thought instinctively.

But once her vision cleared, she knew it wasn't him. The man sitting there was short, like a child, with a large square head, wearing a knit hat. The knit hat was stretched out oddly because of the shape of his head. He had a green muffler wrapped around his neck and wore a navy-blue coat. The muffler was too long, and the buttons on his coat were straining around his stomach, ready to pop. Aomame knew this was the *child* she had seen last night coming out of the park. But this was no child. He was more near middle age. He was short and stocky, with short limbs. And his head was abnormally large, and misshapen.

Aomame remembered what Tamaru had said about the man with a head as large as a Fukusuke good-luck doll, the one they had nicknamed Bobblehead. The person who had been loitering around outside the Azabu Willow House, checking out the safe house. This man on top of the slide perfectly fit the description Tamaru had given her last night. That weird man hadn't given up on his investigation, and now he had crept up on her. *I have to get the pistol. Why of all nights did I leave it back in the bedroom?* Aomame took a deep breath, let the chaos of her heart settle and her nerves calm down. *I mustn't panic. There's no need for the pistol at this point.*

The man wasn't, after all, watching her building. Seated at the top of the slide, he was staring at the sky like Tengo had done, at the very same spot. And he seemed lost in thought. He didn't move a muscle for the longest time, like he had forgotten how to move. He didn't pay any attention to the direction of her room. This confused Aomame. *What's going on? This man came here searching for me. He's probably a member of Sakigake. No doubt at all he's a skilled pursuer. I mean, he was able to follow the trail all the way from the Azabu mansion to here. For all that, there he is now, defenseless, exposed, staring vacantly at the night sky.*

Aomame stealthily rose to her feet, slid open the glass door a crack, slipped inside, and sat down in front of the phone. With trembling hands she began dialing Tamaru's number. She had to report this to him – that she could see Bobblehead from where she was, on top of a slide in a playground across the street. Tamaru would decide what to do, and would no doubt deftly handle the situation. But after punching in the first four numbers she stopped, the receiver clutched in her hand, and bit her lip.

It's too soon, Aomame thought. *There are still too many things we don't know about this man. If Tamaru simply sees him as a risk factor and takes care of him, all those things we don't know about him will remain unknown. Come to think of it, the man is doing exactly what Tengo did the other day. The same slide, the same pose, the same part of the sky, as if he's retracing Tengo's movements. He must be seeing the two moons as well.* Aomame understood this. *Maybe this man and Tengo are linked in some way. And maybe this man hasn't noticed yet that I'm hiding out in an apartment in this building, which is why he's sitting there, defenseless, his back to me.* The more she thought about it, the more persuasive she found this theory. *If that's true, then following the man might lead me right to Tengo. Instead of searching me out, this guy can serve as my guide.* The thought made her heart contract even more, and then start to pound. She laid down the phone.

I'll tell Tamaru about it later, she decided. *There's something I have to do first. Something risky, because it involves the pursued following the pursuer. And this man is no doubt a pro. But even so I can't let this golden opportunity slip by. This may be my last chance. And from the way he looks, he seems to be in a bit of a daze, at least for the moment.*

She hurried into the bedroom, opened the dresser drawer, and took out the Heckler & Koch semiautomatic. She flicked off the safety, racked a round into the chamber, and reset it. She stuffed the pistol into the back of her jeans and went out to the balcony again. Bobblehead was still there, staring at the sky. His misshapen head was perfectly still. He seemed totally captivated by what he was seeing in the sky. Aomame knew how he felt. *That was most definitely a captivating sight.*

Aomame went back inside and put on a down jacket and a baseball cap. And a pair of nonprescription glasses with a simple black frame, enough to give her face a different appearance. She wound a gray muffler around her neck and put her wallet and apartment key in her pocket. She ran down the stairs and went out of the building. The soles of her sneakers were silent as she stepped out on the asphalt. It had been so long since she had felt hard, steady ground beneath her feet, and the feeling encouraged her.

As she walked down the road she checked that Bobblehead was still in the same place. The temperature had dropped significantly after the sun had set, but there was still no wind. She actually found the cold pleasant. Her breath white, Aomame walked as silently as she could past the entrance to the park. Bobblehead showed no sign that he had noticed her. His gaze was fixed straight up from the slide, on the sky. From where she was, Aomame couldn't see them, but she knew that at the end of his gaze there were two moons – one large, one small. No doubt they were snuggled up close to each other in the freezing, cloudless sky.

She passed by the park, and when she got to the next corner, she turned and retraced her steps. She hid in the shadows and watched the man on the slide. The pistol against her back was as hard and cold as death, and the feeling soothed her.

She waited five minutes. Bobblehead slowly got to his feet, brushed off his coat, and gazed up one more time at the sky. Then, as if he had made up his mind, he clambered down the steps of the slide. He left the park and walked off in the direction of the station. Shadowing him wasn't particularly hard. There were few people on a residential street on a Sunday night, and even keeping her distance, she wouldn't lose him. He also had not the slightest suspicion that someone was observing him. He never looked back, kept walking at a set pace, the pace people keep when they're preoccupied. *How ironic,* Aomame thought. *The pursuer's blind spot is that he never thinks* he's *being pursued.*

After a while it dawned on her that Bobblehead wasn't heading toward Koenji Station. Back in the apartment, using a Tokyo map of all twenty-three wards, she had gone over the district again and again until she had memorized the local geography so she would know what direction to take in an emergency. So though he was initially headed toward the station, she knew that when he turned at one corner he was going in a different direction. Bobblehead didn't know the neighborhood, she noticed. Twice he stopped at a corner, looked around as if unsure where to go, and checked the address plaques on telephone poles. He was definitely not from around here.

Finally Bobblehead picked up the pace. Aomame surmised that he was back on familiar territory. He walked past a municipal elementary school, down a narrow street, and went inside an old three-story apartment building.

Aomame waited for five minutes after the man had disappeared inside. Bumping into him at the entrance was the last thing she wanted. There were concrete eaves at the entrance, a round light bathing the front door in a yellowish glow. She looked everywhere but couldn't find a sign for the name of the building. Maybe the apartment building didn't have a name. Either way, it had been built quite a few years ago. She memorized the address indicated on the nearby telephone pole.

After five minutes she headed toward the entrance. She passed quickly under the yellowish light and hurriedly opened the door. There was no one in the tiny entrance hall. It was an empty space, devoid of warmth. A fluorescent light on its last legs buzzed above her. The sound of a TV filtered in from somewhere, as did the shrill voice of a child pestering his mother.

Aomame took her apartment key out of the pocket of her down jacket and lightly jiggled it in her hands so if anyone saw her it would look like she lived in the building. She scanned the names on the mailboxes. One of them might be Bobblehead's. She wasn't hopeful but thought it worth trying. It was a small building, with not that many residents. When she ran across the name *Kawana* on one of the boxes, all sound faded away.

She stood frozen in front of that mailbox. The air felt terribly thin, and she found it hard to breathe. Her lips, slightly parted, were trembling. Time passed. She knew how stupid and dangerous this was. Bobblehead could show up any minute. Still, she couldn't tear herself away from the mailbox. One little card with the name *Kawana* had paralyzed her brain, frozen her body in place.

She had no positive proof that this resident named Kawana was Tengo Kawana. Kawana wasn't that common a name, but certainly not as unusual as Aomame. But if, as she surmised, Bobblehead had some connection with Tengo, then there was a strong possibility that this *Kawana* was none other than Tengo Kawana. The room number was 303, coincidentally the same number as the apartment where she was currently staying.

What should I do? Aomame bit down hard on her lip. Her mind kept going in circles and couldn't find an exit. *What should I do?* Well, she couldn't stay planted in front of the mailbox forever. She made up her mind and walked up the uninviting concrete stairs to the third floor. Here and there on the gloomy floor were thin cracks from years of wear and tear. Her sneakers made a grating noise as she walked.

Aomame now stood outside apartment 303. An ordinary steel door with a printed card saying *Kawana* in the name slot. Just the last name. Those two characters looked brusque, inorganic. At the same time, a deep riddle lay within them. Aomame stood there, listening carefully, her senses razor sharp. But she couldn't hear any sound at all from behind the door, or even tell if there was a light on inside. There was a doorbell next to the door.

Aomame was confused. She bit her lip and contemplated her next step. *Am I supposed to ring the bell?* she asked herself.

Or was this some clever trap? Maybe Bobblehead was hiding behind the door, like an evil dwarf in a dark forest, an ominous smile on his face as he waited. *He deliberately revealed himself on top of that slide to lure me over here and take me captive. Fully aware that I'm searching for Tengo, he's using that as bait. A low-down, cunning man who knows exactly what my weak point is. That's the only way he could ever get me to open my door from the inside.*

She checked that no one else was around and pulled the pistol out of her jeans. She flicked off the safety and stuffed the pistol into the pocket of her down jacket so she could get to it easily. She gripped the pistol in her right hand, finger on the trigger, and with her left hand pressed the doorbell.

The doorbell rang inside the apartment. A leisurely chime, out of step with her racing heart. She gripped the pistol tight, waiting for the door to open. But it didn't. And there didn't seem to be anyone peering out at her through the peephole. She waited a moment, then rang the bell again. The bell was loud enough to get all the people in Suginami Ward to raise their heads and prick up their ears. Aomame's right hand on the pistol grip started to sweat a little. But there was no response.

Better leave, she decided. *The Kawana who lives in 303, whoever he is, isn't at home. And that ominous Bobblehead is still lurking somewhere in this building. Too dangerous to stay any longer.* She rushed down the stairs, shooting a glance at the mailbox as she passed, and left the building. Head down, she hurried under the yellow light and headed toward the street. She glanced back to make sure no one was following her.

There were lots of things she needed to think about, and an equal number of decisions she had to make. She felt in her pocket and reset the safety on the pistol. Then, away from any possible prying eyes, she shoved the pistol in the back of her jeans. *I can't get my expectations or hopes up too high,* she told herself. *The Kawana who lived there might be Tengo. And then again he might not. Once you get your hopes up, your mind starts acting on its own. And when your hopes are dashed you get disappointed, and disappointment leads to a feeling of helplessness. You get careless and let your guard down. And right now,* she thought, *that's the last thing I can afford.*

I have no idea how much Bobblehead knows. But the reality is that he's getting close to me. Almost close enough to reach out and touch. I need to pull myself together and stay alert. I'm dealing with someone who is totally dangerous. The tiniest mistake could be fatal. First of all, I have to stay away from that old apartment building. He's hiding in there, scheming how to capture me – like a poisonous, blood-sucking spider who has spun a web in the darkness.

By the time she got back to her apartment Aomame's mind was made up. There was but one path she could follow.

This time she dialed Tamaru's entire number. She let it ring twelve times, then hung up. She took off her cap and coat, returned the pistol to the drawer, then gulped down two glasses of water. She filled the kettle and boiled water for tea. She peeked through a gap in the curtain at the park across the street, to make sure no one was there. She stood in front of the bathroom mirror and brushed her hair. Even after that her fingers didn't work right. The tension remained. She was pouring hot water in the teapot when the phone rang. It was Tamaru, of course.

"I just saw Bobblehead," she told him.

Silence. "By *just saw him* you mean he's not there anymore?"

"That's right," Aomame said. "A little while ago he was in the park across from my building. But he's not there anymore."

"How long ago do you mean by *a little while ago*?"

"About forty minutes ago."

"Why didn't you call me forty minutes ago?"

"I had to follow him right away and didn't have the time."

Tamaru exhaled ever so slowly, as if squeezing out the breath. "Follow him?"

"I didn't want to lose him."

"I thought I told you never to go outside."

Aomame chose her words carefully. "But I can't just sit by when danger's approaching me. Even if I had called you, you wouldn't have been able to get here right away. Right?"

Tamaru made a small sound in the back of his throat. "So you followed Bobblehead."

"It looks like he had no idea at all he was being followed."

"A pro can act like that," Tamaru cautioned.

Tamaru was right. It all might have been an elaborate ruse. Not that she would admit that. "I'm sure you would be able to do that, but as far as I could tell, Bobblehead isn't on the same level. He may be skilled, but he's different from you."

"He might have had backup."

"No. He was definitely on his own."

Tamaru paused for a moment. "All right. So did you find out where he was heading?"

Aomame told him the address of the building and described its exterior. She didn't know which apartment he was in. Tamaru took notes. He asked a few questions, and Aomame answered as accurately as she could.

"You said that when you first saw him he was in the park across the street from you," Tamaru said.

"Correct."

"What was he doing there?"

Aomame told him – how the man was sitting on top of the slide and staring at the night sky. She didn't mention the two moons. That was only to be expected.

"Looking at the sky?" Tamaru asked. Aomame could hear the gears shift in his mind.

"The sky, or the moon, or the stars. One of those."

"And he let himself be exposed like that, defenseless, on the slide."

"That's right."

"Don't you find that odd?" Tamaru asked. His voice was hard and dry, reminding her of a desert plant that could survive a whole year on one day's worth of rain. "That man had run you down. He was one step away from you. Pretty impressive. Yet there he was, on top of a slide, leisurely gazing up at the night sky, not paying any attention to the apartment where you live. It doesn't add up."

"I agree – it doesn't make much sense. Be that as it may, I couldn't very well let him go."

Tamaru sighed. "But I still think it was dangerous."

Aomame didn't say anything.

"Did following him help you get any closer to solving the riddle?" Tamaru asked.

"No," Aomame said. "But there was one thing that caught my attention."

"Which was?"

"When I looked at the mailboxes I saw that a person named Kawana lives on the third floor."

"So?"

"Have you heard of *Air Chrysalis*? The bestselling novel this past summer?"

"Even I read newspapers, you know. The author, Eriko Fukada, was the daughter of a follower of Sakigake. She disappeared and they suspected she was abducted by the cult. The police investigated it. I haven't read the novel yet."

"Eriko Fukada isn't just the daughter of a follower. Her father was Leader, the head of Sakigake. She's the daughter of the man I sent on to the *other side*. Tengo Kawana was hired by the editor as a ghostwriter, and rewrote *Air Chrysalis*. In reality the novel is a joint work between the two of them."

A long silence descended. Long enough to walk to the end of a long, narrow room, look up something in a dictionary, and walk back. Finally Tamaru broke the silence.

"You have no proof that the Kawana who lives in that building is Tengo Kawana."

"Not yet, no," Aomame admitted. "But if he is the same person, then this all makes sense."

"Certain parts do mesh together," Tamaru said. "But how do you know that this Tengo Kawana ghostwrote *Air Chrysalis*? That can't have been made public. It would have caused a major scandal."

"I heard it from Leader himself. Right before he died, he told me."

Tamaru's voice turned a little cold. "Don't you think you should have told me this before?"

"At the time I didn't think it was so important."

There was silence again for a time. Aomame couldn't tell what Tamaru was thinking, but she knew he didn't like excuses.

"Okay," he finally said. "We'll put that on hold. Let's cut to the chase. What you're trying to say is that Bobblehead marked this Tengo Kawana. And using that as a lead, he was tracking down your whereabouts."

"That's what I think."

"I don't get it," Tamaru said. "Why would Tengo Kawana be a lead to find you? There isn't any connection between you and Kawana, is there? Other than that you dealt with Eriko Fukada's father, and Tengo was the ghostwriter for her novel."

"There *is* a connection," Aomame said, her voice flat.

"There's a direct relationship between you and Tengo Kawana. Is that what you're saying?"

"He and I were in the same class in elementary school. And I believe he's the father of my baby. But I can't explain any more beyond that. It's very – how should I put it? – personal."

On the other end of the phone she heard a ballpoint pen tapping on a desk. That was the only sound she could hear.

"Personal," Tamaru repeated, in a voice that sounded like he had spied some weird creature on top of a rock in a garden.

"I'm sorry," Aomame said.

"I understand. It's a very personal thing. I won't ask anymore," Tamaru said. "So, specifically, what do you want from me?"

"Well, the first thing I would like to know is if the Kawana who lives in that building is actually Tengo Kawana. If it were possible, I would like to make sure of that myself, but it's too risky to go there again."

"Agreed."

"And Bobblehead is probably holed up somewhere in that building, planning something. If he's getting close to locating me, we have to do something about it."

"He already knows a certain amount about the connection between you and the dowager. He has painstakingly hauled in these various leads and is trying to tie them all together. We can't ignore him."

"I have one other request of you," Aomame said.

"Go ahead."

"If it is really Tengo Kawana living there, I don't want any harm to come to him. If it's unavoidable that he is going to get hurt, then I want to take his place."

Tamaru was silent again for a time. No more ballpoint pen tapping this time. There were no sounds at all, in fact. He was considering things in a world devoid of sound.

"I think I can take care of the first two requests," Tamaru said. "That's part of my job. But I can't say anything about the third. It involves very personal things, and there's too much about it I don't understand. Speaking from experience, taking care of three items at once isn't easy. Like it or not, you end up prioritizing."

"I don't mind. You can prioritize them however you like. I just want you to keep this in mind: while I'm still alive, I have to meet Tengo. There's something I have to tell him."

"I'll keep it in mind," Tamaru said. "While there's still spare room in my mind, that is."

"Thank you."

"I have to report what you have told me to the dowager. This is a rather delicate issue, and I can't decide things on my own. So I'll hang up for now. Listen – do not go outside anymore. Lock the door and stay put. If you go outside, it could cause problems. Maybe it already has."

"But it helped me find out a few things about him."

"All right," Tamaru said, sounding resigned. "From what you have told me, it sounds like you did an excellent job. I'll admit that. But don't let your guard down. We don't know yet what he's got up his sleeve. And considering the situation, most likely he has an organization behind him. Do you still have the thing I gave you?"

"Of course."

"Best to keep it nearby."

"Will do."

A short pause, then the phone connection went dead.

Aomame sank back into the bathtub, which she had filled to the brim, and while she warmed up, she thought about Tengo – the Tengo who might or might not be living in an apartment in that old building. She pictured the uninviting steel door, the slot for the name card, the name *Kawana* printed on the card. *What kind of place was beyond that door? And what kind of life was he living?*

In the hot water she touched her breasts, rubbing them. Her nipples had grown larger and harder than before, and more sensitive. *I wish these were Tengo's hands instead of mine,* she thought. She imagined his hands, large and warm. Strong, but surely gentle. If her breasts were enveloped in his hands – how much joy, and peace, she would feel. Aomame also noticed that her breasts were now slightly larger. It was no illusion. They definitely were swollen, the curves softer. *It's probably due to my pregnancy. Or maybe they just got bigger, unrelated to being pregnant. One aspect of my transformation.*

She put her hands on her abdomen. It was still barely swollen, and she didn't have any morning sickness, for some reason. But there was a *little one* hidden within. She knew it. *Wait a moment,* she thought. *Maybe they're not after my life, but after this* little one? *As revenge for me killing Leader, are they trying to get to it, along with me?* The thought made her shudder. Aomame was doubly determined now to see Tengo. Together, the two of them had to protect the *little one. I have had so many precious things stolen from me in my life. But this is one I am going to hold on to.*

She went to bed and read for a while, but sleep didn't come. She shut her book, and gently rolled into a ball to protect her abdomen. With her cheek against the pillow, she thought of the winter moon in the sky above the park, and the little green moon beside it. *Maza* and *dohta.* The mixed light of the two moons bathing the bare branches of the zelkova tree. At this very moment Tamaru must be figuring out a plan, his mind racing at top speed. She could see him, brows knit, tip of his ballpoint pen tapping furiously on the desktop. Eventually, as if led by that monotonous, ceaseless rhythm, the soft blanket of sleep wrapped itself around her.

21

TENGO

Somewhere Inside His Head

THE PHONE WAS RINGING. THE HANDS on his alarm clock showed 2:04. Monday, 2:04 a.m. It was still dark out and Tengo had been sound asleep. A peaceful, dreamless sleep.

First he thought it was Fuka-Eri. She would be the only person who would possibly call at this ungodly hour. Or it could be Komatsu. Komatsu didn't have much common sense when it came to time. But somehow the ring didn't sound like Komatsu. It was more insistent, and businesslike. And besides, he had just seen Komatsu a few hours earlier.

One option was to ignore the call and go back to sleep – Tengo's first choice. But the phone kept on ringing. It might go on ringing all night, for that matter. He got out of bed, bumping his shin as he did, and picked up the receiver.

"Hello," Tengo said, his voice still slurry from sleep. It was like his head was filled with frozen lettuce. There must be some people who don't know you're not supposed to freeze lettuce. Once lettuce has been frozen, it loses all its crispness – which for lettuce is surely its best characteristic.

When he held the receiver to his ear, he heard the sound of wind blowing. A capricious wind rushing through a narrow valley, ruffling the fur of beautiful deer bent over to drink from a clear stream. But it wasn't the sound of wind. It was someone's breathing, amplified by the phone.

"Hello," Tengo repeated. Was it a prank call? Or perhaps the connection was bad.

"Hello," the person on the other end said. A woman's voice he had heard before. It wasn't Fuka-Eri. Nor was it his older girlfriend.

"Hello," Tengo said. "Kawana here."

"Tengo," the person said. They were finally on the same page, though he still didn't know who it was.

"Who's calling?"

"Kumi Adachi," the woman said.

"Oh, hi," Tengo said. Kumi Adachi, the young nurse who lived in the apartment with the hooting owl. "What's going on?"

"Were you asleep?"

"Yes," Tengo said. "How about you?"

This was a pointless question. People who are sleeping can't make phone calls. *Why did I say such a stupid thing?* he wondered. *It must be the frozen lettuce in my head.*

"I'm on duty now," she said. She cleared her throat. "Mr. Kawana just passed away."

"Mr. Kawana just passed away," Tengo repeated, not comprehending. Was someone telling him he himself had just died?

"Your father just breathed his last breath," Kumi said, rephrasing.

Tengo pointlessly switched the receiver from his right hand to his left. "Breathed his last breath," he repeated.

"I was dozing in the nurses' lounge when the bell rang, just after one. It was the bell for your father's room. He has been in a coma for so long, and he couldn't ring the bell by himself, so I thought it was odd, and went to check it out. When I got there his breathing had stopped, as had his heart. I woke up the on-call doctor and we tried to revive him, but couldn't."

"Are you saying my father pressed the call button?"

"Probably. There was no one else who could have."

"What was the cause of death?" Tengo asked.

"I really can't say, though he didn't seem to have suffered. His face looked very peaceful. It was like – a windless day at the end of autumn, when a single leaf falls from a tree. But maybe that's not a good way to put it."

"No, that's okay," Tengo said. "That's a good way of putting it."

"Tengo, can you get here today?"

"I think so." His classes at the cram school began again today, Monday, but for something like this, he would be able to get out of them.

"I'll take the first express train. I should be there before ten."

"I would appreciate it if you would. There are all sorts of *formalities* that have to be taken care of."

"Formalities," Tengo said. "Is there anything in particular I should bring with me?"

"Are you Mr. Kawana's only relative?"

"I'm pretty sure I am."

"Then bring your registered seal. You might need it. And do you have a certificate of registration for the seal?"

"I think I have a spare copy."

"Bring that, too, just in case. I don't think there's anything else you especially need. Your father arranged everything beforehand."

"Arranged everything?"

"Um, while he was still conscious, he gave detailed instructions for everything – the money for his funeral, the clothes he would wear in the coffin, where his ashes would be interred. He was very thorough when it came to preparations. Very practical, I guess you could say."

"That's the kind of person he was," Tengo said, rubbing his temple.

"I finish my rotation at seven a.m. and then am going home to sleep. But Nurse Tamura and Nurse Omura will be on duty in the morning and they can explain the details to you."

"Thank you for all you've done," Tengo said.

"You're quite welcome," Kumi Adachi replied. And then, as if suddenly remembering, her tone turned formal. "My deepest sympathy for your loss."

"Thank you," Tengo said.

He knew he couldn't go back to sleep, so he boiled water and made coffee. That woke him up a bit. Feeling hungry, he threw together a sandwich of tomatoes and cheese that were in the fridge. Like eating in the dark, he could feel the texture but very little of the flavor. He then took out the train schedule and checked the time for the next express to Tateyama. He had only returned two days earlier from the cat town, on Saturday afternoon, and now here he was, setting off again. This time, though, he would probably only stay a night or two.

At four a.m. he washed his face in the bathroom and shaved. He used a brush to tame his cowlicks but, as always, was only partly successful. *Let it be,* he thought, *it will fall into place before long.*

His father's passing didn't particularly shock Tengo. He had spent two solid weeks beside his unconscious father. He already felt that his father had accepted his impending death. The doctors weren't able to determine what had put him into a coma, but Tengo knew. His father had simply decided to die, or else had abandoned the will to live any longer. To borrow Kumi's phrase, as a "single leaf on a tree," he turned off the light of consciousness, closed the door on any senses, and waited for the change of seasons.

From Chikura Station he took a taxi and arrived at the seaside sanatorium at ten thirty. Like the previous day, Sunday, it was a calm early-winter day. Warm sunlight streamed down on the withered lawn, as if rewarding it, and a calico cat that Tengo had never seen before was sunning itself, leisurely grooming its tail. Nurse Tamura and Nurse Omura came to the entrance to greet him. Quietly, they each expressed their condolences, and Tengo thanked them.

His father's body was being kept in an inconspicuous little room in an inconspicuous corner of the sanatorium. Nurse Tamura led Tengo there. His father was lying faceup on a gurney, covered in a white cloth. In the square, windowless room, the white fluorescent light overhead made the white walls even brighter. On top of a waist-high cabinet was a glass vase with three white chrysanthemums, probably placed there that very morning. On the wall was a round clock. It was an old, dusty clock, but it told the time correctly. Its role, perhaps, was to be a witness of some kind. Besides this, there were no furniture or decorations. Countless bodies of elderly people must have passed through here – entering without a word, exiting without a word. A straightforward but solemn atmosphere lay over the room like an unspoken fact.

His father's face didn't look much different from when he was alive. Even up close, it didn't seem like he was dead. His color wasn't bad, and perhaps because someone had been kind enough to shave him, his chin and upper lip were strangely smooth. There didn't seem to be all that much difference from when he was alive, deeply asleep, except that now the feeding tubes and catheters were unnecessary. Leave the body like this, though, and in a few days decay would set in, and then there would be a big difference between life and death. But the body would be cremated before that happened.

The doctor with whom Tengo had spoken many times before came in, expressed his sympathy, then explained what had led up to his father's passing. He was very kind, very thorough in his explanation, but it really all came down to one conclusion: *the cause of death was unknown.* None of their tests had ever determined what was wrong with him. The closest the doctor could say was that Tengo's father died of old age – but he was still only in his mid-sixties, too young for such a diagnosis.

"As the attending physician I'm the one who fills out the death certificate," the doctor said hesitantly. "I'm thinking of writing that the cause of death was 'heart failure brought on by an extended coma,' if that is all right with you?"

"But actually the cause of death was not 'heart failure brought on by an extended coma.' Is that what you're saying?"

The doctor looked a bit embarrassed. "True, until the very end we found nothing wrong with his heart."

"But you couldn't find anything wrong with any of his other organs."

"That's right," the doctor said reluctantly.

"But the form requires a clear cause of death?"

"Correct."

"This isn't my field, but right now his heart is stopped, right?"

"Of course. His heart has stopped."

"Which is a kind of organ failure, isn't it?"

The doctor considered this. "If the heart beating is considered normal, then yes, it is a sort of organ failure, as you say."

"So please write it that way. 'Heart failure brought on by an extended coma,' was it? I have no objection."

The doctor seemed relieved. "I can have the death certificate ready in thirty minutes," he said. Tengo thanked him. The doctor left, leaving only bespectacled Nurse Tamura behind.

"Shall I leave you alone with your father?" Nurse Tamura asked Tengo. Since she had to ask – it was standard procedure – the question sounded a bit matter-of-fact.

"No, there's no need. Thanks," Tengo said. Even if he were left alone with his father, there was nothing in particular he wanted to say to him. It was the same as when he was alive. Now that he was dead, there weren't suddenly all sorts of topics Tengo wanted to discuss.

"Would you like to go somewhere else, then, to discuss the arrangements? You don't mind?" Nurse Tamura asked.

"I don't mind," Tengo replied.

Before Nurse Tamura left, she faced the corpse and brought her hands together in prayer. Tengo did the same. People naturally pay their respects to the dead. The person had, after all, just accomplished the personal, profound feat of dying. Then the two of them left the windowless little room and went to the cafeteria. There was no one else there. Bright sunlight shone in through the large window facing the garden. Tengo stepped into that light and breathed a sigh of relief. There was no sign of the dead there. This was the world of the living – no matter how uncertain and imperfect a world it might be.

Nurse Tamura poured hot roasted *hojicha* tea into a teacup and passed it to him. They sat down across from each other and drank their tea in silence for a while.

"Are you staying over somewhere tonight?" Nurse Tamura asked.

"I'm planning to stay over, but I haven't made a reservation yet."

"If you don't mind, why don't you stay in your father's room? Nobody's using it, and you can save on hotel costs. If it doesn't bother you."

"It doesn't bother me," Tengo said, a little surprised. "But is it all right to do that?"

"We don't mind. If you're okay with it, it's okay with us. I'll get the bed ready later."

"So," Tengo said, broaching the topic, "what am I supposed to do now?"

"Once you get the death certificate from the attending physician, go to the town office and get a permit for cremation, and then take care of the procedures to remove his name from the family record. Those are the main things you need to do now. There should be other things you'll need to take care of – his pension, changing names on his savings account – but talk to the lawyer about those."

"Lawyer?" This took Tengo by surprise.

"Mr. Kawana – your father, that is – spoke with a lawyer about the procedures for after his death. Don't let the word *lawyer* scare you.

Our facility has a lot of elderly patients, and since many are not legally competent, we have paired up with a local law office to provide consultations, so people can avoid legal problems related to division of estates. They also make up wills and provide witnesses. They don't charge a lot."

"Did my father have a will?"

"I can't really say anything about it. You'll need to talk to the lawyer."

"I see. Can I see him soon?"

"We got in touch with him, and he'll be coming here at three. Is that all right? It seems like we're rushing things, but I know you're busy, so I hope you don't mind that we went ahead."

"I appreciate it." Tengo was thankful for her efficiency. For some reason all the middle-aged women he knew were very efficient.

"Before that, though, make sure you go to the town office," Nurse Tamura said, "get his name removed from your family record, and get a permit for cremation. Nothing can happen until you've done that."

"Well, then I have to go to Ichikawa. My father's permanent legal residence should be Ichikawa. If I do that, though, I won't be able to make it back by three."

The nurse shook her head. "No, soon after he came here your father changed his official residence from Ichikawa to Chikura. He said it should make things easier if and when the time came."

"He was well prepared," Tengo said, impressed. It was as if he knew from the beginning that this was where he would die.

"He was," the nurse agreed. "No one else has ever done that. Everyone thinks they will just be here for a short time. Still, though ...," she began to say, and stopped, quietly bringing her hands together in front of her to suggest the rest of what she was going to say. "At any rate, you don't need to go to Ichikawa."

Tengo was taken to his father's room, the room where he spent his final months. The sheets and covers had been stripped off, leaving only a striped mattress. There was a simple lamp on the nightstand, and five empty hangers in the narrow closet. There wasn't a single book in the bookshelf, and all his personal effects had been taken away. But Tengo couldn't recall what personal effects had been there in the first place. He put his bag on the floor and looked around.

The room still had a medicinal smell, and you could still detect the breath of a sick person hanging in the air. Tengo opened the window to let in fresh air. The sun-bleached curtain fluttered in the breeze like the skirt of a girl at play. *How wonderful it would be if Aomame were here,* he thought, *just holding my hand tight, not saying a word.*

He took a bus to the Chikura town hall, showed them the death certificate, and received a permit for cremation. Once twenty-four hours had passed since the time of death, the body could be cremated. He also applied to have his father's name removed from the family record, and received a certificate to that effect. The procedures took a while, but were almost disappointingly simple – nothing that would cause any soul searching. It was no different from reporting a stolen car. Nurse Tamura used their office copier to make three copies of the documents he received.

"At two thirty, before the lawyer comes, someone will be here from Zenkosha, a funeral parlor," Mrs. Tamura said. "Please give him one copy of the cremation permit. The person from the funeral parlor will take care of the rest. While he was still alive, your father talked to the funeral director and decided on all the arrangements. He also put enough money aside to cover it, so you don't need to do anything. Unless you have an objection."

"No, no objection," Tengo said.

His father had left hardly any belongings behind. Old clothes, a few books – that was all.

"Would you like something as a keepsake? All there is, though, is an alarm clock radio, an old self-winding watch, and reading glasses," Nurse Tamura said.

"I don't want anything," Tengo told her. "Just dispose of it any way you like."

At precisely two thirty the funeral director arrived, dressed in a black suit. He moved silently. A thin man, in his early fifties, he had long fingers, large eyes, and a single dry, black wart next to his nose. He seemed to have spent a great deal of time outdoors, because his face was suntanned all over, down to the tips of his ears. Tengo wasn't sure why, but he had never seen a fat funeral director. The man explained the main procedures for the funeral. He was very polite and spoke slowly, deliberately, as if indicating that they could take all the time they needed.

"While your father was alive, he said he wanted as simple a funeral as possible. He wanted a simple, functional casket, and he wanted to be cremated as is. He did not want any ceremony, no scriptures read, no posthumous Buddhist name, or flowers, or a eulogy. And he didn't want a grave. He instructed me to have his ashes simply put in a suitable communal facility. That is, if there are no objections . . ."

He paused and looked entreatingly at Tengo with his large eyes.

"If that is what my father wanted, then I have no objection," Tengo said, looking straight back at those eyes.

The funeral director nodded, and cast his eyes down. "Today would be the wake, and for one night we will have the body lie in state in our funeral home. So we will need to transport the body to our place. The cremation will take place tomorrow at one thirty in the afternoon in a crematorium nearby. I hope this is satisfactory?"

"I have no objection."

"Will you be attending the cremation?"

"I will," Tengo said.

"There are some who do not like to attend, and it is entirely up to you."

"I will be there," Tengo said.

"Very good," the man said, sounding a little relieved. "I'm sorry to bother you with this now, but this is the same amount I showed your father while he was still alive. I would appreciate it if you would approve it."

The funeral director, his long fingers like insect legs, extracted a statement from a folder and passed it to Tengo. Tengo knew almost nothing about funerals, but he could see this was quite inexpensive. He had no objection. He borrowed a ballpoint pen and signed the agreement.

The lawyer came just before three and he and the funeral director stood there chatting for a moment – a clipped conversation, one specialist to another. Tengo couldn't really follow their conversation. The two of them seemed to know each other. This was a small town. Probably everybody knew everybody else.

Near the morgue was an inconspicuous back door, and the funeral parlor's small van was parked just outside. Except for the driver's window, all the windows were tinted black, and the jet-black van was devoid of any sign or markings. The thin funeral director and his white-haired assistant moved Tengo's father onto a rolling gurney and pushed it toward the van. The van had been refitted to have an especially high ceiling and rails onto which they slid the body. They shut the back doors of the van with an earnest thud, the funeral director turned to Tengo and bowed, and the van pulled away. Tengo, the lawyer, Nurse Tamura, and Nurse Omura all faced the rear door of the black Toyota van and brought their hands together in prayer.

Tengo and the lawyer talked in a corner of the cafeteria. The lawyer looked to be in his mid-forties, and was quite obese, the exact opposite of the funeral director. His chin had nearly disappeared, and despite the chill of winter his forehead was covered with a light sheen of sweat. *He must sweat something awful in the summer,* Tengo thought. His gray wool suit smelled of mothballs. He had a narrow forehead, and above it an overabundance of thick, luxurious black hair. The combination of the obese body and the thick hair didn't work. His eyelids were heavy and swollen, his eyes narrow, but behind them was a friendly glint.

"Your father entrusted me with his will. The word *will* implies something significant, but this isn't like one of those wills from a detective novel," the lawyer said, and cleared his throat. "It's actually closer to a simple memo. Let me start by briefly summarizing its contents. The will begins by outlining arrangements for his funeral. I believe the gentleman from Zenkosha has explained this to you?"

"Yes, he did. It's to be a simple funeral."

"Very good," the lawyer said. "That was your father's wish, that everything be done as plainly as possible. The funeral expenses will be paid out of a reserve fund he set aside, and medical and other expenses will come out of the security deposit your father paid when he checked into this facility. There will be nothing you will have to pay for out of your own pocket."

"He didn't want to owe anybody, did he?"

"Exactly. Everything has been prepaid. Also, your father has money in an account at the Chikura post office, which you, as his son, will inherit. You will need to take care of changing it over to your name. To do that, you'll need the proof that your father has been removed from the family register, and a copy of your family register and seal certificate. You should go directly to the Chikura post office and sign the necessary documents yourself. The procedures take some time. As you know, Japanese banks and the post office are quite particular about filling in all the proper forms."

The lawyer took a large white handkerchief out of his coat pocket and wiped the sweat from his forehead.

"That's all I need to tell you about the inheritance. He had no assets other than the post office account – no insurance policies, stocks, real estate, jewelry, art objects – nothing of this sort. Very straightforward, you could say, and fuss free."

Tengo nodded silently. It sounded like his father. But taking over his postal account made Tengo feel a little depressed. It felt like being handed a pile of damp, heavy blankets. If possible, he would rather not have it. But he couldn't say this.

"Your father also entrusted an envelope to my care. I have brought it with me and would like to give it to you now."

The thick brown envelope was sealed tight with packing tape. The obese lawyer took it from his black briefcase and laid it on the table.

"I met Mr. Kawana soon after he came here, and he gave this to me then. He was still – conscious then. He would get confused occasionally, but he was generally able to function fine. He told me that when he died, he would like me to give this envelope to his legal heir."

"*Legal heir*," Tengo repeated, a bit surprised.

"Yes. That was the term he used. Your father didn't specify anyone in particular, but in practical terms you would be the only legal heir."

"As far as I know."

"Then, as instructed, here you go," the lawyer said, pointing to the envelope on the table. "Could you sign a receipt for it, please?"

Tengo signed the receipt. The brown office envelope on the table looked anonymous and bland. Nothing was written on it, neither on the front nor on the back.

"There's one thing I would like to ask you," Tengo said to the lawyer. "Did my father ever mention my name? Or use the word *son*?"

As he mulled this over, the lawyer pulled out his handkerchief again and mopped his brow. He shook his head slightly. "No, Mr. Kawana always used the term *legal heir*. He didn't use any other terms. I remember this because I found it odd."

Tengo was silent. The lawyer collected himself and spoke up.

"But you have to understand that Mr. Kawana knew you were the only legal heir. It's just that when we spoke he didn't use your name. Does that bother you?"

"Not really," Tengo said. "My father was always a bit odd."

The lawyer smiled, as if relieved, and gave a slight nod. He handed

Tengo a new copy of their family register. "If you don't mind, since it was this sort of illness, I would like you to check the family register so we can make sure there are no legal problems with the procedure. According to the record, you are Mr. Kawana's sole child. Your mother passed away a year and a half after giving birth to you. Your father didn't remarry, and raised you by himself. Your father's parents and siblings are already deceased. So you are clearly Mr. Kawana's sole legal heir."

After the lawyer stood up, expressed his condolences, and left, Tengo remained seated, gazing at the envelope on the table. His father was his real blood father, and his mother was *really* dead. The lawyer had said so. So it must be true – or, at least, a fact, in a legal sense. But it felt like the more facts that were revealed, the more the truth receded. Why would that be?

Tengo returned to his father's room, sat down at the desk, and struggled to open the sealed envelope. The envelope might contain the key to unlocking some mystery. Opening it was difficult. There were no scissors or box cutters in the room, so he had to peel off the packing tape with his fingernails. When he finally managed to get the envelope open, the contents were in several other envelopes, all of them in turn tightly sealed. Just the sort of thing he expected from his father.

One envelope contained 500,000 yen in cash – exactly fifty crisp new ten-thousand-yen bills, wrapped in layers of thin paper. A piece of paper included with it said *Emergency cash.* Definitely his father's writing, small letters, nothing abbreviated. This money must be in case there were unanticipated expenses. His father had anticipated that his *legal heir* wouldn't have sufficient funds on hand.

The thickest of the envelopes was stuffed full of newspaper clippings and various award certificates, all of them about Tengo. His certificate from when he won the math contest in elementary school, and the article about it in the local paper. A photo of Tengo next to his trophy. The artistic-looking award Tengo received for having the best grades in his class. He had the best grades in every subject. There were various other articles that showed what a child prodigy Tengo had been. A photo of Tengo in a judo gi in junior high, grinning, holding the second-place banner. Tengo was really surprised to see these. After his father had retired from NHK, he left the company housing he had been in, moved to another apartment in Ichikawa, and finally went to the sanatorium in Chikura. Probably because he had moved by himself so often, he had hardly any possessions. And father and son had basically been strangers to each other for years. Despite this, his father had lovingly carried around all these mementos of Tengo's child-prodigy days.

The next envelope contained various records from his father's days as an NHK fee collector. A record of the times when he was the top producer of the year. Several simple certificates. A photo apparently taken with a colleague on a company trip. An old ID card. Records of payment to his retirement plan and health insurance.... Though his father worked like a dog for NHK for over thirty years, the amount of material left was surprisingly little – next to nothing when compared with Tengo's achievements in elementary school. Society might see his father's entire life as amounting to almost zero, but to Tengo, it wasn't *next to nothing*. Along with a postal savings book, his father had left behind a deep, dark shadow.

There was nothing in the envelope to indicate anything about his father's life before he joined NHK. It was as if his father's life began the moment he became an NHK fee collector.

He opened the final envelope, a thin one, and found a single black-and-white photograph. That was all. It was an old photo, and though the contrast hadn't faded, there was a thin membrane over the whole picture, as if water had seeped into it. It was a photo of a family – a father, a mother, and a tiny baby. The baby looked less than a year old. The mother, dressed in a kimono, was lovingly cradling the baby. Behind them was a torii gate at a shrine. From the clothes they had on, it looked like winter. Since they were visiting a shrine, it was most likely New Year's. The mother was squinting, as if the light were too bright, and smiling. The father, dressed in a dark coat, slightly too big for him, had frown lines between his eyes, as if to say he didn't take anything at face value. The baby looked confused by how big and cold the world could be.

The young father in the photo had to be Tengo's father. He looked much younger, though he already had a sort of surprising maturity about him, and he was thin, his eyes sunken. It was the face of a poor farmer from some out-of-the-way hamlet, stubborn, skeptical. His hair was cut short, his shoulders a bit stooped. That could only be his father. This meant that the baby must be Tengo, and the mother holding the baby must be Tengo's mother. His mother was slightly taller than his father, and had good posture. His father was in his late thirties, while his mother looked to be in her mid-twenties.

Tengo had never seen the photograph before. He had never seen anything that could be called a family photo. And he had never seen a picture of himself when he was little. They couldn't afford a camera, his father had once explained, and never had the opportunity to take any family photos. And Tengo had accepted this. But now he knew it was a lie. They *had* taken a photo together. And though their clothes weren't exactly luxurious, they were at least presentable. They didn't look as if they were so poor they couldn't afford a camera. The photo was taken not long after Tengo was born, sometime between 1954 and 1955. He turned the photo over, but there was no date or indication of where it had been taken.

Tengo studied the woman. In the photo her face was small, and slightly out of focus. If only he had a magnifying glass! Then he could have made out more details. Still, he could see most of her features. She had an oval-shaped face, a small nose, and plump lips. By no means a beauty, though sort of cute – the type of face that left a good impression. At least compared with his father's rustic face she looked far more refined and intelligent. Tengo was happy about this. Her hair was nicely styled, but since she had on a kimono, he couldn't tell much about her figure.

At least as far as they looked in this photo, no one could call them a well-matched couple. There was a great age difference between them. Tengo tried to imagine his parents meeting each other, falling in love, having him – but he just couldn't see it. You didn't get that sense at all from the photo. So if there wasn't an emotional attachment that brought them together, there must have been some other circumstances that did. No, maybe it wasn't as dramatic as the term *circumstances* made it sound. Life might just be an absurd, even crude, chain of events and nothing more.

Tengo tried to figure out if the mother in this photo was the mysterious woman who appeared in his daydreams, or in his fog of childhood memories. But he realized he didn't have any memories of the woman's face whatsoever. The woman in his memory took off her blouse, let down the straps of her slip, and let some unknown man suck her breasts. And her breathing became deeper, like she was moaning. That's all he remembered – some man sucking his mother's breasts. The breasts that should have been his alone were stolen away by somebody else. A baby would no doubt see this as a grave threat. His eyes never went to the man's face.

Tengo returned the photo to the envelope, and thought about what it meant. His father had cherished this one photograph until he died, which might mean he still cherished Tengo's mother. Tengo couldn't remember his mother, for she had died from illness when he was too young to have any memories of her. According to the lawyer's investigation, Tengo was the only child of his mother and his father, the NHK fee collector, a fact recorded in his family register. But official documents didn't guarantee that that man was Tengo's biological father.

"I don't have a son," his father had declared to Tengo before he fell into a coma.

"So, what am I?" Tengo had asked.

"You're nothing," was his father's concise and peremptory reply.

His father's tone of voice had convinced Tengo that there was no blood connection between him and this man. And he had felt freed from heavy shackles. As time went on, however, he wasn't completely convinced that what his father had said was true.

I'm nothing, Tengo repeated.

Suddenly he realized that his young mother in the photo from long ago reminded him of his older girlfriend. Kyoko Yasuda was her name. In order to calm his mind, he pressed his fingers hard against the middle of his forehead. He took the photo out again and stared at it. A small nose, plump lips, a somewhat pointed chin. Her hairstyle was so different he hadn't noticed at first, but her features did somewhat resemble Kyoko's. But what could that possibly mean?

And why did his father think to give this photo to Tengo after his death? While he was alive he had never provided Tengo with a single piece of information about his mother. He had even hidden the existence of this family photo. One thing Tengo did know was that his father never intended to explain the situation to him. Not while he was alive, and not even now after his death. *Look, here's a photo,* his father must be saying. *I'll just hand it to you. It's up to you to* figure it out.

Tengo lay faceup on the bare mattress and stared at the ceiling. It was a painted white plywood ceiling, flat with no wood grain or knots, just several straight joints where the boards came together – the same scene his father's sunken eyes must have viewed during the last few months of life. Or maybe those eyes didn't see anything. At any rate his gaze had been directed there, at the ceiling, whether he had been seeing it or not.

Tengo closed his eyes and tried to imagine himself slowly moving toward death. But for a thirty-year-old in good health, death was something far off, beyond the imagination. Instead, breathing softly, he watched the twilight shadows as they moved across the wall. He tried to not think about anything. Not thinking about anything was not too hard for Tengo. He was too tired to keep any one particular thought in his head. He wanted to catch some sleep if he could, but he was overtired, and sleep wouldn't come.

* * *

Just before six p.m. Nurse Omura came and told him dinner was ready in the cafeteria. Tengo had no appetite, but the tall, busty nurse wouldn't leave him alone. You need to get something, even a little bit, into your stomach, she told him. This was close to a direct order. When it came to telling people how to maintain their health, she was a pro. And Tengo wasn't the type – especially when the other person was an older woman – who could resist.

They took the stairs down to the cafeteria and found Kumi Adachi waiting for them. Nurse Tamura was nowhere to be seen. Tengo ate dinner at the same table as Kumi and Nurse Omura. Tengo had a salad, cooked vegetables, and miso soup with asari clams and scallions, washed down with hot *hojicha* tea.

"When is the cremation?" Kumi asked him.

"Tomorrow afternoon at one," Tengo said. "When that's done, I'll probably go straight back to Tokyo. I have to go back to work."

"Will anyone else be at the cremation besides you, Tengo?"

"No, no one else. Just me."

"Do you mind if I join you?" Kumi asked.

"At my father's cremation?" Tengo asked, surprised.

"Yes. Actually I was pretty fond of him."

Tengo involuntarily put his chopsticks down and looked at her. Was she really talking about his father? "What did you like about him?" he asked her.

"He was very conscientious, never said more than he needed to," she said. "In that sense he was like my father, who passed away."

"Huh," Tengo said.

"My father was a fisherman. He died before he reached fifty."

"Did he die at sea?"

"No, he died of lung cancer. He smoked too much. I don't know why, but fishermen are all heavy smokers. It's like smoke is rising out of their whole body."

Tengo thought about this. "It might have been better if my father had been a fisherman too."

"Why do you think that?"

"I'm not really sure," Tengo replied. "The thought just occurred to me – that it would have been better for him than being an NHK fee collector."

"If your father had been a fisherman, would it have been easier for you to accept him?"

"It would have made many things simpler, I suppose."

Tengo pictured himself as a child, early in the morning on a day when he didn't have school, heading off on a fishing boat with his father. The stiff Pacific wind, the salt spray hitting his face. The monotonous drone of the diesel engine. The stuffy smell of the fishing nets. Hard, dangerous work. One mistake and you could lose your life. But compared with being dragged all over Ichikawa to collect subscription fees, it would have to be a more natural, fulfilling life.

"But collecting NHK fees couldn't have been easy work, could it?" Nurse Omura said as she ate her soy-flavored fish.

"Probably not," Tengo said. At least he knew it wasn't the kind of job he could handle.

"Your father was really good at his job, wasn't he?" Kumi asked.

"I think he was, yes," Tengo said.

"He showed me his award certificates," Kumi said.

"Ah! Darn," Nurse Omura said, suddenly putting down her chopsticks. "I totally forgot. Darn it! How could I forget something so important? Could you wait here for a minute? I have something I have to give you, and it has to be today."

Nurse Omura wiped her mouth with a napkin, stood up, and hurried out of the cafeteria, her meal half eaten.

"I wonder what's so important?" Kumi said, tilting her head.

Tengo had no idea.

As he waited for Nurse Omura's return, he dutifully worked his way through his salad. There weren't many others eating dinner in the cafeteria. At one table there were three old men, none of them speaking. At another table a man in a white coat, with a sprinkling of

339

gray hair, sat alone, reading the evening paper as he ate, a solemn look on his face.

Nurse Omura finally trotted back. She was holding a department-store shopping bag. She took out some neatly folded clothes.

"I got this from Mr. Kawana about a year or so ago, while he was still conscious," the large nurse said. "He said when he was put in the casket he would like to be dressed in this. So I sent it to the cleaners and had them store it in mothballs."

There was no mistaking the NHK fee collector's uniform. The matching trousers had been nicely ironed. The smell of mothballs hit Tengo. For a while he was speechless.

"Mr. Kawana told me he would like to be cremated wearing this uniform," Nurse Omura said. She refolded the uniform neatly and put it back in the shopping bag. "So I'm giving it to you now. Tomorrow, give this to the funeral home people and make sure they dress him in it."

"Isn't it a problem to have him wear this? The uniform was just on loan to him, and when he retired it should have been returned to NHK," Tengo said, weakly.

"I wouldn't worry about it," Kumi said. "If we don't say anything, who's going to know? NHK isn't going to be in a tight spot over a set of old clothes."

Nurse Omura agreed. "Mr. Kawana walked all over the place, from morning to night, for over thirty years for NHK. I'm sure it wasn't always pleasant. Who cares about one uniform? It's not like you're using it to do something bad or anything."

"You're right. I still have my school uniform from high school," Kumi said.

"An NHK collector's uniform and a high school uniform aren't exactly the same thing," Tengo interjected, but no one took up the point.

"Come to think of it, I have my old school uniform in the closet somewhere too," Nurse Omura said.

"Are you telling me you put it on sometimes for your husband? Along with white bobby socks?" Kumi said teasingly.

"Hmm – now that's a thought," Nurse Omura said, her chin in her hands on the table, her expression serious. "Probably get him all hot and bothered."

"Anyway . . . ," Kumi said. She turned to Tengo. "Mr. Kawana definitely wanted to be cremated in his NHK uniform. I think we should help him make his wish come true. Don't you think so?"

Tengo took the bag containing the uniform and went back to the room. Kumi Adachi came with him and made up the bed. There were fresh sheets, with a still-starchy fragrance, a new blanket, a new bed cover, and a new pillow. Once all this was arranged, the bed his father had slept in looked totally transformed. Tengo randomly thought of Kumi's thick, luxuriant pubic hair.

"Your father was in a coma for so long," Kumi said as she smoothed out the wrinkles in the sheets, "but I don't think he was completely unconscious."

"Why do you say that?" Tengo asked.

"Well, he would sometimes send messages to somebody."

Tengo was standing at the window gazing outside, but he spun around and looked at Kumi. "Messages?"

"He would tap on the bed frame. His hand would hang down from the bed and he would knock on the frame, like he was sending Morse code. Like this."

Kumi lightly tapped the wooden bed frame with her fist.

"Don't you think it sounds like a signal?"

"That's not a signal."

"Then what is it?"

"He's knocking on a door," Tengo said, his voice dry. "The front door of a house."

"I guess that makes sense. It does sound like someone knocking on a door." She narrowed her eyes to slits. "So are you saying that even after he lost consciousness he was still making his rounds to collect fees?"

"Probably," Tengo said. "Somewhere inside his head."

"It's like that story of the dead soldier still clutching his trumpet," Kumi said, impressed.

There was nothing to say to this, so Tengo stayed silent.

"Your father must have really liked his job. Going around collecting NHK subscription fees."

"I don't think it's a question of liking or disliking it," Tengo said.

"Then what?"

"It was the one thing he was best at."

"Hmm. I see," Kumi said. She pondered this. "But that might very well be the best way to live your life."

"Maybe so," Tengo said as he looked out at the pine windbreak. It might really be so.

"What's the one thing you can do best?"

"I don't know," Tengo said, looking straight at her. "I honestly have no idea."

22

USHIKAWA

Those Eyes Looked Rather Full of Pity

TENGO SHOWED UP AT THE ENTRANCE to the apartment building on Sunday evening, at six fifteen. As soon as he stepped outside he halted and gazed around, as if looking for something. First to the right, then the left. Then from left to right. He looked up at the sky, then down at his feet. But nothing seemed to be out of the ordinary, as far as he was concerned.

Ushikawa didn't follow him then. Tengo was carrying nothing with him. His hands were stuffed in the pockets of his unpleated chinos. He had on a high-neck sweater and a well-worn olive-green corduroy jacket, and his hair was unruly. A thick paperback book peeped out of a jacket pocket. Ushikawa figured he must be going out to eat dinner in a nearby restaurant. *Fine,* he decided, *just let him go where he wants.*

Tengo had several classes he had to teach on Monday. Ushikawa had found this out by phoning the cram school. Yes, a female office worker had told him, Mr. Kawana will be teaching his regular classes from the beginning of the week. Good. From tomorrow, then, Tengo was finally going back to his normal schedule. Knowing him, he probably wouldn't be going far this evening. (If Ushikawa had followed him that night, he would have found out that Tengo was on his way to meet with Komatsu at the bar in Yotsuya.)

Just before eight, Ushikawa threw on his pea coat, muffler, and knit hat and, looking around him as he did, hurried out of the building. Tengo had not yet returned at this point. If he was really eating somewhere in the neighborhood, it was taking longer than it should. If Ushikawa was unlucky, he might actually bump into him on his way back. But he was willing to run the risk, since there was something he absolutely had to do, and it had to be done now, at this time of night.

He relied on his memory of the route as he turned several corners, passed a few semi-familiar landmarks, and though he hesitated a few times, unsure of the direction, he eventually arrived at the playground. The strong north wind of the previous day had died down, and it was warm for a December evening, but as expected, the park was deserted. Ushikawa double-checked that there was no one else around, then climbed up the slide. He sat down on top of the slide, leaned back against the railing, and looked up at the sky. The moons were there, almost in the same location as the night before. A bright moon, two-thirds full. Not a single cloud nearby. And beside it, a small green, misshapen moon snuggled close.

So it's no mistake, then, Ushikawa thought. He exhaled and shook his head. He wasn't dreaming or hallucinating. Two moons, one big, one small, were definitely visible there, above the leafless zelkova tree. The two moons looked like they had stayed put since last night, waiting for him to return to the top of the slide. They knew that he would be back. As if prearranged, the silence around them was suggestive. And the moons wanted Ushikawa to share that silence with them. *You can't tell anybody else about this,* they warned. They held an index finger, covered with a light dusting of ash, to their mouths to make sure he didn't say a thing.

As he sat there, Ushikawa moved his facial muscles this way and that, to make sure there wasn't something unnatural or unusual about this feeling he was having. He found nothing unnatural about it. For better or for worse, this was his normal face.

Ushikawa always saw himself as a realist, and he actually was. Metaphysical speculation wasn't his thing. If something really existed, you had to accept it as a reality, whether or not it made sense or was logical. That was his basic way of thinking. Principles and logic didn't give birth to reality. Reality came first, and the principles and logic followed. So, he decided, he would have to begin by accepting this reality: that there were two moons in the sky.

The rest of it he would think about later. He sat there, trying not to think, completely absorbed in observing the two moons. He tried to get used to the scene. *I have to accept these guys* as they are, he said to himself. He couldn't explain why something like this could be possible, but it wasn't a question he needed to delve into deeply at this point. The question was *how to deal with it.* That was the real issue. To do so he needed to start by accepting what he was seeing, without questioning the logic of it.

Ushikawa was there for some fifteen minutes. He sat, leaning against the railing of the slide, hardly moving a muscle. Like a diver slowly acclimatizing his body to a change in water pressure, he let himself be bathed in the light from these moons, let it seep into his skin. Ushikawa's instinct told him this was important.

Finally this small man with a misshapen head stood up, climbed down from the slide, and, completely caught up in indescribable musings, walked back to the apartment building. Things looked a little different from when he came. *Maybe it's the moonlight,* he told himself. *That moonlight is gradually displacing how things appear.* Thanks to this, he took the wrong turn a number of times. Before he walked inside the building he looked up at the third floor to check that Tengo's lights were still off. Tengo was still out. It didn't seem likely that he had just gone out to eat someplace nearby. Maybe he was meeting somebody? And maybe that somebody was Aomame. Or Fuka-Eri. *Have I let a golden opportunity slip through my fingers?* he wondered. But it was too late to worry about it now. It was too risky to tail Tengo every time he went out. Tengo only had to spot him once to bring the whole operation crashing down.

Ushikawa went back to his apartment and removed his coat, muffler, and hat. He opened a tin of corned beef, spread some on a roll, and ate it, standing up in the kitchen. He drank a container of lukewarm canned coffee. Nothing had any taste. He could feel the texture of the food, but he couldn't taste anything. Whether this was the fault of the food and drink or his own sense of taste, he couldn't say. Maybe it could be blamed on those two moons. He heard a faint doorbell ring somewhere. A pause, then it rang again. He didn't care. It wasn't his chime ringing, but somebody else's, far away, on a different floor.

He finished his sandwich, drained the coffee, then leisurely smoked a cigarette to bring his mind back to reality. He reconfirmed what it was he had to do here, and sat down behind the camera at the window. He switched on the electric space heater and warmed his hands in front of the orange light. It was Sunday evening, not yet nine. Traffic into and out of the building was sparse, but Ushikawa was determined to see what time Tengo returned.

A moment later a woman in a black down jacket came out of the entrance, a woman he had never seen before. She had on a gray muffler up to her mouth, dark-framed glasses, and a baseball cap – the perfect getup to hide yourself from prying eyes. She was empty-handed and was walking briskly, taking long strides. Instinctively Ushikawa switched on the camera's motor drive and snapped three quick shots. He had to find out where she was going, but by the time he had gotten to his feet, the woman had reached the road and vanished into the night. Ushikawa frowned and gave up. At the pace she was walking, by the time he got his shoes on and chased after her, it would be too late to catch up.

He did an instant replay in his mind of what he had just seen. The woman was about five feet six inches tall, and wore narrow blue jeans and white sneakers. All her clothes looked strangely brand-new. He would put her at mid-twenties to about thirty. Her hair was stuffed in her collar, so he couldn't tell how long it was. The puffy down jacket made it hard to tell what sort of figure she had, but judging from her legs, she must be fairly slim. Her good posture and quick pace indicated she was young and healthy. She must be into sports. All these characteristics fit the Aomame that Ushikawa knew about, though he couldn't make too many assumptions. Still, she seemed to be very cautious. You could tell how tense her whole body was, like an actress being stalked by paparazzi.

Let's suppose for the moment, he thought, *that this was Aomame.*

She came here to see Tengo, but Tengo was out somewhere. The lights in his place were off. She came to see him, but there was no answer when she knocked, so she gave up and left. Maybe she was the one who had been ringing the doorbell. But something about this didn't make sense. Aomame was being pursued, and should be trying to stay out of sight. Why wouldn't she have called Tengo ahead of time to make sure he would be at home? That way she wouldn't unnecessarily expose herself to danger.

Ushikawa mulled this over as he sat in front of the camera, but he couldn't come up with a working hypothesis that made any sense. The woman's actions – disguising herself in this non-disguise, leaving the place where she was hiding – didn't fit what Ushikawa knew about her. She was more cautious and careful than that. The whole thing left him befuddled.

Anyhow, he decided he would go to the photo shop near the station tomorrow and develop the film he had taken. This mystery woman should be in the photos.

He kept watch with his camera until past ten, but after the woman left no one else came in or out of the building. The entrance was silent and deserted, like a stage abandoned after a poorly attended performance. Ushikawa was puzzled about Tengo. As far as he knew, he rarely stayed out this late, and he had classes to teach tomorrow. Maybe he had already come home while Ushikawa was out, and had long since gone to bed?

After ten Ushikawa realized how exhausted he was. He could barely keep his eyes open. This was unusual, since he normally kept late hours. Usually he could stay up as late as he needed. But tonight, sleep was bearing down on him from above, like the stone lid of an ancient coffin.

Maybe I looked at those two moons for too long, he thought, *absorbed too much of their light.* Their vague afterimage remained in his eyes. Their dark silhouettes numbed the soft part of his brain, like a bee stinging and numbing a caterpillar, then laying eggs on the surface of its body. The bee larvae use the paralyzed caterpillar as a convenient source of food and devour it as soon as they're born. Ushikawa frowned and shook this ominous image from his mind.

Fine, he decided. *I can't wait here forever for Tengo to get back. When he gets back is entirely up to him, and he'll just go to sleep as soon as he does. He doesn't have anywhere else to come back to besides this apartment. Most likely.*

Ushikawa listlessly tugged off his trousers and sweater and, stripped to his long-sleeved shirt and long johns, slipped into his sleeping bag. He curled up and soon fell asleep. It was a deep sleep, almost coma-like. As he was falling asleep he thought he heard a knock at the door. But by then his consciousness had shifted over to another world and he couldn't distinguish one thing from another. When he tried, his body creaked. So he kept his eyes shut, didn't try to figure out what the sound could mean, and once more sank down into the soft muddy oblivion of sleep.

It was about thirty minutes after Ushikawa fell into this deep sleep that Tengo came back home after meeting Komatsu. He brushed his teeth, hung up his jacket – which reeked of cigarette smoke – changed into pajamas, and went to sleep. Until a phone call came at two a.m. telling him that his father was dead.

* * *

When Ushikawa awoke, it was past eight a.m., Monday morning, and Tengo was already on the express train to Tateyama, fast asleep to make up for the hours he had missed. Ushikawa sat behind his camera, waiting to catch Tengo on his way to the cram school, but of course he never made an appearance. At one p.m. Ushikawa gave up. He went to a nearby public phone and called the cram school to see if Tengo was teaching his regular classes today.

"Mr. Kawana had a family emergency, so his classes are canceled for today," the woman on the phone said. Ushikawa thanked her and hung up.

Family emergency? The only family Tengo had was his father. His father must have died. If that was the case, then Tengo would be leaving Tokyo again. *Maybe he had already left while I was sleeping. What was wrong with me? I slept so long I missed him.*

At any rate, Tengo is now all alone in the world, thought Ushikawa. A lonely man to begin with, he was now even lonelier. Utterly alone. Before he was even two, his mother had been strangled to death at a hot springs resort in Nagano Prefecture. The man who murdered her was never caught. She had left her husband and, with Tengo in tow, had absconded with a young man. *Absconded* – a quite old-fashioned term. Nobody uses it anymore, but for a certain kind of action it's the perfect term. Why the man killed her wasn't clear. It wasn't even clear if that man had been the one who murdered her. She had been strangled at night with the belt from her robe, in a room at an inn. The man she had been with was gone. It was hard not to suspect him. When Tengo's father got the news, he came from Ichikawa and took back his infant son.

Maybe I should have told Tengo about this, Ushikawa thought. *He has a right to know. But he told me he didn't want to hear anything about his mother from the likes of me, so I didn't say anything. Well, what are you going to do? That's not my problem, it's his.*

At any rate, whether Tengo is here or not, I have to keep up my surveillance of this place, Ushikawa told himself. *Last night was that*

mysterious woman who looked a lot like Aomame. I have no proof it's
her, but there's a strong possibility it is. That's what my misshapen head
is telling me. And if that woman is Aomame, she'll be back to visit Tengo
before long. She doesn't know yet that his father has died. These were
Ushikawa's deductions as he mulled over the situation. Tengo must
have gotten the news about his father during the night and set off
early this morning. And there must be some reason why the two of
them couldn't get in touch by phone. Which means she would definitely
be coming back here. Something was so important to her that she
would come here, despite the danger. This time he was going to find
out where she was going.

Doing so might also begin to explain why there were two moons.
This was a fascinating question that Ushikawa was dying to solve. But
really it was of secondary importance. His job was to find out where
Aomame was hiding, and hand her over, nice and neat, to the creepy
Sakigake duo. *Until I do so, whether there are two moons or only one,*
he decided, *I have to be realistic. That has always been my strong point.*
It's what defines me.

Ushikawa went to the photo store near the station and handed over
five thirty-six-exposure rolls of film. Once the film had been processed
and printed, he went to a nearby chain restaurant and looked through
them in chronological order while eating a meal of chicken curry.
Most were photos of people he was now familiar with. There were
three people he was most interested in: Fuka-Eri and Tengo, and last
night's mystery woman.

Fuka-Eri's eyes made him nervous. Even in the photo she was
staring straight into his face. *No doubt about it,* Ushikawa thought.
She *knew* she was being observed. She probably knew about the hidden
camera, too, and that he was taking photos. Her clear eyes saw through
everything, and they didn't like what Ushikawa was up to. That unwavering gaze stabbed mercilessly to the depths of his heart. There was

no excuse whatsoever for the activities he was engaged in. At the same time, though, she wasn't condemning him, or despising him. In a sense, those gorgeous eyes forgave him. *No, not forgiveness,* Ushikawa decided, rethinking it. Those eyes *pitied* him. She knew how ugly Ushikawa's actions were, and she felt compassion for him.

Looking at her eyes, he had felt a sharp stab of pain between his ribs, as if a thick knitting needle had been thrust in. He felt like a twisted, ugly person. *So what?* he thought. *I really am twisted and ugly.* The natural, transparent pity that colored her eyes sank deep into his heart. He would have much preferred to be openly accused, reviled, denounced, and convicted. Much better even to be beaten senseless with a baseball bat. *That* he could stand. But not *this.*

Compared with her, Tengo was much easier to deal with. In the photo he was standing at the entrance, also looking in his direction. Like Fuka-Eri, he carefully examined his surroundings. But there was nothing in his eyes. Pure, ignorant eyes like those couldn't locate the camera hidden behind the curtains, or Ushikawa.

Ushikawa turned to the photos of the *mystery woman.* There were three photos. Baseball cap, dark-framed glasses, gray muffler up to her nose. It was impossible to make out her features. The lighting was poor in all the photos, and the baseball cap cast a shadow over her face. Still, this woman perfectly fit his mental image of Aomame. He picked up the photos and, like checking out a poker hand, went through them in order, over and over. The more he looked at them, the more convinced he was that this had to be Aomame.

He called the waitress over and asked her about the day's dessert. Peach pie, she replied. Ushikawa ordered a piece and a refill of coffee.

If this isn't Aomame, he thought as he waited for the pie, *then I might never see her as long as I live.*

The peach pie was much tastier than expected. Juicy peaches inside a crisp, flaky crust. Canned peaches, no doubt, but not too bad for a dessert at a chain restaurant. Ushikawa ate every last bite, drained the coffee, and left the restaurant feeling content. He picked up three days' worth of food at a supermarket, then went back to the apartment and his stakeout in front of the camera.

As he continued his surveillance of the entrance, he leaned back against the wall, in a sunny spot, and dozed off a few times. This didn't bother him. He felt sure he hadn't missed anything important while he slept. Tengo was away from Tokyo at his father's funeral, and Fuka-Eri wasn't coming back. She knew he was continuing his surveillance. The chances were slim that the *mystery woman* would visit while it was light out. She would be cautious, and wait until dark to make a move.

But even after sunset the *mystery woman* didn't appear. The same old lineup came and went – shopping bags in hand, out for an evening stroll, those coming back from work looking more beaten and worn out than when they had set off in the morning. Ushikawa watched them come and go but didn't snap any photos. There wasn't any need. Ushikawa was focused on only three people. Everyone else was just a nameless pedestrian. But to pass time Ushikawa called out to them, using the nicknames he had come up with.

"Hey, Chairman Mao." (The man's hair looked like Mao Tse-tung's.) "You must have worked hard today."

"Warm today, isn't it, Long Ears – perfect for a walk."

"Evening, Chinless. Shopping again? What's for dinner?"

Ushikawa kept up his surveillance until eleven. He gave a big yawn and called it a day. After he brushed his teeth, he stuck out his tongue and looked at it in the mirror. It had been a while since he had examined his tongue. Something like moss was growing on it, a light green, like real moss. He examined this moss carefully under the light. It was disturbing. The moss adhered to his entire tongue and didn't look like it would come off easily. *If I keep up like this,* he thought, *I'm going to turn into a Moss Monster. Starting with my tongue, green moss will spread here and there on my skin, like the shell of a turtle that lives in a swamp.* The very thought was disheartening.

He sighed, and in a voiceless voice decided to stop worrying about his tongue. He turned off the light, slowly undressed in the dark, and snuggled into his sleeping bag. He zipped the bag and curled up like a bug.

It was dark when he woke up. He turned to check the time, but his clock wasn't where it should be. This confused him. His long-standing habit was to always check for the clock before he went to sleep. So why wasn't it there? A faint light came in through a gap in the curtain, but it only illuminated a corner of the room. Everywhere else was wrapped in middle-of-the-night darkness.

Ushikawa felt his heart racing, working hard to pump adrenaline through his system. His nostrils flared, his breathing was ragged, like he had woken in the middle of a vivid, exciting dream.

But he wasn't dreaming. Something really *was* happening. Somebody was standing right next to him. Ushikawa could sense it. A shadow, darker than the darkness, was looming over him, staring down at his face. His back stiffened. In a fraction of a second, his mind regrouped and he instinctively tried to unzip the sleeping bag.

In the blink of an eye, the person wrapped his arm around Ushikawa's throat. He didn't even have time to get out a sound. Ushikawa felt a man's strong, trained muscles around his neck. This arm constricted his throat, squeezing him mercilessly in a viselike grip. The man never said a word. Ushikawa couldn't even hear him breathing. He twisted and writhed in his sleeping bag, tearing at the inner nylon lining, kicking with both feet. He tried to scream, but even if he could, it wouldn't help. Once the man had settled down on the tatami he didn't budge an inch, except for his arm, which gradually increased the amount of force he applied. A very effective, economical movement. As he did, pressure grew on Ushikawa's windpipe, and his breathing grew weaker.

In the midst of this desperate situation, what flashed through

Ushikawa's mind was this: *How had the man gotten in here?* The door was locked, the chain inside set, the windows bolted shut. *So how did he get in? If he picked the lock, it would have made a sound.*

This guy is a real pro. If the situation called for it, he wouldn't hesitate to take a person's life. He is trained precisely for this. Was he sent by Sakigake? Have they finally decided to get rid of me? Did they conclude that I was useless to them, a hindrance they had to get rid of? If so, they're flat-out wrong. I'm one step away from locating Aomame. Ushikawa tried to speak, to tell the man this. *Listen to me first,* he wanted to plead. But no voice would come. There wasn't enough air to vibrate his vocal cords, and his tongue in the back of his mouth was a solid rock.

Now his windpipe was completely blocked. His lungs desperately struggled for oxygen, but none was to be found, and he felt his body and mind split apart. His body continued to writhe inside the sleeping bag, but his mind was dragged off into the heavy, gooey air. He suddenly had no feeling in his arms and legs. *Why?* his fading mind asked. *Why do I have to die in such an ugly place, in such an ugly way?* There was no answer. An undefined darkness descended from the ceiling and enveloped everything.

When he regained consciousness, Ushikawa was no longer inside the sleeping bag. He couldn't feel his arms or legs. All he knew was that he had on a blindfold and his cheek felt pressed up against the tatami. He wasn't being strangled anymore. His lungs audibly heaved like bellows breathing in new air. Cold, winter air. The oxygen made new blood, and his heart pumped this hot red liquid to all his nerve endings at top speed. He coughed wretchedly and focused on breathing. Gradually, feeling was returning to his extremities. His heart pounded hard in his ears. *I'm still alive,* Ushikawa told himself in the darkness.

Ushikawa was lying facedown on the tatami. His hands were bound behind him, tied up in something that felt like a soft cloth. His ankles were tied up as well – not tied so tightly, but in an accomplished, effective way. He could roll from side to side, but that was all. Ushikawa found it astounding that he was alive, still breathing. *So that wasn't death,* he thought. It had come awfully close to death, but it wasn't death itself. A sharp pain remained, like a lump, on either side of his throat. He had urinated in his pants and his underwear was wet and starting to get clammy. But it wasn't such a bad sensation. In fact he rather welcomed it. The pain and cold were signs that he was still alive.

"You won't die that easily," the man's voice said. Like he had been reading Ushikawa's mind.

23

AOMAME

The Light Was Definitely There

IT WAS PAST MIDNIGHT, THE DAY had shifted from Sunday to Monday, but still sleep wouldn't come.

Aomame finished her bath, put on pajamas, slipped into bed, and turned out the light. Staying up late wouldn't accomplish a thing. For the time being she had left it all up to Tamaru. Much better to get some sleep and think again in the morning when her mind was fresh. But she was wide awake, and her body wanted to be up and moving. It didn't look like she would be getting to sleep anytime soon.

She gave up, got out of bed, and threw a robe over her pajamas. She boiled water, made herbal tea, and sat at the dining table, slowly sipping it. A thought came to her, but what it was exactly, she couldn't say. It had a thick, furtive form, like far-off rain clouds. She could make out its shape but not its outline. There was a disconnect of some kind between shape and outline. Mug in hand, she went over to the window, and looked out at the playground through a gap in the curtains.

There was no one there, of course. Past one a.m. now, the sandbox, swings, and slide were deserted. It was a particularly silent night. The wind had died down, and there wasn't a single cloud in the sky, just the two moons floating above the frozen branches of the trees. The position of the moons had shifted with the earth's rotation, but they were still visible.

Aomame stood there, thinking about Bobblehead's run-down apartment building, and the name card in the slot on the door of apartment 303. A white card with the typed name *Kawana*. The card wasn't new, by any means. The edges were curled up, and there were faint moisture stains on it. The card had been in the slot for some time.

Tamaru would find out for her if it was really Tengo Kawana who lived there, or someone else with the same last name. At the latest, he would probably report back by tomorrow. He wasn't the kind of person who wasted time. Then she would know for sure. *Depending on the outcome,* she thought, *I might actually see Tengo before much longer.* The possibility made it hard to breathe, like the air around her had suddenly gotten thin.

But things might not work out that easily. Even if the person living in 303 was Tengo Kawana, Bobblehead was hidden away somewhere in the same building. And he was planning something – what, she didn't know, but it couldn't be good. He was undoubtedly hatching a clever plan, breathing down their necks, doing what he could to prevent them from seeing each other.

No, there's nothing to worry about, Aomame told herself. *Tamaru can be trusted. He's more meticulous, capable, and experienced than anyone I know. If I leave it up to him, he will fend off Bobblehead for me. Bobblehead is a danger not just to me, but to Tamaru as well, a risk factor that has to be eliminated.*

But what if Tamaru decides that it isn't advisable for Tengo and me to meet, then what will I do? If that happens, then Tamaru will surely cut off any possibility of Tengo and me ever seeing each other. Tamaru and I are pretty friendly, but his top priority is what will benefit the dowager and keep her out of harm's way. That's his real job – he isn't doing all this for my sake.

This made her uneasy. Getting Tengo and her together, letting them see each other again – where did this fall on Tamaru's list of priorities? She had no way of knowing. Maybe telling Tamaru about Tengo had been a fatal mistake. *Shouldn't I have taken care of everything myself?*

But what's done is done. I've told Tamaru everything. I had no choice. Bobblehead must be lying in wait for me, and it would be suicide to waltz right in all alone. Time is ticking away and I don't have the leisure to put things on hold and see how they might develop. Opening up to Tamaru about everything, and putting it all in his hands, was the best choice at the time.

Aomame decided to stop thinking about Tengo – and stop looking at the moons. The moonlight wreaked havoc on her mind. It changed the tides in inlets, stirred up life in the woods. She drank the last of her herbal tea, left the window, went to the kitchen, and rinsed out the mug. She longed for a sip of brandy, but she knew she shouldn't have any alcohol while pregnant.

She sat on the sofa, switched on the small reading lamp beside it, and began rereading *Air Chrysalis*. She had read the novel at least ten times. It wasn't a long book, and by now she had nearly memorized it. But she wanted to read it again, slowly, attentively. She figured she might as well, since she wasn't about to get to sleep. There might be something in it she had overlooked.

Air Chrysalis was like a book with a secret code, and Eriko Fukada must have told the story in order to get a message across. Tengo rewrote it, creating something more polished, more effective. They had formed a team to create a novel with a wider appeal. As Leader had said, it was a collaborative effort. If Leader was to be believed, when *Air Chrysalis* became a bestseller and certain secrets were revealed within, the Little People lost their power, and the *voice* no longer spoke.

Because of this, the well dried up, the flow was cut off. This is how much influence the novel had exerted.

She focused on each line as she read.

By the time the clock showed 2:30, she was already two-thirds of the way through the novel. She closed the book and tried to put into words the strong emotions she was feeling. Though she wouldn't go so far as to call it a revelation, she had a strong, specific image in her mind.

I wasn't brought here by chance.

This is what the image told her.

I'm here because I'm supposed to be.

Up until now, she thought, *I believed I was dragged into this 1Q84 world not by my own will. Something had intentionally engaged the switch so the train I was on was diverted from the main line and entered this strange new world. Suddenly I realized I was here – a world of two moons, haunted by Little People. Where there is an entrance, but no exit.*

Leader had explained it this way just before he died. *The train is the story that Tengo wrote, and I was trapped inside that tale. Which explains exactly why I am here now – entirely passive, a confused, clueless bit player wandering in a thick fog.*

But that's not the whole picture, Aomame told herself. **That's not the whole picture at all.**

I am not just some passive being mixed up in this because someone else willed it. That might be partly true. But at the same time I chose to be here.

I chose to be here of my own free will.

She was sure of this.

And there's a clear reason I'm here. One reason alone: so I can meet Tengo again. If you look at it the other way around, that's the only reason why this world is inside of me. Maybe it's a paradox, like an image reflected to infinity in a pair of facing mirrors. I am a part of this world, and this world is a part of me.

There was no way for Aomame to know what sort of plot Tengo's new story contained. Most likely there were two moons in that world, and it was frequented by Little People. That was about as far as she could speculate. *This might be Tengo's story,* she thought, *but* it's my story, too. This much she understood.

She realized this when she got to the scene where the young girl, the protagonist, was working to create an air chrysalis every night in the shed with the Little People. As she read through this detailed, clear description, she felt something warm and oozy in her abdomen, a sort of melting warmth with a strange depth. Though tiny, there was an intense heat source there. What that heat source was, and what it meant, was obvious to her – she didn't need to think about it. The *little one.* It was emitting heat in response to the scene in which the protagonist and the Little People together weaved the air chrysalis.

Aomame put the book on the table next to her, unbuttoned her pajama top, and rested a hand on her belly. She could feel the heat being given off, almost like a dim orange light was there inside her. She switched off the reading lamp, and in the darkened bedroom stared hard at that spot, a luminescence almost too faint to see. But the light was definitely there – no mistake about it. *I am not alone. We are connected through this, by experiencing the same story simultaneously.*

And if that story is mine as well as Tengo's, then I should be able to write the story line too. I should be able to comment on what's there, maybe even rewrite part of it. I have to be able to. Most of all, I should be able to decide how it's going to turn out. Right?

She considered the possibility.

Okay, but how do I do it?

Aomame didn't know, though she knew it had to be possible. At this point it was a mere theory. In the silent darkness she pursed her lips and contemplated. This was critical, and she had to put her mind to it.

The two of us are a team. Like Tengo and Eriko Fukada made up a brilliant team when they created Air Chrysalis, *Tengo and I are a team for this new story. Our wills – or maybe some undercurrent of our wills – are becoming one, creating this complex story and propelling it forward. This process probably takes place on some deep, invisible level. Even if we aren't physically together, we are connected, as one. We create the story, and at the same time the story is what sets us in motion. Right?*

But I have a question. A very important question.

In this story that the two of us are writing, what could be the significance of this little one? *What sort of role will it play?*

Inside my womb is a subtle yet tangible heat that is emitting a faint orange light, exactly like an air chrysalis. Is my womb playing the role of an air chrysalis? Am I the maza, *and the* little one *my* dohta? *Is the Little People's will involved in all this – in my being pregnant with Tengo's child, although we didn't have sex? Have they cleverly usurped my womb to use as an air chrysalis? Using me as a device to extract another new* dohta?

No. That's not what's going on. She was positive about it. *That's not possible.*

The Little People have lost their power. Leader said so. The popularity of the novel Air Chrysalis *essentially blocked what they normally do. So they must not know about this pregnancy. But who – or what power – made this pregnancy possible? And why?*

Aomame had no idea.

What she did know was that this *little one* was something she and Tengo had formed. That it was a precious, priceless life. She placed her hand on her abdomen again, pressing gently against the outline of that faint orange glow. She let the warmth she felt there slowly permeate her whole body. *I've got to protect this* little one, *at all costs,* she told herself. *Nobody is ever going to take it away from me, or harm it. The two of us have to keep it safe.* In the darkness, she made up her mind.

She went into the bedroom, took off her robe, and got into bed.

She lay faceup, and once more touched her abdomen and felt the warmth there. Her feeling of unease was gone. She knew what had to be done. *I have to be stronger,* she told herself. *My mind and body have to be one.* Finally sleep came, silently, like smoke, and wrapped her in its embrace. Two moons were still floating in the sky, side by side.

24

TENGO

Leaving the Cat Town

TENGO'S FATHER'S CORPSE WAS DRESSED IN his neatly ironed NHK fee collector's uniform and placed inside the simple coffin. Probably the cheapest coffin available, it was a sullen little casket that looked only slightly more sturdy than the boxes for castella cakes. The deceased was a small person, yet there was barely any room to spare. The casket was made of plywood, and had minimal ornamentation. "Is this casket all right?" the funeral director had asked, making sure. "It's fine," Tengo replied. This was the casket his father had chosen from the catalog, for which he had prepaid. If the deceased had no problem with it, then neither did Tengo.

Dressed in his NHK uniform, lying in the crude coffin, his father didn't look dead. He looked like he was taking a nap on a work break and would soon get up, put on his cap, and go out to collect the rest of the fees. The uniform, with the NHK logo sewed into it, looked like a second skin. He was born in this uniform and would leave this world in the same way as he went up in flames. When Tengo actually saw him in it, he couldn't imagine his father wearing anything else. Just like Wagner's warriors on their funeral pyre could only be dressed in armor.

Tuesday morning, in front of Tengo and Kumi Adachi, the lid of the coffin was closed, nailed shut, then placed inside the hearse. It wasn't much of a hearse, just the same businesslike Toyota van they had used to transport his body to the funeral home. This hearse, too, must have been the cheapest available. *Stately* was the last word you would use to describe it. And there was certainly no *Götterdämmerung* music as a send-off. But Tengo couldn't find anything to complain about, and Kumi didn't seem to have any problems with it either. What was more important was that a person had vanished from the face of the earth, and those left behind had to grasp what that entailed. The two of them got into a taxi and followed the black van.

They left the seaside road, drove a short way into the hills, and arrived at the crematorium. It was a relatively new building but utterly devoid of individuality. It seemed less a crematorium than some sort of factory or government office building. The garden was lovely and well tended, though the tall chimney rising majestically into the sky hinted that this was a facility with a special mission. The crematorium must not have been very busy that day, since the casket was taken right away. The casket was gently laid inside the incinerator, then the heavy lid was shut, like a submarine hatch. The old man in charge, wearing gloves, turned and bowed to Tengo, then hit the ignition switch. Kumi turned to the closed lid and put her hands together in prayer, and Tengo followed suit.

During the hourlong cremation, Tengo and Kumi waited in the building's lounge. Kumi bought two cans of hot coffee from the vending machine and they silently drank them as they sat side by side on a bench, facing a large picture window. Outside was a spacious lawn, dried up now in the winter, and leafless trees. Two black birds were on one of the branches. Tengo didn't know what kind of bird they were. They had long tails, and though small, they gave loud, sharp squawks. When they called out, their tails stood on end. Above the trees was the broad, cloudless, blue winter sky. Beneath her cream-colored duffle coat, Kumi wore a short black dress. Tengo wore a black crew-neck sweater under a dark gray herringbone jacket. His shoes were dark brown loafers. It was the most formal outfit he owned.

"My father was cremated here too," Kumi said. "All the people who attended were smoking like crazy. There was a cloud of smoke hanging up near the ceiling. Maybe to be expected, since they were all fishermen."

Tengo pictured it. A gaggle of sunburned men, uncomfortable in their dark suits, puffing away, mourning a man who had died of lung cancer. Now, though, Tengo and Kumi were the only ones in the lounge. It was quiet all around. Other than an occasional chirp from the birds in the trees, nothing else broke the silence – no music, no voices. Peaceful sunlight poured in through the picture window and formed a taciturn puddle at their feet. Time was flowing leisurely, like a river approaching an estuary.

"Thank you for coming with me," Tengo said after the long silence.

Kumi reached out and put her hand on top of his. "It's hard doing it alone. Better to have somebody with you."

"You may be right," Tengo admitted.

"It's a terrible thing when a person dies, whatever the circumstances. A hole opens up in the world, and we need to pay the proper respects. If we don't, the hole will never be filled in again."

Tengo nodded.

"The hole can't be left open," Kumi went on, "or somebody might fall in."

"But in some cases the dead person has secrets," Tengo said. "And when the hole's filled in, those secrets are never known."

"I think that's necessary too."

"How come?"

"Certain secrets can't be left behind."

"Why not?"

Kumi let go of his hand and looked at him right in the face. "There's something about those secrets that only the deceased person can rightly understand. Something that can't be explained, no matter how hard you try. They're what the dead person has to take with him to his grave. Like a valuable piece of luggage."

Tengo silently looked down at the puddle of light at his feet. The linoleum floor shone dully. In front of him were his worn loafers and Kumi's simple black pumps. They were right in front of him but looked miles away.

"There must be things about you, too, Tengo, that you can't explain to others?"

"Could be," Tengo replied.

Kumi didn't say anything, and crossed her slim black-stockinged legs.

"You told me you died once before, didn't you?" Tengo asked.

"Um. I did die once. On a lonely night when a cold rain was falling."

"Do you remember it?"

"I think so. I've dreamt about it for a long time. A very realistic dream, always exactly the same. So I have to believe that it happened."

"Was it like reincarnation?"

"Reincarnation?"

"Where you're reborn. Transmigration."

Kumi gave it some thought. "I wonder. Maybe it was. Or maybe it wasn't."

"After you died, were you cremated like this?"

Kumi shook her head. "I don't remember that far, since that would be after I died. What I remember is the *moment I died*. Someone was strangling me. A man I had never seen before."

"Do you recall his face?"

"Of course. I saw him many times in my dreams. If I ran across him on the street, I would recognize him right away."

"What would you do if you saw him in real life?"

Kumi rubbed her nose, as if checking to see if it was still there.

"I've thought about that too – what I would do if I ran across him on the street. Maybe I would run away. Or maybe I would follow him so he wouldn't notice me. Unless I was actually put in that situation, I don't know what I would do."

"If you followed him, what would you do then?"

"I don't know. But maybe that man holds some vital secret about me. And if I play my cards right, he might reveal it to me."

"What kind of secret?"

"For instance, the reason why *I'm here*."

"But that guy might kill you again."

"Maybe," Kumi said, lips slightly pursed. "I know it's dangerous. It might be better to just run away. But still the secret draws me in. Like when there's a dark entrance and cats can't help but peep in."

The cremation was over, and Tengo and Kumi, following tradition, picked up select bones from his father's remains and placed them in a small urn. The urn was handed to Tengo. He had no idea what he should do with it, though he knew he couldn't just abandon it. So he clutched the vase in his hands as he and Kumi took a taxi to the station.

"I will take care of any remaining details," Kumi told him in the cab. After a moment she added, "If you would like, I could see about interring the bones, too."

Tengo was startled. "You can do that?"

"I don't see why not," Kumi said. "There are some funerals where not a single person from the family attends."

"That would be a big help," Tengo said. And he handed her the urn, feeling a little guilty, but honestly relieved. *I will probably never see these bones again,* he thought. *All that is left will be memories, and eventually they, too, will vanish like dust.*

"I'm from here, so I think I can take care of it. It's better if you go back to Tokyo right away. We all like you a lot here, but this isn't a place you should stay for long."

I'm leaving the cat town, Tengo mused.

367

"Thank you for everything you've done," Tengo said.

"Tengo, do you mind if I give you some advice? I know I have no right to do so."

"Of course."

"Your father may have had a secret that he took with him to the other side. And that seems to be causing you confusion. I think I can understand how you feel. But you shouldn't peep anymore into that dark entrance. Leave that up to cats. If you keep doing so, you will never go anywhere. Better to think about the future."

"The hole has to be closed up," Tengo said.

"Exactly," Kumi said. "The owl says the same thing. Do you remember the owl?"

"Of course."

The owl is the guardian deity of the woods, knows all, and gives us the wisdom of the night.

"Is that owl still hooting in the woods?"

"The owl's not going anywhere," Kumi replied. "He'll be there for a long time."

Kumi saw him off on the train to Tateyama – as though she needed to make sure, with her own eyes, that he had boarded the train and left town. She stood on the platform and kept waving to him, until he couldn't see her anymore.

It was seven p.m. on Tuesday when he got back to his apartment in Koenji. Tengo turned on the lights, sat down at his dining table, and looked around the room. The place looked the same as when he had left early the previous morning. The curtains were closed tight, and there was a printout of the story he was writing on top of his desk. Six neatly sharpened pencils in a pencil holder, clean dishes still in the rack in the sink. Time was silently ticking by, the calendar on the wall indicating that this was the final month of the year. The room seemed even more *silent* than ever. A little *too* silent. Something excessive seemed included in that silence. Though maybe he was imagining it. Maybe it was because he had just witnessed a person vanishing right before his eyes. The hole in the world might not yet be fully closed up.

He drank a glass of water and took a hot shower. He shampooed his hair thoroughly, cleaned his ears, clipped his nails. He took a new pair of underwear and a shirt from his drawer and put them on. He had to get rid of all the smells that clung to him, the smells of the cat town. *We all like you a lot here, but this isn't a place you should stay for long,* Kumi Adachi had told him.

He had no appetite. He didn't feel like working or opening a book. Listening to music held no appeal. His body was exhausted, but his nerves were on edge, so he knew that even if he lay down he wouldn't get any sleep. Something about the silence seemed contrived.

It would be nice if Fuka-Eri were here, Tengo thought. *I don't care what silly, meaningless things she might talk about. Her fateful lack of intonation, the way her voice rose at the end of questions – it's all fine by me. I haven't heard her voice in a while and I miss it.* But Tengo knew that she wouldn't be coming back to his apartment again. Why he knew this, he couldn't say exactly. But he knew she would never be there again. Probably.

He wanted to talk with someone. *Anyone.* His older girlfriend would be nice, but he couldn't reach her. She was *irretrievably lost.*

He dialed Komatsu's office number, his direct extension, but nobody answered. After fifteen rings he gave up.

He tried to think of other people he could call, but there wasn't anyone. He thought of calling Kumi, but realized he didn't have her number.

His mind turned to a dark hole somewhere in the world, not yet filled in. Not such a big hole, but very deep. *If I look in that hole and speak loudly enough, would I be able to talk with my father? Will the dead tell me what the truth is?*

"If you do that, you'll never go anywhere," Kumi Adachi had told him. "Better to think about the future."

I don't agree. That's not all there is to it. Knowing the secret may not take me anywhere, but still, I have to know the reason why it won't. If I truly understand the reason, maybe I will be able to go somewhere.

Whether you are my real father or not doesn't matter anymore, Tengo said to the dark hole. *Either one is fine with me. Either way, you took a part of me with you to the grave, and I remain here with a part of you. That fact won't change, whether we are related by blood or not. Enough time has passed for that to be the case, and the world has moved on.*

He thought he heard an owl hooting outside, but it was only his ears playing tricks on him.

25

USHIKAWA

Cold or Not, God Is Present

"YOU WON'T DIE THAT EASILY," THE man's voice said from behind him. Like he had been reading Ushikawa's mind. "You just lost consciousness for a moment. Though you were right on the edge of it."

It was a voice he had never heard before. Neutral, utterly devoid of expression. Not too high or low, neither too hard nor too soft. The kind of voice that announces airplane departures or stock market reports.

What day of the week is it? Ushikawa thought randomly. *Must be Monday night. No, technically it might already be Tuesday.*

"Ushikawa," the man said. "You don't mind if I call you Ushikawa, do you?"

Ushikawa didn't reply. There was silence for a good twenty seconds. Then, without warning, the man gave him a short, clipped punch to his left kidney. Silent, but a punch with force behind it. Excruciating pain shot through his whole body. All his internal organs clenched, and until the pain had subsided a little he couldn't breathe. Finally he was able to get out a dry wheeze.

"I asked you politely, and I expect a reply. If you still can't talk, then just nod or shake your head. That's enough. That's what it means to be polite," the man said. "It's okay to call you Ushikawa?"

Ushikawa nodded several times.

"Ushikawa. An easy name to remember. I went through the wallet in your trousers. Your driver's license and business cards were in there. Full-time Director, New Japan Foundation for the Advancement of Scholarship and the Arts. A pretty fancy title, wouldn't you say? What would a Full-time Director of the New Japan Foundation for the Advancement of Scholarship and the Arts be doing shooting photos with a hidden camera in a place like this?"

Ushikawa was silent. He still couldn't get the words out easily.

"You had best reply," the man said. "Consider this a warning. If your kidney bursts, it'll hurt like hell the rest of your life."

"I'm doing surveillance on the residents," Ushikawa finally managed to say. His voice was unsteady, cracking in spots. To him, blindfolded, it didn't sound like his own.

"You mean Tengo Kawana."

Ushikawa nodded.

"The Tengo Kawana who ghostwrote *Air Chrysalis*."

Ushikawa nodded again and then had a fit of coughing. The man knew all this already.

"Who hired you to do this?" the man asked.

"Sakigake."

"That much I could figure out, Ushikawa," the man said. "The question is why, at this late date, Sakigake would want to keep watch over Tengo Kawana's movements. Tengo Kawana can't be that important to them."

Ushikawa's mind raced, trying to figure out who this man was and how much he knew. He didn't know who the man was, but it was clear Sakigake hadn't sent him. Whether that was good news or bad, Ushikawa didn't know.

"There is a question pending," the man said. He pressed a finger against Ushikawa's left kidney. Very hard.

"There's a woman he's connected with," Ushikawa groaned.

"Does this woman have a name?"

"Aomame."

"Why are they pursuing Aomame?" the man asked.

"She brought harm to Leader, the head of Sakigake."

"Brought harm," the man said, as if verifying the phrase. "You mean she killed him, right? To put it more simply."

"That's right," Ushikawa said. He knew he couldn't hide anything from this man. Sooner or later he would have to talk.

"It's a secret within the religion."

"How many people in Sakigake know this secret?"

"A handful."

"Including you."

Ushikawa nodded.

"So you must occupy a very high position."

"No," Ushikawa said, and shook his head, his bruised kidney aching. "I'm simply a messenger. I just happened to find out about it."

"In the wrong place at the wrong time. Is that what you're saying?"

"I think so."

"By the way, Ushikawa, are you working alone?"

Ushikawa nodded.

"I find that strange. Normally a team would conduct surveillance. To do a decent job of it, you would also need someone to run supplies, so three people at the minimum. And you're already deeply connected with an organization. Doing it all alone strikes me as unnatural. In other words, I'm not exactly pleased with your reply."

"I am not a follower of the religion," Ushikawa said. His breathing had calmed down and he was finally able to speak close to normally. "I was hired by them. They call on me when they think it's more convenient to hire an outsider."

"As a Full-time Director of the New Japan Foundation for the Advancement of Scholarship and the Arts?"

"That's just a front. There's no such organization. It was mainly set up by Sakigake for tax purposes. I'm an individual contractor, with no ties to the religion. I just work for them."

"A mercenary of sorts."

"No, not a mercenary. I'm collecting information at their request. If anything rough needs to get done, it's handled by other people."

"So, Ushikawa, you were instructed by Sakigake to do surveillance here on Tengo, and probe into his connection with Aomame."

"Correct."

"No," the man said. "That's the wrong answer. If Sakigake knew for a fact that there's a connection between Aomame and Tengo Kawana, they wouldn't have sent you by yourself on the stakeout. They would have put together a team of their own people. That would reduce the chance for mistakes, and they could resort to force if need be."

"I'm telling you the truth. I'm just doing what the people above me told me to do. Why they're having me do it alone, I have no idea." The pitch of Ushikawa's voice was still unsteady, and it cracked in places.

If he finds out that Sakigake doesn't yet know the connection between Aomame and Tengo, Ushikawa thought, *I might be whacked right here and now. If I'm no longer in the picture, then nobody will be any the wiser about their connection.*

"I'm not very fond of incorrect answers," the man said in a chilly tone. "I think you of all people are well aware of that. I wouldn't mind giving your kidney another punch, but if I hit you hard my hand will hurt, and permanently damaging your kidney isn't what I came here to do. I have no personal animosity toward you. I have just one goal, to get the right answer. So I'm going to try a different approach. I'm sending you to the bottom of the sea."

The bottom of the sea? Ushikawa thought. *What is this guy talking about?*

The man pulled something out of his pocket. There was a rustling sound like plastic rubbing together, and then something covered Ushikawa's head. A plastic bag, the thick freezer bag kind. Then a thick, large rubber band was wrapped around his neck. *This guy is trying to suffocate me,* Ushikawa realized. He tried breathing in but got a mouthful of plastic instead. His nostrils were blocked as well. His lungs were screaming for air, but there wasn't any. The plastic molded tight to his whole face like a death mask. Soon all his muscles started to convulse violently. He tried to reach out to rip away the bag, but his hands wouldn't move. They were tied tight behind his back. His brain blew up like a balloon and felt ready to explode. He tried to scream. He *had* to get air. But no sound came out. His tongue filled his mouth as his consciousness drained away.

Finally the rubber band was taken from his neck, the plastic bag peeled away from his head. Ushikawa desperately gulped down the air in front of him. For a few minutes he bent forward, breathing mightily, like an animal lunging at something just out of reach.

"How was the bottom of the sea?" the man asked after Ushikawa's breathing had settled down. His voice was, as before, expressionless. "You went quite deep down. I imagine you saw all sorts of things you've never seen before. A valuable experience."

Ushikawa couldn't respond. His voice wouldn't come.

"Ushikawa, as I have said a number of times, I am looking for the correct answer. So I'll ask you once again: Were you instructed by Sakigake to track Tengo Kawana's movements and search for his connection with Aomame? This is a critical point. A person's life is on the line. Think carefully before you answer. I'll know if you're lying."

"Sakigake doesn't know about this," Ushikawa managed to stammer.

"Good, that's the correct answer. Sakigake doesn't know yet about the connection between Aomame and Tengo Kawana. You haven't told them yet. Is that correct?"

Ushikawa nodded.

"If you had answered correctly from the start, you wouldn't have had to visit the bottom of the sea. Pretty awful, wasn't it?"

Ushikawa nodded.

"I know. I went through the same thing once," the man said, as easily as if he were chatting about some trivial gossip. "Only people who have experienced it know how horrible it really is. You can't easily generalize about pain. Each kind of pain has its own characteristics. To rephrase Tolstoy's famous line, all happiness is alike, but each pain is painful in its own way. I wouldn't go so far, though, as to say you *savor* it. Don't you agree?"

Ushikawa nodded. He was still panting a little.

The man went on. "So let's be frank with each other, and totally honest. Does that sound like a good idea, Ushikawa?"

Ushikawa nodded.

"Any more incorrect answers and I'll have you take another walk on the bottom of the sea. A longer, more leisurely stroll this time. We'll push the envelope a bit more. If we botch it, you might not come back. I don't think you want to go there. What do you say, Ushikawa?"

Ushikawa shook his head.

"It seems like we have one thing in common," the man said. "We're both lone wolves. Or maybe dogs who got separated from the pack? Rogue operators who don't fit in with society. People who have an instinctive dislike of organizations, or aren't accepted by any organization. We take care of business alone – decide things on our own, take action on our own, take responsibility on our own. We take orders from above, but have no colleagues or subordinates. All we depend on is our brain and our abilities. Do I have it right?"

Ushikawa nodded.

The man continued. "That's our strength, but also at times our weak point. For example, in this case I think you were a little too eager to be successful. You wanted to sort it out by yourself, without informing Sakigake. You wanted to wrap things up neatly and take all the credit. That's why you let your guard down, isn't it?"

Ushikawa nodded once more.

"Why did you have to take things that far?"

"Because it was my fault Leader died."

"How so?"

"I'm the one who ran the background check on Aomame. I did a thorough check on her before letting her see Leader. And I couldn't find anything suspicious at all."

"But she got close to Leader hoping to kill him, and actually did deliver a fatal blow. You messed up your assignment, and you knew that someday you would have to answer for it. You're just a disposable outsider, after all. And you know too much for your own good. To survive this, you knew you had to deliver Aomame's head to them. Am I correct?"

Ushikawa nodded.

"Sorry about that," the man said.

Sorry about that? Ushikawa's misshapen head pondered this. Then it came to him.

"Are you the one who planned Leader's murder?" he asked.

The man didn't respond. But Ushikawa took his silence as not necessarily a denial.

"What are you going to do with me?" Ushikawa asked.

"What indeed. Truth be told, I haven't decided yet. I'm going to take my time and think about it. It all depends on how you play this," Tamaru said. "I still have a few questions I want to ask you."

Ushikawa nodded.

"I would like you to tell me the phone number of your contact at Sakigake. You must report to someone there."

Ushikawa hesitated a moment, but then told him the number. With his life hanging in the balance, he wasn't about to hide it. Tamaru wrote it down.

"His name?"

"I don't know his name," Ushikawa lied. Tamaru didn't seem to mind.

"Pretty tough characters?"

"I'd say so."

"But not real pros."

"They're skilled, and they follow orders from the top, no questions asked. But they're not pros."

"How much do they know about Aomame?" Tamaru asked. "Do they know where she's hiding?"

Ushikawa shook his head. "They don't know yet, which is why I stayed here doing surveillance on Tengo Kawana. If I knew where Aomame is, I would have moved operations over there a long time ago."

"Makes sense," Tamaru said. "Speaking of which, how did you figure out the connection between Aomame and Tengo Kawana?"

"Legwork."

"How so?"

"I reviewed her background, from A to Z. I went back to her child-hood, when she was attending the public elementary school in Ichikawa. Tengo Kawana is also from Ichikawa, so I wondered if there could have been a connection. I went to the elementary school to look into it, and sure enough, they were in the same class for two years."

Tamaru made a low, catlike growl deep in his throat. "I see. A very tenacious investigation, Ushikawa, I must say. It must have taken a lot of time and energy. Impressive."

Ushikawa said nothing. There wasn't a question pending.

"To repeat my question," Tamaru said, "at the present time you are the only one who knows about the connection between Aomame and Tengo Kawana?"

"*You* know about it."

"Not counting me. Those you associate with."

Ushikawa nodded. "I am the only one involved who knows, yes."

"You're telling the truth?"

"I am."

"By the way, did you know that Aomame is pregnant?"

"Pregnant?" Ushikawa said. His voice revealed his surprise. "Whose child is it?"

Tamaru didn't answer his question. "You really didn't know?"

"No, I didn't. Believe me."

Tamaru silently considered his response for a moment, and then spoke.

"All right. It does appear that you didn't know this. I'll believe you. On another topic: you were sniffing around the Willow House in Azabu for a while. Correct?"

Ushikawa nodded.

"Why?"

"The lady who owns it went to a local sports club and Aomame was her personal trainer. It seems they had a close personal relationship. That lady also set up a safe house for battered women on the grounds of her estate. The security there was extremely tight. In my opinion, a little too tight. So I assumed Aomame might be hiding in that safe house."

"And then what happened?"

"I decided that wasn't the case. The lady has plenty of money and power. If she wanted to hide Aomame, she wouldn't do it so close at hand. She would put her somewhere far away. So I gave up checking out the Azabu mansion and turned my attention to Tengo Kawana."

Tamaru gave a low growl again. "You have excellent intuition. You're very logical, not to mention patient. Kind of a waste to have you be an errand boy. Have you always been in this line of work?"

"I used to be a lawyer," Ushikawa said.

"I see. You must have been very good. But I imagine you got carried away, botched up things, and took a fall. These are hard times now, and you're working for next to nothing as an errand boy for this new religious group. Do I have this right?"

Ushikawa nodded. "Yes, that about sums it up."

"Nothing you can do about it," Tamaru said. "For mavericks like us it's not easy to live a normal, everyday life. It might look like we're doing okay for a while, but then we definitely trip up. That's the way the world operates." Tamaru cracked his knuckles, a sharp, ominous sound. "So does Sakigake know about the Willow House?"

"I haven't told anyone," Ushikawa replied truthfully. "When I said that something about the mansion smells fishy, that was my own conjecture, nothing more. The security was too tight for me to confirm anything."

"Good," Tamaru said.

"You were the one who made sure of that, weren't you?"

Tamaru didn't answer.

"Up till now you've answered truthfully," Tamaru said. "In general, at least. Once you sink to the bottom of the sea, you lose the power to lie. If you tried to lie now, it would show in your voice. That's what fear will do to you."

"I'm not lying," Ushikawa said.

"Glad to hear it," Tamaru said. "No one wants to feel any more pain than they have to. By the way, have you heard of Carl Jung?"

Under the blindfold Ushikawa instinctively frowned. *Carl Jung? What was this guy getting at?*

"Carl Jung the psychologist?"

"Exactly."

"I know a little about him," Ushikawa said carefully. "He was born at the end of the nineteenth century in Switzerland. He was a disciple of Freud's, but broke with him. He coined the term 'collective unconscious.' That's about all I know."

"That's plenty," Tamaru said.

Ushikawa waited for him to continue.

"Carl Jung," Tamaru said, "had an elegant house in a quiet lakeside residential area of Zurich, and lived an affluent life with his family. But he needed a place where he could be alone in order to meditate on weighty issues. He found a small parcel of land on one corner of the lake in an area called Bollingen and built a small house there. Not exactly a villa or anything that grand. He piled the stones one by one himself and constructed a round house with high ceilings. The stones had been taken from a nearby quarry. In those days in Switzerland you had to have a stonemason's license in order to build anything out of stone, so Jung went to the trouble of obtaining a license. He even joined the stonemasons' guild. Building this house, and doing it with his own hands, was very important to him. His mother's death also seemed to be one of the major factors that led to him constructing this home."

Tamaru paused for a moment.

"This house was dubbed the 'Tower.' He designed it so it resembled the village huts he had seen on a trip to Africa. The inside was one big open space where everything went on. A very simple residence. He felt this was all one needed to live. The house had no electricity, gas, or running water. He got water from the nearby mountains. What he found out later, though, was that this was just an archetype and nothing else. As time went on, he found it necessary to build partitions and divisions in the house, and a second floor, and later he added on several wings. He created paintings himself on the wall. These were suggestive of the development and split in individual consciousness. The whole house functioned as a sort of three-dimensional mandala. It took him twelve years to complete the entire house. For Jungian researchers, it's an extremely intriguing building. Have you heard of this before?"

Ushikawa shook his head.

"The house is still standing on the banks of the lake in Zurich. Jung's descendants manage it, but unfortunately it's not open to the public, so people can't view the interior. Rumor has it, though, that at the entrance to the original tower there is a stone into which Jung carved some words with his own hand. 'Cold or Not, God Is Present.' That's what he carved into the stone himself."

Tamaru paused again.

" 'Cold or Not, God Is Present,' " he intoned, quietly, once more.

"Do you know what this means?"

Ushikawa shook his head. "No, I don't."

"I can imagine. I'm not sure myself what it means. There's some kind of deep allusion there, something difficult to interpret. But consider this: in this house that Carl Jung built, piling up the stones with his own hands, at the very entrance, he found the need to chisel out, again with his own hands, these words. I don't know why, but I've been drawn to these words for a long time. I find them hard to understand, but the difficulty in understanding makes it all the more profound. I don't know much about God. I was raised in a Catholic orphanage and had some awful experiences there so I don't have a good impression of God. And it was always cold there, even in the summer. It was either really cold or outrageously cold. One or the other. If there is a God, I can't say he treated me very well. Despite all this, those words of Jung's quietly sank deep into the folds of my soul. Sometimes I close my eyes and repeat them over and over, and they make me strangely calm. 'Cold or Not, God Is Present.' Sorry, but could you say that out loud?"

" 'Cold or Not, God Is Present,' " Ushikawa repeated in a weak voice, not really sure what he was saying.

"I can't hear you very well."

" 'Cold or Not, God Is Present.' " This time Ushikawa said it as distinctly as he could.

Tamaru shut his eyes, enjoying the overtones of the words. Eventually, as if he had made up his mind about something, he took a deep breath and let it out. He opened his eyes and looked at his hands. He had on disposable latex gloves so he wouldn't leave behind any fingerprints.

"I'm sorry about this," Tamaru said in a low voice. His tone was solemn. He took out the plastic bag again, put it over Ushikawa's head, and wrapped the thick rubber band around his neck. His movements were swift and decisive. Ushikawa was about to protest, but the words didn't form, and they never reached anyone's ears. *Why is he doing this?* Ushikawa thought from inside the plastic bag. *I told him everything I know. So why does he have to kill me?*

In his head, about to burst, he thought of his little house in Chuorinkan, and about his two young daughters. And the dog they owned. The dog was small and low to the ground and Ushikawa never could bring himself to like it. The dog never liked him, either. The dog wasn't very bright, and barked incessantly. It chewed the rugs and peed on the new flooring in the hallway. It was a totally different creature from the clever mutt he had had as a child. Still, Ushikawa's final conscious thoughts in this life were of the silly little dog scampering around the lawn in their backyard.

Tamaru watched as Ushikawa, his body tightly bound into a ball, writhed on the tatami like some huge fish out of water. Ushikawa's arms and legs were tied behind him, so no matter how much he struggled, the neighbors next door wouldn't hear a thing. Tamaru knew very well what a hideous way to die this was. But it was the most efficient, cleanest way to kill someone. No screams, no blood. Tamaru followed the second hand on his Tag Heuer diver's watch. After three minutes Ushikawa stopped thrashing around. His body trembled slightly, as if resonating to something, and then the trembling stopped. Tamaru looked at his wristwatch for another three minutes. He felt Ushikawa's wrist for a pulse and confirmed that all signs of life had vanished. There was a faint whiff of urine. Ushikawa had lost control of his bladder again, this time emptying it completely. Understandable, considering how much he had suffered.

Tamaru removed the rubber band and peeled away the plastic bag. The bag had been partly sucked into his mouth. Ushikawa's eyes were wide, his mouth open and twisted to one side in death. His dirty, irregular teeth were bared, his tongue with its greenish moss visible. It was the kind of expression Munch might have painted. Ushikawa's normally misshapen head looked even more lopsided. He must have suffered terribly.

"I'm sorry about this," Tamaru said. "I didn't do it because I wanted to."

Tamaru used his fingers to relax the muscles of Ushikawa's face, straighten out the jaw, and make his face more presentable. He used a kitchen towel to wipe away the drool from Ushikawa's mouth. It took a while, but his face began to look a bit better. At least a person looking at it wouldn't avert their eyes. But no matter how hard he tried, he couldn't get Ushikawa's eyes to shut.

"Shakespeare said it best," Tamaru said quietly as he gazed at that lumpish, misshapen head. "Something along these lines: if we die today, we do not have to die tomorrow, so let us look to the best in each other."

Was this from *Henry IV*, or maybe *Richard III*? Tamaru couldn't recall. To him, though, that wasn't important, and he doubted Ushikawa wanted to know the precise reference. Tamaru untied his arms and legs. He had used a soft, towel-like rope, and he had a special way of tying it so as to not leave marks. He took the rope, the plastic bag, and the heavy-duty rubber band and stowed them in a plastic bag he had brought with him for that purpose. He rummaged through Ushikawa's belongings and collected every photo he had taken. He put the camera and tripod in the bag as well. It would only lead to trouble if it got out that Ushikawa had been conducting surveillance. People would ask who he was watching, and the chances were pretty good that Tengo Kawana's name would surface. He took Ushikawa's notebook, too, crammed full of detailed notes. He made sure to collect anything of importance. All that was left behind were the sleeping bag, eating utensils, extra clothes, and Ushikawa's pitiful corpse. Finally, Tamaru took out one of Ushikawa's business cards, the ones that said he was Full-time Director, New Japan Foundation for the Advancement of Scholarship and the Arts, and pocketed it.

"I'm really sorry," Tamaru said again as he was leaving.

Tamaru went into a phone booth near the station, inserted a telephone card into the slot, and dialed the number Ushikawa had given him. It was a local Tokyo number, Shibuya Ward by the look of it. The phone rang six times before someone answered.

Tamaru skipped the preliminaries and told him the address and room number of the apartment in Koenji.

"Did you write it down?"

"Could you repeat it?"

Tamaru did so. The man wrote it down and read it back.

"Ushikawa is there," Tamaru said. "You are familiar with Ushikawa?"

"Ushikawa?"

Tamaru ignored what he said and continued. "Ushikawa is there, and unfortunately he isn't breathing anymore. It doesn't look like a natural death. There are several business cards with Full-time Director, New Japan Foundation for the Advancement of Scholarship and the Arts on them in his business card holder. If the police find these, eventually they will figure out the connection with you. That wouldn't be to your advantage, I imagine. Best to dispose of everything as soon as you can. That's what you're good at."

"Who are you?" the man asked.

"Let's just say I'm a kind informant," Tamaru said. "I'm not so fond of the police myself. Same as you."

"Not a natural death?"

"Well, he didn't die of old age, or very peacefully."

The man was quiet for a moment. "What was this Ushikawa doing there?"

"I don't know. You would have to ask him the details, and as I explained, he's not in a position to respond."

The man on the other end of the line paused. "You must be connected with the young woman who came to the Hotel Okura?"

"That's not the sort of question to which you can expect an answer."

"I'm one of the people who met her. Tell her that and she'll understand. I have a message for her."

"I'm listening."

"We're not planning to harm her," the man said.

"My understanding is that you are trying your best to track her down."

"That's right. We've been trying to locate her for some time."

"Yet you're telling me you don't plan to harm her," Tamaru said. "Why is that?"

There was a short silence before the response came.

"At a certain point the situation changed. Leader's death was deeply mourned by everyone. But that's over, finished. Leader was ill, and, in a sense, he was hoping to put an end to his suffering. So we don't plan to pursue Aomame any further regarding this matter. Instead, we would simply like to talk with her."

"About what?"

"Areas of common interest."

"That's just what *your people* want. You may feel the need to speak with her, but maybe that isn't what she wants."

"There should be room for discussion. There are things that we can provide you. Freedom, for instance, and safety. Knowledge and information. Can't we find a neutral place to discuss this? Name the location. We will go wherever you say. I guarantee her safety, one hundred percent – and not just hers, but the safety of everyone involved. There's no need to run away anymore. I think this is a reasonable request, for both sides."

"That's what you say," Tamaru said. "But there is no reason I should trust you."

"At any rate, I would appreciate it if you would let Aomame know," the man said patiently. "Time is of the essence, and we're still willing to meet you halfway. If you need more proof of our reliability, we'll provide it. You can call here anytime and get in touch with us."

"I wonder if you could give me a few more details. Why is she so important to you? What happened to bring about this transformation?"

The man took a short breath before he replied. "We have to keep hearing the voice. For us it's like a never-ending well. And we can't ever lose it. That's all I can tell you at this time."

"And you need Aomame in order to keep that well."

"It's hard to explain. It's connected, but that's all I can say."

"What about Eriko Fukada? You don't need her anymore?"

"No, not anymore. We don't care where she is, or what she's doing. Her mission is finished."

"What mission?"

"That's sensitive information," the man said after a pause. "I'm sorry, but I can't reveal anything more at this time."

"I suggest you consider your position very carefully," Tamaru said. "In this game we're playing, it's my serve. We can get in touch with you anytime we want, but you can't get in touch with us. You don't even know who we are. Correct?"

"You're right. You do have the advantage. We don't know who you are. But this isn't something we should speak about on the phone. I've already said too much, more than I'm authorized to."

Tamaru was silent for some time. "All right. We'll consider your proposal. We need to talk it over on our end. I will probably be getting in touch with you later."

"I will be waiting to hear from you," the man said. "As I said before, this could be to the advantage of both sides."

"What if we ignore your proposal, or reject it?"

"Then we would have to do things our way. We have a certain amount of power, and unfortunately, things might get a little rough. This could cause problems for everyone involved. No matter who you are, you won't come through this unscathed. I don't see how that could be the ideal outcome for either of us."

"You may be right. But it will take a while before we get to that point. And as you said, time is of the essence."

The man gave a small cough. "It might take time. Or maybe not so much."

"You won't know unless you try."

"Exactly," the man said. "There's one more important thing I need to point out. To borrow your metaphor, in this game it's your serve.

387

But it doesn't seem to me like you're familiar with the basic rules of the game."

"That's another thing you can't know unless you actually try it."

"If you do try it and it doesn't work, that would be a shame."

"For both of us," Tamaru said.

A short, suggestive silence followed.

"What do you plan to do about Ushikawa?" Tamaru asked.

"We'll take charge of him at the earliest opportunity. As early as tonight."

"The apartment is unlocked."

"Much appreciated," the man said.

"By the way, will you all deeply mourn Ushikawa's death?"

"We deeply mourn any person's death."

"You should mourn over him. He was, in his own way, a capable man."

"But not capable *enough*. Is that what you're saying?"

"No man is capable enough to live forever."

"So you say," the man said.

"Yes, I do think that. Don't you?"

"I'll wait for your call," the man said, without answering, his voice cold.

Tamaru silently hung up the phone. There was no need for any more talk. If he wanted to talk further, he would call them. He left the phone booth and walked to where he had parked his car – an old, drab, dark blue Toyota Corolla van, totally inconspicuous. He drove for fifteen minutes, pulled up next to an empty park, checked that there was no one watching, and tossed the plastic bag with the rope and the rubber band into a trash can. Plus the surgical gloves.

"They deeply mourn any person's death," Tamaru said in a low voice as he started the engine and snapped on his seatbelt. *Good – that's what's most important,* he thought. *Everyone's death should be mourned. Even if just for a short time.*

26

AOMAME

Very Romantic

THE PHONE RANG AT JUST PAST noon on Tuesday. Aomame was seated on her yoga mat, legs wide apart, stretching her iliopsoas muscles. It was a much more strenuous exercise than it looked. A light sheen of perspiration was starting to seep through her shirt. She stopped, wiped her face with a towel, and answered the phone.

"Bobblehead is no longer in that apartment," Tamaru said, as always omitting any sort of greeting. No *hellos* for him.

"He's not there anymore?"

"No, he's not. He was persuaded."

"Persuaded," Aomame repeated. She imagined this meant that Tamaru had, through some means, forcibly removed Bobblehead.

"Also, the person named Kawana who lives in that building is the Tengo Kawana you have been looking for."

The world around Aomame expanded, then contracted, as if it were her own heart.

"Are you listening?" Tamaru asked.

"I am."

"But Tengo Kawana isn't in his apartment right now. He has been gone for a couple of days."

"Is he all right?"

"He's not in Tokyo now, but he's definitely all right. Bobblehead rented an apartment in Tengo's building, and was waiting there for you to come see Tengo. He had set up a hidden camera and was keeping watch over the entrance."

"Did he take my picture?"

"He took three photos of you. It was nighttime, and you had on a hat, glasses, and a muffler, so you can't see any facial details in the photos. But it's you. If you had gone there one more time, things could have gotten sticky."

"So I made the right choice leaving things up to you?"

"If there is such a thing as a right choice here."

"Anyway," Aomame said, "I don't have to worry about him."

"That man won't be trying to do you any harm anymore."

"Because you *persuaded* him."

"I had to adjust some things as we went, but in the end, yes," Tamaru said. "I got all the photos. Bobblehead's aim was to wait until you showed up, and Tengo Kawana was merely the bait he was using to reel you in. So I can't see that they would have any reason now to harm Tengo. He should be fine."

"That's a relief," Aomame said.

"Tengo teaches math at a cram school in Yoyogi. He is apparently an excellent teacher, but he only works a few days a week, so he doesn't make much money. He's still single, and he lives modestly in that simple apartment."

When Aomame closed her eyes she could hear her heartbeat inside her ears. The boundary between herself and the world seemed blurred.

"Besides teaching math at the cram school, he is writing a novel. A long one. Ghostwriting *Air Chrysalis* was just a side job. He has his own literary ambitions, which is a good thing. A certain amount of ambition helps a person grow."

"How did you find all this out?"

"He's gone now, so I let myself into his apartment. It was locked, not that I would count that as a lock. I feel bad about invading his privacy, but I needed to do a basic check. For a man living alone, he keeps his place clean. He had even scrubbed the gas stove. The inside of his fridge was very neat, no rotten cabbage or anything tucked away in the back. I could see he had done some ironing as well. Not a bad partner for you to have. As long as he isn't gay, I mean."

"What else did you find out?"

"I called the cram school and asked about his teaching schedule. The girl who answered the phone said that Tengo's father passed away late Sunday night in a hospital somewhere in Chiba Prefecture. He had to leave Tokyo for the funeral, and his Monday classes were canceled. She didn't know when or where the funeral would take place. His next class is on Thursday, so it seems he will be back by then."

Aomame remembered that Tengo's father was an NHK fee collector. On Sundays Tengo had made the rounds of his father's collection route with him. She and Tengo had run across each other a number of times on the streets of Ichikawa. She couldn't remember his father's face very well. He was a small, thin man who wore a fee collector's uniform. He didn't look at all like Tengo.

"Since there's no more Bobblehead, is it all right if I go see Tengo?"

"That's not a good idea," Tamaru shot back. "Bobblehead was *persuaded,* but I had to get in touch with Sakigake to get them to take care of one last piece of business. There was one particular article I didn't want to fall into the hands of the authorities. If that had been discovered, the residents of the apartment would have been gone over with a fine-tooth comb, and your friend might have gotten mixed up in it too. It would have been difficult for me to wrap up everything by myself. If the authorities spotted me lugging that article out in the middle of the night and questioned me, I don't know how I would talk my way out of it. Sakigake has the manpower and the resources, and that's the sort of thing they're used to. Like the time they transported another article out of the Hotel Okura. Do you follow what I'm saying?"

In her mind Aomame translated Tamaru's terminology into more straightforward vocabulary. "So this *persuasion* got rather rough, I take it."

Tamaru gave a low groan. "I feel bad about it, but that man knew too much."

"Was Sakigake aware of what Bobblehead was doing in that apartment?"

"He was working for them, but on that front he was acting on his own. He hadn't yet reported to his superiors on what he was doing. Fortunately for us."

"But by now they must know that he was *up to something*."

"Correct. So you had best not go near there for a while. Tengo Kawana's name and address have to be on their checklist. I doubt they know yet about the personal connection between you and Tengo. But when they search for the reason Bobblehead was in that apartment, Tengo's name will surface. It's only a matter of time."

"If we're lucky, it might be some time before they discover it. They might not make the connection between Bobblehead's death and Tengo right away."

"If we're lucky," Tamaru said. "If they're not as meticulous as I think they are. But I never count on luck. That's how I've survived all these years."

"So I shouldn't go near that apartment building."

"Correct," Tamaru said. "We made a narrow escape, and we can't be too careful."

"I wonder if Bobblehead figured out that I'm hiding in this apartment."

"If he had, right now you would be somewhere I couldn't get to."

"But he came so close."

"He did. But that was just coincidence, nothing more."

"That's why he could sit there on the slide, totally exposed."

"Right," Tamaru said. "He had no idea that you were watching him. He never expected it. And that was his fatal mistake. I said that, didn't I? That there is a very fine line between life and death?"

A few seconds of silence descended on them. A heavy silence that a person's – any person's – death brings on.

"Bobblehead might be gone, but the cult is still after me."

"I'm not so sure about that," Tamaru said. "At first they wanted to grab you and find out what organization planned Leader's murder. They know you couldn't have done it on your own. It was obvious that you must have had backup. If they had caught you, you would have been in for some tough questioning."

"Which is why I needed a pistol," Aomame said.

"Bobblehead was well aware of all this," Tamaru went on. "He knew the cult was after you to grill you and punish you. But somehow the situation has drastically shifted. After Bobblehead left the stage, I spoke with one of the cult members. He said they have no plans to do you any harm. He asked me to give you this message. It could be a trap, but it sounded genuine to me. The guy explained that Leader was actually hoping to die, that it was a kind of self-destruction. So there's no need anymore to punish you."

"He's right," Aomame said in a dry tone. "Leader knew from the outset that I had gone there to kill him. And he wanted me to kill him."

"His security detail hadn't seen through you, but Leader had."

"That's right. I don't know why, but he knew everything beforehand," Aomame said. "He was *waiting for me* there."

Tamaru paused briefly, and then said, "What happened?"

"We made a deal."

"This is the first I've heard of it," Tamaru said, his voice stiff.

"I never had the opportunity to tell you."

"Tell me what sort of deal you made."

393

"I massaged his muscles for a good hour, and all the while he talked. He knew about Tengo. And somehow he knew about the connection between Tengo and me. He told me he wanted me to kill him. He wanted to escape the terrible physical pain he was in as soon as possible. If I would give him death, he said, he would spare Tengo's life for me. So I made up my mind and took his life. Even if I hadn't carried it out, he already had one foot in the grave, and when I considered the kinds of things he had done, I almost felt like letting him stay as he was, in such agony."

"You never reported to Madame about this deal you made."

"I went there to kill Leader, and I carried out my assignment," Aomame said. "The issue with Tengo was private."

"All right," Tamaru said, sounding half resigned. "You most definitely did carry out your assignment, I'll give you that. And the issue of Tengo Kawana is indeed a private matter. But somewhere either before or after this, you became pregnant. That's not something that can be easily overlooked."

"Not *before or after*. I got pregnant on that very night, the night of the huge rainstorm and terrible lightning that hit the city. On the same exact night when I *dealt with* Leader. As I said before, without any sex involved."

Tamaru sighed. "Considering what we're talking about, I either have to believe you or not believe you, one or the other. I have always found you to be a trustworthy person and I want to believe you, but I can't fathom the logic. Understand, I am a person who can only follow deductive reasoning."

Aomame was silent.

Tamaru went on. "Is there a cause-and-effect relationship between Leader's murder and this mysterious pregnancy?"

"I really can't say."

"Is it possible that the fetus inside you is Leader's child? That he used some method – what that would be I have no idea – and impregnated you? If that's true, then I understand why they're trying to get ahold of you. They need a successor to Leader."

Aomame clutched the phone tight and shook her head. "That's impossible. This is Tengo's child. I know it for a fact."

"That's another thing I have to either trust you on or not."

"Beyond that, I can't explain anything."

Tamaru sighed again. "All right. For the time being I'll accept what you're saying – that this baby is yours and Tengo's, and that you know this for a fact. Still, I don't see how it makes sense. At first they wanted to capture you and punish you severely, but at a certain point something happened – or they found out something. Now they *need you*. They said they guarantee your safety, and that they have something to offer you, and they want to meet directly to discuss this. What could have happened to account for this sudden turnaround?"

"They don't need me," Aomame said. "They need what's inside my belly. Somewhere along the line they realized this."

"Ho, ho," one of the Little People intoned from somewhere.

"Things are moving a bit too fast for me," Tamaru said. He gave a little groan again in the back of his throat. "I still don't see the logical connection here."

Well, nothing's been logical since the two moons appeared, Aomame thought. *That's what stole the logic from everything.* Not that she said this aloud.

"Ho, ho," six other Little People joined in.

"They need someone to *hear the voice,*" Tamaru said. "The man I talked with on the phone was insistent about that. If they lose the voice, it could be the end of the religion. What hearing the voice actually means, I have no idea. But that's what the man said. Does this mean that the child inside you is the *one who hears the voice*?"

Aomame laid a gentle hand on her abdomen. Maza *and* dohta, she thought to herself. *The moons can't hear about this.*

"I'm not – really sure," Aomame said, carefully choosing her words. "But I can't think of any other reason they would need me."

"But why would this child have that kind of special power?"

"I don't know." *In exchange for his life, maybe Leader entrusted his successor to me,* she thought. *In order to accomplish that, on that stormy night he might have temporarily opened the circuits where worlds intersect, and joined Tengo and me as one.*

Tamaru went on. "No matter who the father of that child is, or whatever abilities that child may or may not have when it's born, you have no intention of negotiating with the cult, correct? You don't care what they give you in exchange. Even if they solve all the riddles you've been wondering about."

"I'll never do it," Aomame said.

"Despite your intentions, they may take *what they want* by force. By any means necessary," Tamaru said. "Plus, you have a weak spot: Tengo Kawana. Perhaps the only weak spot you have, but it's a big one. When they discover that, that's where they'll focus their attack."

Tamaru was right. Tengo was both her reason for living and her Achilles' heel.

Tamaru went on. "It's too dangerous for you to stay there any longer. You need to move to a more secure location before they figure out the connection between you and Tengo."

"There are no more secure places in *this world*," Aomame said.

Tamaru mulled over her opinion. "Tell me what you're thinking," he said quietly.

"First, I have to see Tengo. Until that happens, I can't leave here. No matter how dangerous it might be."

"What are you going to do when you see him?"

"I know what I need to do."

Tamaru was silent for a moment. "You're crystal clear on that?"

"I don't know if it will work out, but I know what I have to do. I'm crystal clear on that, yes."

"But you're not planning on telling me what it involves."

"I'm sorry, but I can't. Not just you, but anybody. If I told anyone about it, at that instant it would be disclosed to the whole world."

The moons were listening carefully. So were the Little People. And this very room she was in. She couldn't let it out of her heart, not one centimeter. She had to surround her heart with a thick wall so nothing could escape.

On the other end of the line Tamaru was tapping the tip of a ballpoint pen on a desk. Aomame could hear the dry, rhythmic noise. It was a lonely sound, lacking any resonance.

"Okay, then let's get in touch with Tengo Kawana. Before that, though, Madame must agree to it. The task I've been given is to move you, as soon as possible, to another location. But you said you can't leave there until you see Tengo. It doesn't look like it will be easy to explain the reason to her. You understand that, right?"

"It's very difficult to logically explain the illogical."

"Exactly. As difficult as finding a real pearl in a Roppongi oyster bar. But I'll do my best."

"Thank you," Aomame said.

"What you're insisting on doesn't make sense to me, no matter how I look at it. Still, the more I talk with you, the more I feel that maybe I can accept it. I wonder why."

Aomame kept silent.

"Madame trusts you and believes in you," Tamaru said, "so if you insist on it that much, I can't see her finding a reason not to let you see Tengo. You and Tengo seem to have an unwavering connection to each other."

"More than anything in the world," Aomame said.

More than anything in any *world,* she repeated to herself.

"Even if I say it's too dangerous, and refuse to contact Tengo, you'll still go to that apartment to see him."

"I'm sure I will."

"And no one can stop you."

"It's pointless to try."

Tamaru paused for a moment. "What message would you like me to give Tengo?"

"Come to the slide after dark. After it gets dark, anytime is fine. I will be waiting. If you tell him Aomame said this, he'll understand."

"Okay. I'll let him know. *Come to the slide after dark.*"

"If he has something important he doesn't want to leave behind, tell him to bring it with him. But tell him he has to be able to keep both hands free."

"Where are you going to take that luggage?"

"Far away," Aomame said.

"How far away?"

"I don't know," Aomame said.

"All right. As long as Madame gives her permission, I'll let Tengo know. And I will do my best to keep you safe. But there's still danger here. We're dealing with desperate men. You need to protect yourself."

"I understand," Aomame said quietly. Her palm still lay softly on her abdomen. *Not just myself,* she thought.

After she hung up, she collapsed onto the sofa. She closed her eyes and thought about Tengo. She couldn't think of anything else. Her chest felt tight, and it hurt, but it was a good sort of pain. It was the kind of pain she could put up with. Tengo was so close, almost within reach. Less than a ten-minute walk away. The very thought warmed her to her core. *Tengo is a bachelor, and teaches math at a cram school. He lives in a neat, humble little apartment. He cooks, irons, and is writing a long novel.* Aomame envied Tamaru. If it were possible, she would like to get into Tengo's apartment like that, when he was out. Tengo's Tengo-less apartment. In the deserted silence she wanted to touch each and every object there – check out how sharp his pencils were, hold his coffee cup, inhale the odor of his clothes. She wanted to take that step first, before actually coming face-to-face with him.

Without that prefatory knowledge, if they were suddenly together, just the two of them, she couldn't imagine what she should say. The thought made it hard to breathe, and her mind went blank. There were too many things. Still, when it came down to it, perhaps nothing needed to be said. The things she most wanted to tell him would lose their meaning the moment she put them into words.

All she could do now was simply wait – calmly, with eyes wide open. She prepared a bag so she could run outside as soon as she spotted Tengo. She stuffed an oversized black leather shoulder bag with everything she would need so she wouldn't have to come back here. There weren't all that many things. Some cash, a few changes of clothes, and the Heckler & Koch, fully loaded. That was about it. She put the bag where she could get to it at a moment's notice. She took her Junko Shimada suit from the hanger in the closet and, after checking that it wasn't wrinkled, hung it on the wall in the living room. She also took out the white blouse that went with the suit, stockings, and her Charles Jourdan high heels. And the beige spring coat. The same outfit she was wearing when she climbed down the emergency stairway on Metropolitan Expressway No. 3. The coat was a bit thin for a December evening, but she had no other choice.

After getting all this ready, she sat in the garden chair on the balcony and looked out through the slit in the screen at the slide in the park. Tengo's father died late Sunday night. A minimum of twenty-four hours had to elapse between the time a person died and the time they could be cremated. She was sure there was a law that said that. Tuesday would be the earliest they could do the cremation. Today was Tuesday. The earliest Tengo would be back in Tokyo from *wherever* after the funeral would be this evening. And then Tamaru could give him the message. So Tengo wouldn't be coming to the park anytime before that. Plus, it was still light out.

On his death, Leader set this little one *inside my womb,* she thought. *That's my working supposition. Or maybe I should say intuition. Does this mean I'm being manipulated by the will he left behind, being led to a destination that he established?*

Aomame grimaced. *I can't decide anything. Tamaru surmised that I got pregnant with the* one who hears the voice *as a result of Leader's plan. Probably as an air chrysalis. But why does it have to be* me? *And*

399

why does my partner have to be Tengo? This was another thing she couldn't explain.

Be that as it may, things are moving forward around me, even though I can't figure out the connections, or sort out the principles at work behind them, or see where things are headed. I've just wound up entangled in it all. Until now, that is, she told herself.

Her lips twisted and she grimaced even more.

From now on, things will be different. Nobody else's will is going to control me anymore. From now on, I'm going to do things based on one principle alone: my own will. I'm going to protect this little one, *whatever it takes. This is my life, and my child. Somebody else may have programmed it for their own purposes, but there's no doubt in my mind that this is Tengo's and my child. I'll never hand it over to anyone else. Never. From here on out, I'm the one in charge. I'm the one who decides what's good and what's bad – and which way we're headed. And people had better remember that.*

The phone rang the next day, Wednesday, at two in the afternoon.

"I gave him the message," Tamaru said, as usual omitting any greeting. "He's in his apartment now. I talked to him this morning on the phone. He will be at the slide tonight at precisely seven."

"Did he remember me?"

"He remembered you well. He seems to have been searching all over for you."

It was just as Leader said. Tengo is looking for me. That's all I need to know. Aomame's heart was filled with an indescribable joy. No other words in this world had any meaning for her.

"He will be bringing something important with him then, as you asked. I'm guessing that this will include the novel he's writing."

"I'm sure of it," Aomame said.

"I checked around that humble building he lives in. All looks clear to me. No suspicious characters hanging around. Bobblehead's apartment is deserted. Everything's quiet, but not too quiet. Those guys took care of the article during the night and left. They probably thought it wouldn't be good to stay too long. I made sure of this, so I don't think I overlooked anything."

"Good."

"*Probably,* though, is the operative word here, *at least for now.* The situation is changing by the moment. And obviously I'm not perfect. I might be overlooking something important. It is possible that those guys might turn out to be one notch ahead of me."

"Which is why it all comes down to me needing to protect myself."

"As I said."

"Thank you for everything. I'm very grateful to you."

"I don't know what you plan to do from now on," Tamaru said, "but if you do go somewhere far away, and I never see you again, I know I'll feel a little sad. You're a rare sort of character, a type I've seldom come across before."

Aomame smiled into the phone. "That's pretty much the impression I wanted to leave you with."

"Madame needs you. Not for the work you do, but on a personal level, as a companion. So I know she feels quite sad that she has to say good-bye like this. She can't come to the phone now. I hope you'll understand."

"I do," Aomame said. "I might have trouble, too, if I had to talk with her."

"You said you're going far away," Tamaru said. "How far away are we talking about?"

"It's a distance that can't be measured."

"Like the distance that separates one person's heart from another's."

Aomame closed her eyes and took a deep breath. She was on the verge of tears, but was able to hold it together.

"I'm praying that everything will go well," Tamaru said quietly.

"I'm sorry, but I may have to hold on to the Heckler & Koch," Aomame said.

"That's fine. It's my gift to you. If it gets troublesome to have, just toss it into Tokyo Bay. The world will take one small step closer to disarmament."

"I might end up never firing the pistol. Contrary to Chekhov's principle."

"That's fine, too," Tamaru said. "Nothing could be better than not firing it. We're drawing close to the end of the twentieth century. Things are different from back in Chekhov's time. No more horse-drawn carriages, no more women in corsets. Somehow the world survived the Nazis, the atomic bomb, and modern music. Even the way novels are composed has changed drastically. So it's nothing to worry about. But I do have a question. You and Tengo are going to meet on the slide tonight at seven."

"If things work out," Aomame said.

"If you do see him, what are you going to do there?"

"We're going to look at the moon."

"Very romantic," Tamaru said, gently.

27

TENGO

The Whole World May Not Be Enough

ON WEDNESDAY MORNING WHEN THE PHONE rang, Tengo was still asleep. He hadn't been able to fall asleep until nearly dawn, and the whiskey he had drunk still remained in him. He got out of bed, and was surprised to see how light it was outside.

"Tengo Kawana?" a man said. It was a voice he had never heard before.

"Yes," Tengo replied. The man's voice was quiet and businesslike, and he was sure it must be more paperwork regarding his father's death. But his alarm clock showed it was just before eight a.m. Not the time that a city office or funeral home would be calling.

"I am sorry to be calling so early, but I was rather in a hurry."

Something urgent. "What is it?" Tengo's brain was still fuzzy.

"Do you recall the name Aomame?" the man asked.

Aomame? His hangover and sleepiness vanished. His mind reset quickly, like after a short blackout in a stage play. Tengo regripped the receiver.

"Yes, I do," he replied.

"It's quite an unusual name."

"We were in the same class in elementary school," Tengo said, somehow able to get his voice back to normal.

The man paused. "Mr. Kawana, do you have interest at this moment in talking about Aomame?"

Tengo found the man's way of speaking odd. His diction was unique, like listening to lines from an avant-garde translated play.

"If you do not have any interest, then it will be a waste of time for both of us. I'll end this conversation right away."

"I am interested," Tengo said hurriedly. "Sorry, but what is your connection here?"

"I have a message from her," the man said, ignoring his question. "Aomame is hoping to see you. What about you, Mr. Kawana? Would you care to see her as well?"

"I would," Tengo said. He coughed and cleared his throat. "I have been wanting to see her for a long time."

"Fine. She wants to see you. And you are hoping to see her."

Tengo suddenly realized how cold the room was. He grabbed a nearby cardigan and threw it over his pajamas.

"So what should I do?" Tengo asked.

"Can you come to the slide after dark?" the man said.

"The slide?" Tengo asked. What was this guy talking about?

"She said if I told you that, you would understand. She would like you to come to the top of the slide. I'm merely telling you what Aomame said."

Tengo's hand went to his hair, which was a mass of cowlicks and knots after sleeping. *The slide. Where I saw the two moons. It's got to be* that *slide.*

"I think I understand," he replied, his voice dry.

"Fine. Also, if there is something valuable you would like to take with you, make sure you have it on you. So you're all set to move on, far away."

"Something valuable I would like to take with me?" Tengo repeated in surprise.

"Something you don't want to leave behind."

Tengo pondered this. "I'm not sure I totally understand, but by moving on far away, do you mean never coming back here?"

"I wouldn't know," the man said. "As I said previously, I am merely transmitting her message."

Tengo ran his fingers through his tangled hair and considered this. *Move on?* "I might have a fair amount of papers I would want to bring."

"That shouldn't be a problem," the man said. "You are free to choose whatever you like. However, when it comes to luggage, I have been asked to tell you that you should be able to keep both hands free."

"Keep both hands free," Tengo repeated. "So, a suitcase wouldn't work, would it?"

"I wouldn't think so."

From the man's voice it was hard to guess his age, looks, or build. It was the sort of voice that provided no tangible clues. Tengo felt he wouldn't remember the voice at all, as soon as the man hung up. Individuality or emotions – assuming there were any to begin with – were hidden deep down, out of sight.

"That's all that I need to relay," the man said.

"Is Aomame well?" Tengo asked.

"Physically, she's fine," the man said, choosing his words carefully. "Though right now she's caught in a somewhat tense situation. She has to watch her every move. One false step and it might all be over."

"All be over," Tengo repeated mechanically.

"It would be best not to be too late," the man said. "Time has become an important factor."

Time has become an important factor, Tengo repeated to himself. *Was there an issue with this man's choice of words? Or am I too much on edge?*

"I think I can be at the slide at seven tonight," Tengo said. "If for some reason I'm not able to come tonight, I'll be there tomorrow at the same time."

"Understood. And you know which slide we're talking about."

"I think so."

Tengo glanced at the clock. He had eleven hours to go.

"By the way, I heard that your father passed away on Sunday. My deepest condolences."

Tengo instinctively thanked him, but then wondered how this man could possibly know about his father.

"Could you tell me a little more about Aomame?" Tengo said. "For instance, where she is, and what she does?"

"She's single. She works as a fitness instructor at a sports club in Hiroo. She's a first-rate instructor, but circumstances have changed and she has taken leave from her job. And, by sheer coincidence, she has been living not far from you. For anything beyond that, I think it best you hear directly from her."

"Even what sort of *tense situation* she's in right now?"

The man didn't respond. Either he didn't want to answer or he felt there was no need. For whatever reason, people like this seemed to flock to Tengo.

"Today at seven p.m., then, on top of the slide," the man said.

"Just a second," Tengo said quickly. "I have a question. I was warned by someone that I was being watched, and that I should be careful. Excuse me for asking, but did they mean you?"

"No, they didn't mean me," the man said immediately. "It was probably someone else who was watching you. But it is a good idea to be cautious, as that person pointed out."

"Does my being under surveillance have something to do with Aomame's unusual situation?"

"*Somewhat tense* situation," the man said, correcting him. "Yes, most likely there is some sort of connection."

"Is this dangerous?"

The man paused, and chose his words carefully, as if separating out varieties of beans from a pile. "If you call not being able to see Aomame anymore something dangerous, then yes, there is definitely danger involved."

Tengo mentally rearranged this man's roundabout phrasing into something he could understand. He didn't have a clue about the background or the circumstances, but it was obvious that things were indeed fraught.

"If things don't go well, we might not be able to see each other ever again."

"Exactly."

"I understand. I'll be careful," Tengo said.

"I'm sorry to have called so early. It would appear that I woke you up."

Without pausing, the man hung up. Tengo gazed at the black receiver in his hand. As he had predicted, as soon as they hung up, the man's voice had vanished from his memory. Tengo looked at the clock again. Eight ten. *How should I kill all this time between now and seven p.m.?* he wondered.

He started by taking a shower, washing his hair, and untangling it as best he could. Then he stood in front of the mirror and shaved, brushed his teeth, and flossed. He drank some tomato juice from the fridge, boiled water, ground coffee beans and made coffee, toasted a slice of bread. He set the timer and cooked a soft-boiled egg. He concentrated on each action, taking more time than usual. But still it was only nine thirty.

Tonight I will see Aomame on top of the slide.

The thought sent his senses spinning. His hands and legs and face all wanted to go in different directions, and he couldn't gather his emotions in one place. Whatever he tried to do, his concentration was shot. He couldn't read, couldn't write. He couldn't sit still in one place.

The only thing he seemed capable of was washing the dishes, doing the laundry, straightening up his drawers, making his bed. Every five minutes he would stop whatever he was doing and glance at the clock. Thinking about time only seemed to slow it down.

Aomame knows.

He was standing at the sink, sharpening a cleaver that really didn't need to be sharpened. *She knows I've been to the slide in that playground a number of times. She must have seen me, sitting there, staring up at the sky. Otherwise it makes no sense.* He pictured what he looked like on top of the slide, lit up by the mercury-vapor lamp. He had had no sense of being observed. Where had she been watching him from?

It doesn't matter, Tengo thought. *No big deal. No matter where she saw me from, she recognized me.* The thought filled him with joy. *Just as I've been thinking of her, she's been thinking of me.* Tengo could hardly believe it – that in this frantic, labyrinth-like world, two people's hearts – a boy's and a girl's – could be connected, unchanged, even though they hadn't seen each other for twenty years.

But why didn't Aomame call out to me then, when she saw me? Things would be so much simpler if she had. And how did she know where I live? How did she – or that man – find out my phone number? He didn't like to get calls, and had an unlisted number. You couldn't get it even if you called the operator.

There was a lot that remained unknown and mysterious, and the lines that constructed this story were complicated. Which lines connected to which others, and what sort of cause-and-effect relationship existed, was beyond him. Still, ever since Fuka-Eri showed up in his life, he felt he had been living in a place where questions outnumbered answers. But he had a faint sense that this chaos was, ever so slowly, heading toward a denouement.

At seven this evening, though, at least some questions will be cleared up, Tengo thought. *We'll meet on top of the slide. Not as a helpless* ten-year-old boy and girl, but as an independent, grown-up man and woman. As a math teacher in a cram school and a sports club instructor. What will we talk about then? I have no idea. But we will talk – we need to fill in the blanks between us, exchange information about each other. And – to borrow the phrasing of the man who called – we might then move on somewhere. So I need to make sure to bring what's important to me, what I don't want to leave behind – and pack it away so that I can have both hands free.

I have no regrets about leaving here. I lived here for seven years, taught three days a week at the cram school, but never once felt it was home. Like a floating island bobbing along in the flow, it was just a temporary place to rest, and nothing more. My girlfriend is no longer here. Fuka-Eri, too, who shared the place briefly – gone. Tengo had no idea where these two women were now, or what they were doing. They had simply, and quietly, vanished from his life. If he left the cram school, someone else would surely take over. The world would keep on turning, even without him. If Aomame wanted to *move on somewhere* with him, there was nothing to keep him from going.

What could be the important thing he should take with him? Fifty thousand yen in cash and a plastic debit card – that was the extent of the assets he had at hand. There was also one million yen in a savings account. No – there was more. His share of the royalties from *Air Chrysalis* was in the account as well. He had been meaning to return it to Komatsu but hadn't gotten around to it. Then there was the printout of the novel he had begun. He couldn't leave that behind. It had no real value to anyone else, but to Tengo it was precious. He put the manuscript in a paper bag, then stuffed it into the hard, russet nylon shoulder bag he used when he went to the cram school. The bag was really heavy now. He crammed floppy disks into the pocket of his leather jacket. He couldn't very well take his word processor along with him, but he did add his notebooks and fountain pen to his luggage. *What else?* he wondered.

He remembered the envelope the lawyer had given him in Chikura.

Inside were his father's savings book and seal, a copy of their family record, and the mysterious family photo (if indeed that was what it was). It was probably best to take that with him. His elementary school report cards and the NHK commendations he would leave behind. He decided against taking a change of clothes or toiletries. They wouldn't fit in the now-bulging bag, and besides, he could buy them as needed.

Once he had packed everything in the bag, he had nothing left to do. There were no dishes to wash, no shirts left to iron. He looked at the wall clock again. Ten thirty. He thought he should call his friend to take over his classes at the cram school, but then remembered that his friend was always in a terrible mood if you phoned before noon.

Tengo lay down on his bed, fully clothed, and let his mind wander through various possibilities. The last time he saw Aomame was when he was ten. Now they were both thirty. They had both gone through a lot of experiences in the interim. Good things, things that weren't so good (probably slightly more of the latter). *Our looks, our personalities, the environment where we live have all gone through changes,* he thought. *We're no longer a young boy and a young girl.* Is the Aomame over there really the Aomame he had been searching for? And was he the Tengo Kawana she had been looking for? Tengo pictured them on the slide tonight looking at each other, disappointed at what they saw. Maybe they wouldn't find anything to talk about. That was a real possibility. Actually, it would be kind of strange if it didn't turn out that way.

Maybe we shouldn't meet again. Tengo stared up at the ceiling. *Wasn't it better if they kept this desire to see each other hidden within them, and never actually got together? That way, there would always be hope in their hearts. That hope would be a small, yet vital flame that warmed them to their core – a tiny flame to cup one's hands around and protect from the wind, a flame that the violent winds of reality might easily extinguish.*

Tengo stared at the ceiling for a good hour, two conflicting emotions surging through him. More than anything, he wanted to meet Aomame. At the same time, he was afraid to see her. The cold disappointment and uncomfortable silence that might ensue made him shudder. His body felt like it was going to be torn in half. But he *had* to see her. This is what he had been wanting, what he had been hoping for with all his might, for the last twenty years. No matter what disappointment might come of it, he knew he couldn't just turn his back on it and run away.

Tired of staring at the ceiling, he fell asleep on the bed, still lying faceup. A quiet, dreamless sleep of some forty or forty-five minutes – the deep, satisfying sleep you get after concentrating hard, after mental exhaustion. He realized that for the last few days he had only slept in fits and starts and hadn't gotten a good night's sleep. Before it got dark, he needed to rid himself of the fatigue that had built up. He had to be rested and relaxed when he left here and headed for the playground. He knew this instinctively.

As he was falling asleep, he heard Kumi Adachi's voice – or he felt like he heard it. *When morning comes you'll be leaving here, Tengo. Before the exit is blocked.*

This was Kumi's voice, and at the same time it was the voice of the owl at night. In his memory the voices were mixed, and hard to distinguish from each other. What Tengo needed then more than anything was wisdom – the wisdom of the night that had put down roots into the soil. A wisdom that might only be found in the depths of sleep.

At six thirty Tengo slung his bag diagonally across his shoulders and left his apartment. He had on the same clothes as the last time he went to the slide: gray windbreaker and old leather jacket, jeans, and brown work boots. All of them were worn but they fit well, like an extension of his body. *I probably won't ever be back here again,* he thought. As a precaution he took the typed cards with his name on them out of the door slot and the mailbox. *What would happen to everything else?* He decided not to worry about it for now.

As he stood at the entrance to the apartment building, he peered around cautiously. If he believed Fuka-Eri, he was being watched. But just as before, there was no sign of surveillance. Everything was the same as always. Now that the sun had set, the road in front of him was deserted. He set off for the station, at a slow pace. He glanced back from time to time to make sure he wasn't being followed. He turned down several narrow streets he didn't need to take, then came to a stop and checked again to see if anyone was tailing him. *You have to be careful,* the man on the phone had cautioned. *For yourself, and for Aomame, who's in a* tense situation.

But does the man on the phone really know Aomame? Tengo suddenly wondered. *Couldn't this be some kind of clever trap?* Once this thought took hold, he couldn't shake off a sense of unease. If this really was a trap, then Sakigake had to be behind it. As the ghostwriter of *Air Chrysalis* he was probably – no, make that *definitely* – on their blacklist. Which is why that weird guy, Ushikawa, came to him with that suspicious story about a grant. On top of that, Tengo had let Fuka-Eri hide out in his apartment for three months. There were more than enough reasons for the cult to be upset with him.

Be that as it may, Tengo thought, inclining his head, *why would they go to the trouble of using Aomame as bait to lure me into a trap? They already know where I am. It's not like I'm running away and hiding. If they have some business with me, they should approach me directly. There's no need to lure me out to that slide in the playground. Things would be different if the opposite were true – if they were using me as bait to get Aomame.*

But why lure her out?

He couldn't understand it. Was there, by chance, some connection between Aomame and Sakigake? Tengo's deductive reasoning hit a dead end. The only thing he could do was to ask Aomame herself – assuming he could meet her.

At any rate, as the man on the phone said, he would have to be cautious. Tengo scrupulously took a roundabout route and made sure no one was following him. Once certain of that, he hurried off in the direction of the playground.

He arrived at the playground at seven minutes to seven. It was dark out already, and the mercury-vapor lamp shone its even, artificial illumination into every nook and cranny of the tiny park. The afternoon had been lovely and warm, but now that the sun had set the temperature had dropped sharply, and a cold wind was blowing. The pleasant Indian summer weather they had had for a few days had vanished, and real winter, cold and severe, had settled in for the duration. The tips of the zelkova tree's branches trembled, like the fingers of some ancient person shaking out a warning, with a desiccated, raspy sound.

Lights were on in several of the windows in the buildings nearby, but the playground was deserted. Tengo's heart under the leather jacket beat out a slow but heavy rhythm. He rubbed his hands together repeatedly, to see if they had normal sensation. *Everything's fine,* he told himself. *I'm all set. Nothing to be afraid of.* He made up his mind and started climbing up the ladder of the slide.

Once on top, he sat down as he had before. The bottom of the slide was cold and slightly damp. With his hands in his pockets, he leaned against the railing and looked up at the sky. There were clouds of all sizes – several large ones, several small ones. Tengo squinted and looked for the moons, but at the moment they weren't visible, hidden behind the clouds. These weren't dense, heavy clouds, but rather smooth white ones. Still, they were thick and substantial enough to hide the moons from his gaze. The clouds were gliding slowly from north to south.

The wind didn't seem too strong. Or maybe the clouds were actually higher up than they looked? At any rate, they weren't in much of a hurry.

Tengo glanced at his watch. The hands showed three past seven, ticking away the time ever more accurately. Still no Aomame. Tengo spent several minutes gazing at the hands of his watch as if they were something extraordinary. Then he shut his eyes. Like the clouds on the wind, he was in no hurry. If things took time, he didn't mind. He stopped thinking and gave himself over to the flow of time. At this moment, time's natural, even flow was the most important thing.

With his eyes closed, he carefully listened to the sounds around him, as if searching for stations on a radio. He could hear the ceaseless hum of traffic on the expressway. It reminded him of the Pacific surf at the sanatorium in Chikura. A few seagull calls must have been mixed in as well. He could hear the intermittent beep as a large truck backed up, and a huge dog barking a short, sharp warning. Far away someone was shouting out a person's name. He couldn't tell where all these sounds were coming from. With his eyes closed for this long, each and every sound lost its sense of direction and distance. The freezing wind swirled up from time to time, but he didn't feel the cold. Tengo had temporarily forgotten how to feel or react to all stimulations and sensations.

He was suddenly aware of someone sitting beside him, holding his right hand. Like a small creature seeking warmth, a hand slipped inside the pocket of his leather jacket and clasped his large hand. By the time he became fully aware, it had already happened. Without any preface, the situation had jumped to the next stage. *How strange,* Tengo thought, his eyes still closed. *How did this happen?* At one point time was flowing along so slowly that he could barely stand it. Then suddenly it had leapt ahead, skipping whatever lay between.

This person held his big hand even tighter, as if to make sure he was *really there*. Long smooth fingers, with an underlying strength.

Aomame. But he didn't say it aloud. He didn't open his eyes. He just squeezed her hand in return. He remembered this hand. Never once in twenty years had he forgotten the feeling. Of course, it was no longer the tiny hand of a ten-year-old girl. Over the past twenty years her hand had touched many things. It had clasped untold numbers of objects in every possible shape. And the strength within it had grown. Yet Tengo knew right away: this was the very same hand. The way it squeezed his own hand and the feeling it was trying to convey were exactly the same.

Inside him, twenty years dissolved and mixed into one complex, swirling whole. Everything that had accumulated over the years – all he had seen, all the words he had spoken, all the values he had held – all of it coalesced into one solid, thick pillar in his heart, the core of which was spinning like a potter's wheel. Wordlessly, Tengo observed the scene, as if watching the destruction and rebirth of a planet.

Aomame kept silent as well. The two of them on top of the freezing slide, wordlessly holding hands. Once again they were a ten-year-old boy and girl. A lonely boy, and a lonely girl. A classroom, just after school let out, at the beginning of winter. They had neither the power nor the knowledge to know what they should offer to each other, what they should be seeking. They had never, ever, been truly loved, or truly loved someone else. They had never held anyone, never been held. They had no idea, either, where this action would take them. What they entered then was a doorless room. They couldn't get out, nor could anyone else come in. The two of them didn't know it at the time, but this was the only truly complete place in the entire world. Totally isolated, yet the one place not tainted with loneliness.

How much time had passed? Five minutes, perhaps, or was it an hour? Or a whole day? Or maybe time had stood still. What did Tengo understand about time? He knew he could stay like this forever, the two of them silent on top of the slide, holding hands. He had felt that way at age ten, and now, twenty years on, he felt the same.

He knew, too, that it would take time for him to acclimate himself to this new world that had come upon him. His entire way of thinking, his way of seeing things, the way he breathed, the way he moved his body – he would need to adjust and rethink every single element of life. And to do that, he needed to gather together all the time that existed in this world. No – maybe the whole world wouldn't be enough.

"Tengo," Aomame whispered, a voice neither low or high – a voice holding out a promise. "Open your eyes."

Tengo opened his eyes. Time began to flow again in the world.

"There's the moon," Aomame said.

28

USHIKAWA

And a Part of His Soul

THE FLUORESCENT LIGHT ON THE CEILING shone down on Ushikawa's body. The heat was turned off, and a window was open, so the room was as freezing as an icehouse. Several conference tables had been shoved together in the center of the room, and on top of them, Ushikawa lay faceup. He had on winter long johns, and an old blanket was thrown on top of him. Under the blanket, his stomach was swollen, like an anthill in a field. A small piece of cloth covered his questioning, opened eyes – eyes that no one had been able to close. His lips were slightly parted, lips from which no breath or words would ever slip out again. The crown of his head was flatter, and more enigmatic-looking, than it had been while he was alive. Thick, black, frizzy hair – reminiscent of pubic hair – shabbily surrounded that crown.

Buzzcut had on a navy-blue down jacket, while Ponytail was wearing a brown suede rancher's coat with a fur-trimmed collar. Both were slightly ill-fitting, as if they had hurriedly grabbed them from a limited supply of clothing that happened to be on hand. They were indoors, but their breath was white in the cold. The three of them were the sole occupants of the room. Buzzcut, Ponytail, and Ushikawa. There were three aluminum-sash windows on one wall, near the ceiling, and one of them was wide open to help keep the temperature down. Other than the tables with the body, there was no other furniture. It was an entirely bland, no-nonsense room. Placed there, even a corpse – even Ushikawa's – looked like a colorless, utilitarian object.

No one was talking. The room was utterly devoid of sound. Buzzcut had a lot to ponder, and Ponytail never spoke anyway. Buzzcut was lost in thought, pacing back and forth in front of the table that held Ushikawa's body. Except for the moment when he reached the wall and had to turn around, his pace never slackened. His leather shoes were totally silent as they trod upon the cheap, light yellow-green carpeting. As usual, Ponytail staked out a spot near the door and stood there, motionless, legs slightly apart, back straight, staring off at an invisible point in space. He didn't seem tired or cold, not at all. The only evidence that he was still among the living was an occasional rapid burst of blinks, and the measured white breath that left his mouth.

Earlier that day, a number of people had gathered in that freezing room to discuss the situation. One of Sakigake's high-ranking members had been on a trip and it had taken a day to get everyone together. The meeting was secret, and they spoke in hushed tones so no one outside could hear. All this time, Ushikawa's corpse had lain there on the table, like a sample at an industrial machinery convention. Rigor mortis had set in on the corpse, and it would be another three days before that broke and the body was pliable again. Everyone shot the occasional quick glance at the body as they discussed several practical matters.

While they were discussing things there was no sense – even when the talk turned to the deceased – that they were paying respects to him or feeling regret for his passing. The stiff, stocky corpse simply reminded them of certain lessons, and reconfirmed a few reflections on life. Nothing more. Once time has passed, it can't be taken back. If death brings about any resolution, it's one that only applies to the deceased. Those sorts of lessons, those sorts of reflections.

What should they do with Ushikawa's body? They knew the answer before they began. Ushikawa had died of unnatural causes, and if he were discovered, the police would launch an all-out investigation that would inevitably uncover his connection with Sakigake. They couldn't risk that. As soon as the rigor mortis was gone, they would secretly transport the corpse to the industrial-sized incinerator on the grounds of their compound and dispose of it. Soon it would become nothing but black smoke and white ash. The smoke would be absorbed into the sky, the ash would be spread on the fields as fertilizer for the vegetables. They had performed the same operation a number of times, under Buzzcut's supervision. Leader's body had been too big, so they had "handled" it by using a chain saw to cut it into pieces. There was no need to do so this time, for Ushikawa was nowhere near as big. Buzzcut was grateful for that. He didn't like any operations that got too gory. Whether it was dealing with the living or the dead, he preferred not to see any blood.

His superior asked Buzzcut some questions. Who could have killed Ushikawa? And what was Ushikawa doing in that rented apartment in Koenji, anyway? As head of security, Buzzcut had to respond, though he really didn't know the answers.

Before dawn on Tuesday he had gotten the call from that mysterious man (who was, of course, Tamaru) and learned that Ushikawa's body was in the apartment. Their conversation was at once practical and indirect. As soon as he hung up, Buzzcut immediately put out a call to a couple of followers in Tokyo. They changed into work uniforms, pretending to be movers, and headed out to the apartment in a Toyota HiAce van. Before they went inside, they made sure it wasn't a trap. They parked the van and one of them scouted out the surroundings for anything suspicious. They needed to be very cautious. The police might be lying in wait, ready to arrest them as soon as they set foot in the place, something they had to avoid at all costs.

They had brought along a container, the kind used in moving, and somehow were able to stuff the already-stiff body inside. Then they shouldered it out of the building and into the bed of the van. It was late at night, and cold, so fortunately there was no one else around. It took some time to comb through the apartment to make sure no telling evidence was left behind. Using flashlights, they searched every square inch, but they found nothing incriminating, just food, a small electric space heater, a sleeping bag, and a few other basic necessities. The garbage can was mainly full of empty cans and plastic bottles. It appeared that Ushikawa had been holed up there doing surveillance. Buzzcut's sharp eye noted the indentations in the tatami near the window that indicated the presence of a camera tripod, though there was no camera and there were no photographs. The person who had taken Ushikawa's life must have also taken the camera away, along with the film. Since Ushikawa was dressed only in his underwear, he must have been attacked while asleep. The attacker must have silently slipped inside the apartment. It looked like Ushikawa had suffered horribly, for his underwear was completely saturated with urine.

Buzzcut and Ponytail were the only ones in the van when they transported the body to Yamanashi. The other two stayed behind in Tokyo to handle anything that might come up. Ponytail drove the entire way. The HiAce left the Metropolitan Expressway, got onto the Chuo Highway, and headed west. It was still dark out and the expressway was nearly deserted, but they kept their speed under the limit. If the police stopped them now it would be all over. Their license plates – both front and rear – were stolen, and the container in back contained a dead body. There would be no way to talk their way out of that situation. The two of them were silent for the entire trip.

When they arrived at the compound at dawn, a Sakigake doctor examined Ushikawa's body and confirmed that he had died of suffocation. There were no signs of strangulation around the neck, however. The doctor guessed that a bag or something that didn't leave any evidence must have been placed over the victim's head. There were no marks, either, to indicate that the victim's hands and feet had been tied. He didn't appear to have been beaten or tortured. His expression didn't show any signs of agony. If you had to describe his expression, you would say it was one of pure confusion, as if he had been asking a question he knew wouldn't be answered. It was obvious that he had been murdered, but the corpse was remarkably untouched, which the doctor found odd. Whoever had killed him may have massaged his features after his death, to give him a calmer, more natural expression.

"Whoever did this was a real professional," Buzzcut explained to his superior. "There are no marks on him at all. He probably never had a chance to even scream. It happened in the middle of the night, and if he had yelled out in pain, everyone in the building would have heard him. This is the work of a professional hit man."

But why had Ushikawa ended up murdered by a professional killer?

Buzzcut chose his words carefully. "I think Mr. Ushikawa must have stepped on somebody's tail, someone he never should have crossed. Before he even realized what he had done."

Was this the same person who had disposed of Leader?

"I don't have any proof, but the chances are pretty good," Buzzcut said. "And I think Mr. Ushikawa must have undergone something close to torture. I don't know what exactly was done to him, but he definitely was interrogated ruthlessly."

How much did he say?

"I'm sure he told everything he knew," Buzzcut said. "I have no doubt about it. But Ushikawa only had limited knowledge of what was going on. So I don't think that anything he told them will come back to hurt us."

Buzzcut didn't have access to everything that was going on within Sakigake, though he knew a lot more than an outsider.

By professional, do you mean this person is connected to organized crime? the superior asked.

"This isn't the work of the yakuza or organized criminals," Buzzcut said, shaking his head. "They're less subtle and more gory. They wouldn't do something this intricate. Whoever killed Ushikawa was sending us a message. He's telling us he has a sophisticated system backing him up, and if anybody tries anything, there will be consequences. And that we should keep our noses out of it."

It?

Buzzcut shook his head. "What exactly he means by that, I don't know. Ushikawa was working on his own. I asked him any number of times to give me a progress report, but he insisted that he still didn't have enough material. I think he wanted to gather all the facts together by himself first. Which is why he was the only one who knew what was going on when he was murdered. It was Leader himself who had originally singled out Ushikawa. He worked as a kind of independent agent. He didn't like organizations. Considering the chain of command, I wasn't in a position to give him orders."

Buzzcut wanted to make it absolutely clear how far his responsibility extended. Sakigake was itself an established organization. All organizations have rules, and breaking these rules could lead to punishment. He did not want to be blamed for mishandling this affair.

Who was Ushikawa watching in that apartment building?

"We don't know yet. Normally you would expect it to be someone who lives in the building, or in the vicinity. The men I left back in Tokyo are investigating as we speak, but they haven't reported in yet. It will take some time. It might be best if I go back to Tokyo and look into it myself."

Buzzcut wasn't all that confident in the abilities of the men he had left behind. They were devoted, but not the sharpest pencils in the box. And he hadn't explained the situation in much detail to them. It would be much more efficient for him to take charge directly. They should go through Ushikawa's office as well, though the man on the phone might have already beaten them to it. His superior, however, didn't permit him to return to Tokyo. Until things got a bit clearer, he and Ponytail were to stay put. That was an order.

Was Aomame the person Ushikawa had been watching?

"No, it couldn't have been Aomame," Buzzcut said. "If Aomame had been there, he would have immediately reported it. That would have completed his assignment. I think the person he had under watch was connected to – or *might* have been connected to – Aomame's whereabouts. Otherwise it doesn't add up."

And while he had that person under surveillance, someone found out about him, and took steps to stop him?

"That would be my guess," Buzzcut said. "He was getting too close to something dangerous. He may have found some vital clue. If there had been several people on the surveillance work, they could have watched each other's backs and things might have ended up differently."

You spoke directly to that man on the phone. Does it look as though we'll be able to meet Aomame and talk with her?

"I really can't predict. I would imagine, though, that if Aomame isn't willing to negotiate with us, the chances are slim that there will be any meeting. That would be my guess. Everything depends on how she wants to play it."

They should be pleased that we're willing to overlook what happened to Leader and guarantee her safety.

"They want more information. Such as, why do we want to meet with Aomame? Why are we seeking a truce? What exactly are we hoping to negotiate?"

The fact that they want to learn more means they don't have any solid information.

"Exactly. But we don't have any solid information about them, either. We still don't even know the reason they went to all the time and trouble to concoct a plan to murder Leader."

Either way, while we wait for their reply, we have to keep on searching for Aomame. Even if it means stepping on somebody's tail.

Buzzcut paused a moment, and then spoke. "We have a close-knit organization here. We can put a team together and get them out in the field in no time at all. We have a sense of purpose and high morale. People are literally willing to sacrifice themselves, if need be. But from a purely technical perspective, we're nothing more than a band of amateurs. We haven't had any specialized training. Compared with us, the other side are consummate professionals. They know what they're doing, they take action calmly, and they never hesitate. They seem like real veterans. As you're aware, Mr. Ushikawa was no slouch himself."

How exactly do you propose to continue the search?

"At present I think it's best to pursue the *valuable lead* that Mr. Ushikawa himself unearthed. Whatever it may be."

Meaning we don't have any valuable leads of our own?

"Correct," Buzzcut admitted.

No matter how dangerous it might become, and what sacrifices have to be made, we have to find and secure this woman Aomame. As quickly as possible.

"Is this what the voice has directed us to do?" Buzzcut asked. "That we should secure Aomame as quickly as possible? By whatever means necessary?"

His superior didn't reply. Information beyond this was above Buzzcut's pay grade. He was not one of the top brass, merely the head foot soldier. But Buzzcut knew that this was the final message given by *them*, most likely the final "voice" that the shrine maidens had heard.

As Buzzcut paced in front of Ushikawa's corpse in the freezing-cold room, a thought suddenly flashed through his head. He came to an abrupt halt, frowning, his brow knit, as he tried to grab hold of it. The moment he stopped pacing, Ponytail moved. A fraction. He let out a deep breath, and shifted his weight from one foot to the other.

Koenji, Buzzcut thought. He frowned slightly, searching the dark depths of memory. Ever so cautiously, he pulled at a thin thread, tugging it toward him. *Somebody else involved in this affair lives in Koenji. But who?*

He took a thick, crumpled memo pad out of his pocket and flipped through it. Tengo Kawana. His address was in Koenji, Suginami Ward. The same exact address, in fact, as the building in which Ushikawa died. Only the apartment numbers were different – the third floor and the first floor. Had Ushikawa been secretly watching Tengo's movements? There was no doubt about it. The two of them living in the same building was too big a coincidence.

But why, in this situation, did Ushikawa have to trace Tengo's movements? Buzzcut hadn't recalled Tengo's address up till now because he was no longer concerned about him. Tengo was nothing more than a ghostwriter. There had been nothing else about him that they needed to know. Sakigake's interest was now entirely focused on locating Aomame. Despite this, Ushikawa had focused all his attention on the cram school instructor, setting up an elaborate stakeout. And losing his own life in the bargain. *Why?*

Buzzcut couldn't figure it out. Ushikawa clearly had some sort of lead. He must have thought that sticking close to Tengo would lead him to Aomame – which is why he went to the trouble of securing that apartment, setting up a camera on a tripod, and observing Tengo, probably for some time. But what connection could there be between Tengo and Aomame?

Without a word, Buzzcut left the room, went into the room next door – which was heated – and made a phone call to Tokyo, to a unit in a condo in Sakuragaoka in Shibuya. He ordered one of his subordinates to immediately go back to Ushikawa's apartment in Koenji and keep watch over Tengo's movements. Tengo is a large man, with short hair, so you can't miss him, he instructed him. If he leaves the building, the two of you are to tail him, but make sure he doesn't spot you. Don't let him out of your sight. Find out where he's going. At all costs, you've got to keep him under surveillance. We'll join you as soon as we can.

Buzzcut went back to the room that held Ushikawa's body and told Ponytail they would be leaving right away for Tokyo. Ponytail gave a slight nod. He didn't ask for an explanation. He grasped what was asked of him and leapt into action. After they left the room, Buzzcut locked it so that no outsiders would have access. They went out of the building and chose, from a line of ten cars, a black Nissan Gloria. They got in, and Ponytail turned the key, already in the ignition, and started the engine. As per their rules, the car's gas tank was full. Ponytail would drive, as usual. The license plates for the Gloria sedan were legal, the registration clean, so even if they exceeded the speed limit a bit, it wouldn't be a problem.

They had been on the highway for a while by the time it occurred to Buzzcut that he hadn't gotten permission from his superiors to go back to Tokyo. This could come back to haunt him, but it was too late now. There wasn't a moment to lose. He would have to explain the situation to them after he got to Tokyo. He frowned a bit. Sometimes the restrictions disgusted him. The number of rules increased, but never decreased. Still, he knew he couldn't survive outside the system. He was no lone wolf. He was one cog among many, following orders from above.

He switched on the radio and listened to the regular eight o'clock news. When the broadcast was done, Buzzcut turned off the radio, adjusted his seat, and took a short nap. When he woke up he felt hungry – *How long has it been since I've had a decent meal?* he wondered – but there was no time to stop at a rest area for a bite to eat. They were in too much of a hurry.

By this time, however, Tengo had been reunited with Aomame on top of the slide in the park. Buzzcut and Ponytail had no idea where Tengo was headed. Above Tengo and Aomame, the two moons hung in the sky.

* * *

Ushikawa's body lay there in the frozen darkness. No one else was in the room. The lights were off, the door locked from the outside. Through the windows near the ceiling, pale moonlight shone in. But the angle made it impossible for Ushikawa to see the moon. So he couldn't know if there was one moon, or two.

There was no clock in the room, so it was unclear what time it was. Probably an hour or so had passed since Buzzcut and Ponytail had left. If someone else had been there, he would have seen Ushikawa's mouth suddenly begin to move. He would have been frightened out of his wits. This was a terrifying, wholly unexpected event. Ushikawa had long since expired and his body was stiff as a board. Despite this, his mouth continued to tremble slightly. Then, with a dry sound, it opened wide.

If someone had been there, he would no doubt have expected Ushikawa to say something. Some pearls of wisdom that only the dead could impart. Terrified, the person would have waited with bated breath. What secret could he be about to reveal?

But no voice came out. What came out were not words, not a drawn-out breath, but six tiny people, each about two inches tall. Their little bodies were dressed in tiny clothes, and they trod over the greenish mossy tongue, clambering over the dirty, irregular teeth. One by one they emerged, like miners returning to the surface after a hard day's labor. But unlike miners their clothes and faces were sparkling clean, not soiled at all. They were free of all dirt and wear.

Six Little People came out of Ushikawa's mouth and climbed down to the conference table, where each one shook himself and gradually grew bigger. When needed, they could adjust their size, but they never grew taller than a yard or shorter than an inch. When they grew to between twenty-four and twenty-eight inches tall, they stopped shaking and then, in order, descended from the table to the floor. The Little People's faces had no expression. But they weren't like masks. They had quite ordinary faces – smaller, but no different from yours or mine. It's just that, at that moment, they felt no need for any expression.

They seemed neither in a hurry nor too relaxed. They had exactly the right amount of time for the work that they needed to do. That time was neither too long nor too short. Without any obvious signal, the six of them quietly sat down on the floor in a circle. It was a perfect little circle, precisely two yards in diameter.

Wordlessly, one of them reached out and grabbed a single thin thread from the air. The thread was about six inches long, nearly a transparent white, almost creamy color. He placed the thread on the floor. The next person did exactly the same, the same color and thread length. The next three followed suit. Only the last one did something different. He stood up, left the circle, clambered back up on the conference table, reached out, and plucked one frizzy hair from Ushikawa's misshapen head. The hair came out with a tiny *snap*. This was his substitute thread. With practiced hands the first of the Little People wove together those five air threads and the single hair from Ushikawa's head.

And thus the Little People made a new air chrysalis. No one talked now, or chanted out a rhythm. They silently pulled threads from the air, plucked hairs from Ushikawa's head, and – in a set, smooth rhythm – briskly wove together an air chrysalis. Even in the freezing room their breath wasn't white. If anyone else had been there to see it, he might have found this odd too. Or perhaps he wouldn't have even noticed, given all the other surprising things going on.

No matter how intently the Little People worked (and they never stopped), completing an air chrysalis in one night was out of the question. It would take at least three days. But they didn't appear to be rushing. It would be another two days before Ushikawa's rigor mortis had passed and his body could be taken to the incinerator. They were well aware of this. If they got most of it done in two nights, that would be fine. They had enough time for what they needed to do. And they never got tired.

Ushikawa lay on the table, bathed in pale moonlight. His mouth was wide open, as were his unclosable eyes, which were covered by thick cloth. In their final moment, those eyes had seen a house, and a tiny dog scampering about a small patch of lawn.

And a part of his soul was about to change into an air chrysalis.

29

AOMAME

I'll Never Let Go of Your Hand Again

"TENGO, OPEN YOUR EYES," AOMAME WHISPERED. Tengo opened his eyes. Time began to flow again in the world.

"There's the moon," Aomame said.

Tengo raised his face and looked up at the sky. The clouds had parted and above the bare branches of the zelkova tree he could make out the moons. A large yellow moon and a smaller, misshapen green one. *Maza* and *dohta*. The glow colored the edges of the passing clouds, like a long skirt whose hem had been accidentally dipped in dye.

Tengo turned now to look over at Aomame sitting beside him. She was no longer a skinny, undernourished ten-year-old girl, dressed in ill-fitting hand-me-downs, her hair crudely trimmed by her mother. There was little left of the girl she had been, yet Tengo knew her at a glance. This was clearly Aomame and no other. Her eyes, brimming with expression, were the same, even after twenty years. Strong, unclouded, clear eyes. Eyes that knew exactly what they longed for.

Eyes that knew full well what they should see, and weren't going to let anyone get in her way. And those eyes were looking right at him. Straight into his heart.

Aomame had spent the last twenty years somewhere unknown to him. During that time, she had grown into a beautiful woman. Instantly and without reservation, Tengo absorbed all those places, and all that time, and they became a part of his own flesh and blood. They were his places now. His time.

I should say something, Tengo thought, but no words would come. He moved his lips, just barely, searching for proper words in the air, but they were nowhere to be found. All that came out from between his lips were swirls of white breath, like a wandering solitary island. As she gazed into his eyes, Aomame gave a slight shake of her head, just once. Tengo understood what that meant. *You don't have to say a thing.* She continued to hold his hand inside his pocket. She didn't let go, not even for a moment.

"We're seeing the same thing," Aomame said quietly as she gazed deep into his eyes. This was, at once, a question and a confirmation.

"There are two moons," Aomame said.

Tengo nodded. *There are two moons.* He didn't say this aloud. For some reason his voice wouldn't come. He just thought it.

Aomame closed her eyes. She curled up and pressed her cheek against his chest. Her ear was right above his heart. She was listening to his thoughts. "I needed to know this," Aomame said. "That we're in the same world, seeing the same things."

Tengo suddenly noticed that the whirling pillar rising up inside him had vanished. All that surrounded him now was a quiet winter night. There were lights on in a few of the windows in the apartment building across the way, hinting at people other than themselves alive in this world. This struck the two of them as exceedingly strange, even as somehow illogical – that other people could also exist, and be living their lives, in the same world.

Tengo leaned over slightly and breathed in the fragrance of

Aomame's hair. Beautiful, straight hair. Her small, pink ears peeped out like shy little creatures.

It was such a long time, Aomame thought.

It was such a long time, Tengo thought too. At the same time, though, he noticed how the twenty years that had passed now held no substance. It had all passed by in an instant, and took but an instant to be filled in.

Tengo took his hand out of his pocket and put it around her shoulder. Through his palm he could feel the wholeness of her body. He raised his face and looked up at the moons again. Through breaks in the clouds, the odd pair of moons was still bathing the earth in a strange mix of color. The clouds made their way leisurely across the sky. Under that light, Tengo once again keenly felt the mind's ability to relativize time. Twenty years was a long time. But Tengo knew that if he were to meet Aomame in another twenty years, he would feel the same way he did now. Even if they were both over fifty, he would still feel the same mix of excitement and confusion in her presence. His heart would be filled with the same joy and certainty.

Tengo kept these thoughts to himself, but he knew that Aomame was listening carefully to these unspoken words. Her little pink ear pressed against his chest. She was hearing everything that went on in his heart, like a person who can trace a map with his fingertip and conjure up vivid, living scenery.

"I want to stay here forever and forget all about time," Aomame said in a small voice. "But there's something the two of us have to do."

We have to move on, Tengo thought.

"That's right, we have to move on," Aomame said. "The sooner the better. We don't have much time left. Though I can't yet put into words where we're going."

There's no need for words, Tengo thought.

"Don't you want to know where we're going?" Aomame asked.

Tengo shook his head. The winds of reality had not extinguished the flame in his heart. There was nothing more significant.

"We will never be apart," Aomame said. "That's more clear than anything. We will never let go of each other's hand again."

A new cloud appeared and gradually swallowed up the moons. The shadow enveloping the world grew one shade deeper.

"We have to hurry," Aomame whispered. The two of them stood up on the slide. Once again their shadows became one. Like little children groping their way through a dark forest, they held on tightly to each other's hand.

"We're going to leave the cat town," Tengo said, speaking aloud for the first time. Aomame treasured this fresh, newborn voice.

"The cat town?"

"The town at the mercy of a deep loneliness during the day and, come night, of large cats. There's a beautiful river running through it, and an old stone bridge spanning the river. But it's not where we should stay."

We call this world *by different names,* Aomame thought. *I call it* the year 1Q84, *while he calls it the* cat town. *But it all means the same thing.* Aomame squeezed his hand even tighter.

"You're right, we're going to leave the cat town now. The two of us, together," Aomame said. "Once we leave this town, day or night, we will never be apart."

As the two of them hurried out of the park, the pair of moons remained hidden behind the slowly moving clouds. The eyes of the moons were covered. And the boy and the girl, hand in hand, made their way out of the forest.

30

TENGO

If I'm Not Mistaken

AFTER THEY LEFT THE PARK, THEY walked out onto the main street and hailed a cab. Aomame told the driver to take them to Sangenjaya, via Route 246.

For the first time, Tengo noticed what Aomame was wearing. She had on a light-colored spring coat, too thin for this cold time of year. The coat was belted in front. Underneath was a nicely tailored green suit. The skirt was short and tight. She had on stockings and lustrous high heels, and carried a black leather shoulder bag. The bag was bulging and looked heavy. She wasn't wearing any gloves or a muffler, no rings or necklace or earrings, no hint of perfume. To Tengo, what she had on, and what she had omitted, looked entirely natural. He could think of nothing that needed to be added or removed.

The taxi sped down Ring Road 7 toward Route 246. Traffic was flowing along unusually smoothly. For a long time after they got in the taxi, the two of them didn't speak. The radio in the taxi was off, and the young driver was very quiet. All the two of them heard was the ceaseless, monotonous hum of tires. Aomame leaned against Tengo, still clutching his large hand. If she let go she might never find him again. Around them the night city flowed by like a phosphorescent tide.

"There are several things I need to say to you," Aomame said, after a while. "I don't think I can explain everything before we arrive *there*. We don't have that much time. But maybe if we had all the time in the world I still couldn't explain it."

Tengo shook his head slightly. There was no need to explain everything now. They could fill in all the gaps later, as they went – if there were indeed gaps that needed to be filled. Tengo felt that as long as it was something the two of them could share – even a gap they had to abandon or a riddle they never could solve – he could discover a joy there, something akin to love.

"What do I need to know about you at this point?" Tengo asked.

"What do you know about me?" Aomame asked in return.

"Almost nothing," Tengo said. "You're an instructor at a sports club. You're single. You've been living in Koenji."

"I know almost nothing about you, too," Aomame said, "though I do know a few small things. You teach math at a cram school in Yoyogi. You live alone. And you're the one who really wrote *Air Chrysalis*."

Tengo looked at her face, his lips parted in surprise. There were very few people who knew this about him. Did she have some connection with the cult?

"Don't worry. We're on the same side," she said. "If I told you how I came to know this, it would take too long. But I do know that you wrote *Air Chrysalis* together with Eriko Fukada. And that you and I both entered a world where there are two moons in the sky. And there's one more thing. I'm carrying a child. I believe it's yours. For now, these are the important things you ought to know."

"You're *carrying my child*?" The driver might be listening, but Tengo wasn't worrying about it at this point.

"We haven't seen each other in twenty years," Aomame said, "but yes, I'm carrying your child. I'm going to give birth to your child. I know it sounds totally crazy."

Tengo was silent, waiting for her to continue.

"Do you remember that terrible thunderstorm in the beginning of September?"

"I remember it well," Tengo said. "The weather was nice all day, then after sunset it turned stormy, with wild lightning. Water flowed down into the Akasaka-Mitsuke Station and they had to shut down the subway for a while." *The Little People are stirring,* Fuka-Eri had said.

"I got pregnant the night of that storm," Aomame said. "But I didn't have *those sorts of* relations with anyone on that day, or for several months before and after."

She paused and waited until this reality had sunk in, then continued.

"But *it* definitely happened that night. And I'm certain that the child I'm carrying is yours. I can't explain it, but I know it's *true.*"

The memory of the strange sexual encounter he had with Fuka-Eri that night came back to him. Lightning was crashing outside, huge drops of rain lashing the window. The Little People were indeed stirring. He was lying there, faceup in bed, his whole body numb, and Fuka-Eri straddled him, inserted his penis inside her, and squeezed out his semen. She looked like she was in a complete trance. Her eyes were closed from start to finish, as if she were lost in meditation. Her breasts were ample and round, and she had no pubic hair. The whole scene was unreal, but he knew it had really happened.

The next morning, Fuka-Eri had acted as if she had no memory of the events of the previous night, or else tried to give the impression that she didn't remember. To Tengo it had felt more like a business transaction than sex. On that stormy night, Fuka-Eri used his body to collect his semen, down to the very last drop. Even now, Tengo could recall that strange sensation. Fuka-Eri had seemed to become a totally different person.

"There is something I recall," Tengo said dryly. "Something that happened to me that night that logic can't explain."

Aomame looked deep into his eyes.

"At the time," he went on, "I didn't know what it meant. Even now, I'm not sure. But if you did get pregnant that night, and there's no other possible explanation for it, then the child inside you has to be mine."

Fuka-Eri must have been the conduit. That was the role she had been assigned, to act as the passage linking Tengo and Aomame, physically connecting the two of them over a limited period of time. Tengo knew this must be true.

"Someday I'll tell you exactly what happened then," Tengo said, "but right now I don't think I have the words to explain it."

"But you really believe it, right? That the *little one* inside me is your child?"

"From the bottom of my heart," Tengo said.

"Good," Aomame said. "That's all I wanted to know. As long as you believe that, then I don't care about the rest. I don't need any explanations."

"So you're pregnant," Tengo asked again.

"Four months along," Aomame said, guiding his hand to rest on her belly.

Tengo was quiet, seeking signs of life there. It was still very tiny, but his hand could feel the warmth.

"Where are we moving on to? You, me, and the *little one*."

"Somewhere that's not here," Aomame replied. "A world with only one moon. The place where we belong. Where the Little People have no power."

"Little People?" Tengo frowned slightly.

"You described the Little People in detail in *Air Chrysalis*. What they look like, what they do."

Tengo nodded.

"They really exist in this world," Aomame said. "Just like you described them."

When he had rewritten the novel, he had thought the Little People were merely the figment of the active imagination of a seventeen-year-old girl. Or that they were at most a kind of metaphor or symbol. But Tengo could now believe that the Little People really existed, that they had real powers.

"Not just the Little People," Aomame said, "but all of it really exists in this world – air chrysalises, *maza* and *dohta*, two moons."

"And you know the pathway out of *this world*?"

"We'll take the pathway I took to get into this world so that we can get out of it. That's the only exit I can think of." She added, "Do you have the manuscript of the novel you're writing?"

"Right here," Tengo said, lightly tapping the russet-colored bag slung over his shoulder. It struck him as strange. How did she know about this?

Aomame gave a hesitant smile. "I just know."

"It looks like you know a lot of things," Tengo said. It was the first time he had seen her smile. It was the faintest of smiles, yet he felt the tides start to shift all over the world. He knew it was happening.

"Don't let go of it," Aomame said. "It's very important for us."

"Don't worry. I won't."

"We came into *this world* so that we could meet. We didn't realize it ourselves, but that was the purpose of us coming here. We faced all kinds of complications – things that didn't make sense, things that defied explanation. Weird things, gory things, sad things. And sometimes, even beautiful things. We were asked to make a vow, and we did. We were forced to go through hard times, and we made it. We were able to accomplish the goal that we came here to accomplish. But danger is closing in fast. They want the *dohta* inside of me. You know what the *dohta* signifies, I imagine."

Tengo took a deep breath. "You're having our *dohta* – yours and mine."

"I don't know all the details of whatever principle's behind it, but I'm giving birth to a *dohta*. Either through an air chrysalis, or else I'm the air chrysalis. And they're trying to get ahold of all three of us. To make a new system so they can *hear the voice.*"

"But what's my role in this? Assuming I have a role beyond being the father of the *dohta.*"

"You are –" Aomame began, and stopped. The next words wouldn't come. There were several gaps that remained, gaps they would have to work together, over time, to fill in.

"I decided to find you," Tengo said, "but I couldn't. *You* found *me.* I actually didn't do anything. It seems – how should I put it? – unfair."

"Unfair?"

"I owe you a lot. But in the end, I wasn't much help."

"You don't owe me anything," Aomame said firmly. "You're the one who guided me this far. In an invisible way. The two of us are one."

"I think I saw that *dohta,*" Tengo said. "Or at least what the *dohta signifies.* It was you as a ten-year-old, asleep inside the faint light of an air chrysalis. I could touch her fingers. It only happened once."

Aomame leaned her head on Tengo's shoulder. "We don't owe each other anything. Not a thing. But what we do need to worry about is protecting this *little one.* They're closing in. Almost on top of us. I can hear their footsteps."

"I won't ever let anyone else get the two of you – you or the *little one.* Now that we've met each other, we've found what we were looking for when we came to this world. This is a dangerous place. But you said you know where there's an exit."

"I think so," Aomame said. "If I'm not mistaken."

31

TENGO AND AOMAME

Like a Pea in a Pod

AOMAME RECOGNIZED THE SPOT AS THEY got out of the taxi. She stood at the intersection looking around and found the gloomy storage area, surrounded by a metal panel fence, down below the expressway. Leading Tengo by the hand, she crossed at the crosswalk and headed toward it.

She couldn't remember which of the metal panels had the loose bolts, but after patiently testing each one, she found a space that a person could manage to slip through. Aomame bent down and, careful to keep her clothes from getting snagged, slipped inside. Tengo hunched down as much as his large body would allow, and followed behind her. Inside the storage area, everything was exactly as it had been in April, when Aomame had last seen it. Discarded, faded bags of cement, rusty metal pipes, weary weeds, scattered old wastepaper, splotches of hardened white pigeon excrement here and there. In eight months, nothing had changed. During that time, perhaps no one had ever set foot in here. It was like a sandbar on a main highway in the middle of the city – a completely abandoned, forgotten little spot.

"Is this the place?" Tengo asked, looking around.

Aomame nodded. "If there's no exit here, then we're not going anywhere."

In the darkness Aomame searched for the emergency stairway she had climbed down, the narrow stairs linking the expressway and the ground below. *The stairway* has to be here, she told herself. *I have to believe it.*

And she found it. It was actually closer to a ladder than a stairway. It was shabbier and more rickety than she remembered. She was amazed that she had managed to clamber down it before. At any rate, though, here it was. All they needed to do now was climb up, step by step, instead of down. She took off her Charles Jourdan high heels, stuffed them into her bag, and slung the bag across her shoulders. She stepped onto the first rung of the ladder in her stocking feet.

"Follow me," Aomame said, turning around to Tengo.

"Maybe I should go first?" Tengo asked worriedly.

"No, I'll go first." This was the path she had come down, and she would have to be the first to climb back up.

The stairway was colder than when she had come down it. Her hands got so numb that she thought she would lose all feeling. The wind whipped between the support columns under the expressway. It was much more sharp and piercing than it had been before. The stairway was aloof and uninviting. It promised her nothing.

At the beginning of September when she had searched for the stairway on the expressway, it had vanished. The route had been blocked. Yet now the route from the storage area, going up, was still here, just as she had predicted. She had had a feeling that if she started from this direction, she would find it. *If this* little one *inside me,* she thought, *has any special powers, then it will surely protect me and show me the right way to go.*

The stairway existed, but whether it *really* connected up to the expressway, she didn't know. It might be blocked halfway, a dead end. In this world, anything could happen. The only thing to do was to climb up with her own hands and feet and find out what was there – and what was not.

She cautiously climbed up one step after another. She looked down and saw Tengo right behind her. A fierce wind howled, making her spring coat flutter. It was a cutting wind. The hem of her short skirt had crept up to her thighs. The wind had made a mess of her hair, plastering it against her face and blocking her vision, so much so that she found it hard to breathe. Aomame regretted not having tied her hair back. *And I should have worn gloves, too,* she thought. *Why didn't I think of that?* But regretting it wasn't going to be any help. She had only thought to wear exactly the same thing as before. She had to cling to the rungs and keep on climbing.

As she shivered in the cold, patiently climbing upward, she looked over at the balcony of the apartment building across the road. A five-story building made of brown brick tiles, the same building she had seen when she had climbed down. Lights were on in half the rooms. It was so close by she could almost reach out and touch it. It might lead to trouble if one of the residents happened to spot them climbing up the emergency stairway like this in the middle of the night. The two of them were lit up well under the lights from Route 246.

Fortunately, no one appeared at any of the windows. All the curtains were drawn tight. This was only to be expected, really. Who was going to come out on their balcony in the middle of a freezing night to watch an emergency stairway on an expressway?

There was a potted rubber plant on one of the balconies, crouching down next to a grubby lawn chair. In April when she had climbed down she had seen the same rubber plant – a much more pathetic little plant than the one she had left behind at her apartment in Jiyugaoka. This little rubber plant must have been there the whole eight months, huddled in the same exact spot. It was faded and bedraggled, shoved away into the most inconspicuous spot in the world, completely forgotten, probably hardly ever watered. Still, that little plant gave Aomame courage and certainty as she struggled up the rickety stairway, her hands and legs freezing, her mind anxious and confused. *It's okay,* she told herself, *I'm on the right track. At least I'm following the same path I took when I came here, from the opposite direction. This little rubber plant has been a landmark for me. A sober, solitary landmark.*

When I climbed down the stairs back then, I came across a few spiderwebs. And I thought of Tamaki Otsuka, how during summer break in high school we took a trip together, and at night, in bed, we stripped naked and explored each other's bodies. Why had that memory suddenly come to her then, of all times, while climbing down an emergency stairway on the expressway? As she now climbed in the opposite direction, Aomame thought again of Tamaki. She remembered her smooth, beautifully shaped breasts. *So different from my own underdeveloped chest,* she thought. *But those beautiful breasts are now gone forever.*

She thought of Ayumi Nakano, the lonely policewoman who, one August night, wound up in a hotel room in Shibuya, handcuffed, strangled with a bathrobe belt. A troubled young woman walking toward the abyss of destruction. She had had beautiful breasts as well.

Aomame mourned the deaths of these two friends deeply. It saddened her to think that these women were forever gone from the world. And she mourned their lovely breasts – breasts that had vanished without a trace.

Please, she pleaded. *Protect me. I beg you – I need your help.* She believed that her voiceless words had reached the ears of her unfortunate friends. *They'll protect me. I know it.*

When she finally came to the top of the ladder, she was faced with a catwalk that connected up to the side of the road. The catwalk had a low railing, and she would have to crouch low to pass through. Beyond the catwalk was a zigzagging stairway. Not a proper stairway, really, but certainly a far cry better than the ladder. As Aomame recalled, once she ascended the stairs she would come out onto the turnout along the expressway. Trucks barreling down the road sent shocks that rocked the catwalk, as if it were a small boat hit from the side by a wave. The roar of the traffic had increased.

She checked that Tengo, who had come to the top of the ladder, was right behind her, and she reached out and took his hand. His hand was warm. She found it odd that his hand could be so warm on such a cold night, after holding on to a freezing ladder.

"We're almost there," Aomame said in his ear. With the traffic noise and the wind she had to raise her voice. "Once we get up those stairs we'll be on the expressway."

That is, if the stairs aren't blocked, she thought, but she kept this thought to herself.

"You were planning to climb these stairs from the beginning?" Tengo asked.

"Right. If I could locate them."

"And you went to the trouble of dressing like that. Tight skirt, high heels. Not exactly the right outfit to wear to climb steep stairs."

Aomame smiled again. "I had to wear these clothes. Someday I'll explain it to you."

"You have beautiful legs," Tengo said.

"You like them?"

"You bet."

"Thanks," Aomame said. On the narrow catwalk she reached up and gently kissed his ear. A crumpled, cauliflower-like ear. His ear was freezing cold.

She turned back, proceeded along the catwalk, and began climbing up the narrow, steep stairs. Her feet were freezing, her fingertips numb. She was careful not to slip. She continued up the stairs, brushing away her hair as the wind whipped by. The freezing wind brought tears to her eyes. She held on tightly to the handrail so she could keep her balance in the swirling wind, and as she took one cautious step after another, she thought of Tengo right behind her. Of his large hand, and his freezing-cold cauliflower ear. Of the *little one* sleeping inside her. Of the black automatic pistol inside her shoulder bag. And the seven 9mm cartridges in the clip.

We have to get out of this world. To do that I have to believe, from the bottom of my heart, that these stairs will lead to the expressway. I believe, she told herself. She suddenly remembered something Leader had said on the stormy night, before he died. Lyrics to a song. She could recall them all, even now.

> *It's a Barnum and Bailey world,*
> *Just as phony as it can be,*
> *But it wouldn't be make-believe*
> *If you believed in me.*

No matter what happens, no matter what I have to do, I have to make it real, not make-believe. No – the two of us, Tengo and I, have to do that. We have to make it real. We have to put our strength together, every last ounce of strength we possess. For our sake, and for the sake of this little one.

Aomame stopped on a landing halfway up and turned around. Tengo was still there. She reached out her hand, and Tengo took it. She felt the same warmth as before, and it gave her a certain strength. She reached up again and brought her mouth close to his ear.

"You know, once I almost gave up my life for you," she said. "Just a little more and I would have died. A couple of millimeters more. Do you believe me?"

"I do," Tengo said.

"Will you tell me you believe it from the bottom of your heart?"

"I believe it from the bottom of my heart," Tengo replied.

Aomame nodded, and let go of his hand. She faced forward and began climbing the stairs again.

A few minutes later, she reached the top and came out onto Metropolitan Expressway No. 3. The stairway hadn't been blocked. Before she scrambled over the metal fence, she reached up with the back of her hand and wiped away the cold tears in her eyes.

Tengo looked around without saying a word. Finally, he said, as if impressed, "It's Metropolitan Expressway No. 3. This is the exit out of this world, isn't it."

"That's right," Aomame replied. "It's the entrance and the exit."

Tengo helped her from behind as she clambered over the fence, her tight skirt riding up to her hips. Beyond the fence was a turnout just big enough for two cars. This was the third time she had been here. The large Esso billboard was right in front of her. *Put a Tiger in Your Tank.* The same slogan. The same tiger. She stood there in her stocking feet without a word. She inhaled the car exhaust deep into her lungs. This was the most refreshing air she could possibly imagine. *I'm back,* Aomame thought. *We're back.*

The traffic on the expressway was bumper to bumper, just as she had left it. The Shibuya-bound traffic was barely inching along. This surprised her, and she wondered why. *Whenever I come here, the traffic's always backed up. But at this time of day it's pretty rare for the lanes heading into the city on Expressway No. 3 to be like this. There must be an accident somewhere up ahead.* The lanes going the other direction were flowing along nicely but the ones heading into the city were crushingly crowded.

Tengo climbed over the metal fence, lifting one foot up high to nimbly leap over, then came to stand beside her. They stood there together, wordlessly watching the throng of traffic, like people standing beside the Pacific Ocean for the first time in their lives, awestruck at the waves crashing on the shore.

The people in the barely moving cars stared back at them. They seemed confused, uncertain how to react. Their eyes were filled less with curiosity than suspicion. What could this young couple possibly be up to? They had suddenly popped up out of the dark and were standing in a turnout on the expressway. The woman had on a fashionable suit, but her coat was a thin spring one, and she was standing there in stocking feet, with no shoes. The man was stocky, and was wearing a well-worn leather jacket. Both of them had bags slung diagonally across their shoulders. Had their car broken down? Had they been in an accident? There was no sign of any car nearby. And they didn't look like they were asking for help.

Aomame finally pulled herself together and took her high heels out of her bag. She tugged the hem of her skirt down, put the strap of her bag over one shoulder, and tied the belt on her coat. She licked her dry lips, straightened her hair with her fingers, took out a handkerchief, and wiped away her tears. And she once more nestled close to Tengo.

Just as they had done on that December day twenty years earlier, in a classroom after hours, they stood silently side by side, holding hands. They were the only two people in the world. They watched the leisurely flow of cars before them. But they saw nothing. What they were seeing, what they were hearing – none of it mattered. The sights around them – the sounds, the smells – had all been drained of meaning.

"So, we're in a different world now?" Tengo managed to say.

"Most likely," Aomame said.

"Maybe we should make sure."

There was only one way to make sure, and they didn't need to put it into words. Silently, Aomame raised her face and looked up at the sky. At nearly the same instant, Tengo did so too. They were searching for the moon. Considering the angle, the moon should be somewhere above the Esso billboard. But they couldn't find it. It seemed to be hidden behind the clouds. The clouds were flowing toward the south, sedately moving along in the wind. The two of them waited – no need to rush. They had plenty of time. Enough time to recover the time they had lost. The time they shared. No need to panic. A pump in one hand, a knowing smile on his face, the Esso tiger, in profile, watched over the two of them holding hands.

Aomame was struck by a sudden thought. Something was different, but she couldn't put her finger on it. She narrowed her eyes and focused. And then it hit her. The left side of the Esso tiger's face was toward them. But in her memory it was his *right* side that had faced the world. *The tiger had been reversed.* Her face instinctively grimaced, her heart skipped a beat or two. It felt like something inside her had changed course. But could she really say for sure? *Is my memory really that accurate?* Aomame wasn't certain. She just *had a feeling* about it. Sometimes our memory betrays us.

Aomame kept her doubts to herself. She shut her eyes for a moment to let her breathing and heart rate get back to normal, and waited for the clouds to pass.

People continued to stare at the two of them through the car windows. What are these two looking at? And why are they clutching each other's hand so tightly? A number of them craned their heads, trying to see what the couple was staring at, but all that was visible were white clouds and an Esso billboard. *Put a Tiger in Your Tank,* the billboard tiger's profile said, facing to the left, urging those driving by to consume even more gasoline, his orange-striped tail jauntily raised to the sky.

The clouds finally broke and the moon came into view.

There was just one moon. That familiar, yellow, solitary moon. The same moon that silently floated over fields of pampas grass, the moon that rose – a gleaming, round saucer – over the calm surface of lakes, that tranquilly beamed down on the rooftops of fast-asleep houses. The same moon that brought the high tide to shore, that softly shone on the fur of animals and enveloped and protected travelers at night. The moon that, as a crescent, shaved slivers from the soul – or, as a new moon, silently bathed the earth in its own loneliness. *That* moon. The moon was fixed in the sky right above the Esso billboard, and there was no smaller, misshapen greenish moon beside it. It was hanging there, taciturn, beholden to no one. Simultaneously, the two of them looked at the same scene. Wordlessly Aomame clutched Tengo's hand. The feeling of an internal backflow had vanished.

We're back in 1984, Aomame told herself. *This isn't 1Q84 anymore. This is the world of 1984, the world I came from.*

But is it? Could the world really go back so easily to what it was?

Hadn't Leader, just before he died, asserted that there was no pathway back to the old world?

Could this be another, altogether different place? Did we move from one world to yet another, third world? Where the Esso tiger shows us the left side of his face, not his right? Where new riddles and new rules await us?

It might well be, Aomame thought. *At least at this point I can't swear that it isn't. But there is one thing I can say for sure. No matter how you look at it, this isn't that world, with its two moons in the sky. And I am holding Tengo's hand. The two of us entered a dangerous place, where logic had no purpose, and we managed to survive some terrible ordeals, found each other, and slipped away. Whether this place we've arrived in is the world we started out from or a whole new world, what do I have to be afraid of? If there are new trials ahead for us, we just have to overcome them, like we've done before. That's all. But at least we're no longer alone.*

Believing in what she needed to believe, she relaxed, leaning back against Tengo's large body. She pressed her ear against his chest and listened to his heartbeat, and gave herself up to his arms. Just like a pea in a pod.

"Where should we go now?" Tengo asked Aomame after some time had passed. They couldn't stay here forever. That much was clear. But there was no shoulder on the Metropolitan Expressway. The Ikejiri exit was relatively close, but even in a traffic jam like this it was too dangerous for a pedestrian to walk through the backup of cars. They were certain, too, that holding out their thumbs to hitchhike wasn't likely to get them any rides. They could use the emergency phone to call for help from the Japan Highway Public Corporation, but then they would have to come up with a reasonable explanation for why they were stranded. Even if they were able to make it on foot to the Ikejiri exit, the toll collector would be sure to question them. Going back down the same stairs they had climbed up was out of the question.

"I don't know," Aomame said.

She really had no idea what they should do, or where they should go. Once they had climbed the emergency stairway, her role was over. She was too drained to think, or make a judgment call. There wasn't a drop left in her tank. She could only let some other power take over.

O Lord in Heaven, may Thy name be praised in utmost purity for ever and ever, and may Thy kingdom come to us. Please forgive our many sins, and bestow Thy blessings upon our humble pathways. Amen.

The prayer flowed out from her like a conditioned reflex. She didn't have to think about it. Each individual word had no meaning. The phrases were nothing more than sounds to her now, a list of signs and nothing more. Still, as she mechanically recited the prayer, a strange feeling came over her, something you might even call reverence. Something deep inside her struck a chord in her heart. *Despite all that happened, I never lost myself,* she thought. *Thank goodness I can be here, as me. Wherever* here *is.*

May Thy kingdom come, Aomame intoned once more, like she had done in elementary school before lunch, so many years ago. Whatever that might mean, she wished it. *May Thy kingdom come.*

Tengo stroked her hair, as if combing it.

Ten minutes later Tengo was able to flag down a passing taxi. At first they couldn't believe their eyes. A single taxi, absent of any passengers, was slowly making its way along the traffic jam on the expressway. Tengo raised a skeptical hand, the back door swung open right away, and they climbed aboard, quickly, hurriedly, afraid that this phantom would vanish. The young driver, wearing glasses, turned to face them.

"Because of the traffic jam I would like to get off at the Ikejiri exit coming up, if that's all right with you?" the driver asked. He had a rather high-pitched voice for a man, but it wasn't irritating.

"That would be fine," Aomame replied.

"It's actually against the law to pick up passengers on the expressway."

"Which law would that be?" Aomame asked. Her face, reflected in the rearview mirror, wore a slight frown.

The driver couldn't come up with the name of the law that prohibits picking up passengers on highways. Plus, Aomame's face in the rearview mirror was starting to frighten him a little.

"Well, whatever," the driver said, abandoning the topic. "Anyway, where would you like to go?"

"You can let us off near Shibuya Station," Aomame said.

"I haven't set the meter," the driver said. "I'll just charge you for the distance after we get off the expressway."

"Why were you on the expressway with no passenger?" Tengo asked him.

"It's sort of a long story," the driver said, his voice etched with fatigue. "Would you like to hear it?"

"I would," Aomame said. Long and boring was fine by her. She wanted to hear people's stories in this new world. There might be new secrets there, new hints.

"I picked up a fare, a middle-aged man, near Kinuta Park, and he asked me to take him near Aoyama Gakuin University. He wanted me to take the expressway since there would be too much traffic around Shibuya. At this point, there wasn't any bulletin about a traffic jam on the expressway. Traffic was supposed to be moving along just fine. So I did what he asked and got on the expressway at Yoga. But then there was an accident around Tani, apparently, and you can see the result. Once we were stuck, we couldn't even get to the Ikejiri exit to get off. Meanwhile, the passenger spied a friend of his. Around Komazawa, when we weren't moving an inch, there was a silver Mercedes coupe next to us that just happened to be driven by a woman who was a friend of his. They rolled down the windows and chatted and she wound up inviting him to ride with her. The man apologized and asked if he could pay up and go over to her car. Letting a passenger out in the middle of a highway is unheard of, but since we actually weren't moving, I couldn't say no. So the man got into the Mercedes. He felt bad about it, so he added a little extra to what he paid to sweeten the deal. But still it was annoying. I mean, I couldn't move at all. Anyway, bit by bit I made my way here, nearly to the Ikejiri exit. And then I saw you raising your hand. Pretty hard to believe, don't you think?"

"I can believe it," Aomame said concisely.

That night the two of them stayed in a high-rise hotel in Akasaka. They turned the lights out, undressed, got into bed, and held each other. There was a lot they needed to talk about, but that could wait till morning. They had other priorities. Without a word passing between them, they leisurely explored each other's bodies in the dark. With their fingers and palms, one by one, they checked where everything was, what they were shaped like. They felt excited, like little children on a treasure hunt in a secret room. Once they found each part, they kissed it with a seal of approval.

After they had leisurely finished this process, Aomame held Tengo's hard penis in her hand – just like years before, when she had held his hand in the classroom after school. It felt harder than anything she had ever known, miraculously hard. Aomame spread her legs, moved close, and slowly inserted him inside of her. Straight in, deep inside. She closed her eyes in the darkness and gulped a deep and dark intake of breath. Then, ever so slowly, she exhaled. Tengo felt her hot breath on his chest.

"I've always imagined being held by you like this," Aomame said, whispering in his ear as she stopped moving.

"Having sex with me?"

"Yes."

"Since you were ten you've been imagining *this*?" Tengo asked.

Aomame laughed. "No, that came when I was a little older."

"I've been imagining the same thing."

"Being inside me?"

"That's right," Tengo said.

"Is it like you imagined?"

"I still can't believe it's real," Tengo admitted. "I feel like I'm imagining things."

"But this is real."

"It feels too good to be real."

In the darkness Aomame smiled. And she kissed him. They explored each other's tongues.

"My breasts are kind of small, don't you think?" Aomame said.

"They're just right," Tengo said, cupping them.

"You really think so?"

"Of course," he said. "If they were any bigger then it wouldn't be you."

"Thank you," Aomame said. "They're not just small," she added, "but the right and left are also different sizes."

"They're fine the way they are," Tengo said. "The right one's the right one, the left one's the left. No need to change a thing."

Aomame pressed an ear against his chest. "I've been lonely for so long. And I've been hurt so deeply. If only I could have met you again a long time ago, then I wouldn't have had to take all these detours to get here."

Tengo shook his head. "I don't think so. This way is just fine. This is exactly the right time. For both of us."

Aomame started to cry. The tears she had been holding back spilled down her cheeks and there was nothing she could do to stop them. Large teardrops fell audibly onto the sheets like rain. With Tengo buried deep inside her, she trembled slightly as she went on crying. Tengo put his arms around her and held her. He would be holding her close from now on, a thought that made him happier than he could imagine.

"We needed that much time," Tengo said, "to understand how lonely we really were."

"Start moving," Aomame breathed in his ear. "Take your time, and do it slowly."

Tengo did as he was told. He began pumping slowly. Breathing quietly, listening to his heartbeat. Aomame clung to him like she was drowning. She gave up crying, gave up thinking, distanced herself from the past, from the future, and became one with his movements.

Near dawn they slipped on hotel bathrobes, stood next to the large window, and sipped the red wine they had ordered from room service. Aomame took just a token sip. They didn't need to sleep yet. From their room on the seventeenth floor they could enjoy watching the moon to their hearts' content. The clouds had drifted away, and nothing impeded their view. The dawn moon had moved quite a distance, though it still hovered just above the city skyline. The moon was an ashy white, and looked about ready to fall to earth, its job complete.

At the front desk Aomame had asked for a room high up with a view of the moon, even if it cost more. "That's the most important thing – having a nice view of the moon," she said.

The clerk was kind to this young couple who had shown up without a reservation. It also helped that the hotel wasn't busy. She felt kindly toward the couple from the moment she set eyes on them. She had the bellboy go up to look at the room to make sure it had the view they wanted, and only then handed Aomame the key to the junior suite. She gave them a special discount, too.

"Is it a full moon or something tonight?" the woman clerk asked Aomame, her interest aroused. Over the years she had heard every kind of demand, hope, and desire from guests you could imagine. But this was a first, having guests who were looking for a room with a good view of the moon.

"No," Aomame replied. "The moon's past full. It's about two-thirds full. But that doesn't matter. As long as we can see it."

"You enjoy watching the moon, then?"

"It's important to us," Aomame smiled. "More important than you can know."

Even as dawn approached, the number of moons didn't increase. It was just the same old familiar moon. The one and only satellite that has faithfully circled the earth, at the same speed, from before human memory. As she stared at the moon, Aomame softly touched her abdomen, checking one more time that the *little one* was there, inside her. She could swear her belly had grown from the night before.

I still don't know what sort of world this is, she thought. *But whatever world we're in now, I'm sure this is where I will stay. Where we will stay. This world must have its own threats, its own dangers, must be filled with its own type of riddles and contradictions. We may have to travel down many dark paths, leading who knows where. But that's okay. It's not a problem. I'll just have to accept it. I'm not going anywhere. Come what may, this is where we'll remain, in this world with one moon. The three of us – Tengo and me, and the* little one.

Put a tiger in your tank, the Esso tiger said, his left profile toward them. But either side was fine. That big grin of his facing Aomame was natural and warm. *I'm going to believe in that smile,* she told herself. *That's what's important here.* She did her own version of the tiger's smile. Very naturally, very gently.

She quietly stretched out a hand, and Tengo took it. The two of them stood there, side by side, as one, wordlessly watching the moon over the buildings. Until the newly risen sun shone upon it, robbing it of its nighttime brilliance. Until it was nothing more than a gray paper moon, hanging in the sky.

www.vintage-books.co.uk